He made her laugh.

Earlier she'd tried to cover her amusement with sarcasm, but lately Will had a cute way of getting back at her. She felt like a kid again, rather than the dignified woman she'd considered herself to be.

"You're on," she said. "If I love it here, I owe you something big. A seven-course dinner or…" She faltered, realizing she was having a good time.

"I'll make that decision when I collect," he said with a wink over his shoulder.

Above the roar of the engine, he hollered back his usual witty comments, his youthful spirit so evident as they soared across the snow. Youthful, yet he had depth, too, Christine had noticed. She watched the tenderness he had for her grandmother, and Christine also couldn't help but notice how he studied her. She didn't think he'd figured her out yet, but he would.

Gail Gaymer Martin is a multi-award-winning novelist and writer of contemporary Christian fiction with fifty-five published novels and four million books sold. CBS News listed her among the four best writers in the Detroit area. Gail is a cofounder of American Christian Fiction Writers and a keynote speaker at women's events, and she presents workshops at writers' conferences. She lives in Michigan. Visit her at gailgaymermartin.com.

Leigh Bale is a *Publishers Weekly* bestselling author. She is the winner of the prestigious Golden Heart® Award and was a finalist for the Gayle Wilson Award of Excellence and the Booksellers' Best Award. The daughter of a retired US forest ranger, she holds a BA in history. Married in 1981 to the love of her life, Leigh and her professor husband have two children and two grandkids. You can reach her at leighbale.com.

With Christmas in His Heart

Gail Gaymer Martin

&

The Forest Ranger's Christmas

Leigh Bale

LOVE INSPIRED
INSPIRATIONAL ROMANCE

LOVE INSPIRED®
INSPIRATIONAL ROMANCE

Recycling programs
for this product may
not exist in your area.

ISBN-13: 978-1-335-28494-5

With Christmas in His Heart &
The Forest Ranger's Christmas

Copyright © 2020 by Harlequin Books S.A.

With Christmas in His Heart
First published in 2006. This edition published in 2020.
Copyright © 2006 by Gail Gaymer Martin

The Forest Ranger's Christmas
First published in 2014. This edition published in 2020.
Copyright © 2014 by Lora Lee Bale

This edition published by arrangement with Harlequin Books S.A.

For questions and comments about the quality of this book,
please contact us at CustomerService@Harlequin.com.

Love Inspired
22 Adelaide St. West, 40th Floor
Toronto, Ontario M5H 4E3, Canada
www.Harlequin.com

Printed in U.S.A.

CONTENTS

WITH CHRISTMAS IN HIS HEART

Gail Gaymer Martin

Acknowledgments

A huge thank-you to Kay Hoppenrath,
a year-round resident of Mackinac Island, who
kindly provided me with so much wonderful
information about the island life, especially in
winter, so that my story could be real. Though I
tried to be accurate, I occasionally took a novelist's
prerogative. Mackinac Island has given me and all
visitors wonderful memories. It is a special place
that takes me back in time to a world we don't
know anymore. What a blessing. Also, thanks to
bookseller Tamara Tomac, who found Kay
as a willing ear for my questions.

To Shelly Gaponik, my niece, who helped me
with my snowmobile lingo. Hopefully I got it right.

Thanks to physician Mel Hodde and writer friends
Marta Perry and Carol Steward, who provided me
with accurate stroke information.

As always to my husband, Bob, who is my right arm
and my dearest friend and who provided me
with stained glass information.

In his heart a man plans his course,
but the Lord determines his steps.
—*Proverbs* 16:9

Chapter One

Christine Powers clung to the railing of the ferry, chilled to the bone yet hot under the collar, a cliché her father often used.

Her father. Her parents. How could she begrudge them an anniversary cruise? Yet while they swayed in the tropic breezes, she had been trapped into this freezing trip to Mackinac Island to care for her grandmother.

Important projects were piled on her desk back in Southfield. Her clients' deadlines had been pushed back as much as they could be so she could make the trip that had rankled her from the moment her father had asked.

She loved her grandmother. She loved her parents. But she also loved her career, and putting it in jeopardy hadn't sat well with her.

The ferry bumped against the pier, giving her a jolt, and Christine watched a crew member toss a line to a dockhand. Her gaze moved up the long wooden pier to the island town. Through the swirling snowflakes she could see Fort Mackinac sitting proudly on a hill, its white concrete walls providing a barricade when, hundreds of years earlier, many nations entered the Michigan waters to take over the island.

In the summer, Christine loved Mackinac Island. She loved its history and landscape and the uniqueness that captured tourists from all over. But she didn't love it now—not when she felt mired in the midst of too many projects that needed completion. She had advertising copy to edit, two ad campaigns to finalize and a new client to impress. The Dorset account would make her shine in the eyes of her firm.

A ragged sigh escaped, leaving a billow of white breath hanging on the air. She lifted her shoulders and grasped her carry-on bag, determined to get through the next few days.

When she heard the clang of the gangway, she maneuvered through the expansive benches toward the front of the boat to disembark. As she neared, she surveyed the prow, where she hoped to see her other bag, but the area stood bare.

A crewman flagged her forward, and she stepped onto the slippery ramp, clutching the railing until her feet hit the pier.

"Careful," a crewman called.

She muttered a thank-you and had taken two steps forward when her foot slipped on the icy planking. She skidded, her arms flailing while her carry-on bag landed on the pier. A hand grasped her arm to steady her, and the crew member who'd warned her gave her a knowing grin.

She managed a smile—better than screaming—and retrieved her bag. She took guarded steps toward the ferry exit, where she eyed a workman unloading the luggage. She looked through the feathery flakes, praying hers was there and not left back in Mackinaw City.

If she weren't so stressed, the snowfall would be appealing. The soft flakes drifted past her, twirling on the frigid breeze that streamed off the straits. Why would anyone want to live on an island so isolated in the winter? By the beginning of January their only escape would be by air until the ice bridge was ready.

A shiver ran through her as she stepped beneath the enclosure and reached the ferry's cargo. Her worry eased when she spotted her suitcase. She set down her small bag and tugged at her luggage beneath the other baggage.

"Let me help."

Her focus shifted to the stranger who'd stepped beside her. She jumped at his closeness, then was thrown off guard by his wide grin.

"Thanks. I have it." She gave another determined tug and settled the suitcase beside her, pulled up the handle and tried to connect the carry-on bag to the larger piece.

The man didn't move from the spot. He shook his head as he watched, then gave a chuckle when her carry-on slipped to the ground.

If she hadn't been so irked, she would have enjoyed his smile, but his laughter rubbed her the wrong way. "That wasn't funny. My laptop's in there."

"Sorry," he said, looking less than sorry with his boyish grin and snapping dark eyes. "I assume you're Christine Powers. I've been waiting for you."

She stopped short. "I'm Christine, but who are you, if I might ask?"

He drew back and looked surprised. "I thought you knew I was coming for you. I'm Will. Will Lambert. I board with your grandmother."

"You board with my grandmother? Since when?"

"For the past year."

She controlled her jaw from sagging a foot. "No one told me."

He shrugged. "I guess you'll have to trust me. I'm trusting you're actually Christine Powers."

That made her laugh despite the cold penetrating her leather gloves. "I wasn't expecting anyone to meet me," she said, anxious to get away from the bitter wind. "I'd planned to take a taxi."

"Then you have your dream come true."

She squinted at him, wondering if he were loony or being humorous. He gestured toward the street. "The taxi's waiting. I offered to meet you because your grand-mother thought you'd have a ton of luggage."

He grasped the handle of her large case and reached for the smaller one, but she clutched it as if it held her life's treasures. "I'll carry this myself."

"Okay," he said, shrugging. "The carriage is this way." He took a step forward and looked back to make sure she was following.

Carriage? The question was fleeting. What else? The unique island had no motorized conveyances except for a couple of emergency vehicles and snowmobiles when there was enough snowfall. Horse and carriage was a common mode of transportation.

Her limbs tensed as she checked the ground for icy patches. Christine eyed the man ahead of her. He had broad shoulders and an easy gait, as if he knew who he was and liked himself. She would enjoy having that feel-ing, but at times, she wasn't sure she knew who she was. The boarder had a casual manner, sort of a rough gal-lantry like a young John Wayne. She could almost pic-ture him in a tilted Stetson.

When Will stepped from under the covering onto the

sidewalk, Christine stopped beneath the enclosure and looked at snow that quickly dissipated to slush beneath the feet of the horses.

Will turned toward her as if wondering why she'd been dawdling, but she didn't hurry. Let him wait. She studied him, watching his breath puff in a white mist. He wore a dark leather jacket and a dark blue scarf around his neck. He had a youthful look yet a face that appeared seasoned by life.

Christine had learned to study people first and form an opinion before she let down her guard. She'd learned to analyze her clients at the firm. Sadly, she hadn't always been as astute at judging people as she was today.

Stepping from beneath the shelter, she turned her attention to Main Street, where buggies lined the road— hotel shuttles, private conveyances and taxis, like the one that would take her to her grandmother's. The town had already captured the feeling of Christmas. Large wreaths with bright red ribbons hung from the old-fashioned streetlights, and the dusting of snow created a Christmas-card setting.

The scent of winter sharpened the air and softened the scent of horse muck that steamed from the cold ground. She recoiled again, amazed she'd agreed to do this "little favor" for her parents.

As the driver loaded her case behind the seat, the horse's flank quivered, and it stomped its foot as if ready to be on its way. Will reached for her smaller case, and this time she relinquished it. He handed it to the driver, who put it behind the seat with her other bag. He told the driver where they were headed, then offered to assist her.

She placed her hand in his, feeling his warm palm and long fingers clasping hers to give her a lift into the buggy.

The cab tipped as Will joined her and pulled a lap robe over her legs. "This will keep you warmer."

The driver looked over his shoulder through the front window. "Ready?" he asked.

"We're all set," Will called. When he settled against the seat, his eyes sought hers, and she must have grimaced, because his look softened. "You'll get used to this. It takes a while. Modern conveniences are a habit, not a necessity."

He said it with a self-assured tone that seemed patronizing. Christine liked conveniences. In fact, she liked luxuries, and she wasn't planning to apologize for her taste.

The horse jerked forward and moved down Huron Street, its clip-clop rhythm rocking the floorboards. Her shoulder hit Will's, and he shifted. A cool spot filled the space, and she almost wished he would have stayed closer.

The driver snapped the reins again and the horse picked up its pace. She studied the scene, noting many shops appeared closed as they trotted past, their interiors dark and the displays gone from the windows. A wreath on the door gave sign that the restaurant was open, and more Christmas decor brightened the pharmacy and grocery store.

Will was quiet, and she wondered what he had on his mind.

He glanced at her, as if realizing she'd been looking at him. "Life here is different from the big city. Can you imagine not having to lock your doors?"

"Not really," she said, turning toward the scenery.

But her quiet didn't stop him. He talked about the community while she viewed the passing landscape. She didn't want to get caught up in his lighthearted prattle.

She'd been miserable about coming here, and she planned to stay that way. Her attitude jolted her. She was being childish, but right now she didn't care.

Ahead, Huron Street veered right past the visitor's center. Christine viewed the wide lawn of the fort now hidden beneath a fine blanket of snow. The jingle of the horse's bells set her in a holiday mood, despite her opposition to being here.

The driver pulled the reins, and they turned up Fort Road. As they climbed Fort Hill, the wind nipped at their backs and sent a chill down Christine's spine.

"Cold?" Will asked, tucking the blanket more securely around her legs. "If you move closer to me, I'll block the wind."

She noted his masculine frame and, though feeling odd nestled beside a perfect stranger, she shifted toward him, grateful for the offer. When she moved, he slid his arm around her shoulders.

For a fleeting moment she drew away, but the wind lunged across her again. Reconsidering, she settled beside him. Pride and independence held no value if she froze to death.

Steam billowed from the horse's nostrils as it trotted along, its hooves clopping on the asphalt road and breaking the deep silence.

"How long will you be here?"

"Only a week or so." Her breath ballooned like a white cloud.

"That's right. Your parents went on a cruise."

She eyed him, wondering what else he knew about her family. "A Caribbean cruise."

"Warm weather in the Caribbean. Sounds nice, although I like winter," he said. As a second thought, he added, "Nice you're filling in for them."

Nice probably wasn't the word. She'd resented it, but she'd come. "They're celebrating their fortieth wedding anniversary."

Will drew her tighter against his shoulder. "Forty. That's great. Your parents are nice Christian people."

"They are," she said, feeling on edge again. Her Christian upbringing had taught her to honor her parents and show compassion, but while her parents followed those rules, she wasn't always very good at it.

The road veered to the right, past the governor's summer residence, then at the fork, the driver turned onto Cupid's Pathway. When she saw the house ahead of her, she pulled away from Will's protection, hoping to regain her composure.

"Here we are," he said, as the driver reined in the horse beside the lovely Victorian home. The house tugged at her memories—summer memories, she reminded herself.

Will jumped off the rig and extended his hand. She took it, thinking he was not just irritatingly charming but a gentleman. When her foot touched the ground, Christine felt off balance. She steadied herself, not wanting to let Will know how addled she felt.

He released her and scooted around to the back of the carriage while the driver unloaded her luggage. When the large bag hit the road, Will pulled out the extension handle, grasped her carry-on and paid the driver.

Will led the way, and by the time she'd climbed the porch steps, he'd given a rap on the door, opened it and beamed his toying smile. "I live here."

Christine gave a nod, thinking he might live in the house, but her grandmother wasn't his. She hoped he remembered that. Hearing her grandmother's welcoming voice, she surged past him.

"Grandma," she said, sweeping into the cozy living room. She set her case on the carpet and opened her arms to her grandmother, noticing the droopiness on the right side of her face. Seeing her made the stroke seem so much more real. "You look good, Grandma Summers. As beautiful as ever."

Her grandmother shook her head, her hair now white, her body thinned by age and illness. "That's a wee bit of stretching the truth, Christine, but thank you. The truth is, you're as lovely as ever." Though her words were understandable, Christine noted a faint slur in her diction.

Christine ached seeing her grandmother's motionless left side. Her mind flew back to the first time she was old enough to remember a visit from her grandmother. Ella Summers had appeared to her as a tall, well-dressed woman with neat brown hair the color of wet sand and a loving smile. Today she still had a warm, but lopsided smile.

Choked by the comparison, Christine leaned down to embrace her. When she straightened, she glanced behind her, wondering what had happened to Will.

"I'm happy you're here," her grandmother said, "but I'm sorry it's because of my health. I feel so—"

"Just get better, Grandma. Don't worry about feeling guilty." Let me do that, Christine thought, as her grandmother's words heightened her feeling of negligence.

She slipped off her coat, but before she could dispose of it, a sound behind her caused Christine to turn.

Will stood with his shoulder braced against the living room doorjamb. He had removed his jacket, and she noticed his chestnut-colored sweater, nearly the color of his eyes. She pulled her attention away and focused on her grandmother.

"Now that I'm out of the hospital's rehab and you're here, I'll get better sooner," Ella said, trying to reach for her hand without success.

The picture cut through her. "Mom and Dad told me what happened, but I'd like to hear it from you." She draped her coat on the sofa, then sat in a chair closer to Grandma Summers.

Her grandmother's face pulled to a frown. "You know, Christine, my memory fails me when it comes to those first days. I can remember details of my childhood, but all I remember about my stroke is Will found me and called nine-one-one. I'm not even sure if I remember that or if he told me about it."

"I can tell you what happened," Will said, stepping more deeply into the room.

Christine ignored his offer. She'd heard secondhand details. She wanted it from her grandmother. "I see the stroke affected your arm," Christine said, watching her grandmother's frustration grow when she'd tried to gesture.

"My left arm and leg. My leg doesn't cooperate, and I'm a little off balance." Discouragement sounded in her voice. "But I've made progress."

Christine patted her hand. "I'm so sorry."

"Where do you want her bags, Grandma Ella?"

Christine froze. Grandma Ella? At least, he could call her Grandma Summers. Even better, Mrs. Summers. She opened her mouth to comment.

"The room at the top of the stairs," her grandmother said.

Will winked and tipped an imaginary hat—cowboy

hat in Christine's mind—before he headed up the staircase with her luggage.

"How long has he been here?" Christine asked, fighting the unexpected interest she had in him.

"Will's such a nice young man." Ella turned her gaze from the staircase to Christine. "He moved in at the beginning of the season last year in May. I decided I'd like to have someone around, and he's been a blessing. He's like a grandson."

A grandson? Christine weighed her grandmother's words, confounded by the unknown relationship. "Mom and Dad approved?"

"Certainly. They met him on visits before my stroke, but they became much better acquainted when they were here recently. You should come here more often, dear. You're out of the loop."

Christine could have chuckled at her grandmother's modern lingo, but guilt won out. An occasional trip to the island wouldn't hurt her.

"Will's been through so much with me. He's the one who called nine-one-one when he realized something was wrong. He saved my life."

She realized her grandmother had already told her that, but it was a point she couldn't forget. How could she dislike someone who had saved her grandmother's life?

Will's footsteps bounding down the stairs drew Christine's attention to the hallway. He whipped around the corner like a man who owned the place.

"How about some cocoa?" he asked. He gave her grandmother a questioning look.

"That would be nice," Ella said. "And you can bring in some of the cookies Mrs. Fields baked."

Christine chuckled.

"It's really Mrs. Fields, the neighbor. Not the franchise," Will said.

Christine watched him head into the next room, tired of his knowing everything. Right now, she really did feel out of the loop.

"Linda Fields has been helping me in the morning since your mother left. Dressing myself is difficult. She does other things for me when Will's at work. She's been so kind."

Christine felt herself sinking lower in the chair. "You can't dress yourself?"

"I had therapy." She rubbed her temple with her right hand. "Occupational therapy, I think is what they call it. They showed me how to get dressed, but sometimes it's so frustrating. The therapist guarantees me I'll be as good as new again."

The vision of a neighbor helping her grandmother dress wavered in Christine's mind. She'd never dressed anyone, and the indignity for her grandmother seemed unbearable. "How long?"

"She's been coming in since your mother and father left."

"No. I meant how long before you'll be good as new?"

"It's up to the progress I make in my therapy. Judy, she's my therapist, only comes twice a week to see me, and I have to do the routine myself a couple times a day."

"Who helps you now?"

"Will or Linda, but Will's devoting too much time to me. He has his work."

Apparently he'd become her grandmother's superhero. "Mom'll be here soon, and you won't have to worry." Christine hated the feeling of inadequacy. She'd never nursed anyone. Apparently Will had. Will this. Will that.

With Will permeating her thoughts, another question struck her. "Who is he, Grandma Summers?"

Her eyes shifted with uncertainty. "He? You mean she. Judy's my therapist."

"No, I mean Will. Who is he?"

"He's a nice young man who needed a place to stay. I thought I told you."

"You did, but you mentioned he has a job. Is it here on the island?"

Her grandmother's eyes brightened. "Not just a job. He owns a store in town."

"Really?" So Will Whatever-His-Name was a businessman. "What kind of a store?" Hardware, she figured.

"He's an artist. Stained glass. It's so beautiful." Her grandmother's left arm twitched, and a look of despair washed over her. "I keep forgetting," she said, then gestured to the window with her right arm.

Christine looked to her left and saw a glass angel glinting in the growing sunlight. A rainbow decorated the carpet. She rose and wandered to the faceted design. Clear beveled glass shaped the figure about eight inches high. The angel clasped a vibrant floral bouquet, the only color in the lovely artwork.

"It's beautiful." The unbidden words slipped from Christine's mouth.

"Thank you."

His voice jarred her, and she turned toward Will, standing beside her grandmother, holding a tray.

He looked away and set it on the old chest her grandmother used as a coffee table. "Here you go," he said, handing her grandmother a mug.

Christine grimaced as she watched Ella struggle to grasp the drink with one hand.

"Sorry," he said, retrieving the heavy crockery and pulling a straw from his pocket. "You've always been so independent it's hard to remember." His warm smile seemed attentive as he tore the paper wrapper from the straw and lowered it into her cocoa, then held it up for her to sip.

The chocolate aroma wafted in the air and reminded Christine of the years she was a child and her mother would make her hot chocolate in the evening as a lure toward bedtime.

Christine observed his attentiveness. He was not only a gentleman, but a gentle man. It seemed strange to her, and she couldn't help but question his motives.

When Will finished, he grasped another mug and offered it to Christine. The movement brought her back from her thoughts. "Thanks," she said, accepting the drink.

He pushed her coat to the far end of the sofa and sat. In silence, they sipped the chocolate, and Christine sensed each of them had sunk into their own thoughts. Hers asked questions about the man who sat across from her looking as if he belonged there while she knew she didn't. She belonged behind a desk at Creative Productions, where she generated unique promotion ideas for other companies' ad campaigns. The whole situation coursed through her like a bad case of stomach flu.

When she lifted her head, Will was eyeing her as if trying to read her thoughts. She turned to her grandmother. "Does your therapist fly in from St. Ignace?"

"She's from Vital Care located in St. Ignace," Will said, "but the nurse is on the island. She works at the Medical——"

"I was asking my grandmother," Christine said pointedly.

Ella shook her head. "Will knows the answers to all your questions, Christine."

"I know that, Grandma Summers, but—"

"He's been through the whole thing with me. He and Linda."

Christine lowered her gaze, reeling from her grandmother's subtle reprimand. She looked at Will. "I appreciate your help."

Ella's frown thawed. "Now that you're here, Christine, you can take over, and we can give Linda and Will a break."

Christine blinked. Bathe her grandmother? She worked in a think tank, not a bathtub. She paused while indignity coursed through her, not for herself but for her grandmother. How did she feel having to allow others to help her with tasks most people took for granted? "And Mom will be here soon," she said.

Ella lifted a warm gaze to Will. "Did I thank you for meeting Christine at the ferry dock?"

"No thanks necessary." He set down his mug and rose. "I should get over to the studio. I have a big project I'm trying to finish."

Christine watched him stride toward the door, then pause and look back at them with his casual grin. A young John Wayne, she thought again.

He wasn't such a bad guy, she supposed, but he seemed way too familiar with her grandmother. He had to have an ulterior motive, and she felt determined to learn what it was.

Chapter Two

Will stood inside the small stable and placed the saddle pad on the horse. She whinnied and stamped her foot as if to say she wanted to go and wanted to go now. The action reminded him of Grandma Ella's granddaughter. She seemed to lack patience worse than the mare. And trust? She had less trust than a mother bird. He pictured her clinging to her carry-on at the ferry station, as if she had the crown jewels inside the little case.

He shifted to reach the saddle and lowered it on the horse's back, adjusting it on the pad to make sure it didn't rub the horse's withers. He gave Daisy a pat. Women. He didn't understand Christine at all, and rubbing? He must have rubbed her the wrong way. She didn't like him, and since the moment he'd met her, he'd trudged through his thoughts trying to imagine how he'd offended her. He must have, because she obviously had an attitude toward him with a capital *A*.

Still, she was prettier than the baroque glass he worked with in some of his stained-glass artwork. Like the glass, she had texture and lines—very pretty lines, he had to admit. Working with his art, he could lay out his pattern and select the most unique whorls and designs in the glass created by the melding colors, but with Ella's granddaughter, he had to deal with the whole of her. He couldn't lop off the parts that weren't as nice. Her attitude fell into that category.

Will bent down and buckled the cinch snug around the horse's belly. He checked the tightness, then adjusted the stirrups. When he rose, he paused a moment while Christine's image filled his mind. When he'd stood beside her near the taxi, he'd noticed she was only a couple inches shorter than his six feet, and she was as slender as a bead of solder. She was a work of art with a bad attitude.

He could still picture how her golden hair fell in waves and bounced against her shoulder. In the taxi, he couldn't help but admire her glowing skin, her wide-set eyes that studied him so intently. Hazel eyes, he guessed, as changeable as she seemed to be.

Will reached for the bridle and moved to the horse's left side. He placed his hand on the horse's forelock and pressed gently. Daisy lowered her head, and he grabbed the headstall, separated the mouthpiece from the reins and held it to the horse's mouth. She opened it, and he slipped the bit gently inside, then pulled the headstall over the horse's ears. After he adjusted the chin strap, he gave Daisy's shoulders a pat.

"You're not bad-looking yourself, young lady." He tucked his hand into his pocket and pulled out a sugar cube. Daisy sensed it and lifted her head to nibble the sweet from the palm of his hand.

An unexpected thought came to him. What treat could he use to have Christine nibbling out of his palm? He wiped his hand on his jeans and gathered the reins. He leaned against the stall as once again his thoughts filtered through the morning's events. The woman had a message in her eye, warning that she didn't trust him and didn't want to try. He'd seen the same look of disdain on his father's face more often than he wanted to remember.

Will pulled his back away from the boards and led Daisy to the stable doorway, then shifted his focus toward the house.

He needed a plan. If he had to spend a week with this woman hovering beside Ella—her granddaughter no less—he had to find a way to get along with her. Daisy's sugar cube entered his mind again.

He kicked a stone with the toe of his boot and grunted. Get along? He got along fine with everyone else. The problem belonged to Christine.

Christine stepped into her guest bedroom and found her suitcase lying on the bed. Will had placed her small bag on a table beneath the window. Will again. He was like a woodpecker—irritating but intriguing.

Winter sunshine spread a spiderweb design on the table's wooden top. She wandered to the window and pushed back the lacy curtain. Will stood below just inside the stable doorway with a horse, saddled and ready to ride. Knowing he couldn't see her, she watched him staring into space as if his mind were faraway.

Seeing him with the horse, his hand on the reins, brought the same gentle cowboy to mind. She grinned at her imaginings. She'd daydreamed as a teenager but not as a woman with brains in her head.

A ragged sigh escaped her. What was it about the handsome man that she disliked? From the moment she'd laid eyes on him, he'd set her on edge, and it made no sense. She could only reason she was killing the messenger. He'd picked her up at the island ferry—a place she hadn't wanted to come.

She let the curtain drop and reminded herself the visit was only a week—eight days at the most. She had her laptop and her cell phone. Though it wouldn't be easy, business could be conducted that way, she hoped, for a short time.

She thought of her friend, Ellene, who'd had a similar gripe earlier in the year when she was stranded on Harsens Island in Lake St. Clair. She'd blown off Ellene's concern about island life, and now her friend was married to Connor and lived there. Amazing what love could do.

Love. She didn't really like the word. She'd been bitten too badly to trust. At thirty-nine, marriage seemed an unlikely prospect.

Christine returned to the window and peeked out. Will had vanished from the doorway. She could see the horse's imprints in the mounting snow. Perhaps he'd gone to work. Good. He needn't worry about her grandmother any longer now that she was there. He could spend the whole day at his job.

Stained glass. A businessman and a creative type. He seemed too—she couldn't find the word—too lackadaisical for a man who had to make a living running a business. Why hadn't he dropped her off and gone back to work instead of making them hot chocolate?

The delicate stained-glass angel filled her mind—a perfect gift for her grandmother, who'd always been a strong Christian. She could only deduce Will was a believer.

Sadness wove like tendrils into her conscience. She was a believer, but—but what? "Admit it," she mumbled.

"The Bible says faith and actions work together, and faith is made complete by a person's good deeds."

Letting the thought fetter away, Christine slipped back the curtain again and scanned the yard. She had an empty feeling, thinking about her lack of compassion for others. It wasn't that she didn't care. She just didn't take the time.

She backed away and turned her attention to her luggage, slipped her pants into a drawer and her sweaters into another, then hung up a few items. Easy when she knew how to travel light. She pulled up her shoulders and drew in a lengthy breath.

"Be nice," she whispered to herself. The man had been kind to her grandmother. The next time she saw him she knew she should show her gratitude.

She left the bedroom and descended the staircase into the large foyer. She loved her grandmother's house with all the nooks and crannies of an elegant Victorian home. So many lovely homes had been built on the island in the late 1800s.

The first floor greeted her with silence. She paused to listen. Still hearing nothing, she crossed the tiles to the living room doorway and saw her grandmother seated where she'd left her, her head resting against the wing of the chair. Her eyes were closed, and her chest rose and fell in an easy rhythm.

She studied her grandmother's face a moment, the classic lines—a well-sculpted nose, wide-set eyes as green as a new leaf, a full mouth that always curved upward into a pleasant grin, her mother's features in her grandmother's face.

Christine smiled at her grandmother's quiet beauty. Even though the stroke had left its mark, she felt confident her grandmother would get well.

"Nice smile."

Christine's heart jolted, and she swung toward the window seat that looked out to the garden. She poked her index finger into her chest. "Me?" she whispered, not wanting to wake her grandmother.

He gave a quiet chuckle and tilted his head toward the sleeping form. "She's not smiling so it must be you." His voice was hushed, and he glanced toward her grandmother as if to make sure he hadn't awakened her.

Christine tiptoed across the carpet and settled onto the next window seat. "Why are you sitting in here?"

"Waiting for you."

"Me?"

Will tilted his head. "She's sleeping so I'm not—"

"Waiting for her, I know." The man confounded her. "Why are you waiting, and where's your horse?"

His eyebrows raised, and she realized she'd given herself away.

"You were watching me?"

"No. I happened to look out the window."

He flashed her a teasing smile. "Daisy's tied up outside ready to go. I thought you might need something in town."

She frowned, looking for his motive.

Will rose, his grin fading to match her scowl. "I'm trying to be nice. I want you to feel welcome."

"I always feel welcome at my grandmother's."

"But I've never seen you here in the past year and a half. Maybe since you've visited last, she's moved the silverware to a different drawer."

His barb added another notch to her guilt. "I can find the silverware. Thank you."

He shook his head and strutted to the doorway. "Have a nice day."

"You, too," she said, thinking hers would be nicer with him gone, but the thought gave her a kick. She was being so unfair. Jealousy? Was that it? Was she being that childish about ownership of her grandmother? The idea hounded her as she hurried from the room.

"Will," she called, having distanced herself from the living room doorway. She headed in the direction she suspected he'd gone. "Will."

He didn't respond, and she dropped her arms to her sides.

"You called?"

Her neck jerked upward, and she looked at him near the back hallway. Now facing him, her apology knotted in her throat. "Look, I'm—I'm sorry. It's not your fault that I'm here. It's no one's fault. My parents planned their trip, and my grandmother didn't know she was having a stroke. I—" She stopped, not knowing what else to say.

He looked at her questioningly. "It's okay. Sometimes things happen that we don't expect, and it's difficult to adjust plans. My parents like planning everything to the letter. My father wishes I would, but I don't. As he would say in the words of Shakespeare, 'Ay, there's the rub.'"

"You're quoting Shakespeare?"

He laughed, and the look in his eyes unsettled her. His rich smile reflected in the sparkling brown of his iris. "Like everyone, I took English lit at university."

"You were a college man?"

His smile faded. She studied him, curious why her question had triggered the negative look.

He seemed to regroup. "For nearly three years."

No degree? "What was your major? Art?" she asked.

"Business."

Business. She drew back, startled by the new information. "So where does the art come in?"

His eyes drifted, and she could see he was uncomfortable with the probing.

"I left U of M and went to Creative Studies in Detroit, then to Carnegie Mellon in Pittsburgh."

Now that really knocked her off guard. "I'm impressed."

"Don't be," he said.

His comment was so abrupt Christine didn't understand what happened. "I don't mean to keep you."

"I'm on my way." He took a step backward. "Drop by the studio sometime."

"If I have time. My grandmother's my priority."

He gave a quick nod and headed out the front door. She followed and watched him through the Victorian glass window. He put his foot into the stirrup, flung his trim leg over the saddle and snapped the reins. The horse took off at a good gait and, before long, he'd vanished around the bend.

She let out a sigh. The conversation had been strange. Strange and strained. Something bothered Will, and she wondered if her grandmother knew his problem.

With her grandmother in mind, Christine returned to the living room, and when she came through the doorway, her grandmother opened her eyes. "I guess I caught a little catnap."

"Naps are good for you. I unpacked and talked with Will a few minutes."

Her grandmother straightened. "Why don't you like Will, Christine?"

"Why don't I what?"

"I can see you don't like Will, and I can't understand why. I'm sure Will sees it, too."

"I apologized to him before he left. I know I was a little abrupt."

"But why, dear?"

Christine wandered deeper into the room and sank into a nearby chair. "I—I keep thinking he must have an ulterior motive."

"Will? He's as gentle as a lamb and so kindhearted."

She ached watching her grandmother try to gesture again. "But why is he so thoughtful? You're his landlady."

Her grandmother straightened in the chair. "Because he follows God's Word. He clothes himself with compassion and kindness. You're a Christian. You should understand that."

"I—" She felt her heel tapping against the carpet and tried to stop herself before her grandmother noticed. Christine knew she would disappoint her if she admitted her faith had paled from the actions of her youth.

"What motive do you think he has?" Her grandmother's sentence came out disjointed.

"I don't know." She wanted to end the direction of the conversation. "I just think a mature male would have better things to do than to be a nursemaid to—"

"An old lady."

Christine flinched. "I didn't mean it that way, Grandma." She wished she could just keep her mouth shut. Where was the tact she used in the business world?

"I know." Her vivid green eyes captured Christine's.

Christine could barely look in her eyes. "I'm—"

"You're a career woman," Ella said. "You make important deals and enjoy success. I'm proud of you, but you can also be kind and still be successful. God says, there will be a time for every activity, a time for every deed. In fact, success is even greater when it's done with a humble heart and a desire to please the Lord."

Christine fought her tears. She felt like a child being chastised by her parents for misbehaving, but this was Grandma Summers, and grandmothers were supposed to be supportive and forgiving.

Yet her grandmother was right. Christine had been unpleasant, but she'd thought she'd had good reason. "I did apologize."

"I know. You told me." She eased back and didn't say any more.

Christine's mind slid back to that moment. "What's in the back hall off the foyer? Will came from that way."

"It's the back entry. He can come from the apartment that way or leave to go outside. I can lock that door, but it's been convenient for me."

"Is that how he found you after you had the stroke?"

"It was. He came in one morning to see if I wanted anything from the store in town. He found me confused and weak. At least that's what he tells me. I tried to walk and couldn't. That's when he called for help. Fast thinking."

"I'm glad he was here," Christine said, and meant every word. She rose and kissed her grandmother's cheek. "So what can I do for you? Can I help you with your therapy?"

She glanced around the room and noticed dust on the table. "I can dust and run the vacuum." She crossed the room and gathered shoes and a jacket from the floor. "What should I do with these?"

The shoes were definitely not her grandmother's. They were men's shoes, and so was the jacket. "Will's?"

Her grandmother chuckled. "He drops his belongings like a teenager, but I don't mind. It's nice to have someone here."

"Well, he shouldn't cause you extra work. He has his own home. I'll talk to him."

Her grandmother shook her head. "Sometimes Will forgets. Don't worry about cleaning. Will pitches in, and I should really hire a cleaning lady for a while."

"Mom will be here. She won't want a cleaning lady. You know Mom. You do it her way or no way." She chuckled, then realized she'd almost described herself.

Her grandmother gave a nod, then gestured toward a table with a toss of her head. "See that little ball? Would you hand it to me? I'm supposed to squeeze it off and on during the day to strengthen my muscles."

Christine handed her the ball and had turned to discard Will's belongings when the telephone rang. "I'll get it." She headed toward the small secretary and picked up the receiver. "Summers residence."

When she heard her father's voice, her spirit lifted. "Daddy, where are you?"

She covered the mouthpiece and turned to her grandmother. "They're in Jamaica. I can hear the steel drum band." Christine longed to be on some exotic island with sunshine and balmy breezes. "Are you having fun?"

"A great time. Fantastic." His voice boomed.

"I'm really happy for you, Dad."

"How's Grandma? And be honest, Christine."

"Grandma's fine." She couldn't believe he'd told her to be honest. "Really. We're doing okay, and you'll be here soon. We'll see you on Monday, right?"

Her heart sank a little with his answer.

"Okay, Wednesday will work. I can leave on the afternoon ferry if you're early enough. Love you both."

She hung up and faced her grandmother. "It's eighty-five degrees there."

"I'm sure they're having a wonderful time," she said, her eyes searching Christine's.

Guilt blanketed her again. She needed to fix her attitude. The problem was timing. Timing? Face it, she thought, no time was ever good for Christine. She liked to plan her course and sail away with no waves, but things didn't always happen the way she wanted. She needed to learn to roll with the tide. Will's comment about things not always going as planned echoed in her thoughts.

"I'd like to go to church tomorrow," Ella said. "It's difficult, but I have the wheelchair. Would you like to go?"

"Church?" She stood in the middle of the room and looked out the wide front window and across the porch to the splotches of white and tried to envision what good a wheelchair would do in the snow. "But how—"

"Will can handle it. We'll get a taxi. It's just a short ride down Fort Hill."

Christine stopped herself from rolling her eyes. Will again. "Is it worth the trouble, Grandma?"

"Worth it? What has more worth than spending time with the Lord?"

She closed her mouth before she put her foot in it again. "I meant it's so difficult for you."

"My therapist said I should try to get out. I've been too embarrassed to have anyone see me so useless. My face is drooping. I can see that in the mirror."

Christine knelt beside her grandmother. "You're not useless. I'm sorry I said anything. I—"

Her grandmother patted her arm with a weak hand.

"You didn't make me feel that way, Christine. I'm just..." She paused and looked at her unaccommodating fingers. "Did I ever tell you about when I was a girl?"

Christine figured she'd heard every youthful tale of her grandmother's, but she'd already hurt her feelings enough. "I don't know, Grandma."

Ella gave her a tender look and leaned back in her chair. "When I was a girl, my mother sent all of us to Bible school during the summer. It was like a summer camp but at the church. We learned so much about compassion and giving to others. We memorized Bible verses. One of my favorites was that whatever you do, whether in word or deed, do it all in the name of the Lord Jesus. Even as a girl, I realized that our deeds reflect our faith."

Christine recalled thinking that same thing earlier that day, and she wondered if the Lord was pounding a lesson into her head. "I know, Grandma, but—"

"No buts. We had a project one year at the Bible camp. We visited a hospital to bring little gifts we made to some of the elderly patients. I saw a woman there unable to use her limbs. At the time I didn't know anything about strokes, but I'm sure that's what it was. She couldn't speak well, either. That very day I promised the Lord I would always be kind to people in need. So being useless myself makes it doubly hard because of the promise I made to God."

How could she argue with her grandmother's way of looking at her vow? Christine figured God was the one who had allowed her grandmother to have a stroke. He knew she couldn't continue to be helpful, so He'd have to forgive her breaking her vow. But she couldn't verbalize that to her grandmother.

"Then, I think, it's most important that you get better. Right, Grandma?"

"Right," she said, a gentle look in her eyes. "And that's why I want to go to church."

"Then you and I will go to church," Christine said.

"You and me and Will."

Christine managed to smile. "You and me and Will."

Chapter Three

"There, that wasn't so bad." Will stomped the snow from his shoes on the porch mat. Today when he'd awakened, he was surprised to see a heavy snow had fallen while he'd slept, leaving the island shrouded in white.

He wheeled Grandma Ella through the front door to the middle of the foyer. "Let me take your coat."

"I can get her coat," Christine said, bustling toward him.

He shrugged. "It's all yours." He tried to figure out the big deal. Either one of them could help her. It wasn't like a jump ball in a basketball game.

Christine hung her grandmother's coat in the foyer closet, then hung up her own and closed the door without a glance his way.

Will shook his head and passed her, removed his wet shoes and left them by the living room archway, not wanting to dirty Ella's carpet. He headed across the carpet, shrugged off his jacket and hung it on a chair, then settled on the sofa.

Yesterday's newspaper lay on the floor. Will lifted it to his lap and swung his feet around to spread out on the cushions. Though he tried to focus on the first page, his attention had shifted over the top of the paper toward the foyer.

Christine came through the doorway pushing Ella's wheelchair. He really wished Grandma Ella would get out of the thing. She needed to get her legs working and strengthen the muscles. That would alleviate her unsteadiness. He'd encouraged her to use the walker, but she said she felt like an old lady.

Christine turned his way, and her expression let him know she wasn't pleased to see him sprawling on the sofa.

Will dropped the paper onto the floor and swung his feet to the carpet. "Sorry. Usually on Sundays, I keep Grandma Ella company for a while. Am I taking up too much space?"

A pink tinge lit Christine's cheeks. "No." She sank onto the chair with a sigh. "Not at all."

"What's wrong, dear?" her grandmother asked.

"Nothing."

"You look unhappy."

"Really. I'm fine."

A look of uneasiness filled her face, and she gave Will a smile that looked a little forced to him.

She studied her fingernails for a moment. "I need to go into town. I should have thought of it while we were there for church. I noticed at breakfast we need a few things from the grocery store."

Will glanced at his watch. "It's Sunday. The store's just about to open. I'll take you," he said. "I need to drop by the studio anyway and pick up some paperwork I forgot to bring home."

"You have a tandem bike, or am I supposed to ride

with you on the horse?" As the words left her, she concocted another grin.

The look on her face made him laugh. "No, but that's a good idea. Daisy would love to go for a good run this morning. She leaves for the mainland tomorrow."

Christine looked surprised "Leaves?"

He loved to confound her. "Once the heavy snow begins, Daisy is stabled at a farm on the mainland. Only the horses used for taxis and drays stick around here for the winter."

Christine gave him a look. "The horses are smarter than people, I think."

He chuckled, but he got her point. He jumped up and headed for the doorway. "We'll take my sled... or you can ride your grandmother's."

"Sled?"

He laughed aloud this time. "Snowmobile."

"You want me to drive myself? I don't know a thing about snowmobiles."

"One day I'll give you a lesson then."

"Yes," Grandma Ella said, "that's a good idea."

Christine held up her hand in protest. "I'm leaving next week. Save the lesson for my mom." She chuckled.

Will enjoyed her unexpected good humor and wished he could always see that side. "You can ride with me. I'd like you to see my studio anyway."

"You'll enjoy seeing the shop," her grandmother agreed.

She paused a moment, then said, "Okay."

Will glanced back to make sure he had heard her correctly. No argument?

"Who can I call to stay with you, Grandma Summers?" Christine asked.

Her grandmother waved her away. "I'm not a baby. I can stay by myself for an hour. Put the portable phone next to me, and set my walker here. I'll use it if I need to get up."

"We won't be gone long," Will assured Christine, then turned to Grandma Ella, "and we can check on you, okay?"

"I'll be fine. You can't tie an old horse down for long."

Christine chuckled. "If you were a horse, Will would be shipping you over to St. Ignace."

Will gave her a high five, and to his amazement, she responded and took a step backward toward the foyer.

"I'll change and make a list," she said.

"Keep it short," Will said. "We go to the mainland for the bulk of the groceries."

Christine stopped and motioned toward the window. "But what about when—"

"No ferry service? Then supplies are flown in." He enjoyed teaching this strong-willed woman about island life.

She arched a neatly trimmed brow. "As I said, island living isn't very convenient, is it?"

"No, but then if you're looking for convenience you don't live on an island."

Christine gave him a see-I-told-you-so look.

Will didn't bother to comment. "I'll change and be ready in a minute. And remember, we're not going back if you forget anything."

She looked as if she wanted to say something but didn't.

Christine stood outside the small barn, eyeing Will's snowmobile and trying to imagine herself seated on it. She'd surprised herself by agreeing to ride the thing, but she needed to get around, and walking down and up hills to town in snow appealed to her even less than riding with Will.

She felt like the Abominable Snowman, with a sweatshirt and down jacket over her sweater. She could barely move. With two pairs of socks under the tall boots she had borrowed from her grandmother—already a little tight—she tromped through the snow like Frosty on a bad day.

"Are you warm enough?" Will asked.

"I hope so." She could only deduce that his silly expression was lighthearted sarcasm. She shifted her attention to the snowmobile. "You want me to get on this thing?"

Will lifted his hand. "Hang on a minute." He walked back into the stable and came out carrying two helmets. "You're not going anywhere without this."

He tossed her one, and she nearly dropped it. "I'm supposed to wear this?"

"You're not only supposed to—you will. It's for your safety. No one gets on my sled without one."

Sled? She pictured the little red sled from her childhood, then eyed the monstrosity he was telling her to get on. She gazed at the helmet and then at him. How much danger was she in?

"Put it on," he said, slipping some kind of hood over his head.

"What's that?"

"A smock. You'll have to get one." He slid the helmet onto his head and attached the strap.

She followed what he'd done, attached the strap and felt as if she had a cooking pot on her head with a large shield over her face. "I look stupid."

"You don't look stupid," he said, accentuating the word *look*.

"I hear a *but* in that statement."

"I'm not going there," he said, a teasing smile growing on his face.

Will looked amazingly handsome, his broad shoulders accentuated beneath his sledding jacket. Below the helmet, his eyes sparkled when he looked at her. "Okay, Bigfoot, can you climb on?"

He made her laugh. She liked that but not his I-know-more-about-island-life-than-you-do attitude. Earlier she'd tried to cover her amusement with sarcasm, but lately he had a cute way to get back at her. She felt like a kid again, rather than the dignified woman she'd considered herself to be.

She'd studied Will, weighing his boyish charm and easy manner, and had pondered how old he might be. She'd wanted to know, but she knew good manners, and one couldn't blatantly ask. She'd be irked if he asked her.

Christine straddled the vehicle as best she could, then plopped onto the seat, scooting back as far as she could to make room for him. She felt her cell phone press against her leg. She'd tucked it in her pocket.

He waited for her to get settled, then slipped in front of her. "I made it. You're not as fat as you look."

She gave him a jab. "I feel undignified enough. Don't add to it."

"Dignity is nothing without a sense of humor."

"I don't mind laughing *with* someone, but I don't want to be laughed *at* by someone," she said.

"Then next time, you'll have to leave about half that garb at home." He grinned. "You need a bib."

"A bib? I'm not eating lobster."

"Snow pants, to you," he said, chuckling. "You'll get used to it, and if I were a betting man, I'd wager you'll get to love the island even in winter."

"You're on," she said. "If I love it here, I owe you something big. A seven-course dinner or—" She faltered, realizing she was having a good time.

"I'll make that decision when I collect," he said with a wink over his shoulder. "Now keep your feet on the foot board." He pulled the cord and started the engine. He revved the motor to warm it, sending another grin with each vroom-vroom sound. "Ready?"

"Absolutely," she said, then jolted backward when the sled shot forward. She let out a squeal and clung to him, her arms wrapped around his waist, praying her feet were glued to the footrest.

He paused at the end of the driveway. "Lean with me on the turns," he called over his shoulder.

She nodded, and he rolled forward, then made a right toward Custer Road.

Above the roar of the engine, he hollered back his usual witty comments, his youthful spirit evident as they soared across the snow. Youthful, yet he had depth, too, Christine had noticed. She saw the heavy thoughts in his eyes. She watched the tenderness he had for her grandmother, and Christine couldn't help but notice how he studied her. She didn't think he'd figured her out yet, but he would.

The wind whipped past, and Christine clung to Will's body for warmth and security. A chill rolled down her back despite her heavy clothing, or wasn't it the wind at all? She'd never done anything quite so daring, and perhaps it was only the adventure that took her breath away and sent excitement prickling up her spine.

Will seemed to be in his element—relaxed and care-free. She wished she could be more like him, more easy-going, and definitely more trusting.

The snow-burdened trees shimmered in the muted winter sun, and occasionally the clouded sky opened to let a bright ray stream down to earth and drop sequins in the snow. She closed her eyes from the glitter.

"Hang on," Will called.

Her heart rose to her throat as they made a curve past the governor's house and flew down Fort Hill and the whitewashed buildings flashed past her. She clung to him even tighter, enjoying the unfamiliar feeling of holding a man in her arms.

Instead of heading to Main Street, Will slowed and turned onto Market Street. They shot past the medical center and post office. Along the way, the quaint shops and homey bed-and-breakfasts lined the road, adorned with green-and-red wreaths and garland announcing Christmas. Finally he decelerated and pulled to the curb. "Here we are."

She looked at the store beside her. The window held displays of magnificent stained-glass windows, and sun catchers in all shapes and sizes hung from the French panes. The brilliant colors glinted in the afternoon rays.

The quiet street seemed so different from the hustle and bustle she recalled from the summer afternoons when tourists packed the streets—*fudgies,* the residents called them, because most visitors left the island with boxes of homemade fudge purchased in the famous island fudge shops.

Will climbed from the sled and extended his hand. Christine looked at it and at her feet adhered to the running board, her body cramped from clinging to Will's waist as they flew across the unblemished snow. "I'm not sure I can move."

He pulled off his helmet, his grin as wide as the Mackinac Bridge, and shook his head. "Let me help."

She gave him her hand and dismounted, her knees trembling from the bumpy vibration of the sled. "I need to get my land legs."

He drew closer, balancing her in his arms. "You'll get used to it."

But could she ever become used to being held in a wonderful man's arms? The thought rushed down her limbs, and, embarrassed, Christine stepped away and pulled off her helmet.

Will took it from her and hung it with his on the handlebars.

For a moment, Christine felt overwhelmed by the newness of her experiences, but she had to admit she felt exhilarated. The fresh air, the wind nipping at her cheeks, the unspoiled beauty of the landscape, the feel of Will's arms—it all had painted a memory in her mind and on her senses.

She drew in another breath, filling her lungs with pure air. "It smells wonderful."

"The cold freezes the horse dung."

His surprising comment made her laugh. "That's very romantic." As the word left her, she tried to stop it, but it was too late. Why would she say *romantic* to a man she barely knew and probably would never see again once she returned home?

"Thanks," he said. "I'm glad I can make a good impression on someone in this world."

Though he smiled, Christine sensed an undertone in his voice. She eyed him, but he didn't give a hint of what he had meant and she didn't know him well enough to pry, although she was tempted.

Will pulled a ring of keys from his pocket and headed for the door while Christine moved closer to the shop window to take a better look at his artwork. She saw the name on the window, Sea of Glass. She'd heard that phrase before.

Her mind shifted back to Will's behavior. He was hiding something or… Maybe he was more like she was than she'd thought. Now that she'd gotten through her own murky days as a naive businesswoman, she had gained confidence and had also developed a deep curiosity to look more deeply into people.

People said much more below the surface than their words expressed. Subliminal messages were important in the advertising business. She needed curiosity to sense what the company really wanted to convey in their ads, and then needed it again to express the underlying message to the consumer. If Will was playing games, he didn't know with whom he was messing.

Will pushed open the door, and a bell tinkled, catching her attention. Christine followed him inside, feeling the warmth of the building and the varied aromas of raw wood, dust and all the products that went into stained-glass art. She knew nothing about it, but she was awed by what she saw.

"This is beautiful, Will." She paused beneath a large window hanging from the ceiling. A rich tapestry of colors created a pastoral scene with flowers, a river, sun and shade—multiple hues of greens and blues. "How do you do this? It's amazing."

"Very carefully," he said, the playful tone returning to his voice.

Her admiration rose as she turned in a circle to view the magnificent pieces of glass designs that adorned the store. "You learned to do this in college?"

He shrugged. "It's like anything. You learn techniques, and then you let your creativity take flight. You must do something creative in your own work—maybe something different than me, but still unique and your own style."

She searched his face, surprised at the matter-of-fact way he discussed his art. Something bothered him. "I suppose I do, but it's very different."

He stood a moment in silence. "Why is it different?"

"In advertising, I create ads and promotional campaigns for clients."

"That's creative." He gave one of his sun catchers a poke. "It's the same. You didn't learn everything in college."

"That's very true." She thought of all the mistakes she'd made and her feeble attempts to cover them. "I work with a team. I can always blame them for my errors in judgment. You can't."

"No, but what's the difference. You know you made the mistake, the same as I do."

His comment left her flailing. He'd pinpointed an important issue that hit too close to home. No matter what she had done wrong, she knew about it herself—and so did God.

She looked at Will's expectant face, his eyes searching hers as if filled with questions he didn't have the nerve to ask. Something about him was endearing. "I'm really impressed." She made a sweeping gesture around the store, seeing wooden crates filled with gigantic pieces of marvelous glass in many colors and textures.

"I figured you'd like some of my things."

"Some? Everything is unique."

His questioning look faded, and a grin replaced it. "Then come into my back room and see some more of my work."

Will winked, then smiled at her over his shoulder.

Christine had to admit he had a wonderful smile that seemed contagious. She wanted to grin back, but she wasn't planning to let him know she found him attractive.

He passed through the doorway. "This is my studio where I make all of these things."

She followed him through the door and paused. She'd seen the supplies he sold in the front of the store, but in the back she surveyed worktables laden with projects and crates with a mixture of glass nearby.

"Where did you get the name for the shop—Sea of Glass?"

He turned to face her. "It's in the Bible. Revelations. Those who were victorious over Satan stood beside the sea of glass as clear as crystal." He gestured toward the lake. "The studio's only a couple blocks from the water. I thought it was fitting."

"It is. I like it."

"Glass is like people," he said, holding up a piece. "If you just glance at it, you see one thing, but if you really look inside—" he held it toward the light "—you see all kinds of nuances and textures."

She ran her finger over the swirled design, wondering what he'd seen inside her. "What kind of glass is this?"

"Baroque." He slid the large piece back into the rack, then selected another. "This is water glass."

Christine looked at the texture appearing like raindrops.

"And this is a smooth ripple. Here's an opal glass, bull's-eye, English muffle and cathedral glass."

"You've lost me."

He lowered the glass and then stepped closer and tousled her already messed hair. "No, I haven't. You're right here. See." He stepped closer and gave her a quick hug.

The embrace surprised yet pleased her. Will looked different in the studio, as if he were in control of his life. She saw confidence, and a look on his face that intrigued her—pride and a kind of wholeness. She wished she felt that way.

"You love this work," she said. "I can see it on your face."

"I do. It's like cheating. I earn a living doing something that I have to do because I can't help myself."

"That's not cheating. It's finding the right job."

He patted a stool beside the tall raw-wood table. "Sit here."

She slid onto the stool, and he leaned his hip against the table.

"Have you found the right career?" he asked.

"I like to think so. When we do a good job and make the client happy, I can sit back and see the result of my work. It feels good."

"That's what counts." He shifted away, but his response left her questioning her own decisions. She saw a specific difference between Will's attitude toward his work and hers.

"Would you like to see how I do any of these things?" He motioned toward the projects scattered around the room.

"I'd love to, but I think we'd better get going. I'm nervous about leaving my grandmother too long."

He nodded, then reached beneath his worktable and pulled out a large folded paper. "A pattern I'm designing. I'll show you back at the house."

"I'd like that," she said. "Let's go. We still have to stop at the grocery store."

As the words left her, her cell phone played its familiar tune. She dug into her pocket, curious yet concerned. "I left the number with Grandma. I hope she's okay." She stared at it, afraid to answer.

"You'll know, if you answer that thing."

The melody stopped when she hit the green button. "Hello," she said, expecting to hear her grandmother's voice, but who she heard instead gave her a start. "Dad. Where are you?"

She heard the upset in his voice, and she listened as her pulse pounded in her temple.

"You're in Florida? Why?"

Her stomach tightened as her world crumpled. She turned her head toward Will, unable to believe what she'd just heard.

She closed her eyes, then opened them again. "My mother fell and broke her hip, jogging."

Chapter Four

Christine watched Will's jaw drop. "Your mother broke her hip jogging? Where?"

"On the ship's promenade deck." She crumpled back onto the stool. "I can't believe this. This is a bad dream."

Will rose and rested his hand on her back. His warmth rushed through her. "I'm sure she'll be fine. She's in Florida, you said. Don't worry about—"

"Not that. I'm stuck here, Will. Don't you understand? I need to get back to my job. I thought I'd be home in a few days. Now what?"

She could see he'd been taken aback. His dark eyes flashed with disbelief, and she tried to recover from his look. "Naturally I'm concerned about my mother, but like you said, she'll be okay. I just wasn't planning on something like this happening."

"We don't plan for bad things to happen, Christine, but they do."

She stared at him, wanting to say something, to explain, to have someone understand her stress, but she knew it was useless. Will didn't know her at all. He had no idea about her work or how hard it was to stay at the top. "I'll figure out something."

Will pulled his hand away, leaving a cold spot where warmth had been. Her mood felt the same. Without expecting it, she'd enjoyed the outing and new experience of the snowmobile, but now the fun had faded.

She rose from the stool. "We'd better get moving. I'm sure my grandmother is upset about this, too. Daddy called there first. I know Grandma's fine, but she'll be worried about me."

"That's just like your grandmother," Will said, walking ahead of her and snapping off the lights. He tucked the folded paper inside his jacket and waited at the door for her, his hand on the knob.

Outside, the wind seemed colder than it had felt earlier. Christine sank onto the sled, scooted back and waited for Will to climb on and help block the bitter air. Tears filled her eyes, and she brushed them away with her gloves. She felt sorry for herself, and she hated the feeling. *Lord, I'm trying to make this a go. I want to be thoughtful and compassionate, but this isn't helping.*

God's voice didn't fill her head with an answer. The only sound she heard was the rev of the engine as they sped away. She wrapped her arms around Will's trim waist, his broad shoulders blocking the wind—just as he seemed to want to protect her from her problems.

"Hang on," he called.

That's what she needed to do—hang on. But to what?

When Will stopped outside Doud's Mercantile, Christine saw a smart-looking snowmobile on display. "They sell sleds at the grocery store?"

Will grinned. "No. It's for the Christmas Bazaar the first weekend in December. They hold a fund-raiser, and the prize is this sweet-looking baby right here." He gave the sled a pat. "It's the best of its line."

"It's really nice. Tell me what to do, and I'll donate to the fundraiser, but I never win prizes. If I do, I'll give the sled to you."

Will gave her shoulder a squeeze.

Christine flew through the grocery store, paid for the purchases, donated to the fund-raiser, then headed back to her grandmother's in silence, her mind having slipped back to her problem.

The fun had vanished from the trip as quickly as the sun had hidden behind the heavy clouds and refused to come out. The cold penetrated her body, as did her dismay, and she felt icy to the bone.

Will put away the sled while Christine hurried into the house. She dropped her packages on the kitchen counter, then rushed toward the living room while she pulled off her coat. When she came through the doorway, her grandmother's concerned eyes lifted to hers.

Christine dropped her coat on a chair and put her arms around her grandmother's shoulders. "What a predicament, Grandma Summers. Poor Mom."

Ella's face reflected her concern, but her demeanor negated the look. "I'll manage, dear, but tell me what happened. Your father only told me your mother had broken her hip, of all things."

Christine shared the story that her father had told her. "It was the wind, I guess. He said the prow of the ship has a powerful wind. Mom lost her balance and fell."

"But he said they were in Florida," Ella said.

"Yes, they airlifted her there. They have a doctor on board, but they can't do surgery like that on the ship."

Her grandmother shook her head. "How long be-fore—"

"Daddy didn't know." The back door banged closed, and Christine lifted her head. "Mom'll need surgery and rehab. It'll be weeks."

"Many weeks, I'd guess," Will said from the doorway. He strutted in and plopped into a chair. "Looks like you'll need a snowmobile lesson after all."

Christine didn't like the faint grin he tried to hide without success.

"Don't jump to conclusions," she said. "I have to go back to work. Somehow." She felt the air leave her lungs.

He pinched his thumb and index finger and slid them across his mouth. "Zip."

"Zip?"

"I've zipped my mouth shut."

Good, she thought, then had second thoughts. He was a nice guy—an appealing man—but she certainly didn't want to hear his jokes about her predicament.

She turned back to her grandmother. "Don't worry. I'll see you have good care. I'm sure you'll get better and better each day."

Christine wondered if she was trying to convince her-self of that even more than her grandmother. Good care could come from a professional. Christine's mind began to snap with ideas.

Her grandmother's expression broke her heart. "I know," she said, "but this is difficult for you all the way around."

"I'd better get dinner," Christine said, rising and mo-tioning toward the kitchen. "I left the groceries on the counter." Anxious to think by herself, she didn't wait for a response but hurried into the kitchen.

She stood inside the doorway, taking in the tall painted cabinets and tiled countertops. She shifted to the groceries and pulled items from the shopping bags, totally oblivious to what she'd planned to make her grandmother for Sunday dinner.

As she clung to the refrigerator, Christine's mind raced. Tomorrow she had work to do. First she needed to alert her boss of the complication, with a guarantee she would be back on the job soon. Next she needed to let her parents know she couldn't stay. How could she break that news to her father, who was already under so much stress and worry?

"Can I help?"

Christine spun around to face Will. So much for time to think. His gentle look eased through her senses. "No thanks. I have things under control."

"You don't look like it," he said, closing the distance and taking a box of cereal from her hands. "Cereal goes in the cabinet." He opened the door and looked at her over his shoulder. "Milk goes in the refrigerator."

He lifted the milk from the cabinet and carried it back to her, leaned past her, and set the carton on the shelf. Then he moved her aside and closed the door. "Perhaps you'd better sit for a minute and get a grip."

She studied him, wanting to make some kind of retort but had nothing in her head to say. Milk in the cabinet and cereal in the refrigerator did nothing to convince him of her solid state of mind.

Christine did as he said and sank onto a kitchen chair, putting her face in her hands. She rubbed her eyes, willing herself not to cry. She'd figured she could handle the seven or eight days from her work, but now?

Will's warm hand rested on her shoulder again and

gave her taut muscles a squeeze. "It'll be all right. Things will work out the way God planned them."

She looked at his face, filled with sincerity. "But what about what I planned? I have a job and I have to answer to someone. I'm not like you. I'm not my own boss. I work with a team. I'm responsible for what I do." She slapped her hand against the table. "I have clients."

"Me, too," he said, his voice as calm as a mother's reassurance.

She lifted her head and looked at him. "What clients?"

"I do special orders. I set deadlines, and I keep them. I'm proud of my work, and I do well. And I have a boss."

"You do? I thought you owned the business."

"I do," he said, using his thumbs to massage away the tension from her shoulders. "My big boss is the Lord. Whatever I do I answer to Him."

"It's not the same," she said, uneasy with his half-joking comments.

Will pulled his hand away and captured her chin and lifted it. "I'm not kidding with you. I answer to the Lord, and that's much more powerful than answering to the head of a corporation. One situation deals with a lifetime, the other eternity."

Christine pulled her chin away. "I know that, but I can't be lighthearted about my career." She turned her head.

"Neither can I. I've given up a lot for it. More than I should have."

He'd piqued her curiosity, and she turned back to look at him. "What does that mean?"

Will pursed his lips and shook his head. "That's my problem. You have enough of your own."

She didn't want to deal with her own. Christine wanted

the problems to go away, to fade with the evening sun. She drew in a breath and managed to rise. "It's dinner-time."

"I know. I'm hungry. Let me help."

She gave him a quick look. "Don't you have your own kitchen?"

"A small one. Haven't you ever seen my apartment?"

She ignored his question. "I'm making dinner for my grandmother."

"I pay room and *board*," he said. "That means your grandmother cooks for me when she's well."

Room and board. The phrase sank in. He paid her grandmother for his food. She thought he'd eaten there last night because her grandmother had invited him. She gathered her thoughts, ashamed of her reaction to his attempt to be kind. "Okay, you can help. Do you know how to make a salad?"

"Sure. I make a great salad, but—" He hesitated, a deep frown on his face. "I think I'll go out for a while. Don't worry about me for dinner."

Christine opened her mouth to apologize, but he'd already shot from the room. She heard the back door bang closed, and she stood there staring at an empty room and feeling even more empty inside.

Will pushed the burger around on his plate and stared out the window of the Mustang Lounge. The view was nothing spectacular, no shoreline, just small shops across the street and new flakes drifting down to whiten the graying ground from the day's traffic.

Will had tried to understand Christine's attitude. She'd been disappointed by her father's news, but he didn't like the way she dealt with letdowns. It really wasn't his business, but he had to live with the woman or stay holed up in his small apartment, and he wished he could smooth things over for her.

He'd probably shoved too much Bible at her. He knew she'd been raised a Christian from meeting her parents, but she'd lost something along the way. In his opinion, she'd be a happier lady if she settled her disagreement with the Lord. God kept His promises, and Christine could use some reassurance right now.

But he suspected she had deeper issues. Christine's glowing comments about her job left him with questions. She seemed a woman who'd worked hard to get where she was, but she had internal fears. Either she'd failed too often and questioned her own ability, or the job she praised wasn't as fulfilling as she tried to lead him to believe.

What difference did it make? He tossed the napkin onto the table and signaled Jude for more coffee.

The man gave him a nod, then went on to finish whatever he was doing behind the counter.

The lounge was quiet this time of day. The business would probably pick up in the evening, or maybe the first big snowfall had people scrambling to get their sleds ready for use. Only three or four customers had come in to eat, which was unusual for one of the only restaurants open year-round.

Will rarely came to the lounge on Sunday. Usually he ate at Grandma Ella's. He enjoyed those quiet evenings when he'd make a fire in her fireplace and loll around, listening to her stories or watching TV, or sometimes even playing a game of dominos with her. Often she beat the socks off of him. She'd had the mind of a steel trap before the stroke.

Will's thoughts shifted back to his coffee request. When he looked up, he saw Jude wandering over with the pot, so he eased back, not needing to give another call.

"Sorry for the wait," Jude said, and filled Will's cup. He stood a moment, looking at him with questioning eyes. "You don't look too happy."

Will shrugged. "I'm okay."

"How's Ella doing? Troubles? Why no dinner today at the Summers' house?"

"Grandma Ella's okay. Her granddaughter's there to help out. She's been a handful."

"Who? Ella?"

Will grinned at his error. "No. Her granddaughter."

"Teenager?"

His question surprised Will. "No, she's a woman."

Jude set down the pot and made an hourglass shape with his hands. "That kind of woman?"

"I haven't noticed."

Jude let out a guffaw. "Come on. You noticed." He slid into the booth across from Will and folded his arms over his chest. "Either she's old enough to be your mother or ugly as sin. Which is it?"

"Neither." Will focused on his refreshed coffee then lifted the mug to take a drink. The hot liquid burned his tongue, and he pulled the mug back, sloshing coffee onto the table. He grabbed his wrinkled napkin and swiped at the wet spot.

"She's got you addled," Jude said, letting go another loud cackle. "So what's up? She won't give you a second look?"

"That's not it at all. Where's your mind? She's as mean as a cornered opossum." Will heard himself and chuckled at his description. "She's not real happy here taking care of Ella, so she has an attitude." Will told Jude the story about her mother's fall. "So now she's stuck here. She's one of those high-powered business women, I guess."

"I always thought of you as a pretty good business-man yourself."

"Thanks, but it's different. She's in advertising. It's kind of dog-eat-dog, she says. She's apparently afraid to be away too long." His earlier conjecture came to mind.

"Big-city woman in a small town."

Will gave his head a toss. "Something like that." But with his quick response, he pictured Christine's ruddy cheeks and sparkling eyes when she'd climbed off the sled. He saw her surprise and admiration when she'd stepped into his shop, but she'd changed in a moment, sliding right back to her edgy ways when she got the bad news.

"Bring her in. I'll put a smile on her face."

"Right," Will said, making sure Jude heard the sarcasm in his voice.

"Do I see a little jealousy?" Jude asked, slipping from the seat and grabbing the coffeepot from the table.

"Me? You're kidding." Will gave him an evil eye and did a playful toss of his head. "Get out of here."

Jude walked away laughing, while Will sat there trying to make sense out of their conversation. Jealous? Jealous of what? Sure she was a pretty woman, and yes, she could be fun to be with, but he barely knew her and half of what he knew he didn't understand.

He pushed his hip away from the bench and pulled his wallet from his back pocket. If Miss Powers hadn't been so nasty, Will would have been at Grandma Ella's eating a home-cooked meal. *Powers*. Fitting, he thought.

He chuckled at his observation, then rose and headed for the cash register to pay his bill.

The next time he saw Christine, he would tell her that was the last time he'd walk away from dinner. He grinned at an idea that came to mind. Maybe he'd give the mighty Miss P a taste of her own medicine.

Will sat in his room, moping. He'd thought of charging into the house and telling Christine what he thought of her behavior, but then he stopped himself. It would do no good. She would be there for a while, and he didn't like stress. He'd had that on the mainland with his dad and life in general. The island had mellowed him. Now he put his energy into creating works of art rather than works of get-even.

He stared at his apartment TV, the program not registering in his mind. He'd turned it on for noise. He'd hoped he would become distracted, but that hadn't happened.

The room had darkened, and light from the television flickered on the walls. As he rose to turn on a light, he heard a rap at his door.

He snapped on the lamp and grabbed the doorknob. When he pulled it open, he drew back. Christine stood at the door with a dish in her hand. He looked at the plate, then at her. "Yes?"

She stood a moment searching his eyes. "I brought dessert. It's cherry pie. Michigan cherries." She extended the dish. "I made it myself."

He didn't take the plate although he wanted to. His half-eaten burger hadn't filled a corner of his stomach.

"Can I come in?" she asked.

The request surprised him, and he stepped back without thinking.

She took a cautious step forward, still holding out the plate for him.

Will took it and closed the door after her.

Christine stood a moment, scanning the room. "Now that I'm here, I realize I've been in here before, but it's smaller than I remember."

"Thanks for the pie," he said, setting it on the short counter that served as the bulk of his kitchen. He had a compact sink, a microwave over a two-burner stove, and an apartment-size refrigerator in the small kitchenette.

She stood just inside the door, looking as if she wanted to talk but didn't.

"Would you like to sit?" He gestured at a chair.

She took a hesitant step toward it while he moved to his recliner. "Would you like some coffee?"

"Only if you're having some."

"It'll be good with the pie," he said, taking the five steps to the kitchen counter. She didn't speak while he filled the brewer and snapped the switch. By the time he'd slid the canister back in the cabinet and wiped off the spilled grounds, the aroma of coffee filled the air.

He returned to the living room area and slipped into his chair.

She looked at him, her discomfort evident. "I want to apologize—again," she added.

"You're getting good at that," he said, then wished he'd kept his mouth closed when she flinched with his comment.

"I know. I don't mean to behave like this. I—"

"It's your grandmother that I care about, Christine. You can dislike me for whatever reason, but I'm not happy when I see you hurting your grandmother."

Concern spread over her face. "I'm not trying to hurt her. I only—"

"You're not trying to, but I can read your expression, and I'm sure your grandmother can. She knows you don't want to be here, and it makes her feel that she's to blame."

"But she's not to blame. My mother—" She rose in mid-sentence and wandered around the room. "It's no one's fault but my own. I can't control everything that happens in my own life let alone anything that happens in the world."

"None of us can. I used to fight life, but being on the island has helped me to see things in perspective. It's also helped me grow in my faith." He faltered, wanting to be honest. "I sense you don't like me talking about the Bible and God."

She spun around. "That's not true." Her shoulders sagged. "It's not exactly true. I feel guilty when you talk about the Bible. I've drifted so far away from church attendance. My faith has weakened. It all seems so useless to me."

Will rose. "It's not useless. It's the only thing that we can be sure of." He pointed at the chair again. "Please, sit, and I'll get the coffee."

She waited a moment before she ambled back and sank into the cushion. Her lovely face looked stressed, and he wished he could say something. Her concern seemed deep.

When she was seated, he crossed to the cabinet and took out two mugs. "Is there a boyfriend at home that you're worried about?" He glanced at her over his shoulder.

"A boyfriend? No. Not at all. It's my job. There are twenty people waiting for my position at the agency. If

I can't be there, I don't know if I'll have a job when I'm able to go back. I can't ask them to give me a month-or-two leave."

He poured the coffee and turned. "Milk? Sugar?"

"Black," she said, rubbing the back of her neck.

He felt sorry for her. No one wanted that kind of job stress. "So what will you do?" He crossed the room and set her coffee on the table beside her.

"I don't know. I have to call tomorrow and see how much they're willing to bend."

While she talked, he pulled the covering off the pie and grabbed a fork, then collected his mug and wandered back to the sofa. "If the firm likes your work—"

She shook her head. "No. It's competitive. We each struggle to present the best promotional package. It's a catfight sometimes." She hesitated. "I can't trust my boss—people steal ideas."

"That's why I like stained glass. It's my idea and no one is there to take credit but me." He drew up his shoulders and gave a faint laugh. "But I also have to carry the brunt of a failure."

Christine seemed to be listening. "Is that why you left the business major?"

"The business world wasn't for me. I knew it in my gut." He pressed his hand against his stomach. "You know how you feel something right here. Right in the core of your being."

She nodded. "Eat your pie. I hope you like it."

He lifted the fork and delved into the dessert, then slipped it into his mouth. The pie was a perfect blend of tart and sweet, just the way he liked it. "It's great." He gestured with his fork.

Christine smiled. "Thanks."

"Let me just add, you make a mean crust."

She said thank-you and grinned, and Will's heart felt good to see her so real again.

"By the way, I accept your apology and I really love your peace offering."

"You're welcome," she said, trying to hide her smile.

Will's mind slid back to the day he'd given Daisy the sugar cube. He hadn't come up with the sweet treat to get Christine eating out of his hand, but she certainly had. He dug into the rich crust and ate another bite of pie.

Chapter Five

Christine sat in her bedroom, staring at her cell phone. She had to call the office, but she didn't want to. Even though she still had a week's vacation, she couldn't rest until she had dealt with the problem.

Her mind kept drifting back to Will's comment the day before. "You know how you feel something right here. Right in the core of your being," he'd said about his work, but Christine wasn't sure if she'd ever felt that certain about anything. She often felt fear in the core of her being.

She fiddled with the cell buttons while trying to phrase her opening sentences. What should she say that would get the point across about her delay without alarming Chet?

Chet. Her stomach twisted. Chet, the man she had trusted and the one who'd stabbed her in the back. The memory of her naiveté suddenly overwhelmed her. As she rehearsed her dialogue, it fell apart, as it did so often when confronting her boss.

Instead of worrying about Chet, she turned her idea to a new direction. If she could work via cell and e-mail for a few days—just as a test—then he would have fewer complaints with her delay in returning to work. The idea sank as fast as it rose, but she had no other plan.

She hit the memory dial and heard the connection. "Sandy? Hi, this is Christine."

"Hey, girlfriend, how's the vacation?"

"It's okay, but—"

"But no handsome men around?"

"That's not the problem."

She chuckled. "Too many choices?"

"No. There's one man—my grandmother's boarder, but he's another issue. Listen to me." She swallowed. "I've run into a problem."

"Problem? What kind?"

Christine summarized her newest challenge in between Sandy's questions and her vocalized groans of sympathy.

"When's the next team meeting?" Christine asked.

"In an hour."

She cringed and looked at her watch. "That soon."

"I thought you were on vacation."

"Yes, I know I'm on vacation, but—"

"Forget the but. Tell me about this boarder. Looks. Age. Prospects."

"I don't know. He's good-looking." Good-looking, beguiling, sweet. "Will owns a store on the island. He's a stained-glass artist."

"Hmm? The artistic type. Clever. Married or—"

"Single. Now can we—"

"Age?"

"I have no idea." She pictured Will's youthful spirit, but he'd accomplished so much she could only speculate. "My age, I suppose. Late thirties maybe, but that has nothing to do with anything. I need to see how I can function long distance, or else how can I impress Chet that I can stay away and still work?"

"That's a hard call, Christine. I don't think it's possible."

Christine tossed the comment aside. "I want to give it a try." She drew up her shoulders. "How about trying a conference call? Do you think that would work?"

Sandy's voice flagged again before she came back with a semipositive comment.

Christine tried to keep up her hopes. "Would you ask the team, then give me a call? I'll sit in on the meeting and see what happens. I have to make this work, Sandy."

"I'll do what I can, Christine, but you're really asking the impossible. What about the visuals—graphics, charts, PowerPoint—"

Her coworker's commiseration did little to assure Christine. "I know, but you can do it."

"Thanks for the vote of confidence," Sandy said.

"Thanks for pitching them the idea for me. I can work on the brochure from here. Tell them that, okay?"

When she'd hung up, she felt defeated. Sandy's reminder of the visuals gnawed at her. The team would spend too much time trying to explain those to her unless… Her spirit lifted. If Sandy could scan the material and send it, she could at least see it on her computer.

Will stopped at the kitchen doorway. "What's wrong?"

Christine shook her head, her face more full of frustration than he'd seen since she arrived. "Nothing."

"For nothing, you look as if you lost your best friend." His heart skipped. "Don't tell me something's wrong with Grandma Ella."

Christine rose and pushed the computer lid closed. "She's fine. The therapist came today, and it tired her. She's napping."

He eyed the computer a moment, then her face, seeing something had upset her. "Did you help Judy with the therapy today?"

"No, I was busy." She heaved a deep sigh. "It was bad timing."

Bad timing. He wondered why Christine didn't understand the importance of therapy. Frisking for a solution, Will wandered to the cookie jar and looked into the empty cavern, then slid the lid back on and moved to the refrigerator. "I can show you what I know. Christine, do you realize the longer it takes her to get back into gear, the harder it'll be?"

As if she hadn't heard, Christine lifted the laptop from the table without a response.

He grabbed an apple from the fridge fruit drawer and closed the door, then leaned his back against it. "You came here to help your grandmother, didn't you?"

"Who are you? The therapy police?" She plopped the computer back onto the table.

"Therapy police?" He laughed.

She looked at him finally and laughed with him. Will loved her smile—when she had one.

"Look, I don't mean to be sharp, but I'm having some problems. I don't know how this is going to work with me on the island and my work in Southfield." Frustration flooded her face. "You don't understand, because your work is here."

"I'm sorry about—" He shook his head, not knowing what to say. Instead he tried a different tack. "Anything I can do to help?"

She stared into space a moment, then gave a single head shake. "Not unless you have a trick form of transportation that can get me to Southfield and back in a couple of minutes."

He slipped into a chair and took a bite of the apple. The skin broke and the loud crack punctuated the silence. "Sorry. I can't help you with that, either."

"No one can," she said, her head lowering.

He waited, then saw her darkened face tinge a brighter shade.

"Or maybe there is." She lifted her eyes to his.

He could see the wheels turning. "What is it?"

"What did you call that service? The place where the therapist works?"

"Vital Care." Disbelieving, he waited for her idea.

"I'll call my dad. I'm sure they have full-time nursing staff. I know it's costly, but Grandma must have insurance and—"

"She only has Medicare. Your folks already checked."

Her head shot upward. "What does that mean?"

"They checked."

"And?"

"I don't want you to bite my head off."

"I won't."

"I don't know all the details, but your dad looked into a temporary full-time caregiver to take over until they returned. It wasn't possible."

She pursed her lips and opened her mouth, then closed it. "I'll still talk to my dad."

"Go ahead." He patted the chair beside him. "Sit for a minute. I have three college years in business. What's your problem at the firm? Maybe I can help."

She looked distrusting at first, then seemed to have

second thoughts and sank back into the chair. "It's just difficult. We met today on a conference call." She pulled her cell phone from her pocket and glanced at the phone. "The power's low on my cell." She slipped it back. "It's difficult. Everyone talks at once. I can't see the visuals. I asked Sandy about scanning them or sending attachments ahead of time so I can view them on the computer, but she doesn't have time or access to the ad ideas before the meeting."

Will rallied his courage. "You're on vacation, right?"

"Yes, but that's for little more than a week. I only have a couple more weeks' vacation after that, and I don't want to use them all for—"

"Here's a thought." He managed a smile. "The quicker your grandmother can function alone, the faster you'll get home. Her therapy is vital. Instead of worrying about your job right now, concentrate on helping your grandmother."

Christine's expression caused him to backpedal. "I know your work is your career and your life, but for the next week, let's see how much progress she can make. Between Linda and me, maybe we can take over so you can go home."

Christine's gloom began to fade. "Do you think she'll improve that fast?"

He had to be honest. "A week will give you time to make decisions, and every improvement adds to the possibility."

"You're right," she said.

I am? he almost said aloud. "So with that settled, let's think about dinner." He sent her an approving smile.

He received an arched eyebrow in return.

* * *

Christine sat nearby, listening to the therapist's instructions.

"Okay, Ella," Judy said, "now place your arms at your sides, then slowly lift them over your head and then lower them. We'll do this ten times today."

Watching her grandmother's struggle gnawed at Christine's emotions. Something so simple appeared very difficult. Ella raised her right arm, but it seemed forever before the left rose above the mattress.

"Good," Judy said. "Now again."

Christine averted her gaze and looked out the window at the dancing snow. Snow. Time had flown. Thanksgiving had passed the week before, and now Christmas seemed on their doorstep. She had so much to do for the holiday. She hadn't finished her shopping, and nothing seemed open on the island.

"Do you understand, Christine?"

Judy's voice jerked her back to the therapy. "Yes, ten times over her head."

Her frown gave Christine a warning she'd let her attention drift too far.

"Then she will sit up and do ten more." She supported Ella's back and helped her raise her left arm. "After a couple, she can try it herself. Right, Ella?"

"Right," Ella said, with a look of despair.

Christine nodded. "Ten times lying down and ten sitting up."

"Yes, and then on Friday, add five more. And I want you to pick up a jigsaw puzzle. That'll be great exercise for Ella's hands and fingers. It aids dexterity."

"A jigsaw puzzle."

"Yes. They probably have them at the drugstore."

Christine's thoughts left the jigsaw puzzle and shifted to Will. He'd tried so hard to help her, and she had been terribly ungrateful. He made her laugh and forget her troubles, but she fought him every step. Why? She shook her head, having no answer except the one she didn't want to face—envy of his relationship with her grandmother.

Christine's focus drifted back to her grandmother's quivering limbs. Sadness washed over her.

Judy helped Ella rise. "And now we're going to do laps."

"Laps?" That statement triggered Christine's attention. "Where?"

"From the living room through the foyer into the kitchen and around the table and back." She turned to Ella. "You'll use your walker, but soon I want you on a cane. You want to get well, don't you?"

"Do I look stupid?" Ella said.

Christine laughed.

"Now, now, Ella. You're a smart lady," Judy said, "and that's why I know you can do this. But you must have someone work with you. Don't try walking with the cane alone for a while."

The truth of the situation sank into Christine's head. She couldn't walk away and leave her grandmother unless she had professional help, and if Will had been accurate, that seemed hopeless. Maybe he'd been wrong.

As the thought drifted into her mind, Christine heard the hallway door open and close, and Will appeared in her grandmother's bedroom doorway. "How's it going?"

The scent of winter rode in on his jacket—a crispy fragrance of outdoors and fresh air.

"I'm going to be doing a few pirouettes before you know it," Ella said. "Just you wait and see."

"I never doubted that," Will said. He strode toward Judy. "Are you finished?"

"We'll do some laps, but I think Christine's done."

"That's who I wanted," he said. "Are you going to be here for a few more minutes?"

Judy nodded. "Another half hour or so."

"Great," he said, running his fingers through his snow-dampened hair. "I want to show Christine a couple of things if I can steal her."

"She's all yours." Judy looked from Christine to Will and back again. "Are you taking her to the tree-lighting ceremony tonight? It's a beautiful sight."

"Tree lighting? I hadn't—"

"At dusk," Ella said, gesturing with her good arm. "Christine would enjoy that, Will. I'm sure Linda will come in to stay for an hour while you go."

Christine's focus wasn't on the tree lighting. Instead she wondered why Will wanted to steal her, but anything seemed better than watching her grandmother grimace with pain.

"No problem for me," Judy said, supporting Ella's calf as she lifted her leg. "Take a good half hour."

Will beckoned to Christine.

She rose without argument and followed him into the hallway, admiring his broad shoulders yet concerned about his coy smile. "Where are you taking me?"

"Put on your coat and boots. It's lesson time."

Lesson time? "I've had about as many lessons as I need for one day. I'm a full-fledged therapist as we speak."

Will grinned, and the look won her over.

"I have something in mind besides therapy." He pointed toward the foyer. "Coat and boots."

"Is that an order?"

He nodded and led the way.

"Daisy's on the mainland, right? I'm not learning to horseback ride."

"No, but you should learn how to use the sled in case you need to get away when I'm not here. I'll just show you how to start it and take it for a short spin." He gestured toward the doorway. "There's new snow, and it'll be a smooth ride."

"Please, Will, I don't want—"

"Shush!" He walked up behind her and slipped his hand over her mouth, his face against her hair. She heard him draw a deep breath. "You smell like cookies. Vanilla wafers?"

"It's my lotion," she said, feeling his warm breath on her cheek. "And I suppose I'd better bake some cookies, since I've seen you looking into the empty container."

He turned her around, his eyes capturing hers. "I like cookies."

But his eyes said he liked her, and the feeling wavered down her limbs. She looked away and wrapped a scarf around her neck. "Let's get this over with. If I break a hip, then you're going to be nursemaid to everyone."

"You won't break anything but a few hearts, Christine."

A few hearts. Her pulse skipped, and she gave a sarcastic laugh, hoping their conversation would get back to normal. She hadn't met a man in a long time who could rattle her equilibrium like Will.

He guided her through the kitchen to the porch. Her grandmother's smaller sled sat beside his. She eyed it as if it were a rocket and she were going to the moon.

Though the snow had deepened, the sun felt warmer than the last time Christine had faced a snowmobile.

She squinted at the light glinting from the fresh powdery crystals, then looked into the clear blue sky. She understood why David had written the Psalms. On days like this, if she were a poet, she would write a beautiful praise.

Her thoughts of the Lord surprised Christine as she moved through the snow. Perhaps a place like the island gave her more time to think about things other than competition and survival in the mad rush of life at home.

"I'll warn you," Christine said, "I can never start a lawn mower."

Will grinned. "This one is different." He stood beside the smaller sled, dangling a key. "It has a regular ignition. No pull starter."

"Whew!" She adored his cute grin. "I'm relieved."

Will patted the seat. She slipped into it and felt like a seasoned sledder.

He poked the key into the ignition. "Now pull out the choke about halfway." He pointed to the right side of the handlebars. "It's that tab marked by the circle with a diagonal line through it."

Will was leaning so close to her, she breathed in his subtle scent of spice. He turned to look at her, his breath puffing in a white stream and blending with hers.

She steadied her emotions and did as he told her.

"That's right," he said.

His face, spotlighted by the sun, looked so handsome in the bright light. The creases she'd seen around his eyes seemed to have vanished.

"Now," he said, turning back to the gauges, "when you turn the key and the engine sounds steady, push in the choke." He chuckled. "Hopefully the sled will stay running on its own."

"Okay," Christine said, looking at all the gadgetry

in front of her and doing as he'd told her. The sound of the engine hammered the afternoon air. She glanced at the floorboard. "But where's the gas pedal and brake?"

He brushed his palm against her hair. "You're too funny. It's here." He pointed to the handlebars. "Put your hands here and find the lever on the right side. That's the throttle. Use your thumb to gain speed."

"And the brake?" she asked, feeling more panicky.

"The lever on the left. The sled will slow automatically by releasing pressure on the throttle, especially in soft snow. That's why I thought you should have the lesson today."

"Throttle on the right. Brake on the left."

"That's it. And remember to lean into the turn. If you don't, you can flip over."

"Thanks," she said, raising her hands in the air. "That's enough lesson for me."

He caught her hand and gave it a squeeze. "Come on. Be a sport." He cupped his other hand around hers, and the warmth penetrated her gloves.

"If you want independence, you'll need to ride this thing."

Will walked away, slipped on his helmet and started the engine. He sat a moment before rolling forward and stopping beside her. "Ready?"

She covered her head with the helmet and drew in a hasty breath, her voice catching in her throat. She could only nod.

"Let's go." He motioned forward and glided down the driveway to the snow-covered road.

Christine followed his instructions as best she could remember, then jerked forward and stalled.

Will grinned and waited.

She started the engine again, and this time kept it going. As she rolled forward, Will shot onto the street.

Christine eased out to the road, fear and adventure knotted in every sinew. She pressed the throttle, and the sled gunned forward. Soon she was behind Will, feeling like a baby bird learning to fly.

The wind nipped at her nose, and each breath seemed to crystalize inside her lungs, but it awakened her spirit. She heard her laughter sail on the air. She couldn't remember feeling so free and happy in a long time.

Ahead Will slowed, then made a great loop into a snow-covered field and headed back up Cupid's Pathway. The street name made her grin. It sounded like a children's tale of princes and princesses.

In only a few minutes, they returned home, and she felt disappointed the lesson was over. She parked and climbed off, her heart thundering in her chest and pride billowing in her heart. "Not bad," she said, pulling off the helmet and shaking her hair free.

Will hurried to her side, drew her into his arms, lifted her above the ground, then plopped her back to earth.

She caught her breath, stunned at their play.

"You were wonderful," he said. "The best student I've ever had."

"And how many is that?"

"One, but you were very good."

"Thanks. It was fun."

His gaze searched hers and made her nervous. He was an attractive man.

"You look like a teenager," Will said. "Look at those rosy cheeks and that sparkle in your eyes. You're a beautiful woman, Christine."

He'd taken her aback with his comment. "Forget that

teenage comment. I'm far from that. I'll accept the rosy cheeks. I can feel them burning."

Will tilted her face upward and studied her again. "You're timeless, I'd say."

She felt her heart flutter, and the sensation set her on edge. What was she thinking? She checked her watch. "I think it's time to get back in."

He rested his hand on her shoulder. "Good job on the sled."

"Thanks."

"I'll put it in the stable and be heading back to work. I'll pick you up later for the tree lighting." He gave her a wink and pivoted away toward the sleds.

"See you later." She gave a quick wave while her heart did a loop-the-loop.

The Christmas tree stood near the chamber of commerce building on Main Street. Christine's eagerness grew as she watched the schoolchildren's excitement as they gathered around the tree. Will stood behind her, his hands on her shoulders.

The evening wind felt nippier than what she'd experienced earlier in the day; a chill prickled along her spine. Will moved beside her and slid his arm around her. He gave her an easy smile, and she smiled back, for once comfortable with his closeness.

Snowflakes began to fall like a picture-perfect Christmas scene. They drifted on the breeze and twirled on the chilling air. Will held her close, and she warmed at his touch.

The ceremony began, and soon the tree lights glowed, with cheers and oohs from those who were gathered. The friendly chatter and handshakes felt so different from the life she led at home. She shifted to leave, but Will held her close. "Now we sing carols."

"Really?"

She saw the glow in his eyes and guessed the same glow was in hers. The music began and the children's voices filled the crisp air with songs like "Joy to the World," "Away in a Manger," and "Silent Night."

With each song, Will's baritone voice joined the singers. At first, she sang with timidity, then found her voice lifting along with his. Joyous sounds filled with the spirit of the season—a kind of music and feeling she'd only thought of in dreams.

"Fun?" he asked.

"Wonderful." She gazed into his eyes, sparkling brighter than the tree lights, and in the joy of the moment she had an urge to kiss him. "Thank you," she said, tiptoing up to plant a quick kiss on his lips.

Though he looked surprised, he smiled. "Tell me what else I can do to win another one of those."

She chuckled liked a schoolgirl, then caught herself. What was she doing? She was Christine Powers, businesswoman, devoted to her job, a dynamo in advertising. How could a tree-lighting ceremony three hundred miles from home turn her into a giggly teenager?

Will bent and kissed her cheek. "I'm glad you're having a good time. I won't forget tonight."

She looked at the snowflakes resting on his hair, his beguiling smile, and the warmth in his eyes. She would never forget tonight, either.

Chapter Six

"So Mom's doing well, you think?"

Christine's shoulders relaxed hearing her father's positive response.

"Can I talk with her?"

"Just a minute. I'll wake her."

"No, Dad. I can talk another time."

"How's your grandmother?"

"She's doing fine. I'm learning how to help her with the therapy. I think she's improving every day...so I have a question."

She heard silence on the line.

"This is theoretical, but let's say I can't get a leave or I can't work from here, and my boss insists I return. If that happened, I was thinking that—"

"Christine, did you ask for an extension?"

"No, but I'm afraid that—"

"Wait. Don't you have more leave time?"

"Yes, I have a couple more weeks' vacation, but I'd like to have some time during the summer to—"

"You know there's no one else to send." His voice was weighted with frustration. "Chad's—"

"I know Chad can't leave his family and come here at the holidays. I understand, but—" Her father's comment about her married brother bristled down her back. "I feel I'm being punished for being single. I have a life, too, and…"

This time her father didn't stop her, and she didn't know where to go.

"What about professional full-time care for Grandma? She must have insurance, and I thought—"

She listened to the same thing Will had told her.

"That doesn't seem right," she said.

"Do you want us to put your grandmother in a home?"

"No." Her hand had tensed on her cell phone, and she longed to lay it down, to disconnect, to cancel the call if she could. The conversation had gone as badly as she imagined it would. She asked herself why she'd bothered.

"I'll call my boss next Monday, and see what I can do."

The conversation bogged down with her mother's prognosis—two months or more before she would be able to travel. When Christine hung up from her father, tears filled her eyes. She couldn't stay that long, and she saw no other solution.

Rarely had Christine prayed in recent years. Today she bowed her head and talked with God. The Lord had ways of solving problems that a human couldn't even imagine. She had to depend on God's mercy.

Feeling calmer, Christine headed downstairs, putting on her I'm-just-fine expression. At the bottom of the steps, she heard her grandmother's voice talking to her.

"I didn't hear you, Grandma Summers. I was upstairs." She stepped into the living room and stopped. Her grandmother was speaking on the telephone, her face lit with a smile.

"Who was that?" Christine asked when she'd hung up.

"One of the circle ladies from church. Some of them thought I looked good when they saw me on Sunday."

"You did. I told you."

"Tomorrow they're coming to visit and bringing some casseroles for our dinners. I don't know how many, but I thought you'd like to hear that."

Christine didn't know which she enjoyed hearing more, the news about the prepared dinners or the ladies' visit.

"And you'll have some free time to enjoy yourself for a change," her grandmother added.

That thought had already crossed her mind. "That's thoughtful, Grandma, but the best thing is to see the smile on your face."

"I hadn't realized how much I miss my church friends," Ella said. "A few came to see me in the hospital, and I had many cards and some food gifts when your folks were here, but you know how it is. Time passes, and it's easy to forget about those who are sick. I must keep that in mind when I'm doing well again."

"I have no doubt you will," Christine said, remembering the vow her grandmother had made when she was a girl. "Are you ready to tackle your therapy?"

The grin faded.

"The stronger you become the faster you'll be up and active again." Will's words spilled from her as his face rose in her thoughts. He always said the right thing.

"I know," Ella said, giving a toss of her head.

"Let's get at it."

Will glanced at his desk calendar to check the deadline date for a stained-glass window he was making for a customer. He'd selected clear glass of varying textures to complement the bevel cluster. The windows were big sellers.

As his eyes shifted over the November dates, he realized his error and flipped the page to December. Time was flying, and he'd promised to have a table at the Christmas Bazaar the coming weekend. He drew back, amazed at how forgetful he'd become. He'd mentioned the event to Christine only days earlier.

His mind wandered, knowing he needed to select his art pieces and box them to transport to the Community Hall. Too much to do, and too little time. He scanned the December dates again, noting he had plenty of time to complete the customer's beveled window, but what else waited to be done?

As the calendar came into view again, his thoughts took a detour. He scanned the excellent still life photograph of the stone church on Grand Hill, the evergreen branches weighted with snow against the gray stone and the one bright spot—a cardinal sitting on the fir. He'd wanted to spend a day taking photos for the annual calendar contest that the island held each year. The judging would be at the Winter Festival in February, and if he wanted to enter, he needed to get the photographs taken. He rubbed his neck, wondering which way to turn. Christine had thrown his schedule out of whack.

He eyed his watch. Lunchtime. His chest tightened with awareness. Normally he'd stay at the studio and eat a cold sandwich or heat up a commercial microwave soup, but lately, he'd taken time to go back home to eat. He didn't have to question his motives. Christine. She filled his mind.

Grabbing his jacket, he switched the light off with

his other hand and headed outside. He locked the door, jumped on his sled and headed up Market Street. Home seemed to pull him like a magnet.

The day seemed perfect—a crisp breeze but an abundance of sunshine. The scenery flashed past, and as he neared his apartment, his pulse raced. He knew he was being foolish. He already suspected Christine was older and wiser than he. He certainly wasn't the kind of man who would interest her, so why open himself for rejection?

The question led him into a new line of thought. He enjoyed her company. He hadn't met any younger woman on the island that captured his interest as Christine had. Maybe it was her spunk or her business prowess. He respected that. More likely he was drawn to the Christine she let him see when she let down her guard. She could make him laugh, and he loved that. Why not enjoy her company while she was here and let it go at that?

He let the answer slip away, aware of the flashing warning sign he didn't want to face. He drove up Grandma Ella's driveway and entered through the back door. A tangy scent greeted him along with a smile from Christine.

"What's cookin'?" He slipped off his shoes in the back hallway and hung his jacket on a chair near the door.

"Sloppy Joes. I haven't eaten one for years."

He stood close to her, enjoying the rich aroma of the meat-and-tomato blend, along with her nearness. "Can I help?"

"You can open the buns."

He spotted the package on the counter and opened the cellophane. Before he removed them from the wrapper, he moved to the sink to wash his hands.

"And you can get the chips. They're on the fridge."

Will set out three plates, placed an open bun on each, then tore open the bag of potato chips. "I'm glad I came home."

"So am I," she said. "Grandma Summers has friends coming in tomorrow, so I'll have a couple of free hours. I need to do some Christmas shopping. Any ideas?"

His mind surged to the calendar he'd perused earlier. "The Christmas Bazaar is Saturday at the Community Center. You can pick up some handmade items and even have an ice-cream sundae while you're there."

"A bazaar? I'm not sure that's the best place to buy quality gifts." She reached for a plate.

He moved closer and held the dish while she piled the meat mixture onto the bun. "Sure it is. Wait until you see the great things they have. I have a booth there."

"Your stained glass?" She stood transfixed with the spoonful of meat hovering over the plate.

"Smaller items. I will probably bring a few windows, sun catchers, Christmas ornaments, some jewelry."

"Jewelry?"

"It's made with fused glass. You'll be surprised." He turned and placed the dish on the table. "Lots of things. We have a talented island. Scarves, mittens, winter caps." He fought the temptation to run his fingers through her waves. "You could use a cap."

"If I go, I'll have to find someone to stay with—"

"Bring her along. She needs to get out. You're doing her laps, right?"

She drew back. "Yes, Mr. Therapy Police. I had her doing laps today."

He grinned. "The more she realizes what she's missing the harder she'll work to get better."

Christine nodded. "She mentioned today how much she misses everyone."

"Going will make her happy then. I think the walker will work for Saturday. There are benches where she can sit and visit."

"Good idea." Christine turned off the burner and slid the pot off the heat. "Can you bring in Grandma while I get the drinks?"

"Sure thing," he said, whistling a rambling tune as he headed into the living room.

Ella grinned at him when he came through the doorway She looked sunnier than he'd seen her in days, and it made him feel good. "Lunchtime." He strode across the room and plopped her walker in front of her. "If you don't get walking, you'll miss the best Sloppy Joes ever made."

"I smell them," she said, struggling to rise with only one strong hand.

He let her struggle, knowing that the more she forced herself to do, the better off she'd be. When she'd managed to grab hold of the walker with both hands, she shuffled forward while he stayed close by her side. He could see the difference even in the past couple days that Christine had been making her do laps two or three times a day.

When they gathered around the table, Ella reached toward Christine to take her hand. Will noticed and grasped Ella's left, but Ella didn't begin the prayer. Her eyes were focused on the broken circle. Will eyed Christine, and she reached over and took his hand.

Grandma Ella began the prayers, thanking God for the day, the food, family and friends. Will tried to concentrate, but his mind skipped off on its own to the pleasant sensation of Christine's delicate hand in his, her tapered fingers nestled against his palm.

"And Lord, we ask You for patience and perseverance. We don't always understand Your ways, but we know You are directing our steps. Keep us mindful of Your mercy and grace. Keep us attentive to Your love and forgiveness. Amen."

In the silence as each of them delved into the savory sandwich, Will's mind marched back to Christine's sweeter manner. He liked what he'd seen the past two days—the sled ride and today the camaraderie. Grandma Ella's words about love and forgiveness sank into his thoughts. How long would it take before he and Christine might be real friends?

He looked up and saw Christine watching him. When they were alone, he planned to invite her on his photography venture. He wondered if she might inspire something unique and amazing in his photographs. She'd already inspired his imagination.

"Now don't you worry," Darlene Baxter said. "We'll keep Ella busy for a couple of hours, and then I thought I'd stay on a while and help her with her therapy. She can tell me what to do."

"That's so nice of you," Christine said.

"Ella says you're devoting too much time to her, and she wants you to enjoy yourself."

Christine winced with the comment. "You're too kind, Mrs. Baxter. Thanks again." Guilt pressed against her shoulders, knowing she'd only been devoted to her grandmother the past couple of days. Before she had only whined.

"I'm going to run a few errands while you're here."

"Have fun," Ella said, as Christine strolled into the

foyer. She paused to look out the door's beveled window and saw Will pulling into the driveway.

Perfect timing, she thought, as she slipped on her jacket and boots.

Before she'd finished, he gave a tap and opened the door. "Looks like I'm right on time."

"I have to find my scarf and gloves." She tiptoed to peek onto the top shelf.

Will came forward and reached over her head. "Here you go," he said, pulling them down from the top shelf.

She wrapped the plaid blue scarf around her neck—one that belonged to her grandmother—and Will took the end and gave an extra pull. Christine loosened the scarf, giving his gleeful expression a frown.

He opened the door, and she slipped on her gloves as she stepped outside. "Bye, Grandma," she called.

Muffled voices sent back a greeting as Will closed the door. "It's a great day," he said. "This past week's been wonderful. Would you like to have a diversion before you run your errands?"

He'd piqued her interest. "What kind of diversion?"

"A photo shoot."

"Photo shoot?"

"For the island calendar. They hold a contest during the Winter Festival and select twelve photos taken of scenes on the island for next year's calendar."

"Do you have one in this year?"

His smile faded. "Never. So I thought maybe you'd inspire me. Bring me luck, maybe."

"How long?"

He shrugged. "As long as it takes."

"I have only an hour."

She noticed he didn't comment. He ushered her toward his sled, and she settled onto the seat, then scooted back. Once he was on, he maneuvered the sled from the driveway, and they were off.

They headed into town and stopped to take photos of a streetlamp adorned with a Christmas wreath, then off to Market Street where Will photographed the quiet setting looking toward the fort. The still beauty wrapped around Christine's spirit.

Will looked content, setting his aperture for the best lighting and distance. He moved from one angle to another. He shifted beneath a tree and aimed the camera upward through the snow-burdened branches to the amazing blue sky.

"I bet that was beautiful," Christine said, shifting her weight and bumping a limb.

Before Will could move, an avalanche of snow fell from one branch to the next and blanketed him in a snow pile. "Thanks," he said, jumping away and grabbing a cloth to wipe the camera.

"I'm sorry."

He shook his head and chucked her cheek. "Forgiven. No damage as long as I get the snow off fast."

She hovered over him, fearful that she'd destroyed his camera. He raised it without her expecting and snapped her photo.

"Why did you do that? I wasn't smiling."

"You looked lovely—concerned and guilty. That's just the way I like you."

She folded her arms. "No photos unless I have a warning."

"Okay," he said. "Be warned." He moved the f-stop and snapped another photo.

"I thought the calendar was scenery."

"It is, but I took these for me."

"Why?"

"To remember you by."

Her breath left her for a moment, realizing one day she would be gone. Her job and her life waited for her in Southfield, not the island.

He stood a minute, looking into the sky.

"Something wrong?"

"Thinking."

She waited beside him and thought, too, about the fun she'd had since she stopped fighting Will and her grandmother's care, but she knew that in a few more days, she had to face reality. If her boss didn't approve a leave—and she feared he wouldn't just for spite—she would be in a bind. Chet would love to get her out of the company. But she had the goods on him, and he knew it.

"What are you thinking?" she asked finally.

"I want something unique. Special. This time of year my photos will be for snow months—November through March. Everyone does the Christmas wreath, the fort, the snow piled in the fields. I want a different idea. Something other than Thanksgiving, Christmas or New Year's Eve."

"That leaves February," Christine said.

"What happens in February other than a short month that takes forever?" he asked.

"Valentine's Day."

His head shot upward. "Hearts, flowers, cupids, love."

"How about a photo on Cupid's Pathway?" she asked.

His eyebrows raised. "Okay. You have something there, but what? Not just a street view. That's not original. Something to do with Valentine's Day."

"A heart."

"Whose?"

She chuckled. "Not mine. A heart...in the snow."

"Yes!" He twirled around on one heel as if spinning would bring an idea. "Drawn by a finger." He looked at her hands. "With red gloves. Instead of carving a heart with initials on a tree, a girl spells it in snow."

"I like it," she said. "We can find fresh snow near the house."

"But color? Is the glove enough?" He snapped his finger. "Let me run into the shop a minute." He beckoned her to follow.

They hurried up the road a couple of shops, and Will opened the door and ran into the back. Christine waited by the door gazing around the room. She could purchase some wonderful Christmas gifts from Will's shop. She headed for a display, but he reappeared, looking empty-handed, and waved her toward the door.

"I thought you—"

He patted his pocket. "I have what I need. Wait and see."

She followed him outside, and when he locked the door, they climbed on the sled and raced up Cadotte Avenue to Hoban Road into Harrisonville. When they turned right onto Cupid's Pathway, Will slowed and scanned the roadside. "I need fresh snow."

She pointed to a patch of open snow, unblemished and glistening in the winter sun.

"That's great," he said, pulling the sled to the road's edge and turning it off.

He stepped out and grabbed his camera.

Christine sat on the sled, watching him move from right to left, close, then farther away using his zoom lens. He crouched down and focused on the snow, then rose again and tossed a stick onto one area and studied it through the lens.

"What are you doing?" Christine called out.

"Checking for light and shadow." He beckoned to her.

She slipped off the sled and headed his way, tucking her hands into her pockets away from the nippy air.

"Look through the lens at the stick," he said, handing her the camera.

She put her eye against the viewfinder while Will stood close beside her, his hand resting on her shoulder. She located the broken limb. Sunlight from the left caused a definite shadow on the snow. "The stick leaves a fine shadow."

"It will broaden as the sun lowers in the sky, but it's enough." He studied her face as he took the camera from her.

"Interesting," Will said, wondering if he meant the shadows or her.

He hung the camera on his neck, then moved to an unmarred snowbank. He crouched and took his finger and drew a large heart on the snow. The shadow highlighted it with a fine line of gray.

Christine admired the almost perfect heart. She waited to see what was next, curious about what he'd brought from the studio.

Will paused a moment, looking through the lens again, and then squatted and marked his initials—W. L.—into the snow. Below the letters he marked a plus sign. Finally, he rose.

"Your turn." He glanced at her hands. "Where are your gloves?"

"In here," she said, pulling her hands from her pockets.

"Good. Now crouch like I did and draw your initials,

but don't lift your finger when you get to the end of the letter *P*."

Rattled, she turned to him. "You want me to use my initials?"

"Sure." He gave her a wink. "Why not?"

She had no answer for that, but it didn't seem appropriate for her to be making a heart with their initials. The whole idea unsettled her.

"Go ahead," he said, standing back and focusing.

If she refused, she'd be making a big deal out of nothing, so she knelt and stretched her arm over the heart and scratched her initials beneath the plus sign. C. P. She heard the lens click, then click again.

"Hold it," he said, shifting and snapping two more shots. "Okay. That's it."

She rose, her legs feeling tingly from lack of blood and from the cold.

"Want to see?" he asked.

"See? But you brought something with you, I thought."

"Red glass globs. I thought I'd outline the heart, but I don't need them. Look at it." He beckoned her.

She hurried to his side.

"Here." He handed her the digital camera, hit a button, and the photograph appeared. The effect startled her— the stark white snow, the shadow heart and initials, then her bright red finger. "It's really great, Will. Beautiful in its simplicity."

"And perfect for February. I'll title it *Love on Cupid's Pathway*."

Love on Cupid's Pathway. She looked back at the heart and their initials and felt a flush rise up her neck. "We'd better go, don't you think?"

He grasped her hand and pulled her closer. "Are you upset?"

"No, I—I'm just looking at the time." She glanced at her watch.

"Thanks for the inspiration," he said.

She saw it coming and didn't move. Will bent over and planted a kiss on her cold cheek. The warmth radiated through her, and she had to fight the desire to turn her cheek and kiss his mouth.

Chapter Seven

"I have a matching bracelet if you're interested," Will said to customer Myra Holt. He dug beneath the table, located it and handed it to her.

"This is gorgeous, Will. I love the colors."

"Thanks." His attention drifted toward the doorway, looking for Christine, then back to Myra.

She eyed the price tag and didn't flinch. "Let me get Gus, and see what he says. I'll be right back." She sent him a smile and headed down the aisle looking for her husband.

Will leaned back in the folding chair, grabbing a moment's break before the next customer arrived. Everyone knew everyone on the island, so the Christmas Bazaar seemed one big party.

A woman passed wearing a red jacket, and the color took him back to yesterday afternoon when he'd had the nerve to insist Christine write her initials in the snow. She'd flushed, he'd noticed, and he wasn't sure if she was embarrassed or flattered. He hoped it was the latter.

Something about Christine had worked its way into his thoughts and wound around his heart as tightly as tendrils on a morning glory. He felt the spiral squeeze, and his pulse raced. The dream was ridiculous. He wanted to ask Grandma Ella Christine's age, but he didn't have the nerve. Anyway, it was difficult to talk with Ella alone. Christine always seemed to hover nearby like flies at a picnic.

Will grinned to himself. He loved her hovering, but not when he hoped to talk privately to her grandmother. Will wasn't sure what difference it would make, but sometimes age bothered women. He liked her maturity. At times, she seemed girlish, like the times they'd spent on the sled when her smile lit up the sky and her laughter rekindled his longing for someone to share his life.

Will knew the day would come when she would leave. Maybe sooner than he thought. On Monday, she'd said she had to call her boss. Could he say no to a family's need? She'd hinted that she had a difficult relationship with him, and Will had wondered what that was about. Had it been a romance or some work-related conflict? He drew in a deep breath. So many things he would probably never know.

"Here it is," Myra said, returning. She held the bracelet and pendant toward her husband.

The man looked at it with a blank face, obviously not interested. "If you like it, buy it," he said, after a cursory look.

"Are you sure? You could wrap it for Christmas," Myra said.

"Wouldn't that be dumb? You know what it is."

"Maybe by then I'd forget."

Gus brushed her off with a hand motion. "Buy it. Enjoy it."

Her glum look brightened, and she turned back to Will. "He said it's okay."

"I'm sure you'll enjoy these pieces, Myra." Will slipped them onto the cotton and put a lid on the white nondescript box he used for the jewelry. He pulled out the gold foil Sea of Glass sticker and added it to the top. When he lifted his head, Christine stood beside Myra. He felt a smile grow on his face.

"Hi," he said. "I wondered if you would come."

"It took a little longer getting Grandma here."

Will realized he was still holding Myra's package. He handed it to her. "Myra, this is Christine. She's Ella Summers's granddaughter from Lower Michigan."

The women greeted each other while Will's gaze wandered over Christine's form. She carried her jacket on her arm, and he could see her attire. She'd worn a sweater the color of autumn leaves—shades of orange, coral, red and gold—that highlighted her honey hair and hazel eyes. She looked like an Indian-summer day.

Myra stood between them for a moment, and when the conversation didn't go anywhere, she said goodbye and headed in the direction Gus had gone.

"What do you think?" Will asked.

"About the bazaar?"

He nodded.

"It's nice. I've only been here a few minutes."

"Where's your grandmother?"

"She found a seat by one of her circle ladies. She's selling quilted things—toss pillows and baby blankets."

She glanced over her shoulder as if checking on her grandmother, and Will rose and came out from behind the table.

"I have a friend who'll sit in for me for a while when you'd like some ice cream."

She turned back. "Thanks. I'll pass for now. Maybe later. I want to see what you're selling."

He backed away and allowed her room to study the glass pieces he had on display. She admired his work, and he enjoyed hearing her oohs and aahs.

"I'd like to buy a few things for gifts. It's beautiful stuff, Will." She eyed the table again and then shifted to the jewelry. "How do you do this?" She studied the pendant, holding it to the light. "Is it really glass?"

"Fused glass. I have some fluted bowls and dishes back at the studio made in the same way."

"Really?" She shifted to a bracelet, then earrings. "It's amazing. Tell me how it's made."

"I heat it in a kiln to various degrees until it's fused. You can see some is rough—the glass has melted together and adheres, but you can feel the ridges of each color." He lifted her hand and ran her finger along the piece of glass.

He loved the feel of her hand in his, her fingers warm and soft like smooth glass cooling from the kiln.

"Or you can fire it at a higher temperature, around eighteen hundred degrees, and then—"

"You get this," she said, raising a pendant, the colors melded together in one smooth piece.

"That's it," he said, squeezing the hand that he held in his. His confidence rose, knowing she hadn't pulled away from him. That had been real progress with Christine.

"If you come to my studio sometime, I'll show you how to make glass beads like these."

She grasped the strand of flowing beadwork and turned it in her hand. "I love this. The colors and—" She looked at him in what he could only call admiration.

"You have a gold mine here, Will. I'm amazed." She laid the necklace down on the velvet-covered table. "How does this work? Do you donate some of your profits?"

He shook his head. "It's all donated. I'm giving these items away."

"Giving? You're kidding."

"That's the spirit of Christmas. The money's divided five ways—the four churches on the island and the medical center."

"But this is worth so much." She gestured toward the display.

"The churches and medical center are worth much more. Where would we be without them?"

"I suppose." Her eyebrows lifted as she turned to view a sun catcher, then hung it back on the stand. She paused a moment. "I have some ideas for you."

He managed to hold his stance, but his instinct was to draw back. Ideas meant interference. He wanted no part of strategies. His father admired those. Will grimaced inwardly, realizing, instead of interfering, perhaps she had a jewelry design idea. He changed the subject.

"Visit the studio, and I'll show you how to make glass beads. They're easy, really."

She grinned. "For you maybe."

He drew her closer and gave her a squeeze. "You'll just have to trust me. Now stay right here, and I'll get someone to cover my booth so we can take a walk."

Christine watched him walk away, her mind spilling out marketing ideas. She turned again to study the jewelry, wondering how much promotion he did and what yearly income he netted. She could double it. He could hire other workers to do the simpler steps—like the bead making—and he could use his time for the artistic creativity.

Her skin prickled with excitement, anxious to tell him about her thoughts. When she looked at the crowd and the buzz of activity around her, she wondered if this was a practical time to talk. She could see Will in the distance, cornered by two people who seemed determined to carry on a lengthy conversation. He'd gestured her way, but that hadn't stopped them.

Small towns. She'd never seen anything like the friendliness she'd noticed here. Besides church, in stores and on the street, people called to Will by name, and not just a few, but about everyone he passed.

Even yesterday, the postman had called her by name. The postman. Obviously she had a postman in Royal Oak, but to have him call her Christine seemed beyond her comprehension. She didn't know a tenth of the people who worked in the office building where Creative Productions had their suite let alone a whole town.

Finally, she saw Will make his way down the aisle. After two more stops, this time shorter, he returned to her side, and within seconds, so did a woman.

"Christine, this is Janet Deacon. She works for me part-time in the store during the tourist season."

Christine took the woman's hand in greeting. She was an attractive lady, perhaps her age, and Christine eyed Will to see if she was more than a part-time employee, but Will's eyes were on her, and she let the question fade. When her mind made queries like that one, it set her on edge.

"We'll only be a half hour or so," Will said.

"No problem, Will. I'm happy to help." She sent him

a smile, which he returned, then he took Christine's arm and led her away from the table.

"Where's the booth you left Grandma Ella at?" he asked, craning his neck to look along the busy aisles.

"This way," she said, pointing.

He walked beside her, stopped every few minutes for conversation and introductions. Christine figured they'd never get to the ice-cream area.

Finally her grandmother came into view. "How are you doing?" Christine asked as she approached.

"Okay," Ella said, looking a little tired but happy.

"You want to leave?"

"No, I'm fine for a while. Enjoy yourself."

"How about an ice-cream sundae?" Will asked, patting her shoulder in the gentlest way, which made Christine's heart surge. He would be a good father, she could tell.

"We had a sundae a few minutes ago, but thanks."

"You did?" Christine asked.

"Darlene's son brought them to us. The best ice cream. Fattening, but who cares?" Ella said.

Christine grinned. "I care."

Will shook his head. "Does this lovely woman look overweight to you?"

Darlene chuckled. "No, not even without love in my eyes."

The comment startled Christine, but she forced herself to laugh. What were people thinking? She studied Darlene, who prattled on about her son and her sales. What did the woman see in Will's eyes? What did she see in Christine's?

"Ready?" Will asked, clasping her arm.

"Sure," she said, the word nearly inaudible. She

needed to get a grip. Darlene didn't know romance from friendship.

Will guided her along the aisles toward the ice-cream stand, but before they reached it, he stopped by a table of handmade knitted items.

"Can I help you, Will?" the woman asked as he plowed through the scarves.

"I'm looking for a red one."

She laid down her knitting needles and leaned below the table. When she straightened, she held a bright red scarf. "Like this?"

"Perfect," he said. "I'll take it."

She watched him pay the woman, and when she slipped it into a plastic grocery bag, he turned and handed it to Christine.

"For me?"

"To match your red gloves."

She grinned at his endearing expression. "But it's not even Christmas."

"It's always Christmas in my heart," he said, steering her to the back of the building where ice-cream chairs and tables had been placed.

Christine stared at the plastic bag, touched by the unexpected gift. So many of her experiences on the island had been unexpected. "Thanks. You're too good to me."

As they walked, she couldn't help but compare him to other men she knew—men at her office and men who lived in her apartment building. Some were nice, but they either seemed patronizing or pushy or with a goal in mind—a goal she didn't share.

At the stand, she and Will designed their sundaes,

amid others in line who knew Will's name and soon learned hers.

When they'd settled at the table, her thoughts moved from Will's charm to her business ideas.

"How do you like the bazaar?" he asked, dipping into the mixture of ice cream, syrups, cherries, nuts and sprinkles topped with whipped cream.

"Fun. Different. Life here seems easy. Not easy really, because things like shopping and dentist appointments are more complicated, but easygoing. Sort of cozy."

He gave that some thought. "It's definitely close-knit and friendly."

"I can see that," she said, eager to move along to another topic. "I wanted to talk to you about those ideas I mentioned."

"Jewelry ideas?" Concern settled on his face.

"All your products. I'm just curious if you do marketing and promotion?"

He laughed. "We have an automatic market when the tourists arrive. They hit every shop on Main Street and Market. It's what they do."

"But after tourist season? What then?"

He slipped his hand over hers and gave it a pat. "Then we get cozy."

Cozy. The word came back to bite her. Apparently Will didn't have her drive for success. She imagined he could double his income, triple it, maybe, with Internet marketing. Items handcrafted on the island would automatically have a draw. Before she could speak her mind, Will spoke.

"Talking about business. Tell me about Creative… What's it called again?"

"Creative Productions. We develop marketing strategies and create commercial advertising for different venues—TV, radio, newspaper, magazines—you get it."

"Sounds challenging. How long have you been there?"

"Twelve years or so. I worked at Commercial Design for about three years out of college."

A look came over him that Christine couldn't read.

Will delved into his sundae and the conversation faded. He hadn't seemed interested in hearing her ideas and he certainly didn't like something she'd said about her work.

"I'd better get back to the booth," he said.

His abruptness startled her. "I need to get Grandma home, too." Yet she faltered, not wanting to leave with the tension she sensed between them. "I'll walk with you to the booth so I can—"

"I have much more at the studio. I think that's better."

She wasn't sure what he meant by that. Was it better she buy her gifts another time or was it better she leave? Hurt by his behavior, she clutched her gift to her chest. "I'll head over to Grandma then."

"See you later." He gave her a quick wave and walked away.

She stood a moment trying to collect herself and to hold back tears that threatened to sneak from behind her eyes.

Will kept moving forward. He wanted to turn back and look at her, but he couldn't. He felt like a heel, pushing her away like that, but she'd thrown him a curve when she answered his question.

His addition was good. Twelve years and three years

equaled fifteen. She'd gotten out of college at least fifteen years ago. Fifteen years ago he'd been a freshman in high school. Will didn't care, but he feared Christine would. They'd become friends, and they'd just begun to have fun together. Once she realized his age—and she would—it was all over, and he knew it.

Someone grabbed his arm and, when he turned, Jude stood beside him with a grin on his face.

"So that's the chick you were telling me about," he said.

Will drew back. Chick? He'd never considered Christine a chick. "She's the *woman*," he said, hoping to make a point.

"She's not bad at all," Jude said. "So how's it going?"

"Good. Sales are better than last year, I think."

Jude punched his shoulder. "Not the sales. I mean with her. How's that going?"

"Fine. We've come to an amiable agreement. As long as she's here, we can tolerate each other, I think."

"Tolerate? Dude, where are your eyes? That lady's a better prize than that new sled outside Doud's."

"Do you want me to put in a good word for you, Jude?"

"Would you?" His eyes widened.

"No. And remember that."

Jude drew back and held up his hand. "I'm only kidding, Will. You said you're not interested, but apparently I have that wrong. Sorry, man."

Will opened his mouth to rebut, but nothing came. He was interested in Christine. Why try to pretend he wasn't? "It's okay," Will said, extending his hand.

"Sure, man," Jude said, giving him a curious look. He rattled on about the restaurant and Doud's sled, but Will's mind had stopped at his own admission.

He liked Christine, and he feared his feelings had headed off in directions he couldn't control. He barely knew the woman, but he sensed a pull that only God could cause. The attraction made no sense to him.

Chapter Eight

"Chet, you know I'd be back if I could. I didn't tell my mom to break her hip."

She listened to his superior attitude, and she controlled herself from knocking it down a peg. She had the ammunition, but she thought better of it. If she reminded him of his underhanded ways with her, she'd only put herself in a deeper hole.

"Look, Chet, think compassion. Can you do that?"

"What's that?" he asked her.

She wanted to give a smart remark back. "I don't know what you expect me to do. I'm all my parents have, and they—"

He cut her off and his question struck her.

"Yes, I have a brother, but he's married and lives out of state. My dad—"

She cringed at his next demand. "Look, I have two more weeks' vacation." Her vacation. Her stomach knotted. This wasn't the way she wanted to spend her vacation, but Chet wasn't going to manipulate her. "That'll nearly take me to the Christmas holidays. She's improving every day. Maybe by then, I'll—"

Chet's demand charged through her as he cut her off.

Her hopes fell to the ground. "I realize I have clients and yes, I'm going to talk with them today. I'll work out something about the meeting."

Christine hung up and fell backward on her bed. Tears slipped from the corners of her eyes and dripped to the quilt beneath her. Chet had made the threats she'd expected. She could go over his head, but it could destroy her. Right now, she needed to keep things low-key and try to cooperate as best she could.

She'd forgotten about a meeting she had with a client in less than a week, a big client who needed a sizable ad campaign. She wasn't the type to forget, but she wouldn't dwell on this now. She'd promised them mountains, and she'd better get busy. If she couldn't keep her appointments, someone else could. She'd be slipping from her status at the company.

As the outcomes swirled in her head, she pushed the heels of her hands against her eyes to stop the welling of tears. She refused to feel sorry for herself.

She rose and slid forward, her feet dangling from the mattress. Since she'd been here, she'd learned to enjoy some things about being laid-back—*cozy,* as she'd called it a couple days earlier. But it was more than cozy. The world had a sense of calmness and acceptance. Life had stresses, but they were different. They lacked the panic and the tension that she'd come to accept in her work and in city life.

She recalled the traffic jams on Southfield Road and I-696. She'd line up for miles. Her time would be frittered away while she directed her anger at drivers cutting her off and driving down the shoulder to sneak in ahead of her.

But here on the island, traffic? She smiled. Traffic was two horses and a carriage or two snowmobiles passing on a quiet road. She found something about that image soothing. No wonder her grandmother still looked so good even after her stroke. A little droopy in the face, perhaps, but she still had a sparkle in her eyes and a will to live fully.

Christine's thoughts slipped back to Will. She still felt troubled about what had happened at the bazaar. Yesterday he'd been busy at the event, too, and they hadn't really talked. Today he'd slipped away without a hello or goodbye. She longed to know what she'd done.

She pictured Will in the studio—his confidence and sense of being, sense of control. She admired his creativity, and though she was certain he had deadlines and responsibilities, he could pace himself. He could say yes or no to a job. He could take a day off without having his director threaten him. He could come home early and go in late if the fancy struck him.

She lowered her head in her hands. She'd been so excited to tell him about her great ideas for his store, and now she felt depressed and miserable. Being upset solved no problems. She'd find an answer.

Christine forced herself to rise. She dabbed powder around her eyes to cover the redness. The last thing she wanted was for her grandmother to know she had become upset again. Her grandmother mentioned a couple of the circle ladies were bringing her some jigsaw puzzles after her therapy. Christine hoped she could take the snowmobile—she looked to heaven and begged for mercy—and drop by the studio. She had to find out what was wrong.

Will lifted his head from his work, and his breath left him. Christine stood in the doorway of the studio, a smile on her face, but her eyes were questioning. What could he tell her? Not the truth. First he needed to figure out what he wanted and where he wanted this to go.

"Hi," he said, trying to remove the apprehension from his voice. "What brings you here?"

"Christmas gifts. You told me to drop by, and Grandma Summers has company."

"Great," he said, before pausing to ask his next question. "How did you get here?"

"The sled. You give good lessons."

That made him grin. "Thanks."

"How was the bazaar on Sunday?"

"Just about as busy as Saturday."

"Who won Doud's sled?"

He shrugged. "A year-round resident."

"Oh," she said. "Then it wasn't me."

"No, it wasn't you." He knew they were batting around the inevitable, so he took a different tack. "Sorry about Saturday. I didn't mean to let my mood affect our fun."

She drew closer, resting her hand against a display case. "What was that all about? I figured I did something, but I didn't know what."

"It was me," he said, feeling less than capable.

"What?" Her eyes narrowed as if his response had confused her.

"You're so sure of yourself in business. You have tremendous drive. I've seen it since you've gotten here. Your mind never stops."

She drew back. "It comes across that much?"

He shrugged. "I'm not saying it's bad, but I know you're anxious to get back to your work, and I—I'm not as anxious to have you go."

She studied his face. "I've been a diversion, I know."

"Diversion? Christine, you're more than a diversion. I really like you. You're great to be with. You make me laugh. I—"

"And somewhere in there I make you feel less confident and less capable. That doesn't make sense. You should want me to leave."

"It's difficult to explain. The longer you've been here, the more you've let down your..." He struggled for the words. "You've let go of your job at times. I see the love you have for your grandmother despite your drive to get back to work. You—"

"I know."

He felt his eyes widen at her admission.

"You look surprised that I see that in me, but I do. Let me tell you what happened today. I called my boss."

He listened while she told him her plight. He had to admit she'd fought a good fight. The vacation days were the biggest evidence. She'd once said she didn't want to give those up. "What will you do?"

She lowered her head and shook it. "I don't know. I'll do what I can and pray that Grandma Summers improves enough for me to go back when the time comes. Or..."

Her voice faded, but he wanted to know more. "Sounds as if your boss is trying to get even for some reason. Do you know why?"

She shook her head. "I really don't want to talk about it today. I need to decide what I can do. There are clients I need to talk with, and I may have to go back to the office for a day or so this week." She lowered her head again, then lifted it. "I hate to ask you but—"

"If you need me, Linda and I can handle it. I'm sure."

"Really?"

"We handled it a couple days before you got here, and your grandmother is doing better now."

"Thanks, Will. I feel much better with your offer. I can't tell you how much."

"I have some news," he said, the words blurting from him more loudly than he expected. He noticed the surprised look on Christine's face.

A frown wrinkled her forehead. "What kind of news?"

"My parents are coming up on the weekend for an early Christmas."

Her expression showed her confusion. "That's good news, isn't it?"

"Right," he said, trying to convince himself.

"Why early?"

"They have their Christmas traditions, and I said I couldn't get there this year so they're coming here."

She fell quiet, as if trying to understand. "Are you worried about Grandma Summers? Is that why you're not going home?"

"That's a small part of it." He turned away, afraid to look into her eyes for fear she'd read the truth. "I don't enjoy the family's social calendar. They either drag me with them—not always happy about it because I don't have the proper clothes—or I stay with the family and wish I were here." He finally looked at her.

She became quiet again, her eyes shifting from him to the distance. "I look forward to meeting them."

Her comment twisted in his stomach. "Say that after the fact." He heard the bitterness in his voice, and he regretted letting her see it.

He steadied himself. "Ready to look around for your gifts? I always give my friends a great bargain."

She gave him a pleasant look, but her voice seemed strained. "My credit card is ready. Show me the way."

Christine lowered her cell phone and pulled back her shoulders. Done. She had to go back tomorrow for an overnight stay. She'd hinted at changing the appointment, but her client hadn't been receptive to change, and she knew if she wanted to keep the company happy, she'd better make the trip.

Flying from the Pellston Regional Airport to Detroit Metro, then renting a car seemed easier than driving the five hours home. She checked the flight schedule. The trip flying would take about an hour and twenty minutes. She could even fly back to the island the same day, but she wouldn't. She wanted to see her mother while she was there.

Christine rubbed the gritty feeling from her eyes. She hadn't slept well. All night, she'd waded through the subliminal undertones of Will's reasons to stay on the island for Christmas. Bitterness seemed to rise from the mix of emotions she sensed in him—bitterness and disapproval. His attitude made her curious, and she was anxious to meet his parents.

When he'd suggested she look at his stock, she'd been relieved. It had distracted her from speculating.

Will's talent amazed her. The beadwork had been lovely, and he'd promised her a lesson. He told her bead making was simple, but that would seem the same as her telling him planning an advertising campaign was easy. It could be when the person had expertise.

She'd purchased a number of items to use as Christmas gifts—a gorgeous molded plate made with crushed glass for her mother. Will called it frits—a whole new language for her. She selected a string of beads in shades of blue for her sister-in-law, stained-glass barrettes for her two nieces, and a butterfly sun catcher for her coworker Sandy. She'd admired one for herself but let it pass. She'd spent enough money, and she still had numerous gifts to buy. Perhaps if she could spare a few hours, she could shop in the Detroit area when she went home.

Home. She pictured her loft in Royal Oak, looking over the store-front business area. The only trees were in the distance, appearing over housetops. She liked her place, but lately the image of the wide-open space seemed stark and empty. It wasn't like her grandmother's house, with doors sprawling along hallways, nooks and crannies and rooms she hadn't used in years.

With her decision made, Christine headed to the first floor. She stood in the doorway watching Judy encourage her grandmother to lift her arms and legs. The progress seemed slow but steady, and that gave Christine hope.

"How's it going?" Christine asked as she sat nearby. "You're using the sofa today."

"It's lower and firmer," Judy said. "It adds to the challenge, but I can see an improvement."

She turned to Christine. "You know, the insurance only covers three more weeks. That gets you up to Christmas. I hope you or someone can continue the therapy here, rather than sending her—"

"We'll work something out," Christine said, stopping the woman from suggesting they send her grandmother to an assisted-living complex. She'd seen the look in her grandma's eyes. She couldn't do that to her.

"Grandma." Christine faltered. "I'm going to have to go home for a couple of days—I need to get online and make my reservations—but Will said he and Linda could stay with you while I'm gone."

"We'll do fine. Don't worry."

Her grandmother said the words, but Christine saw a look of concern on her face.

"I promise I'll be back. I'm planning an overnight visit home—Wednesday, I think, and I'll be back Thursday evening."

"I know this is a hardship for you," her grandmother said. "If I could make it any different—"

"Grandma, don't say that. We'll talk later." She patted her grandmother's hand and headed upstairs to her cell. She needed to make reservations for the flight and car, then tell her father she was coming for a brief visit, and while she was at it, she wanted to make lunch plans with her friend, Ellene, and see how married life had affected her.

When Christine came down the stairs, she found her grandmother in the living room, her Bible in her hands.

She waited a moment before Ella looked up from her reading. "Judy said you're doing well."

"That's what she said."

Christine sat across from her grandmother. "I made plans, and I called Linda. She's ready to come in to help you in the morning and get your meals, and when she can't be here, Will said he has no problem getting home early."

"I know. I'm frustrated, I guess, and when that happens, I seek God's Word. I always find comfort in this book." She rested her hands on the Bible.

Christine leaned back, ready to be open with her grandmother. "When I came here, I'd been drifting from church attendance. The last two Sundays have been nice being with you in church. I love the hymns, and the lessons haven't hurt me, either."

Her grandmother only looked at her.

"I'm sure you didn't know but—"

"But I did." A faint, lopsided grin settled on her face.

"You did?"

"You can't fool an old lady, Christine. I knew you didn't want to go to church, and I could tell from your attitude that you'd drifted a little too far from the Lord, but I see the difference, and it does my heart good."

"But I didn't say anything." She searched her grandmother's face.

"No, but I saw it in your manner. Actions speak louder than words. I know you've heard that a thousand times, but it's true."

Christine hung her head. She remembered saying the same. "Faith without positive action was a dying faith."

"But remember that we're saved by grace alone, and not good works. The Bible tells us that, but when the Lord has blessed us, then we want to show our love by doing as He would want. Those are the things that everyone can see."

A smile pulled at Christine's mouth. "I remember a song I sang in the teen group years ago—"They Will Know We Are Christians By Our Love."

"I remember that song." She shifted the Bible and fondled the page. "It reminds us of our behavior. Since the stroke, I can't do as much, and I get frustrated with my fumbling arms and a leg that either stays glued to the floor or tries to trip me up."

"But you're getting much better now."

"I am, and I'm still filled with self-pity, but lately

when that happens, I read from Psalms because they are a beautiful blend of prayer and praise.

"When I feel sorry for myself, I think of what could have happened with my stroke, and then I'm filled with thankfulness. Here's what I just read. It's from Psalms 142:3. 'When my spirit grows faint within me, it is You who knows my way.'" She drew her attention from the scripture. "This verse is for you, too."

The verse wrapped around Christine's heart. She'd always struggled to find her own way, forgetting to ask God to guide her.

"And speaking of seeing change," her grandmother said. "In the past week, you glow. You're not like you were the day you came. I know you're still feeling stressed from your work, but you're not as determined— aggressive." She nailed Christine with her gaze. "You were aggressive when you arrived, but you've softened. You're a lovely woman, and now it shows."

Tears grew behind Christine's eyes. She had no idea she'd appeared aggressive to her grandmother. She opened her mouth to apologize, but she choked on the words.

"Don't be upset," her grandmother said. "You did nothing wrong, but now I see you and Will laughing about things. You're going off on the sled and coming back with rosy cheeks and a vibrance I haven't seen in you for years. The island can get in your heart and change you."

Had it been the island or her grandmother's love? And Will. He'd impacted her, too, by making her face herself. She pressed her hand against her chest, feeling the beat of her heart and the rise and fall of her lungs. She felt alive on the island, much more alive than she had at home.

"I love you, Grandma," she said. She rose and kissed the elderly woman's soft cheek.

"And I love you, too, Christine—more and more each day. I'll miss you when you go back home, and I know you must. I don't mean for this little trip, but later when I'm doing well. You've been good for me."

"You've been even better for me." She clasped her hand. "And now, let's work on the jigsaw puzzle. We need to get those fingers moving."

Chapter Nine

Will rose from the fireplace and waited a moment to see if the kindling caught the flame. When he was satisfied, he moved to the sofa, mesmerized by the fire sparking inside the hearth.

"That looks nice," Christine said, coming into the room. "Grandma decided to go to bed early. A couple of ladies from her circle are coming over to visit tomorrow."

She stepped past him heading for a chair, but Will reached out and pulled her down beside him. "The view's better from here."

Christine gave him a curious glance, then watched the flames licking along the log and settled back.

Will hunkered down beside her. "I'm glad people are beginning to treat her as if she's going to live. I know they mean well, but sometimes they only called or dropped off food, and they didn't stay. She misses her normal relationship with them."

"I know it's been hard on her."

"I suppose it has on you, too, missing your friends." A questioning tone accentuated his voice.

Her head lifted from the cushion. "That's funny."

"What?"

Her expression shifted from awareness to surprise. "I don't miss my friends, because I don't have many."

"You don't?"

"Not really. My life has been so filled with work that I come home exhausted and don't really socialize much."

"You must do something. Even I hang around with a few people."

"I have a good friend who moved when she got married, and I'm hoping to see her when I go to Detroit on Wednesday. I'll call her and see if we can meet for lunch or dinner."

"She's married?"

"Yes, I was her maid of honor. She's younger than I am, but we've been like sisters."

The reference to her age caught him again, and he struggled to keep from reacting. He needed to talk with her about that, but he feared if she knew the truth, she'd not give them a chance. Chance? He had a fleeting chance as it was. The woman lived near Detroit. He lived three hundred miles away on an island. That situation could undo any chance in itself.

"You're quiet," she said, leaning her head back again.

He turned to her, watching the firelight dance across her face. The golden glow glinted in her hair, and her eyes sparkled even more brightly. "If you lived on the island, you'd have a good friend."

Will cringed hearing his inane comment, like a love-sick puppy. He expected her to laugh, but she didn't.

"I know. Grandma and I had a talk today about change. She thinks I've changed since I've come here."

The urge to touch her hair tangled his thoughts. He fought the desire until he couldn't control it any longer.

He eased his finger upward and brushed a lock from her cheek. "You have. I've seen it, and I like it."

She didn't flinch as he swept the spun gold from her face. "You look worn-out."

"It's the trip. I hate leaving and dumping this on you and Linda. I'll be back the next day, but it's asking a lot."

He motioned to his shoulder and drew her head toward it. Her gaze drifted to his hand, and as she shifted closer, he slid his arm around her shoulders. "I wouldn't have volunteered if I hadn't wanted to help. I love your grandmother."

Christine lifted her head, and he wanted to kick himself for making a statement that caused her to shift away.

She looked at him closely. "I know you do, and that's another thing I couldn't understand. When I first met you, I thought you had an ulterior motive."

"Ulterior motive?" She'd thrown him with the comment. "What do you mean?"

"I don't know. I couldn't understand a man being so accommodating to an elderly woman without wanting something."

"Like what?"

"Like her money."

"Her money? I didn't know she had any money. That wouldn't have entered my mind." Now he'd straightened up and removed his arm from around her.

"You see, that was my bad attitude. I'm really sorry."

She fell against the cushion, and Will took advantage of her upset to embrace her again and draw her closer. "I hope you know—"

"My grandmother was shocked that I'd even said it."

"You told your grandmother?"

"She put me in my place. She talked about Christian love and compassion. That's something I lack so much."

He nestled his head against hers again. "Not anymore. You're willing to fight your boss for time to spend with your grandmother. That's not the action of someone who's not caring. I see your love every day that you're standing over her forcing her to do her therapy or encouraging her to work on the jigsaw."

"And it feels good." She turned toward him, her mouth so close to his he could feel her breath against his lips. "I've never imagined that helping someone could give me such a sense of purpose and—" she shrugged "—I don't know, happiness, I guess."

"It's because it happens right here." He lifted her hand and pressed it against his heart. "When things affect you here, instead of up there—" he used his free hand to motion to his head "—then it's a special gift. It's what God wants us to do, because we're doing it for Him."

A tender look moved to her face. "It's that Christmas heart you talked about." She snuggled closer, and he ran his finger over the soft flesh of her arm.

In the quiet, he listened to the snap of the log in the fireplace and watched the ash sprinkle down like glowing confetti.

"You'll be back Thursday," he said, breaking the silence.

"Probably around four in the afternoon. My meeting is in the morning, and I hope to leave after lunch."

"If we can get someone to stay with Grandma Ella, would you like to help me pick out a Christmas tree?"

"So early?"

"My folks will be here Saturday afternoon, and—"

Christine shifted. "Yes, that's a good idea. I forgot

they were coming so soon. We want the house to look like Christmas."

"Just a little one for my place," he said.

"No, we'll put one up here, too. They'll come to dinner. You shouldn't just take them to a restaurant or feed them a microwave frozen dinner."

He chuckled. "I suppose you're right."

"We'll make a holiday meal. This will be fun."

He didn't want to destroy her plans, but nothing was very much fun with his family—unless Christine could work a miracle on them, and even God hadn't done that.

Christine stood at the car rental checking the time. She'd agreed to meet Ellene for lunch and a little shopping before she headed for the office. She decided to work on the project in the evening after most everyone had gone. The building would be quieter, and she wouldn't be distracted by co-workers dropping in to find out how she'd fared on the island. Later she would visit her parents. She missed them.

"Here you go," the clerk said, slipping her the paperwork. "Go through that door on the left, and they'll direct you to your car."

"Thanks," Christine said, picking up her overnight bag and following the clerk's directions.

Once she pulled away from Detroit Metro airport, she headed east on I-94. The pavement was dry with no signs of snow, but the barren trees and gray sky told her that winter was not far-off.

Traffic sped along on the highway, and she followed the signs and veered onto the Southfield Freeway merging with traffic. The familiar landmarks whipped past her window and left her feeling lonely. She pictured her grandmother doing her exercises—the laps they'd gotten to enjoy as they talked while pacing the familiar path through the house. Her grandmother seemed stronger every day.

And Will. His smile filled her mind and his silly humor that she'd grown to love. She knew he had problems, but he carried them well, not like the burdens she lugged around so often—her fears of falling short on her job, the competition that kept her awake at night—but for a short while, that had changed.

The freeway merged into a regular road, and she braked for the stoplight. She'd be on time, she noted, glancing at her watch. As she approached Ten Mile Road, the restaurant sign caught her eye—Wing Hong. She liked Chinese food and so did Ellene, and the restaurant wasn't noisy like so many were at lunchtime.

She pulled into the parking lot and entered the restaurant lobby. When she looked into the dining area with its red-and-black Asian decor, she saw Ellene's bright smile. She waved, and Christine hurried forward, her arms open.

"It's so good to see you," she said, grasping her friend to her chest. "I hope you didn't wait long."

"I was just seated," she said, holding Christine back and eyeing her from all directions. "What's up with you? You look better than I've seen you in so long. Something must agree with you up there."

Christine shrugged. "It's been a battle, but I'm surviving." She pulled off her coat, threw it on the bench and slipped into the booth.

"If it were a battle, you've come out the victor. You have the brightest glow, Christine, even more than when we spent an hour at the gym. I'm telling you, it must be the fresh air."

Christine laughed. "Can you picture me driving a snowmobile?"

Ellene shook her head. "You're kidding. Is that your only transportation?"

"Now with the snow. I didn't know what I was doing until Will gave me a lesson. I was so determined—"

Ellene grabbed her arm. "Hold on. Will? Who's Will?"

Christine tried to keep her voice calm, but she longed to talk about him. "He's my grandmother's boarder."

"Really?"

She studied Christine, and her scrutiny made Christine uneasy. "Really. I didn't know she had a boarder until he met me at the ferry depot."

"On a white steed?"

"No, with a taxi—horse and carriage no less."

Ellene grasped her hand and squeezed. "Please tell me. Something's going on, and I'm so excited for you. You like him, right?"

"I didn't want to, but I do, Ellene, and it makes no sense. I barely know him, and yet I feel I've known him forever. I was very edgy at first, but I came to my senses."

"Edgy?"

Christine told her how she'd worried about Will's motives, her jealousy with his closeness to her grandmother, and his island know-it-all. "But that's changed. He owns a business, and I have so many ideas for him."

"Is he open to that? You know a man and his business. If you interfere—"

"You order?" the Asian woman asked.

"I haven't looked." Christine flipped open the menu

and gave it a quick scan. "I'll take the number six luncheon plate with wonton soup."

The waitress nodded, and after Ellene placed her order, the woman left.

"I mentioned ideas to him, and he didn't say anything." Or did he? Was that one of his silent moments?

"I don't mean to interfere, but I know how you are about business. You have set ideas, and they don't always work for someone else."

Christine was taken aback. "Do you really think I'm pushy?" *Aggressive.* Her grandmother's word made her wince.

"I didn't say pushy exactly. Your ideas are strong and you think they're right."

Was that so bad? Christine pondered what Ellene had said for a moment. "I do know a lot about marketing and that's where Will's business is weak. I think the Internet could be a boon to making him a—"

"Success?" Ellene frowned. "Do you think a man wants to hear you don't consider him a success? You know I did that to Connor, and it almost ruined our relationship. I don't want to see you ruin something before it has a chance to succeed."

"He knows I admire him."

"You say you admire him, but what you do really tells the tale." She brushed the air with her hand. "Look. Ignore me. It's none of my business. Just tell me about him."

Christine let her friend's comments slide, but they stuck in the back of her mind as she told her about Will. Ellene's smile was as broad as her own when she talked about the sled lessons and the conversations in front of the fireplace. "I like him a lot, but it's sad."

"Sad?"

"Because I live here, and he lives there. He'd never come back to the city. I would stake my job on it."

"That's a pretty strong comment."

They paused while the waitress brought their soup and egg roll with a pot of Chinese tea.

"You'd have to meet him. The island has made a mark on him—a good mark. He belongs there. Remember how you felt about Harsens Island and how much Connor loved it."

"He still does, and guess what—so do I now that I'm there. Caitlin is so happy, too." She took a spoonful of soup. "I'd love to meet Will, but obviously that's not possible."

"I know, but wouldn't it be nice."

The conversation drifted to Ellene's construction business, her husband Connor's new sports store, and the reason Christine had come to town, but her thoughts clung to things Ellene had said. Her grandmother had talked about her aggressiveness, and now her friend had called her pushy and interfering.

Was that really how she'd acted?

"It's quiet here without Christine."

Will turned his head and looked at Grandma Ella. "I was thinking that, too. Funny how a person can get used to scratchy long johns." He chuckled, and so did Grandma Ella.

"She did come across as a little abrasive around the edges, didn't she? But not anymore."

"She has you to thank for that," Will said, helping Ella with her laps. "It's great to see you on a cane."

"It's good to be on it. You can throw that walker into the garbage as far as I'm concerned."

He chuckled.

"I think two things made a difference in Christine's life," Ella said. "You and the Lord."

Will faltered. "Me? I didn't do a thing but teach her how to drive a sled."

"That was part of it. She got a taste of life on the island, and the Lord did the rest."

"But you were the catalyst."

Ella chuckled. "I did get her to church and shared some Bible verses with her, and she was open to that. Christine came here with a lot of guilt, and it's fading fast like the evening sun."

Will thought about what she'd said. Christine had arrived with a frown on her face and a negative attitude. They had faded until now he saw a radiant woman who'd discovered a lighthearted way of looking at things…at least most of the time.

"You've fallen in love with her."

Will tripped over his foot. "I what?"

"You can't hide it, Will. You're like a kid with a gift you've wanted forever, like a teenager with car keys. You can't get your fill of her. When my son, who's been gone a long time now, passed his driving test and got his license, he'd run to the grocery store at the drop of a hat."

"On the island?"

"No." She grinned. "When I lived in Detroit. I moved here when the house was left to me by my parents."

"I didn't know that."

"Lots of things you don't know." She gave him a wink. "But some things I do know, and you're in love."

"And I can't do a thing about it, Grandma Ella. Christine is a big-city girl. She has a job she loves, and a home in Royal Oak. I can't compete with that."

"Oh, Will, love doesn't compete. Hand me my Bible, and I'll tell you about love in First Corinthians."

"I know," he said. "Love is kind. It doesn't boast. It isn't rude. Love never fails. It protects. It doesn't envy. I know I forgot some."

"The most important. Love is patient. Give it time, Will, and pray about it. Nothing would make me happier than you and Christine finding a love that's blessed. But be patient. She's made long strides, but she'll stumble. It's part of her, but she's grown and that's been God's doing."

Love is patient. Will grasped on to that thought. Grandma Ella knew about life and the Lord. He'd trust her to give him good advice, and he trusted God to answer his prayers.

"So how did it go?"

Christine's head shot upward and she frowned. "Very well, Chet. Thanks."

He sauntered into her office and sat on the edge of her desk. "Is the deal set, then?"

"No, but it's close. They'll look it over and take it to their board meeting, but they sounded pleased with the presentation. They said they'd be in touch by tomorrow. I asked them to e-mail, since I won't be here."

He stood and put his hands on the desk, his face thrusting closer to hers. "You can't be a long-distance employee, Christine. I know you think you have all the good ideas, but we have others here who can do your job."

She rose and pushed back her chair. "Listen, Chet. You thought I had great ideas once. Remember?" She narrowed her eyes, hoping to nail him to the spot.

Instead he laughed. "That was a long time ago, Christine." He moved closer. "When you were gullible. You should have known better than to listen to my promises."

"That's water under the bridge, Chet. I'm not afraid of you, but I want to do my job here. People have problems sometimes—illness, emergencies—and I have one of those. I'm the only person available to help my grandmother. I'll take my two weeks' vacation. In fact I put in for that already, and it was approved."

"Really, and what about the Dorset project? Can you handle that long-distance?"

"If I must, I will."

"We'll see about that. You have to be ready in January. I'm thinking your team needs another leader."

"They'll be fine without me physically present. I'm in contact by e-mail and on the phone. I haven't died, Chet. I'm just a few miles away."

He grabbed the calendar from his desk. "Let's see. Those two weeks' vacation should take you to December fifteenth. We'll see you back here on December eighteenth then. You'll be home for Christmas."

Christine managed to hide her frustration. She needed longer, and she'd get it somehow. She'd looked forward to Christmas on the island.

Chet's smirk eroded her patience, and an idea came from nowhere. "FMLA, Chet, you've heard of FMLA, right? Family Medical Leave Act. I'm entitled to that. Twelve weeks of it, if I must. That's not what I want, but if I'm needed, that's what I'll have to do."

"We'll see about that, my friend. I've already told the big guy upstairs that I had to help you with the Emerson project since you were on vacation."

Her pulse escalated. "You out-and-out lied?"

"No, I did talk to them on the phone and said the meeting was set for today. I did help you, didn't I?"

He spun on his heel and vanished around the corner.

Christine sank into her chair and lowered her face into her hands.

Chapter Ten

Will grabbed the phone on the second ring.

"I'm back."

Christine's voice bubbled over the line, and Will felt a smile grow on his face. "How was it?"

"Pretty good. I had a nice visit with my friend over Chinese food, my mom seemed fine despite her hip, and the meeting with the client went well, I think."

"Then why only pretty good?"

She hesitated before she spoke. "It's a long story. I'll tell you later."

"Are you going with me to pick out the Christmas trees?"

"Where is the lot?"

"Down by the Chamber Riding Stables on Market and Cadotte. The junior class sponsors the tree sale."

"Sure, I'll go." He heard a pause. "But how do you get the tree back on the sled?"

He shook his head. "You have much to learn. In the sled's caboose or we can have it delivered."

"I do have a lot to learn."

Will heard another pause and wondered if her statement held more meaning than the reference to sleds.

"I picked up a couple things to add to the tree while I was shopping yesterday," she said.

"You've got my attention."

She laughed. "You'll have to wait. It's a surprise."

He loved the sound of her voice, and his chest grew tight, picturing her face. "I'll leave here shortly."

Will said goodbye and hung up, feeling as if he'd been given a gift by her call. He'd missed her so much while she was gone—only a day and a half, he knew, and the idea stressed him. What would he do when she left for good? Their relationship was like a shipboard romance, doomed to end when the boat docked at the final port.

He finished cutting the glass pieces he'd marked and closed the studio. A gloomy sky had lowered over the island the day before, reflecting the funk he'd been in, but it lingered today and didn't fit the mood he now felt.

Christine had returned, and the evening would be dedicated to Christmas—decorating the trees and listening to carols—and maybe having a cup of hot chocolate.

Will sped along the frozen earth, the snow forming a landscape of glass that glinted when the sun accidentally peeked from behind the clouds before it vanished again. The house appeared ahead, and he knew Christine was waiting inside.

She opened the door as he came up the walk.

"Ready?" he called. She held up her index finger, and in a moment, she darted outside dressed in her jacket and wearing the bright red scarf he'd bought to match her gloves.

He opened his arms, and she went into them. He teetered in surprise, yet thrilled to her candid action. It was what he'd wanted to happen.

"So tell me," he said, easing back. "Why was your time only pretty good?"

"It's Chet, my boss. He's pulling things on me again. He has a history of it. It's my fault. I fell for it one time, and once more he's manipulating things. I'll survive."

A gust caught them, and he saw her shiver. He noticed something more in her face, something that revealed the story was deeper and more serious than she wanted to admit.

"Let's go," he said, letting her climb onto the sled before he joined her.

While he waited, the lowering sun tried to peak from beneath the thick bank of clouds, but only a flicker lit the sky, then vanished again, leaving him with an unsettled feeling.

"It looks pretty," Christine said, standing back to admire her grandmother's tree. "I love these old Christmas balls."

"I was given some of them when I was a child," her grandmother said. "And many are from my mother's ornaments. They're antiques."

"And beautiful," Christine said. "These are the things we cherish about Christmas. It's not the gifts under the tree, but the memories—good memories."

Will drew closer to her and touched her shoulder. "I've never heard you so nostalgic."

"I know," she said, feeling his gentle touch shimmer down her arm. "Sometimes I amaze myself."

He grinned and gestured toward the foyer. "Let's

tackle my tree. That won't take long, and then we'll have a treat."

"Don't worry if I'm not here when you come back in. I'm thinking of heading for bed."

Christine shifted to her side and rested her hand on her grandmother's arm. "Grandma, it's too early. Are you feeling all right?"

"I'm feeling wonderful, and you know what's the most special?"

Christine studied her face, wondering what she was about to say. "No."

"You calling me Grandma."

"I've always called you Grandma."

"No. I was Grandma Summers. It's nice just hearing the plain old Grandma. More loving, I think."

Christine's chest tightened. "I've always loved you, but now it's more personal, I guess."

"It's how we should be with Jesus," her grandmother said. "When we get personal is when He's our closest friend."

"I'll add a second to that," Will said.

The comments bounced around in Christine's thoughts. Had she ever had that kind of personal feeling about Jesus? Since she'd been on the island, she'd drawn closer.

"Ready?" Will asked, beckoning her to follow.

Christine bent and kissed her grandmother's cheek. "I love you."

Her grandmother's crepey hand pressed against hers. "I love you, too."

"I'll come back and check on you shortly." She gave a wave and followed Will into the foyer and through the back entrance leading to his apartment. Knowing her grandmother was within a few steps relieved the normal tension she felt when she was away, and Ella's getting steadier on the walker—even the cane—brought Christine joy. "Thank You, Lord." The praise lingered in her mind.

Will had already set his tabletop tree into a stand, and Christine waited while he dragged out a small box of decorations. She wasn't sure why he wanted his own tree. Yet as she watched the delight on his face—like a child on Christmas morning—she recognized the joy he had in preparing for Christmas.

"Help me untangle these," he said, pulling out a knotted string of miniature lights.

She shook her head at the task but took a section and began solving the puzzle. "This reminds me of my grandmother's jigsaw. I insist she use her left hand when I'm watching her. It's difficult, but she'll get there. I see the determination in her face."

Will reached across the space and brushed her cheek. "You're a very devoted granddaughter. It looks so good on you."

"Thanks. I'm enjoying the time with her, and I mean that. I can't help but worry about my job, but…"

He let the string of lights sag in his hand and gazed at her. "Tell me about this guy—your boss."

"Chet." She drew up her shoulders while frustration charged through her again. "You'll ruin my evening if you make me talk about him."

"Sorry, but I'd like to understand what you're going through."

"It's something I'm ashamed of, Will. I haven't told anyone, and it's been eating at me. I was gullible and naive. *Stupid* is an even better word."

He let the string drop to the ground and moved two steps toward her. He took the lights from her hand and drew her closer. "Whatever you did or said, it's easier to live with when it's out in the open."

She noticed his expression and suspected he also had things in his life he'd rather forget.

Christine looked into his eyes, and as his discomfort faded, she saw the same gentleness arise that she'd seen when he cared for her grandmother. Will's natural inclination toward compassion aroused her longing. She wished she had the same ability to put others first always.

He guided her to the sofa and motioned for her to sit. She wanted to pull away and to decorate the tree rather than bare her past—the embarrassing, disgusting truth of her gullibility.

Will didn't move, and she gave in and sat. She tried to hide her trembling hands, but Will noticed.

"When you say things aloud, Christine, it gets rid of them." He slipped his arm around her shoulders. "Tell me about Chet. Don't let the past spoil what we have."

Don't let the past spoil what we have. But what did they have? She knew what she longed for, but she also knew a relationship with Will was destined to failure. They were worlds apart, and the knowledge squeezed against her heart.

Yet she looked at his face, so open to hearing, and realized he'd offered her a gift. What difference did it make? If nothing were to become of their relationship, then she had nothing to lose except finally confessing her wrongdoing—a sin that had eaten at her for years and for which she'd already paid a depressing price.

She swallowed, then lowered her head to collect her thoughts. How had it all begun? "Chet was a new, up-

coming man in the company when I met him. I'd joined
the team a few months before he had." The words tasted
bitter, and the acrid memory churned in her throat. "He
flirted. I flirted. After a few weeks, we dated. He told me
how much he admired my work. My ideas. Me."

Will shifted and rested his hand on her arm, his finger brushing along her skin.

"He started talking commitment. Life plans." She
sorted her thoughts, trying to remember what had happened first. "He told me how good our lives would be if
he became a top adman. He suggested I help him. We'd
brainstorm, and he'd present the idea as his own." She
turned to look at Will. "I'd become very respected when
I joined the company. They said I had innovative ideas
with a touch of wit."

"That doesn't surprise me," Will said. "I love your
spunky attitude."

"Spunky?" She thought back and agreed she had been
spunky with him from the beginning. "Chet wanted the
top guns to think the ideas were his and not mine. He
said it would be better for our relationship and our status as a couple."

"That's chauvinistic," Will said, the disapproval evident in his voice.

"But I was smitten. I fell for it. I was flattered and
foolish. I gave him my best ideas, and he became their
golden boy over the next few months."

"How could you do that? You're so strong."

"I am now. I wasn't then. But when I saw what was
happening, I started to back away. I told him he was set,
and I needed to show I had talent."

"What did he do?"

"He said he wanted to marry me." She swallowed

again, feeling tears fill her eyes. "He said once we were married and settled, then it wouldn't matter. He would be my director. I'd be his wife, and he knew my talent."

"Slick move. Disgusting, but slick."

"That's not the worst. He knew me well." Christine swallowed back the revulsion that the memory evoked and wondered how Will would react. "Without a wedding or a wedding date, we became—became involved, and I felt trapped. He knew that I had a Christian upbringing and I had morals. If I revealed the truth, he could do the same. I felt sick."

Will released a deep groan, and she felt him flinch, but his finger kept its steady rhythm along her arm.

"When he was promoted with his own office, he suddenly lost interest. I realized I'd been duped, and I was disgusted with myself."

"Christine. I don't know what to say." He lowered his head and was quiet while she struggled with what he was thinking.

"I shouldn't have told you. I knew you'd think less of me."

"No, I don't. You were naive. Those are the reasons I didn't want to go into corporate business. I don't play games. I don't stab my friends in the back. I don't lie or use people."

"I know you don't, Will."

"Couldn't you do anything?"

"What? He had me in the middle. I'd make a fool of myself no matter what I did or said. First I'd have to admit what I'd done, and then, he could say it was all sour grapes. I felt trapped in my own sin."

"And now?"

"He's confident I still won't say anything. I'm very

respected. Once his promotion became solid, he didn't need to prove anything. He's the team director, and he knows I'll continue to work hard and give the company what they want—innovative ads with a unique twist."

"Why is he fighting you now? You'd think he'd be happy to have you on leave for a couple of months."

"It's control. It's cat and mouse. He loves the torment. He threatened my job."

"To fire you?"

"No. To give my clients to someone else to direct. I don't have much to stand on when I'm not there. It means struggling to get a foothold again when I get back. It's the principle of the thing, but I'm not going to sit back and take it. I have rights, and I'll go to the top if I must."

"I would expect nothing else. God knows the truth, Christine, and the truth will win out."

His words wove through her mind. Will's faith amazed her. She longed to understand. "Will, I really want to know—"

Before she finished the sentence, he'd risen and held his hands out to her. "We need to get this tree finished. It's late and my parents arrive tomorrow."

She glanced at her watch. Nearly ten o'clock. She rose, and he drew her into his arms and gave her a reassuring hug. She held her question and joined him in untangling the tree lights.

Lights led to the ornaments, and when he began hanging them, Christine darted from the room and found the surprises she'd purchased for him. When she returned, he was standing back and looking at the tabletop tree.

"Not bad," he said. "A little scanty, but that's okay. I'll enjoy your grandmother's more than this one."

"I can fill in a couple of gaps."

He gave her a tender look when he saw the two packages in her hand.

She extended the one. "This is probably silly, but I thought it was lovely."

Will took the bag and pulled out an orb wrapped in bubble wrap. "Why is it silly?" He peeled away the protective covering while the question hung in the air. When the ball appeared, he lifted it and held it to the light. "Christine, it's beautiful. This is handblown."

"I know, but you could probably make one yourself."

"What difference does that make? This was from you and that makes it special." He turned to eye the tree, and when he located a larger opening in the branches, he added a hook to the ornament and hung it there. The ball twirled below the limb, the light refracting in the swirls of color.

"It is pretty," she said, pleased that he really seemed to like it. She fingered the next package and felt color rising up her neck, wondering if she'd made a mistake with this gift. She prayed he didn't misunderstand.

"So what's in the other bag?" he asked.

"Don't laugh and don't embarrass me with this one. I spotted it in the mall at one of those craft booths, and I couldn't resist. Please take it in the spirit it's given."

A questioning frown filled his face. She handed him the package. When he opened it, the frown shifted to a broad smile.

"I'm taking this in the spirit that I prefer. I hope you don't mind." He looked at her with eyes that made her melt. "I love it."

"I thought it would remind you of the photo you entered in the calendar contest."

"It reminds me of more than that."

She looked at the white handcrafted wooden heart personalized with their initials in red and the plus sign, just as they'd written it in the snow.

"This deserves a prominent spot," he said, moving an ornament to place the heart at the front of the tree. "And the gift deserves a real hug." He turned and opened his arms to her.

She stepped into his embrace, amazed at the feeling of comfort and familiarity that washed over her.

When she eased away, he urged her closer. "I bought a surprise, too," he said, reaching beneath the tree.

His hand reappeared from under the branches, and she caught her breath. A sprig of mistletoe hung between his fingers. His eyes captured hers as he raised the mistletoe above her head, his eyes asking if it was okay.

She couldn't respond, her own heart fighting for and against his action. They were spiraling even more deeply into a whirlwind relationship too fragile to withstand a gale.

He gathered her into his arms, his mouth finding hers. When she closed her eyes, her thoughts swirled like the colors of the lovely glass ornament. The gentle touch, the warmth that swept through Christine stunned her. His hand holding the mistletoe lowered to her back, nestling her closer as his mouth found hers again.

Reality smacked her. Why had she allowed this to happen? Sadness pried at the lovely liquid emotion that washed along her limbs. Nothing could undo their differences.

Will must have sensed her reserve, because he eased back, confusion spreading to his face. "What is it?"

She lowered her head. "Nothing you can fix."

"It's not the past, is it? I understand about that. Please, don't let those memories ruin what we have."

Ruin what we have? Again the words wove through her mind. "It's not that, Will." What did they have? A new friendship? Was it more? It couldn't be. "It's us. My work is downstate. Yours is here. I live in the city. You live on an island."

He rested his index finger on her lips. "Shush. I have no idea what this means, but God is in charge, and with Him all things are possible."

If God were in charge, He'd made a bungle of her life. She looked into Will's pleading eyes but couldn't tell him she disagreed. All things were not possible. She knew that for certain.

Chapter Eleven

When Christine heard Will calling her from the back hallway, she headed toward his voice.

He beckoned to her. "I want you to meet my parents." He appeared stressed even though he smiled.

"I'd like to meet them," she said, anxious to find out why their son had the negative feelings he seemed to have.

She walked through the doorway, then into his apartment. The couple was seated on the only two comfortable chairs in the crowded room. They looked out of place—his father in a dark business suit and his mother in a shirtwaist burgundy dress, her neck adorned with a string of pearls and her feet covered with fur-topped boots. They gave the illusion of a wealthy family dropping by to visit Tiny Tim at Christmas. The scene was paradoxical.

"This is Christine," Will said.

His parents studied her with suspicion in their eyes, and sadly, the look took her back to her own scrutiny of Will when she came to the island.

"Hello," she said, moving forward to offer her hand.

His mother's fingers brushed hers, then his father gave a firmer handshake, but his eyes continued to probe questioningly.

"I'm Ella's granddaughter. Ella is Will's landlady, as you know."

Will's mother looked her over again. "And you live here, too."

Christine heard the insinuation in his mother's voice. "No. I'm from the Detroit area, as you are. I've been staying here to help with Ella's therapy until my parents can arrive." She saw their glazed look. "My mother broke her hip on a cruise. Will probably told you my grandmother had a stroke."

Will slid a kitchen chair behind her, and Christine sat as his mother's eyebrows lifted.

"No, he didn't," she said.

"That's a shame," Will's father said. "Will must be a burden on your grandmother."

Will opened his mouth but Christine cut him off, shocked at their comment. "Not at all. He's been very helpful." Her thoughts shot back to her criticism of Will's belongings scattered around her grandmother's house. The problem had faded in her eyes. She looked at Will, and he grinned back. She hoped his parents witnessed the friendship between them. One smiling face, at least, was needed among this scowling group.

Will pulled up an ottoman and sat beside the table holding the Christmas tree.

Mr. Lambert turned his attention to her. "So you're from the city."

Christine nodded.

"And what do you do there?"

"I'm in advertising. I work for Creative Productions."

He shot a look at Will. "You see, Will. This woman has a head on her shoulders."

"Dad, I—" Will let his comment drop with the shake of his head.

Christine's back stiffened. "Have you been to Will's studio? He's extremely talented."

"We'd hoped he would make glass his hobby," his mother said. "We'd had such expectations."

"It's not a hobby," Will blurted, "and we don't need to hear that again, Mom. I'm doing very well, and I know I've disappointed you."

"Will has a thriving business," Christine added, then turned to him. "You'll have to take them there."

Out of nowhere, she became uneasy with her involvement in their discussion, and changing the subject became her mission. "How was your trip?"

"Long," Mrs. Lambert said. "Too long. We should have flown."

Mr. Lambert gave her a fleeting frown, then redirected his focus. "You could have flown home for the holiday, Will. Your room is waiting for you."

His room? Christine flashed him a look. She no longer had a room at home. Her mother turned it into a craft room—scrapbooking, sewing, needlework—as each hobby caught her fancy.

Will let the comment roll off his shoulders. "I'm busy here. I have a number of projects that need to be completed for the holidays. My customers come first. I think you'd appreciate that motto."

Christine cut in to the conversation again, fearing it was heading for an argument. "Before you leave, my grandmother is looking forward to meeting you, and she'd like you to have some refreshments."

Mrs. Lambert's eyes flashed from Will to her husband and back as if she hadn't heard. "I thought you had a real apartment, Will."

He grinned. "This is a real apartment, but it's small and not set up for socializing. You'll have more room at Grandma Ella's."

His father grunted. "If you were in the business at home, Will, you'd be successful and have a home of your own. A large home."

"I'm happy here, Dad."

"You appear to be an older woman," Mrs. Lambert said, turning to Christine. "I suppose you have your own home."

Older woman? Christine flinched, wondering what she meant. She glanced around the room for a mirror. She'd thought she looked pretty good today. "I have a loft in Royal Oak. I like it there."

"One of those new lofts. They're very popular," Mr. Lambert said. "That's what you need, Will. Some space to call home, and that reminds me."

His father dug into his breast pocket and pulled out a checkbook. Christine's mouth gaped as she watched him scribble a check and tear it off the pad. He extended it to Will. "We didn't know what you needed so we thought you could use this."

Will took the check, glanced at it and handed it back. "Dad, I don't need this amount of money. I don't need anything."

His father flexed his palm to stop him. "No. I'm sure you have needs." The tone of his voice made the meaning clear. "You can find a real condo on the island." He turned to Christine. "You look like a bright woman. Can't you convince this boy to find an attractive condo to live in?"

Christine reeled with his comment. *This boy?* She looked at Will's manly profile and shook her head. "I have no influence on your son, Mr. Lambert. I think that's his decision."

Will laid the check in front of his father. "Thank you, Mom. Dad. I'm happy living here, and I have everything I need." He glanced toward Christine with a telling look. "Nearly everything I need."

She squirmed with discomfort, understanding his innuendo.

Will rose. "By the way, I have something for you." He disappeared into his bedroom.

They sat the seconds in silence, watching the doorway. Will returned with a large narrow box—one of his large stained-glass windows, Christine guessed.

"Merry Christmas," Will said, setting the gift in front of his parents.

His father eyed the carton.

Will lowered himself onto the ottoman. "I'm sorry, I didn't gift wrap it."

His father pulled the tape from the box, and when he struggled to withdraw the gift, Will rose to help him pull out the glass.

"Will, it's beautiful," Christine said, amazed that he'd never shown her the wonderful landscape—distant trees scattered along the rolling hills where a winding path led away into an amazing sunset.

His parents gaped, then passed each other looks as if they were pleasantly surprised.

"This is very lovely," his mother said. "I didn't know you worked with such large pieces of glass."

"I thought it could hang in the large window in the library or maybe the living room picture window. Whichever you prefer. I'll show you how to hang it before you leave."

His father studied the scene. "Now what would you get for something like this?"

"At least two or three hundred dollars," his mother said, looking at Will with question.

"I've sold similar for fourteen hundred dollars."

His mother's eyes widened. "Really?"

"Glass is priced by the square foot, the type of glass, and the complexity of the design." Will helped his father slide the piece back into the carton. "It's heavy, Dad. Would you prefer me to mail it home rather than your carrying it?"

"Mail it? No, it would cost you a fortune."

"I can afford to send it home."

His father shook his head. "I'll have them handle it at the ferry, and someone can help me get it into the car."

Will didn't ask again and rose. "You can leave your coats here. Why don't we go and have some refreshments with Grandma Ella?" Will motioned his parents toward the door.

Christine went on ahead, her mind rolling with what she'd observed and heard in their bouncing conversation. They treated Will as if he were a child, as if he didn't have a brain in his head. No wonder he had negative feelings about their visiting. The astounding relationship set her back. Why couldn't these people accept Will's decision to be a craftsman of such lovely artwork?

She led them to the doorway and paused to usher them in. Her grandmother sat in her favorite chair, a sweet smile on her face. She'd been anxious to meet Will's family, and Christine prayed the visit didn't disappoint her.

After her grandmother had been introduced, the Lamberts settled on the sofa, and Christine headed for the kitchen, puzzled about the difficult relationship Will had with his parents. They'd wanted to guide his life, and he'd rebelled. How could he honor his parents when he didn't think it was best for him?

Before she could fill the teapot, Will stood behind her.

"What can I do?" he asked, touching her shoulder.

Warmth swept down her arm. She turned, his lips so close to hers, producing a strong desire to kiss away the sadness she saw in his eyes. "You can entertain your parents while I bring in the tray."

"They'll do better alone with Grandma Ella."

Christine didn't argue. "How about filling the coffee carafe while I get the teapot ready."

As she worked, she grinned, thinking they had their personal Mrs. Fields to supply them with unending cookies. The neighbor had brought over a new supply of homemade Christmas treats. She arranged the items on a plate, then loaded it all onto a tray.

"All set," she said, eyeing Will.

Though he smiled, his face looked strained.

She whisked past him into the living room, feeling him close behind. His familiar scent, citrus and spice, captured her senses.

"Here we are," Christine said, lowering the tray to the chest in front of the sofa. She managed to give Will's mother a pleasant look though tension snapped in the room.

Christine poured the coffee and tea, then offered the sugar and cream. She handed the Lamberts dessert plates, but they appeared to accept them as a social nicety rather than wanting to be social.

"We have room for you and Mrs. Lambert to stay

here," Christine offered, doing it out of courtesy and not desire.

"Thank you, but we have a lovely room at the Market Street Inn," Mrs. Lambert said. "It's near Main Street."

"That's very close to my store," Will said.

"We're sure having strangers in the house would be difficult for you." Will's father gestured toward him. "Even Will has overstayed his visit."

"Visit?" Ella's head bent back as if the comment had knocked her off balance. "Will's no guest here. He's like a grandson, and he's been very good company for me." Her gaze shifted to Will's as if she wondered if he'd said something to his parents. "I enjoy having him here, and I always thought he felt the same."

"I do, Grandma Ella. Don't worry about that."

Her shoulders eased. "He saved my life, you know." She began the long story about her stroke and Will's part in saving her. "You can see I think a great deal of your son."

"That's very nice," Mrs. Lambert said, "but shouldn't a young man have friends his own age?"

"Mother, I have friends of all ages." Irritation sparked in his voice for the first time. "My parents forget I'm not their teenager anymore."

"Sometimes, I wonder," his mother mumbled.

Mr. Lambert patted his wife's arm. "We would have preferred a different life for Will," Mr. Lambert said, looking at Ella.

"You're unhappy with Will's choices?" Ella asked as if she couldn't believe what she'd heard. "You can be very proud of your son. He's so talented, and he's a fine Christian man."

His father gave her a feeble grin. "We have standards

in our family, and we had hoped our only son would follow in my footsteps."

Ella gave him a steady look. "When I was a young mother, I always wanted my children to have a life better than me, not the same."

Mr. Lambert eyed her. "That's what I mean. We wanted him to be successful."

Ella folded her hands in her lap. "But he is."

Mrs. Lambert lowered her teacup. "Perhaps we define success differently."

"Perhaps. But you should know that your son is creative and very well liked by everyone on the island. Think of parents who have children who use drugs, curse, lie and cheat—even abuse their families."

"My son doesn't have his own family," Mrs. Lambert said.

Ella drew up her shoulders. "On the island, he has a large family."

Christine watched her grandmother's dark regard brighten as her left hand shifted toward the Bible. The action lifted Christine's heart. She pictured her only weeks earlier unable to move the hand.

Ella looked at the Bible and back at the Lamberts. "And remember what the Lord says in Proverbs Sixteen. 'In his heart a man plans his course, but the Lord determines his steps.' You see, the plan isn't yours or mine to make, really. It's what the Lord has set for our purpose."

"I—I—" Will's father sputtered before stretching his neck higher. "I don't totally agree with you, Mrs. Summers, but we each have our own philosophies."

"Oh, but this isn't a philosophy. It—"

Christine touched her grandmother's shoulder, and she ended the discussion. Christine could see it would go nowhere but cause greater stress. "Please, have some cookies. They're homemade by our neighbor."

Mrs. Lambert eyed the dish and selected one. "Thank you," she said. She examined the miniature treat and took a tiny bite.

"Dad, I'd like you to see the studio. How long are you staying?"

"Only tonight, son. We have some social engagements. You know the Christmas season."

Will gave a nod. "I sure do, Dad. So let's call a taxi and head for the store. I'd like you to see it. Then, I think, Christine is planning to cook dinner."

"Oh, no," his father said. "We planned to take you out to dinner. We saw a restaurant open on Hoban that looks acceptable. The Village Inn, I think."

Will gave Christine a discouraged look, then turned back to his parents. "We can talk about it later."

His father felt his breast pocket as if making sure no one had pickpocketed his wallet and checkbook.

Christine observed the discussion unfold as if it were a wrestling match.

His father tucked his hand inside the pocket and withdrew an envelope. "I don't want to forget this. Here's mail for you that came to the house."

"Mail?" Will reached for the envelope and checked the return address. "This is from John Skinner."

"I recognized the name," his mother said. "You graduated from high school with him."

"Right," Will said, eyeing the envelope.

Mrs. Lambert's focus settled on the letter. "I wonder what John's doing. He was such a bright boy. I know he must be involved in something worthwhile."

Will's jaw tightened as he slipped his finger under the

tab and opened the envelope. He glanced at it and laid the letter on the table. "It's nothing. Just my high school class reunion announcement."

"You'll go," his mother said.

Will shook his head. "Probably not. I haven't seen those people in years."

"It's your tenth. You should go."

Tenth? His tenth high school class reunion. Christine's heart stopped, and she clamped her jaw to keep her mouth from gaping. Tenth? That meant he was— She faltered. If he graduated when he was eighteen, he was only twenty-eight. She was nearly forty.

Chapter Twelve

After Will left with his parents, Christine hurried into her bedroom and slammed the door. She'd known he had a youthful manner, but he seemed mature and capable— wonderful really. But eleven years?

She sank onto the bed and held her face in her hands. Her dreams—dreams she wanted to dispel but dreams that had persisted—sagged like the surrealistic paintings of Dali's drooping clocks. She'd be the laughingstock of everyone if they knew she'd finally given her heart to a man nearly young enough to be her son.

And she'd kissed him on the mouth. She felt mortified.

She wanted to talk to someone. She needed someone's opinion. Ellene's face soared into her mind. She pressed the buttons on her cell. If Ellene could come for a visit, if she could meet Will and see them together, if she could— The thought hung on the air as reality flew back in her face. This was temporary. She would be leaving in another month, and Will would be a memory.

Sadness flooded her. She didn't want a memory. She wanted the impossible dream. Her thoughts wavered. Will had changed her. He'd been good for her and cared about her. Will's career could be successful in the Detroit area. Better even. Maybe... Could she influence him to even consider moving back to Detroit?

The cell address book had darkened, and she hit the buttons again and this time pushed the call symbol.

When Ellene's voice came on the line, Christine's heart picked up pace. "I need you. Can you come for a visit?"

"What's wrong?"

"Nothing. Everything." She rubbed her temple, not making sense out of anything. "I want you to meet Will. I need you to meet him. Ellene, I'm so confused. I feel so strongly about him, and we've only met. He's different, and I want to know if this is just a shipboard romance or is it real."

"It's not shipboard," Ellene said, laughter in her voice. "But you are stranded on an island and that can be dangerous. Just ask me."

"That's not funny, Ellene. Something in my heart tells me this is special." She pressed her hand against her chest, feeling thunder beneath her palm. "Ask Connor if you can come up for a couple of days. Fly up. It's not too expensive, and I'll pay your way."

"Shush. You don't have to pay my way. Let me think."

The line went silent except for Ellene's breathing, and Christine's pulse throbbing against the receiver.

"I was planning to call you," Ellene said, "but maybe it would be more fun in person. I'll check with Connor, but I don't think he'll mind at all. I'll call you."

"I'd be so grateful, Ellene. Truly. I know I sound like a babbling teenager, but it's not that. It's far from that. Today I feel very old."

"Christine, what's wrong with you? Look, I'll tell Connor it's an emergency."

"You're a dear friend," Christine said.

"You, too. I'll call back with the details."

When the phone had disconnected, Christine sat staring into space, wondering how Will was faring with his family. She'd given up on making them dinner. They seemed very set on their plans, and she knew they didn't include her, and she thought it was best. She hoped Will did, too.

He needed time with his parents. Maybe once they saw his studio—his store with so many wonderful gifts—they would realize he wasn't a boy any longer.

Boy. The word zipped through her like a dart. No. He was a man. She'd spent more than two weeks with him, enjoying his company and seeing him as a peer. What was eleven years? Eleven years. She cringed at the question.

Will charged up the back steps, stomped into the hallway and slammed the door to his apartment. He took off his coat and flung it on the chair, then caved into the recliner, tilting it back and closing his eyes.

Fiasco.

He pictured the look on Christine's face when she observed his parents and him in action. Shame filled him. The Bible said to honor his parents. He hadn't, but he believed in his heart that he'd done what he had to do, and he prayed the Lord had led him in that direction. Yet it still bothered him.

One event had been a positive when—

A knock on his door drew his attention. He rose and answered it.

"Christine," he said, searching her face. "Come in."

She gave him a cautious grin and walked into the room as if she were uncomfortable.

He motioned toward a chair. "Have a seat." He leaned over and snapped on the Christmas tree lights. Anything to remind him that this was a joyous time of year. "What's up?"

She loosed a ragged sigh. "I just wondered how you fared today."

He sank into the recliner. "I'm so sorry about the dinner. I didn't think they'd be that rude, but by that time, I decided you'd be grateful not having to listen to any more of the tension."

"I understand, Will."

"They're not bad people, Christine. I know they think they have only the best in their mind for me, but their best and mine are different."

"I saw that." She lowered her head.

"My father wanted me to follow in his footsteps. That's typical of successful parents, and I tried. I went to business school for three years as I told you. Then I couldn't take it anymore. It's not what I wanted to do. I loved the arts. I knew God had given me a creative talent, but in the business administration field, it was mired by the wayside. I broke my father's heart when I told him I was dropping out of University of Michigan and going to Creative Studies. He's never accepted that decision."

"But you have a business and an art career. You've accomplished both. I would think—"

"I know. It's hard to understand. I should enjoy their visit, but it's difficult when they're so determined to force me back into their world."

"Funny thing, Will, when I first came here—" She

stopped in mid-sentence as if struggling for the words. "When I first came here, I felt the same way. At least, similar to them. I questioned why anyone with a right mind would want to live on the island."

He leaned closer, wanting to make sure he'd really heard what she'd said. "Are you saying you feel differently now?"

She didn't answer but studied him for a moment, a frown settling on her face as if she were fighting the thoughts. "For you, I do. You're so suited to the island life."

"I'm glad to hear you say that. At least I know I have one person on my side."

"Two. Grandma. She adores you."

His eyes captured hers. "And you?"

"I—I admire you so much, Will. You're a wonderful...man."

She faltered, and he wondered if his parents' constant references to *boy* and *son* caused her to see him in another way. "Thanks," he said, trying to make his words sound real.

He gazed at her. Yes she was older, but not that much, he didn't think. Yet it didn't matter. He cared about her more than he could explain. Admiration wasn't what he wanted to hear. Yes, her admiration was nice, and so was respect, but he wanted to be loved.

Christine broke the silence. "Was the whole time with them as stressed as it was here?"

"You mean my parents?"

"Yes. After you left, did it—"

"Get better? Yes. In fact, I was just sitting here thinking about it. When I showed them the store and my studio, both of them seemed to be knocked sideways. I don't know what they thought I had here, but they were impressed. I could see my mother's mental calculator adding the value of the large windows hanging in the store."

Christine chuckled, and it sounded so good to him.

"My dad began grilling me about sales. I showed him my books. His eyes widened like an owl. I think the part that bothered him was the quiet winter. He began talking marketing. That part's just not in me."

"I know," she said.

Will realized it was in her, and she'd mentioned wanting to talk with him about ideas. He hoped not tonight. He couldn't bear to hear any more criticism right now. "How was your day?"

"Good. My friend Ellene is coming next Friday for the weekend. I think you'll like her."

"I'm glad she's coming," he said, not meaning it. He'd have to share her with someone for the weekend, and he wanted to keep her for himself.

"Are your parents leaving in the morning?" she asked.

"I thought about meeting them for brunch. They mentioned eating before they catch the early-afternoon ferry. They don't go to church."

"I wondered about that."

"They attend church occasionally, but they don't have the same kind of relationship with God that I have."

"I guessed that from the conversation with Grandma." She looked uneasy. "I'm afraid they don't like me very much. Still, I'm sorry I didn't have a chance to say goodbye."

"Then join us. I think my dad admired you. He's hard to read, but remember, he thought you had brains—which is what I seem to lack."

She grinned.

"Church service is early," he said. "I'm not going to meet them until eleven. Please come with me."

"I'll talk with Grandma. Maybe I will if you're sure they won't mind."

He didn't really care if they did.

She rose and moved toward the door. "You need to rest. It's been a difficult day, I know."

Will stood and caught her hand, pulling her closer. She seemed to resist, then in the next moment relaxed in his arms. He didn't want to push his luck. Will lowered his lips and kissed her temple. He sensed he should take it easy or risk driving her away. Had it been his parents' behavior or something else that had created a new wedge between them?

"Are you sure they won't be upset?" Christine climbed off Will's sled and joined him as he headed into Sinclair's.

"I think they'll be fine," he said, opening the door.

The sweep of heat washed over her as they entered.

"There they are," Will said, pointing toward a table on the far side of the room.

His father noticed him and motioned to his wife. She looked up, a mixture of surprise and question on her face.

"We didn't know if you were coming," his father said, gesturing to the two extra chairs.

"I wasn't sure if I would, but Christine wanted to say goodbye and so do I."

"That's thoughtful," his mother said.

Christine tried to read a tone in her voice, but she didn't hear one.

Mrs. Lambert turned to her. "I was rather impressed with Will's business."

The statement surprised Christine and opened the

door for Christine's thoughts. "Amazing, really. Will's work is exquisite. He can price his work at a high rate because of the quality, and he's innovative. Besides the stained-glass pieces, he's created other art—jewelry and decorative plates and bowls—by fusing glass. I hope he showed them to you."

She realized her mouth raced like a revving engine, and she caught her breath to let them respond.

Mrs. Lambert glanced at her husband, then Will. "Yes, I believe he did show us."

"I brought out a few pieces," Will said. "Mother particularly liked the fluted bowl in the shades of coral and pink. I think you saw that, didn't you?"

Christine nodded. "Yes. It's lovely. All of your work is."

"You're prejudiced." He gave her a private look.

The waitress arrived with coffee and halted their conversation while she told them about the Sunday buffet. When she walked away, the conversation continued as if it had never stopped.

"I worry about the winter months. No income really." His father pushed his coffee cup with his finger. "A man needs year-round work."

"Dad, I told you I have a number of projects to complete for the holidays. People call me for custom orders, and when I'm not busy with those, I need the time to work on new stock for the summer. I do a tremendous business then."

"Yes, I saw that," he said, pulling his finger from the cup and leaning back in the chair as if calculating what he wanted to say next.

"Let's check out the buffet," Will suggested, standing and pulling out Christine's chair as she rose.

His mother and father followed, and they went through the line selecting their breakfast fare. Will looked relieved that the earlier conversation had ended.

At the table, they spent quiet moments delving into the good food, with comments made about the various dishes and little else. When Will's father pushed his plate back, he studied Christine. "Do you enjoy island life, Christine?"

The question surprised her, and she choked on her drink. "I think the island life is wonderful for some people." She set her fork on the edge of her plate. "But I have mixed feelings for me, personally. My work is in Southfield."

She looked at Will and weighed the question. "For Will this is a perfect setting. He has the winter's quiet to prepare for the mass of tourists that arrive in May and stay until October. He loves it here. I can't imagine him in another setting." The words pained her, but she knew they were true. "Some of us can live in the city and thrive on the big corporations. Some prefer the small towns and can thrive as well. I wish—" What? She wished so many things.

Mr. Lambert eyed her. "You wish you had the stomach for island life?" The gaze drifted from her to Will, and she sensed he noticed the heated flush rising up her neck.

"I wish I didn't have to cope with the stress of big-city life and still have the benefits."

Mr. Lambert shook his head. "You're an honest woman."

"Will," his mother said, drawing his attention, "I will admit that I'm impressed with your talent. I had envisioned your work so differently."

Christine's heart jumped, hearing his mother's confession. She tried to listen to the private conversation, but his father caught her eye and leaned toward her in a conspiratorial manner. "We know Will has talent," he said, speaking in a near whisper, "but we'd like him to stretch his wings in a more aggressive business style. Think of what he could do."

She felt her face pull into a frown. She'd tried to suggest those things. "But that's not what Will—"

"Wants," his father said, completing her statement. "I know, but you're a wise woman. My wife senses you have feelings for Will, and his life here and yours there—"

"I respect Will's talent, and he's a wonderful friend, but we barely know each other."

"You're a woman with some sense in her head. We think you could influence him to—"

Christine patted his arm to stop him. "I said I respect Will. That means I also respect his decision. I have no idea where our relationship could lead, but I know one thing for sure. If I really loved him, I would never drag him away from something this important to him. Then my love wouldn't be true."

His father's eyes darkened. "This is more of your Bible talk, I suppose."

Christine couldn't help but smile. "Bible talk? That's my grandmother. I came here like you, Mr. Lambert, a weak Christian."

He drew back, his brows lifting.

"I'm sorry for being honest." She glanced to make sure Will's attention was on his mother. It was, and she returned to her private dialogue. "Yes, it's in the Bible, but I mean what I say. I rarely went to church. I was a title Christian."

His frown deepened.

Christine didn't let that stop her. "Will has a deep faith, as does my grandmother, and recently I heard her description of love, and I went to the Word and studied it for myself because I needed to know the truth. Love is not self-seeking. It keeps no record of wrongs. Love protects and hopes and trusts." She looked at Will's father. "I trust Will. I trust that he knows what he's doing. If you love him, you will, too."

He leaned back, his gaze connected with hers, but she saw a new look in his eyes. He didn't speak, and Christine feared she'd done greater harm than good.

Finally, he leaned forward. "You've made a point."

"Thank you," she said, releasing a pent-up breath as the waitress arrived with their bill.

Chapter Thirteen

"I'm grateful for those church ladies," Will said, standing beside Christine in his studio.

She chuckled, knowing what he meant, because she agreed.

"I noticed they're even helping with her therapy now. Those women deserve stars in their crowns."

"I told them that, but they love it. Grandma is a blessed woman to have so many people care about her."

"The only thing I don't like," he said, pulling supplies from drawers beneath his workbench, "is the quicker she gets better, the faster you'll be leaving."

Christine didn't want to think of the inevitable either. Her mind shot back to the conversation with Will's father five days earlier. Will had never asked what they were talking about, and, being preoccupied with his mother's conversation, she hoped he hadn't noticed.

She shook her head. "Don't think about that now. I'm here until my vacation's over, and then longer if I use a family medical leave, and I'm thinking I may do that. All I can hope is Chet doesn't push too hard. He could make life very difficult for me at the office if he follows through."

"I don't want to see that happen, Christine. I know you love your work."

She looked at the sincerity in his eyes, and her pulse skipped. She'd always said she loved her work, but watching Will in the studio—the joy he had in creating, the lack of stress, the delight in living—sometimes she wondered about her situation at Creative Productions. Still, that's the work she knew, and that's where she excelled.

"Okay, ready to learn about making beads?" He slipped on his safety glasses and lit a torch he'd clamped to his worktable.

Beads. She'd wanted time to talk with him. She'd thought about what she'd said to his father, and she told herself she wasn't trying to change him, but just make things better for him. But she observed his eagerness with the beads. "Sure," she said, though her heart wasn't in it.

"I've already coated the mandrel with bead release. That's a fireproof coating."

"Great, but what's a mandrel?"

His mouth curved to a grin. "This metal rod." He lifted it from the equipment on the table. "You need this to make beads."

"Okay," she said, feeling the heat of the torch.

She watched him heat the mandrel, then warm the glass rods, rotating them until they formed what appeared to be a honey-type liquid blob. As the glass melted, he touched the mandrel tip to the glass and rotated it to form a circle. When it reached what he apparently thought was the right size, he pulled away the rod and continued to rotate the bead to a smooth surface. She felt her mouth gape at the ease with which he created the lovely bauble.

"Want to try this?"

She stepped back. "I don't think so, Will. That's your talent. Mine is advertising and marketing. Now that, I could help you with."

He moved back the mandrel and rolled the bead on a special surface, then lowered it onto a cooling mixture. When he looked at her, disappointment had registered on his face. "Did my father succeed in influencing you?"

She drew back at his question. "No. Not at all. I told you a long time ago I had some ideas. I would never do that to you." Her shoulders tensed with his accusation.

In a heartbeat, he lowered the mandrel and turned off the torch, then drew her to him. "I'm sorry, Christine. I shouldn't have said that."

She felt as if he'd slapped her.

"I have no excuse," he said, his voice strained. "I saw my father talking to you at the restaurant. He seemed intense, and so were you. You haven't mentioned the conversation, and I hated to ask. I figured you'd say something."

"I'm sorry I didn't." She hadn't wanted to tell him that his father had tried to influence her. She'd prayed for reconciliation between them.

"When you didn't say anything, I started assuming what he talked about. Naturally I figured he wanted you to coerce me back to Detroit."

Her muscles knotted as disappointment spread over her. "I'm sorry you'd think I'd do that, Will."

"No, Christine. It's me. I get this way with my dad. My mother had eased a little, and I thought maybe—"

"I defended you. I told your father that real love had nothing to do with forcing someone's will. It had to do with trust and confidence in them. I'd never try to manipulate you, and I'm disappointed that you think I would do that."

He stepped away and turned his back. "I was wrong to accuse you, but you know, I've sensed you pulling away since my parents came. I realized our friendship is…temporary. It's—"

"I don't want to hear that. Please. I treasure the time we've spent together. I've changed, and I attribute that to my grandmother and you. I've learned something about myself. It's nothing to do with how I feel about you. It's—" She stopped herself. Not now. She needed to think, to weigh her feelings and take a long look at her life. She needed time.

"Let's leave it at that." He picked the bead from the fiber and rolled it between his fingers, then dropped it into her hand. "So what are your thoughts?"

"About us?"

"No. You mentioned your ideas."

Her ideas seemed so unimportant now. She weighed the value of causing more tension between them with sharing the strategies she'd thought of earlier. She couldn't help herself. Marketing was her work.

"This has no reflection on your father's opinion. When I first came here and saw the great merchandise you have—all those wonderful pieces of art—I thought about marketing. I know you have a captive audience in the summer, but you could enhance the late autumn, winter and early spring months by using the Internet."

"You mean selling online?"

She nodded, her enthusiasm growing. "All you need is a Web site that offers photographs of your work—the jewelry, sun catchers, small windows, vases, things easy to mail—and a brief description with the price. Once you know the shipping cost, you can set up a secure site and use charge cards or an Internet bank service, and that's it. You could hire someone to do packaging and handling or do it yourself."

Her heart pumped at the thought of how his sales could rise. "Do you know how many people shop on the Internet? It's amazing."

His eyes widened and glazed. "I don't mean to sound ignorant, but, Christine, I don't know anything about creating Web sites and finding secure sites. I'm an artist."

"But some people do." She swallowed, fearing where she was headed. "I do. I could help you get started. You're a great photographer. You can take the photos, or I can, and I'll—"

"Christine, I'm not sure I want to do this. Once you're gone, then what do I do?"

"I—" She stopped herself, seeing the expression on his face. She remembered what Ellene had said. "You have a wonderful business, Will. I don't know why I'm even suggesting this. It's just a gold mine for you." His expression reminded her of the truth. Will didn't seem to want a gold mine. He loved his simple life, so why change it?

"It's not that I don't appreciate your ideas," he said, relaxing and moving closer. He took her in his arms and kissed the top of her head. "You're suggesting what is so natural for you. I need to think about the reason I would do this. Why complicate my life?"

She wondered if she had already complicated his life by just being there. Christine lifted her gaze to his and her stomach rolled with a sweet sensation. "You're right, Will."

"As always," he said, a smile brightening his face. "Let me think. I need some time to weigh what you've said."

I need some time. So did she. Christine shrugged, wishing she could learn to keep her ideas to herself.

"Don't be sad," he said, tilting her chin upward. His gaze drifted to her lips, and her heart squeezed in anticipation.

Will's mouth bent to hers, but this time the gentle touch deepened. He held her close, his hand cupping her head, his fingers plying her hair while his free hand held her shoulders with a tenderness that made her knees weak. Emotion took away her breath, and her lungs cried for air.

Will eased back and kissed the tip of her nose. "I'm thinking," he said, his mouth so close she could feel his lips move against hers.

A smile tugged at the corner of her mouth, but before it could reach the surface, his lips met hers again.

Dear Lord, she thought, *I'm lost in this man's arms. I've never felt this way, but how can it ever be? He's so young. I'm so much older. My heart is fighting my head, and I'm so afraid I'll be hurt again. Help me, Lord.*

"Should we leave for the airport?" Will asked.

"Ellene said she wouldn't take off until noon, so we have time…"

Christine looked gorgeous with her legs tucked beneath her in his recliner. Will wished he owned a sofa so he could hold her in his arms. Maybe his parents were right about one thing at least. He needed a bigger apartment if he was ever going to find someone to share his life.

He patted his lap. "Come here a second."

"Why?"

"I want you near me."

"That's silly. We'll break the chair."

"Not so, but if we do, I'll buy another one."

She laughed, her long hair sweeping over her face as she gave him a coy look as if playing hard to get.

"Please," he said, sending her a coaxing smile.

She pulled herself from the recliner and sauntered toward him, an elfish look in her eye. "This is silly, you know."

"Sometimes it's fun to be silly." He reached forward and grasped her hand, pulling her down.

Christine rested her head on his shoulder, and he wrapped his arms around her, loving the feeling of being close to her.

"See. This is perfect."

She wriggled as if to get comfortable. "I'm sorry about the bead making, Will. Maybe one day I can concentrate. I'd love to learn how to make them."

"Like you said, it's not your expertise."

"No, but I expected you to build a Web site and sell online. That's not yours, either. I have a controlling nature, and I'm not really happy with it anymore."

"I'm happy with everything about you."

"That's because you're so…you. It's your natural way. You have every fruit of the spirit. I wish I knew how you do it."

"I don't do it, Christine," he said, running his finger along the arm of her sweater. "It's the Lord."

"But how do you get Him to do it?"

He couldn't help but laugh at her question. "I don't know. I study the Word. I pray for God's direction."

"I've been doing that. I really have."

"And I allow the Lord to work in me. Your grandmother talks so often about the fruits of the spirit, and they're almost inseparable from Jesus's new commandment."

"You mean there's an eleventh commandment?" She tilted her head upward, smiling at him.

He shook his head. "You're teasing," he said, enjoying the sweet scent of her perfume. "Jesus said 'I give you a new commandment and that is to love one another as I have loved you.' So it's easy. We respond to things in the best manner we can to emulate Jesus."

"Easy? I find that very hard."

"No one's perfect, but we can try."

She swung her legs downward and shifted to sit more upright. "Do you mean that by trying to be more like Jesus we become closer to Him?"

"I think so. I know that the Lord is beside me now." He brushed his fingers against her soft cheek.

"If you have all of us on your lap, this chair is really going to break."

He gave her a teasing poke. "Stop. We're being serious now. Jesus is always with me. It's that personal kind of relationship that people talk about. I can just toss out my concerns, and I know He is here and He hears me. He's beside you, too."

She lowered her head. "Funny, but since I've been on the island, I can better understand what you're saying. Maybe it's less distractions or—"

"Less competitiveness, less media, less traffic, less of the things that aren't important. On an island, you depend on people—on personal relationships. That's what's important. Then kindness and compassion are natural."

"Why are you so young yet so wise?"

Will felt her tense as if the comment was something she hadn't wanted to deal with. Her reaction rocked him.

Was that why she'd become so withdrawn after brunch with his father? He'd felt it, then watched it fade as they spent time together. But it really hadn't faded at all.

"Do you want to talk about this?" he asked.

She lowered her head, dismay on her face. "I'm sorry I said anything. I've been trying to not let it bother me. We're only friends. We can—"

"Christine."

She faltered when he said her name, and she lifted her gaze to his, her eyes filled with concern.

"Do you really believe we're only friends?" He waited, watching her face shift from one emotion to another, until he saw tears well in her eyes.

"Please," Will said, drawing her against his chest again, "don't be upset. Age is a state of mind. I guessed a while ago I was a little younger than you, but I hoped it wouldn't bother you."

"When your parents were here and I heard some of the conversation, I calculated you're twenty-eight or so." She looked at him with question.

"I'll be twenty-nine in January."

"Do you know how old I am?"

"I don't care."

"Yes, you do."

"You mean too much to me to let something as finite as age affect our relationship. What we have is precious."

"What do we have, Will? That's what I want to know. I live in metro Detroit. You're up here. I can never see you leaving the island. I can't picture me living here. I'm bossy and stressed much of the time. You're easygoing and so wonderful."

"Remember what I said. Let the Lord handle this. I don't have all the answers, but if the feelings I have for you are real, then I know God has the answer. I trust in Him."

He felt her tense against him. She turned and clasped his face in her hands. "I can't believe I'm saying this, but I trust Him, too."

He drew his fingers along her hair and brushed the softness of her neck. "I can't tell you how happy I am to hear you say that."

They were silent a moment, each perhaps in their own thoughts.

Then she stirred. "I'm thirty-nine, Will. I could almost be your mother."

Chapter Fourteen

Christine looked at Will's startled expression, and it broke her heart. He could deny it all he wanted, but she could tell he hadn't realized exactly how old she was.

"You're being dramatic," he said. "A few years means nothing to me."

She slipped from his lap and headed toward the kitchenette for water. "I'm just making a point."

"I know, and I'm ignoring it. I don't care if you're fifty. I care about you, and that's all that matters."

With a glass in her hand, she turned and studied him, wondering if the expression she'd seen had been only her imagination. "You were shocked when I told you my age. Admit it."

"What shocked me was the thought of your being my mother. I would have been very disappointed."

"Disappointed? Why?"

"Because then I would never have known you as I do."

Christine swung back to the faucet and ran the tap as she weighed his words, facing his determination but pondering the wisdom.

She took a long drink, then glanced at her watch. "We'd better get to the airport. Ellene will be waiting."

Will rose and grabbed his jacket from the back of a kitchen chair. "I'd like you to think about what I've said, Christine. This conversation isn't over."

She shook her head. "Will, let's just drop it. I have so much going in my life that I don't know which end is up. I like you. You know that."

He reached for her arm and stared into her eyes, his question obvious.

"Okay, so it's more than like. I really care about you, and I wish things were different, but they're not. I can't answer the questions I know you have. I want to enjoy what we have. Can we do that?"

Will was silent as he zipped his jacket.

"Please," she said.

"For now. Enjoy your friend's visit for the weekend, but we can't stop, Christine. My heart's on the line, and—"

Christine pressed her finger against his lips. "Mine is, too, Will."

His gaze captured hers, and she felt drawn like a hummingbird to nectar. She leaned closer and brushed a kiss on his lips.

They stood a moment without speaking, then he pressed his palm to her cheek. "We'd better go. Dress warm."

She slipped into her boots and jacket, wrapped the red scarf around her neck and covered her ears with a new pair of red earmuffs.

As they strode outside, she pulled her gloves from her pocket. They'd agreed to her driving her grandmother's snowmobile so Ellene could ride with Will. She'd warned

Ellene to dress warm, and she hoped her friend knew what that meant.

The sun's warmth hadn't penetrated the nippy breeze, and Christine shivered, but once settled on the sled, the heat of excitement embraced her as she started the engine and waited for it to warm. Will gave a wave, and she followed him, opening the throttle and gliding to the street, then zooming toward the airport.

Will headed left to Hoban Road, slowed near Annex and made another left. She could see the airport driveway to her right, and her excitement grew as she anticipated seeing Ellene. She needed a friend. She needed an honest appraisal of the crazy thoughts leading her into an unknown way of life. She needed common sense, and she'd find that in her friend.

When they pulled up to the terminal building, she turned off the engine and hurried up the walk. Will trailed behind her, giving her a chance to greet Ellene alone, she guessed.

Ellene appeared at the doorway, her wild dark hair held bound by a knitted cap. "I'm ready," she said, opening her arms to Christine, who ran into them with the speed of light.

"Thanks for coming." Christine looked at her and noticed her attention had shifted beyond her shoulder. Christine turned around to see Will's smiling face.

"Ellene, this is Will Lambert. Will, Ellene Farraday."

They moved closer and shook hands, each eyeing the other.

"Will's going to be your taxi."

"Really," she said. "That sounds interesting."

"My sled will be," he said, understanding her humor. "Do you have luggage?"

"Just this case." She extended her carry-on bag. "I'm only here for a weekend."

Will chuckled. "Christine said she was only here for a week and look what happened."

"My husband would never forgive me," she said with a smile.

"Ready to face the elements?"

"As ready as I'll ever be," Ellene said, linking arms with Christine as they headed toward the sleds.

An icy shiver charged down Christine's back, and she feared it wasn't the wind but the outcome of Ellene's visit. What did she expect from her friend? She wanted Ellene to like Will, and yet she feared she would. The paradox made no sense, but the worry felt real.

Now that she'd asked for help, perhaps she'd sought the wrong person. She thought of what Will had said earlier. Jesus walked beside him every minute. Why couldn't she let the Lord handle her confusion and not drag Ellene into the quandary?

"I've never liked Scrabble," Will said as Christine added up her twenty-three-letter word. "She makes everyone else look like they're ignorant."

She couldn't help but grin at his upset. "No I don't. I have a strategic eye."

Ella concentrated on the game, gathered her letters together and placed her word on the board.

"You can't use *saith*," Christine said. "The rules say no foreign words." She knew the word but loved teasing her grandmother.

Everyone laughed. "It's in the Bible, Christine," Ella said. "And God's Word can't be wrong."

"She got you," Will said, studying his letters for his

turn. "It's getting late." He looked around the table and ended with Christine. "Is this about over?"

"You want to give up and let me win?" Christine wrinkled her nose at him.

"Sounds good to me. You're going to win anyway."

"For someone who's known you only a few weeks," Ellene said, "this man has your number."

Will chuckled and banged the table. The board loped upward as words divided and skidded across its face.

"I suppose we have to quit now." Christine shook her head. "You did that on purpose."

"I really didn't, but I think it was providence."

They slid their letters into the box, and Christine folded the board while Ellene gathered the letter stands, putting everything inside the game box.

Will stood. "Now, I think it's time for me to say goodnight." He leaned over and grasped Ellene's hand. "It's nice to get to know one of Christine's friends. Your husband sounds like a man I'd like to meet."

"Maybe you will," she said, giving a telling glance toward Christine, then back to him.

Christine cringed with her obvious meaning. They hadn't talked yet. She'd avoided saying anything to Ellene, because she wanted her to get to know Will without her influence.

Will tipped his imaginary hat and slipped into the foyer.

Christine heard the back door close, and she looked at Ellene, wanting so badly to talk but not with her grandmother present.

When she turned toward her grandmother, Ella gave a wide yawn. "I think I'll get cozy in bed and read my

Bible for a while before I go to sleep. You girls need time to talk."

"Don't rush off because of me," Ellene said.

"No, dear, not at all. Shuffling around with one leg still not cooperating is very tiring. And you saw the work-out Christine gave me with my therapy."

"She is a taskmaster," Ellene said.

"Anyway," she continued, "I love to read God's Word all snuggled up in bed."

"Let me help, Grandma," Christine said, rising and handing her the footed cane they'd moved out of the way.

She took her grandmother's arm to steady her and they made their way to the door. "I'll be right back," Christine said over her shoulder.

Christine's heart had lifted as she watched her grandmother's improvement. Her left hand had more strength, and though her fingers needed still greater coordination, she had some use of them.

When her grandmother had undressed, Christine hung up her clothing or dropped items in the hamper, then helped her with the buttons on her flannel gown. Christine shifted her grandmother's Bible closer on her night-stand, then leaned down to give her a kiss on the cheek. "Good night, Grandma."

"Good night, Christine. I hope you and Ellene have a good talk. I think she likes Will."

Christine bit her cheek. She should be happy, but her emotions headed off to dark corners. "I think she does, too."

"But I want you to remember one thing." Her grandmother lifted the Bible with her right hand and rested it on the blanket. "Proverbs says, 'There is no wisdom, no insight, no plan that can succeed against the Lord.'"

Christine stood a moment, trying to decipher what her grandmother meant.

"You don't understand?"

"I—"

"I know you invited Ellene here because you're concerned about Will."

Christine thought a moment. "No, not Will. I'm concerned about me."

"It's one and the same, dear. You see Will in your future, and it frightens you. You want your friend's advice. Just remember that all the advice in the world cannot shake the Lord's path for you."

"I know, Grandma, it's just—" She paused, trying to decide if she wanted to say it or not. "Do you realize how old Will is? Do you know how old I am?"

Her grandmother chuckled. "I've never seen anything in the Bible that states who has to be older or younger, but remember what I've told you before—a person plans his course, but the Lord determines his steps."

Christine drew back. How many times had she been reminded that she could plan until she turned purple but the Lord guided her steps?

"Will may be younger than you, Christine, but he is a God-fearing Christian man who thinks the world of you. I've seen it. What is more important, that a man be older than a woman or that a man treats the woman as if she is a gift from heaven?"

A ragged breath shivered from Christine. She touched her grandmother's hand. "Thanks, Grandma. I'll heed your words."

"That's all we want, dear."

"We?"

"The Lord and me."

A faint grin found Christine as she placed the table lamp remote button closer to her grandmother. "I love you," she whispered as she closed the door and headed down the hallway, realizing she couldn't sneak anything past her grandmother.

"That didn't take too long," Christine said, walking into the living room.

Ellene had turned on the television but snapped it off and laid the remote onto the lamp table. "Tell me. I'm curious."

Christine faltered. "Curious? About what?"

"What's your problem?"

"You mean with Will?"

"Yes. You told me you were so different. I understand he lives here and you live in Royal Oak. That's different, but personality-wise, the two of you fit like gloves. I love his humor, and you play off it like a fine-tuned instrument." She paused and leaned forward, sincerity filling her face. "Christine, the man's a gem."

Christine fell back against the sofa cushion. "I know. I know."

Ellene rose and shifted to her side. "So what is it? The island versus the big city?"

"Yes, part of it. That is a problem. My work. His work. He doesn't want to leave the island. I can't work here."

Ellene took her hands. "How important is that, Christine? Does your career mean everything in the world to you?"

"Certainly it does." She lowered her head. "It always has until—"

"Until what?"

Christine struggled with her thoughts. What was the real problem? She knew Will had strong feelings for her, but could she trust him? She wanted to say yes, but she feared being wrong. She'd been wrong before. And then the age issue. Ellene hadn't mentioned their ages.

Ellene waited, then asked again.

"Part of it is reality. You remember what happened with Chet. Do I keep my head when my heart's involved?"

"But Will isn't Chet. He's as far from being Chet as I am from being the Queen of England."

"I know. He's a wonderful Christian. I'm working on being a better one myself." A deep sigh escaped her. "It's my career, too. Who would I be without it?"

"A wife who supports her husband's work. A mother someday."

"A mother?" The age factor shook her again. "I'm nearly forty. That's another issue."

"If you are in love and you marry, you still have time. I know the clock is ticking, but lots of women make the decision later in life."

"This is stupid," Christine said, realizing how far astray the conversation had gone. "He hasn't asked me to marry him."

"Not yet, but I can see it coming."

The comment smacked her between the eyes. "You mean you really see that?"

"I'd be blind if I didn't."

The news made her reel. She knew Will cared. She cared, but— "Okay, but do you see nothing else about age? You don't see any problems?"

Ellene frowned. "Are we playing guessing games?" She shook her head. "Is he younger than you?"

Christine veered back. "You have to ask?"

"Yes, I guess I do. Both of you have a youthful spirit—

especially here, Christine. I've never seen you so light-hearted. When I saw you on the snowmobile, laughing and later playing Scrabble— You two are like kids."

"That's because he is a kid."

Ellene froze, then recovered. "He might be younger, but he's a man. Either that, or I'm deluded."

"He's twenty-eight. Twenty-nine in January. I'm eleven years older than he is."

"Ten after his birthday," she said, a light tone in her voice. She wrapped her arms around Christine's shoulders. "My dear friend, don't hold back a chance at pure happiness because of a few years, an island life and a career. I want to tell you my life is tremendous since I fell in love again with Connor."

"You do look wonderful," Christine said, noticing the bloom in her cheeks. "You look as if life has been good."

"It's been more than that, and I'll tell you in a minute, but let's finish this. So the man is younger. If it's not important to him, then it shouldn't be to you. If he's as strong a Christian as you say, he won't play lightly with marriage. Christians believe their vows—until death parts them. I can't envision him playing games with marriage."

Christine knotted her hands and dropped them to her lap. "But does he know his mind?"

Ellene lowered her arms and drew back. "Here's the truth. I think Will is a catch. I think he could make a wonderful husband and a great father. I think he's as honest as he is sincere, but I have doubts."

"You do?" Christine felt her heart tug. She wanted to know those doubts, but she wanted Will more. Her mind tossed like a tree in a hurricane.

"If you're this unsure, then I think you should be cau-

tious. You want a career and the big city. You can't have
that here. You can manipulate him to move—then you
can have both—but should you? I think not. If the love
isn't strong enough to stand the test, then it won't hold
up under marriage."

Christine rose and paced the floor. She'd said the same
to Will's father. She didn't know what she wanted anymore. Fear charged through her thoughts and nailed her
to the floor. "You said your marriage was wonderful. You
were happy. So why the change of heart?"

"I am happy. I'm ecstatic. Marriage is wonderful and
blessed, but it's not perfect and it's not easy."

"There isn't much that is." Christine pressed her fingertips against her temple to quell the pounding.

"No, but all of the problems are minor to the joy.
That's why love can see you through it all, but the love
must be sure and strong."

Christine's mind glided back to her talks with Will,
the sled rides, watching him work in the studio, seeing
his tenderness with her grandmother, his loving kisses.
How could she push that away because of fear? "I need
to think, Ellene. I thought it was the age that bothered
me, and it does. But you're right—what's age? My grandmother reminded me—more than once—that I can plan
my life down to the nth degree, but it's God in charge."

"Your grandmother's right."

Christine returned and sank to the sofa. She pushed
the palms of her hands into her eyes, willing the head-
ache to vanish. While she thought, Ellene remained quiet
like the good friend that she was.

"Thanks," Christine said finally. "Those were things
I needed to hear, and it will give me food for thought."

"I'm glad."

Ellene's smile radiated, and Christine looked at her sitting beside her like a woman who had a secret bursting to be released. Her mind shot back to Ellene's earlier comment. "When I said you looked as if life has been good, you said it's been more than that. So what does that mean?"

"Can't you guess?"

Christine eyed her again as the truth fell into her mind. "Really?" She glanced at her belly and noticed the faint roundness. "You're pregnant."

"I am. We're so excited and so is Caitlin."

Christine threw her arms around Ellene's neck. "Do you know what the baby is?"

"No, but I'd love a boy for Connor. Still I adore Caitlin as if she were my own and would be thrilled with a little girl. Whatever the Lord blesses us with is fine with me."

"I'm so happy for you. A baby. It's wonderful."

"You can't believe how wonderful. My career has taken a back step now. I don't care about proving anything like I did a year ago. I wanted my dad to be proud of me—a woman contractor. Dad is, I know, but he's even more thrilled to be a grandfather."

"Our values change, I guess."

"That's what I've been telling you, my friend. Weigh what's important in your life. Love and family. Career and success. Sometimes a little of both, but God's will be done."

"I'll say amen to that." Christine closed her eyes and gave Ellene another hug. Warmth spread through her, knowing God had the solution, and she needed a clear answer from the Lord.

Chapter Fifteen

Will stood back near the sled, letting Christine say her goodbye.

"I can't tell you how much I appreciate your coming, Ellene." Christine hugged her friend, then gave her belly a tender pat. "I can't wait to meet the new little Farraday. Keep me posted."

"Godmother?" Ellene asked, giving Christine a questioning look.

"I'd be honored. Give Caitlin a hug, and tell Connor how happy I am."

"I will," she said, stepping backward toward Will.

Will helped Ellene into the sled with less assurance than he had when she arrived. Then he hadn't realized she carried a child in her belly, and he worried about the bumpy ride. "You sure you'll be okay?"

She grinned up at him from the sled. "I arrived two days ago. I haven't changed that much." She gave another wave to Christine. "See you when you get back."

Christine moved forward. "Are you sure you don't mind my not riding to the airport? If I hadn't checked my e-mail this morning, I wouldn't know about the snafu at my office."

"No problem. I'll be boarding as soon as I arrive. Love you."

"Love you back." Christine waved.

Will revved the engine, rolling forward a minute before making sure Ellene was settled and comfortable.

"I'm ready," she said. "Anytime."

Will sent a wave to Christine and glided toward the end of the driveway, then headed onto the road.

The day was the warmest it had been since Ellene had arrived. They'd spent Saturday at Will's studio while Ellene raved about his work and agreed with Christine about the Internet sales. He'd given it thought but still hadn't felt comfortable with the idea. As a businessman, he knew expanding sales had value, but his inexperience with the Internet set him back.

Ellene clung to him tightly, the way Christine had when she first started riding. Now Christine's hold had lessened, not from foolishness but with confidence. He loved the feel of Christine behind him on the sled.

Trying to talk seemed pointless, but he checked on Ellene once in a while to make sure she felt secure, and in minutes, they'd arrived at the airport.

He helped her from the sled while his mind clung to Christine and her need to call the office. He wondered if they were putting pressure on her to return, and he feared what she would do.

"I enjoyed meeting you so much, Will," Ellene said as he carried her bag to the terminal.

"Same here." But he wanted to know so much more. He opened the door, and they stepped inside the terminal.

Ellene turned to face him. "Be patient with Christine. She's finding her way."

He knew he'd frowned at her comment, because the expression on her face changed. "I'm not sure what you mean?"

Ellene smiled. "You think a lot of her, I've deducted."

"Yes. Very much."

"She cares very much about you, but she's dealing with some old fears and some new ones." She shook her head and chuckled. "I know I sound cryptic, but trust me. She's looking to the Lord for answers, and that can't be bad."

Will smiled back. "That's good news. We all have problems. I have my own problems." He saw the question on her face. "I've been open with Christine. There are no surprises."

"Good," she said, glancing out the window at the runway. "I suppose I'd better get going."

Ellene extended her hand, and Will grasped it, feeling a sense of peace. "Thanks for your candid comments."

Ellene held her finger to her lips. "Those were between you and me, okay?"

He nodded and handed her the carry-on bag. "Safe flight," he called as she headed to the tarmac.

She wiggled her fingers in a wave and exited through the doorway.

Will watched her go, hoping she was right. What had she and Christine talked about and what had been said? He knew the problem had been careers and the island. Now they'd added the age factor.

Age? He couldn't see that as a factor. Christine was spring to him. She was blossoming flowers and humming bees, the wings of birds and the flutter of butterfly wings. She was a delight, even those first days when her attitude nearly darkened the glow of the real woman.

Will turned and headed back to the sled. New snowflakes twirled on the wind, and he tugged on his gloves while feeling a smile grow on his face. He'd become almost poetic thinking of Christine. With her, his creativity flew. He could only imagine what it might be like to have her in his life always.

Christine clutched the telephone against her ear. "Tell me the truth, Sandy. What's happening?"

She listened to Sandy's dire story of Chet's tactics.

"He wants to replace me on the project or for good?" Christine asked. "He can't do that."

Sandy's voice lowered. "I shouldn't be telling you this, but you've been a good friend. Chet is really on a rampage. I can't make sense out of it."

Christine's mind swam with possibilities. "Do you think his job is on the line? We've done well with the clients, haven't we? I thought my last meeting on the Dorset project went well. They gave us the contract."

"I know. I don't have a clue."

"If he's in trouble, then I know he'll try to blame us. Watch out for yourself, Sandy. Chet comes across like cream, but underneath, he's cottage cheese."

Sandy chuckled. "You don't like cottage cheese, do you?"

"I hate it, but it's an analogy. He's not as smooth as he tries to make himself out to be."

"I got it," Sandy said.

"Just watch it, and keep me posted if you learn anything."

"I will," she said, but Christine heard a tone in her voice.

"I know I'm going to take off more time. I talked to my mom this morning. She's making progress, but she can't be any help to my grandmother while she's taking care of her own problems."

"I'm sorry you're going through all of this."

"Thanks. I'm okay with it."

"That's good. I'm beginning to think you're right, Christine." She lowered her voice again. "Chet's gone to a corporate meeting in Chicago. I wonder if they've caught up with him. Did you know they're requiring the execs to turn in a monthly strategic-planning report on their teams? That's not just what we're doing but what he's doing."

"You're kidding."

"No, we've been hearing the buzz for a couple of weeks."

Christine massaged the back of her neck. "I doubt if Chet can cover himself with corporate." She paused, her heart sinking. "Unless he can prove he has a few incompetents under him."

"But you've already answered that. We've had good campaigns. They're not stupid at corporate."

She weighed what Sandy had said. "Chet's going to have to cover himself some other way."

"So we all need to keep our eyes open. I'm glad you called, Christine."

"When does Chet get back into the office?"

"Wednesday afternoon, he said."

"I'll call him then. We both know he's up to something. I can't believe I fell for that man."

Silence hung over the line.

Christine's arms tingled. "Sandy?"

"You weren't the only one." Sandy's lengthy sigh rattled over the phone.

"No. Not you." Sadness flooded her.

"Afraid so."

Christine finished the conversation and hung up, feeling mortified that she'd ever thought Chet had been a man worth moping over. And poor Sandy. He'd used her, too. Maybe he was running out of women who were willing to sell their ideas for his attention. A chill shivered down her back at the memories.

For a fleeting moment, Christine didn't care what happened. Her grandmother needed her for a while longer, and she wasn't budging until after Christmas.

She looked toward heaven asking for help. As prickles swept down her spine, a calm spread over her, and she knew the Lord had heard her prayers.

Will lifted his head when he heard a knock on the shop door. He laid down the copper foil and headed toward the sound. Christine stood at the window waving, and his heart squeezed, seeing her there with her nose pressed against the door's stained glass.

"This is a surprise," he said as she stepped inside.

She stomped the snow from her boots. "Linda came over with a new jigsaw puzzle and scooted me out of the house. She said she'd help with the therapy today. Grandma knows the routine, she just needs someone to keep an eye on her."

Will kissed the tip of her cold nose. "You sound like you feel guilty leaving her. You shouldn't."

"I know." She unbuttoned her coat and pulled the scarf from around her neck. "What are you doing?"

"A last-minute Christmas project. Everything else is finished." Just saying it, tension left his shoulders. "I love the work, but when I'm under a deadline, I feel the pressure."

"But you don't show pressure. That's what's so wonderful. I do. Chet's back today, and I have to call him this afternoon."

"What'll happen?"

"I don't know." He saw the confusion in her eyes before she lowered her head.

He drew her into his arms and nestled her against his chest. The snow from her jacket melted against his knit shirt, but her warmth compensated. "I've been thinking."

"About what?" She tilted her head upward to look at him.

"About your marketing ideas."

"Really?" Her eyes sparkled with anticipation.

"If you were here long enough to get me set up, maybe I could give it a try." The words seemed to croak from his throat. "I'm nervous, I'll admit, and I'd start small. Maybe just jewelry and stained-glass boxes."

"You're really willing to give that a try?"

"Yes, but I need your help, and I won't know how to update the site. I'm not a graphic artist."

She brightened. "Neither am I, exactly, but I know enough about doing a Web site, and—"

"Did you hear what I said?" He gave her a squeeze. "You have to be here to do that, and it will take some time."

She drew back, suspicion glowing on her face. "Are you doing this to keep me captive?"

"Not really, but that's a bonus."

She laughed, then gazed down at his shirt. "I got you all wet."

"I don't care." He drew her back into his arms, his mind flooding with things he wanted to say, but the store wasn't the place. "Have time for a ride?"

"Ride where?"

"Up the road. Maybe to Arch Rock."

"It's snowing."

"I know, and that makes it all the better."

She shrugged. "Sure, I'll go if it won't take too long."

"Let me grab my camera."

He hurried into the studio, slipped into his bib and realized Christine needed warmer clothing, too. He grabbed his camera and tripod, then headed toward her.

"Let's go," he said, grasping her hand and leading her outside.

Soft flakes drifted from the sky, and the sun shone as if it had no idea it was winter. Will motioned to his sled. "Let's take mine," he said, "unless you prefer to drive yourself."

"No. I like riding with you."

She slipped into the seat and scooted back, making room for him. He dropped the tripod into the caboose and tucked the camera beneath his jacket, then started the engine.

"Here we go," he said, easing away from the curb, then headed down Market Street to the Fort Hill.

The wind whipped in his face, sending snowflakes shooting past like a torn feather pillow in a pillow fight. Christine leaned with him when they rounded the fort and raced up Arch Rock Road. He had an idea what he wanted to do, but his heart knotted in his throat. Now he had hope. If he spoke his mind, his hope could crumble.

At Arch Rock, the rugged bluff spread ahead of him like a fresh white sheet. Not one track blemished the pristine landscape. He hesitated, not wanting to mar the beauty. Instead, he pulled to the side of the road. "Look at that," he said, motioning to the expanse of white that stretched along the bluff.

He took Christine's hand and helped her from the sled, brushing the snow from her pants. With her hand in his, they walked along the bluff to Arch Rock, which towered one-hundred-and-fifty-feet into the air from the ground below and framed a scenic view of the Straits. Today the water's icy ripples glistened in the bright sun.

Will slipped his arm around Christine's shoulder. "What do you think of the view?"

"Wow! I've seen this in the summer, but there are no words to describe this."

He gave her a moment to enjoy the view, then turned her to face him. "There are no words to describe you, either."

Christine blinked, then smiled. "Thank you. I could say the same about you."

Will was captured by her gaze. Their eyes lingered, searching each other's faces as if time had stood still and the concerns and problems had faded beneath the mounds of crystals winking in the sunlight.

"Let me take your picture framed in the arch," he said. He didn't wait for a response, but darted back to the sled and grabbed his camera and tripod.

She argued, but he didn't listen and took her photograph with the sun glowing in her blond hair and a smile on her face, which brightened his world even more.

"That's enough," she said, shaking her head. "What's the tripod for?"

"For us." He opened its legs and attached the camera to the top. "Stay there, and I'll join you." He focused, set the lens, then the timer before darting to her side.

They stood in an embrace until the beeping stopped and a faint click reached his ears. "Now that didn't hurt, did it?"

Christine gave him a playful look. "Not at all, but I don't want to see myself on a calendar next year."

He wished she could be on every page of next year's edition.

Will took her hands and wove his fingers through hers. Though covered by gloves, he could feel the heat of her radiating through him. "Standing here with you is like a dream. Since you've been here—even when you didn't like me very much—you've captured my imagination, and I saw something inside you that I don't think you even knew was there."

She tilted her head as if trying to understand. "I'm sorry, Will. I guess I didn't like you very much. I was jealous of you, I think."

He grinned. "Jealous? That doesn't make sense. You have so much going for you."

"And you have so much going for you and with so much happiness. My grandmother knew you and loved you, and she barely knew me."

He saw the sadness in her face. "But she does now, and you're precious to her."

"I know, but I'm realizing that I've been longing for the day when I would feel truly confident and self-actualized."

Will reared back. "Now there's a five-dollar word."

"You know what I mean—reaching my potential—and I'm not sure that day will ever come the way I'm headed."

She looked up at him as if asking him to give her the direction, and he knew it only came from the Lord. He shook his head, not knowing what to say.

"I'm praying, Will, and I'm looking for that direction you keep telling me about."

"Do you have faith that God will open the right door?"

"I do." She lowered her gaze. "I'm trying, too."

He heard her intake of breath, and she seemed to rally.

"Yes, I do, Will. You and Grandma can't be wrong."

He drew her closer, his laughter vibrating against her. She rested in his arms, looking at him. His gaze lingered on her mouth. He wanted to kiss her yet needed to speak his mind.

"Christine, I brought you here to this special place because this is how I see you—pure and perfect. You stepped into my life such a short time ago, and I feel as if I've known you a lifetime."

He watched her eyes shift, exploring his as if trying to understand.

"I realize in such a short time, you can't make a life commitment, but, Christine, I want to tell you that I love you. I know it in my soul."

Her head jerked back as if his declaration had startled her.

"Don't speak right now," he said, "but I think I should tell you how much I care about you, and if I had my way, you'd give us the time to get to know each other and to see where it leads. I know I've been led to you."

Tears rimmed her eyes. She closed them and opened them again, but she didn't pull away. Instead, she seemed to cling to him with anticipation. "I've dreamed of you saying these things to me. I fought the feelings for so long, but I've lost the battle."

"Christine, I—"

"No. Let me finish. But you're saying this at the worst time. I have to call Chet, and I'm not sure what's going to happen. I'm scared—scared to the depth of my being. My work has been my life, and I don't know if I can give it up."

She began to shake in his arms, and he had to lean closer to hear the next sentence.

An exhale rattled from her. "But I don't know if I can give you up, either."

"You can't give up on us, Christine. It's not you or me. It's us. Just give us time."

"I want to," she said. "I really want to."

He lowered his lips to hers, her icy mouth warming as his lips moved on hers. He heard her sigh, and his own sigh wove around it. The kiss deepened, and he knew in his heart that Christine could not walk away.

"I love you," he whispered into her hair.

"I don't deserve you."

Her words disappointed him. He'd longed to hear her say those three words that had never meant so much to him as now.

A cold wind lashed against his back, and he lifted his gaze as a cloud hid the sun. "We'd better go."

She nodded, stepping out from his arms and heading back to the sled.

His own thoughts felt as dark as the suddenly dusky sky. He'd told her the truth, and she'd left him feeling empty.

Chapter Sixteen

"I know I've made mistakes," Chet said. "I made you promises that I didn't keep. We need to talk, Christine."

"We are talking," she said, her fingers trembling against the telephone.

"Not on the phone. I need to see you in person. I have plans, and I need you here."

She shook her head. "I can't come, Chet. Not now. Christmas is in five days. I can't leave my grandmother now."

"Just come back for a couple of days. You can go back on the weekend. This is important. I have a promotion lined up for you, but I don't want to talk about it this way."

"A promotion? You're kidding." She'd waited so long to hear this.

"I talked to the vice president at corporate. He gave me the go-ahead."

"Can't you tell me about it on the phone?"

"No. I'm in a little spot here, and I need to know you're serious about this. If you can't take time for me, then how can I trust that you'll give your all to this job?

I put in good words for you, Christine. You can't let me down now."

His offer spun in her head. A promotion. She'd lived and breathed that dream for so long. Chet could make it a reality. "For just two days?"

"Sure. You can go back for Christmas if you must, and then make arrangements for January. We need you here. *I* need you here."

"I'll leave in the morning, Chet. I have to make arrangements for my grandmother's care."

"Good girl, Christine. You won't be sorry. You're my girl, right?"

A gnawing feeling rolled down her spine. "I'll be there tomorrow morning."

When she hung up, her world spun out of control. Promotion? Will? She had to decide. Life as she knew it or life as she'd lived it the past few weeks?

Christine drew in a lengthy breath. Leaving was such bad timing. She had gifts to wrap, Christmas dinner to plan, her grandmother's care. Two days. All she could do was try to get back on Friday. That would give her Saturday and Sunday. Monday was Christmas Day.

Christine bent to kiss her grandmother's cheek. "I'll be back Friday night, I hope. If not, Saturday morning. You'll be okay, right?"

Her grandmother's eyes looked questioning. "I'll be fine, Christine. It's you I'm worried about."

Surprised, Christine stepped back. "Don't worry about me. The plane ride is short."

"I'm not concerned about the plane ride. I'm worried about you."

Christine knew what she'd meant, but the candid

comment still startled her. She tensed, feeling everyone was against her. Will's reaction had been unpleasant. He'd tried to accept her decision, but she knew him well enough now to know he was upset.

Looking through the front window, Christine saw the taxi stop in front. "It's time to go."

Her grandmother craned her neck to look out the window. "Will's not taking you to the airport?"

"No. I didn't want to bother him. I called a taxi." Christine looked outside, watching steam from the horse's nostrils billow into the morning air.

"Linda's dropping by to help with your therapy, and she'll help you in the morning and at night. Will's a phone call away, and some of your ladies will be dropping by for lunch today and tomorrow. Will's agreed to handle dinner."

"You didn't have to do all that. I have to get along on my own now."

Her subtle comment made Christine cringe. The meaning didn't need explanation. "I'll be back Friday night," she said again.

She wrapped the scarf around her neck, remembering that Will had given it to her shortly after she'd arrived on the island. She fingered the fabric, then lifted her overnight case and headed out the front door.

The driver helped her into the carriage, and the horses swayed, then jerked forward, clopping along the snow-covered road. The frosty wind sneaked through the crevices of the rig, and she pulled the blanket over her legs, recalling how Will had tucked her in the day she arrived. She'd had such a bad attitude that day.

Only a few weeks had made a tremendous difference in the way she looked at life. She'd grown accustomed to the easygoing manner that belonged to the people who lived here.

She shivered again as warm tears blurred her vision. How could she turn down a promotion? She knew her grandmother and Will were disappointed. She saw it in their faces and heard it in their voices, but she'd be foolish not to listen to Chet's proposal.

The scenery flickered past, a blend of sun and shadow, almost like the emotions that racked her. The city awaited her. The city. Memories of creeping traffic on the freeways as snow and ice made driving treacherous—cars spinning out of control and vehicles sliding through lights and stop signs—accidents waiting to happen.

Her thoughts faded as the taxi turned into the airport driveway, the lengthy stretch to the terminal and airstrip. She'd be back tomorrow night. The trip wasn't that long and her grandmother would be fine.

The driver helped Christine alight and handed her the overnight bag, then climbed onto the carriage and jingled away.

As she turned, the sound of a sled roared behind her and she looked over her shoulder. Will. She stopped, her pulse charging through her.

He climbed from the sled and hurried to her side. "Do you know what you're doing?"

Will's question startled her. "Why would you ask, Will? I explained yesterday. I—" What was she doing? She looked into his disappointed face, his sparkling eyes shrouded with anguish. "It's the promotion I've always wanted. It's—"

"His lies. His manipulation. You might think he's changed, but he hasn't." He grasped her arms, his gaze riveted to hers. "But I can't make you love me."

Her chest ached. She did love him, but—

"I've said I love you, Christine, and I've tried to show you how I feel. I can't do any more. If you leave, your words have meant nothing. Remember our words belie our actions."

"I'll be back tomorrow, Will."

"Not really. You're already gone, Christine, and it breaks my heart." He pulled her to him and pressed his warm lips against hers, the only warmth that touched her body at that moment.

He released her and spun away before she could think. The engine roared, and with blurred vision, she watched the sled make a turn and fly down the road.

Christine stood a moment until the sled vanished, her heart as empty as the landscape in front of her. She turned toward the terminal, her legs weak as she entered the building.

In a daze, she passed through the boarding gate and onto the tarmac, stepping onto the plane and settling into her seat. She sat a moment, trying to control the tears that welled in her eyes, the throbbing in her temple.

Snowflakes drifted past the window, and she looked out at the diamond-clad snow.

I brought you here to this special place because this is how I see you—pure and perfect. Will's words whispered in her ear. Her chest tightened again, picturing his disappointed expression.

I feel as if I've known you a lifetime. She felt the same—his smile, his strong arms holding her close, his faith. A man any woman would give the world for had told her that he loved her.

A knot twisted in Christine's throat. Her eyes blurred again as she looked out at the landscape.

Chet's words blasted into her thoughts. *I have a promotion lined up for you. I talked to the vice president at corporate. He gave me the go-ahead.*

She could still hear his voice. He sounded desperate. Just as she suspected, Chet was in trouble. He'd admitted it. "I'm in a little spot here," he'd said. She'd heard that line before and all his promises before.

The plane's engine revved as fear prickled down Christine's back. What was she doing? Will's words roared in her ears. *His lies. His manipulation. You might think he's changed, but he hasn't.*

She'd hurt Will to the core, but a promotion. Her dream. Her goal. Her life. Her—

Chet's voice rang in her ears. *I need to know you're serious about this. If you can't take time for me, then how can I trust that you'll give your all to this job? I put in good words for you, Christine. You can't let me down now.*

How can I trust you? Yes, and how could she trust him? Tears rolled down her cheeks. What had she done? Will's anguished face. Her grandmother's expression. She'd hurt them. Terribly. *Oh Lord, help me*, she moaned.

Will looked at his watch and climbed from his sled. He gazed into the sky and saw a plane above the treetops heading for St. Ignace. His heart felt void. He'd trusted and loved, and now he knew he could never trust her again.

He headed into the house, left his jacket in his apartment, and took a deep breath before he opened the door into Grandma Ella's house. He had no spirit to work today. Earlier he'd tried, thinking it would fill his mind, but he'd cut a piece backward, and he'd burned his hand on the soldering iron. His race to the airport had done nothing more than open the wound even deeper.

When he stepped into the living room, Grandma Ella looked up, her face expectant, then sinking to despair. "You're back early," she said.

"I couldn't concentrate." He plopped onto the sofa and stretched his legs along the cushion, ashamed to admit he'd chased Christine to the airport with only a rejection for his efforts.

Will eyed Ella again and noticed she held the Bible in her hand. He'd prayed, but apparently God had other plans for him. He knew the Lord sometimes said no to prayers.

"Any good words for me in there?" he said, motioning toward the Bible.

She lifted her head and gave him a feeble smile. "All the words are good for us."

He nodded and looked away.

"But I did read something that you might need to hear." She opened the Bible and scanned the page. "It's in Proverbs, Chapter three—'Trust in the Lord with all your heart and lean not on your own understanding; in all your ways acknowledge Him, and He will make your paths straight.'"

Straight where? Will asked himself. Straight into the pits. He didn't respond but thought again of the words. *Lean not on your own understanding.* How could a person not try to understand? Today he felt stripped of hope. Not faith, but hope.

"God answers in His time, Will." As if she'd heard his thoughts, Grandma Ella's voice penetrated the silence.

"I know." He slipped his legs off the sofa and leaned

his elbows on his knees, his hands knotted between them. "I really thought she loved me."

"She does, Will. I'm sure of it."

"I'm younger. I know that bothered her more than anything else."

"Age is nothing. She knows that. Age is of the heart, not the years."

He managed a grin. "You're a prime example of that."

"Eventually the years catch up with the body, but the heart knows no age."

"I feel empty inside." He shook his head. "I wish I'd given her the surprise I'd planned." His throat closed as he pictured the special Christmas gift he had for her.

Ella closed the Bible and slid it onto the table. "She'll be back tomorrow. She'll be here for Christmas."

He raised a hand and ran it through his hair. "It's not the same. The gift has no meaning now."

"All gifts have meaning."

A tear escaped his eyes and dripped on his hand. He brushed it away, not wanting Ella to notice. "Can I help you with your therapy?"

"Later." She leaned her head back and closed her eyes. "A little later."

"Okay," he said, staring at the carpet pattern, thinking that his life had gone from delight to heartache in the blink of an eye. He lifted his legs back onto the sofa and closed his eyes.

Sunlight and snow filled him. Christine's face glowing in the wintry air, framed by the Arch Rock. He felt his heart wrench. Christine nestled on his lap by the fireside. Christine watching him work in the studio. His plans, his dreams, his hopes shriveled away like autumn leaves.

Should he blame her? Advertising was her career. It

was her livelihood. It was her pride and identity. If he loved her, how could he ask her to give that up for him?

Though he asked the question, he had no answer. He just wanted her to love him so much that a career didn't matter. Foolish notion. Could he give up his art? Art pumped within him like life-giving blood. He paused. The island. He could give up the island.

He opened his eyes again and stared at the ceiling. He'd miss the place. He loved the island residents' sense of community. He loved the quiet nights, the landscape brimming with natural beauty. Yet he could live in the city if living there meant being with Christine.

They needed to talk. He checked his watch. Did she have her cell phone turned on? She was only a call away, but he'd wait, wait to make sure she'd landed safely.

Will rose and took quiet steps across the room. He gazed out the window, seeing the morning sun rising higher for another bright day. In his peripheral vision, he saw a carriage on the road. A taxi. His heart skipped. Christine? Hope filled his mind.

The driver slowed and stopped, then opened the carriage door. Will's pulse raced. He ran through the foyer and to the front door. Flinging it open, he bounded down the steps.

Christine dropped her carry-on onto the snow and flung herself into his arms. The feel of her clinging to him, the smell of her hair, the touch of her skin melded into a blessing. Her tear-wet lips touched his, and he felt her shudder in his arms.

"I'm sorry," she cried. "I've been a fool."

"No. You came back." He kissed the tears from her cheeks while his fingers caressed her hair, her neck, her cheek. "I love you, Christine. I'll go back to the city with you if you want. I can't lose you now."

"I don't want the city. I want you, and I want the island."

He lifted her in his arms and spun her around as the snow-white world blurred into a sunlit panorama. The carriage moved away, and Will set Christine down to earth, afraid to let her go. Only the cold penetrating his shirt assured him this was not a dream but reality.

"I love you," she said, her eyes searching his.

"That's what I've wanted to hear," he said, swinging her into his arms and carrying her toward the house.

The scent of turkey and stuffing threaded through the room and drew Will from his apartment. The past four days had been beyond his dreams. He'd heard Christine say "I love you" more times than he had ever hoped, and the words meant as much each time he heard them.

Grandma Ella's face had beamed with joy when she saw Christine come through the door. She'd begun praising God from the moment Christine hurried to her arms. Will's heart had been in his throat.

"Is it time for a taste test?" Will asked, coming through the kitchen door. Christine stood with her back to him, pulling the turkey from the oven. He loved seeing Grandma Ella standing nearby helping with the preparations. She had to watch her balance and force her left hand to function, but he could tell she'd nearly become her old self.

He gave the elderly woman a kiss on the cheek as he sneaked past and tore a sliver of turkey from the bird.

Christine gave him a playful smack, then pointed to the electric knife. "Start cutting, and that's an order."

He grinned, wanting to kiss her cream-colored neck where she'd pinned her hair up for church. She wore one of Grandma Ella's aprons tied over her deep purple dress. He looked down to see her in fuzzy slippers.

"I like your outfit," he said, nodding toward her foot-wear.

She ignored him, and he decided the faster he sliced the turkey the quicker they'd eat. He couldn't wait to open gifts, and he was positive his would be a surprise.

Christine's mind flew between preparing the meal, thinking of her amazing journey with Will, then sinking to an abyss when she thought about her conversations with Chet.

The call had been difficult, but when she'd hung up, she'd walked away with confidence. She had nothing to lose anymore by letting corporate know the truth about Chet—how he'd used his charm and idle promises on unsuspecting female coworkers to gain his own success. She'd pondered whether her action was vindictive, but Grandma Ella had convinced her—and Will had agreed—the sinner needed to repent to be forgiven, and Chet had yet to learn that lesson.

When the food was ready, she called everyone to the dining room table set with her grandmother's Christmas dinnerware. As always, they joined hands for prayer.

"Lord," her grandmother began, "we thank You for this day and especially for Your guidance. Nothing could bring me more joy, Father, than to have Christine and Will here together with Your blessing. Help us to always trust Your will and follow the path You make for us to follow. We ask You to bless this food to our body, and we thank You for the gift of Your Son who gives us eternal life. We pray this in Jesus's precious name."

"Amen," Christine said, joining the others, but her amen came with a feeling of relief and joy. She'd finally understood the closeness with the Lord that Will had often talked about. God had guided her off the plane and back into a taxi rather than fly the meaningless journey to Southfield. Life's meaning was right here on the island.

Once the plates were filled, the conversation moved to the two worship services they'd attended both yesterday and that morning, Christine's parents, and plans for the future.

"I have to go back in January and move my things here. Eventually, I'll need to look for an apartment or—"

"You'll do no such thing," her grandmother said. "I'd be delighted for you to stay with me if you would until—"

"Grandma, I'd love to stay here. This house means so much to me. It always holds good memories, and—".

"And here's my gift to you if you'll take it with good intention," Ella said.

Christine lifted her head and lowered her fork. "Gift?" She grinned.

"Maybe this is presumptuous of an old woman, but this house is too big for me. If you decide to stay for good—" She glanced from her to Will. "I'd love to trade. You can enjoy the house, and I'll fit as snug as a bug in the apartment. I want you to have this house, and I know your parents would agree. But if I'd be in your way, then I could—"

"Grandma," Christine said, "you'll never be in my way. If it weren't for you, I'd be sitting in Southfield right now, listening to Chet's lies." She looked at Will. "I knew I loved Will, but like that children's poem, 'The Spider and The Fly,' I was ready to fall into Chet's web again, because I'm too stupid and naive."

"You're too trusting and honest," Will said. "You want to believe, and Chet won't let you."

She reached across the cloth to grasp Will's hand. "I'm ashamed at the things I let worry me. Age. My work. Island life. After I quit fighting, those things meant nothing, and anyway, I have a new job, and I'm excited."

"You have a new job?" Grandma Ella's voice lifted in surprise.

"I'm going to build a Web site for Will and be his webmaster and new marketing director."

"That's wonderful, Christine," her grandmother said, her eyes shifting toward Will as if making sure he was pleased.

"Speaking of gifts, it's gift time," Will said, standing up and pushing in his chair.

His abrupt announcement surprised Christine. "We have to clean up first."

"That can wait, but this can't."

"Why not?"

"I'm too excited." Will caught her elbow and beckoned her to follow.

Confused, she studied her grandmother to see if she knew anything about the surprise, but she looked at her and didn't blink.

Will captured her hand and tugged her through the back door to the porch. She stared ahead, looking at the snow, and wrapped her arms around herself to fend away the cold. "What?"

"Look there," he said, pointing toward the driveway.

When she turned, her heart leaped. "It's a new snowmobile, and what's that in the seat?"

"Your bib."

"You bought me a snow outfit and a sled? But you didn't know if—"

"I have faith," he said, slipping his arms around her cold shoulders. "I won the sled at the Christmas bazaar draw."

"The one at Doud's?" She frowned. "But you told me—"

"It was won by a year-round resident, and that's right. Me. I had Jude keep it at his place, and I sneaked it here this morning after church."

"I can't believe this. You're giving it to me." She looked him in the eyes, amazed at what he'd said. "You really knew I'd stay."

"I hoped with all my heart."

"Your faith is so strong." She tiptoed to give him a quick kiss.

"Yours, too," he said, turning her toward the warmth of the house. "You came back, didn't you?"

She'd come back—back home, and she never wanted to leave.

Chapter Seventeen

Seven Weeks Later

"The ice bridge is ready," Will called as he came into the house, anxious to see Christine.

She pivoted toward him from the table. "What's that mean?"

"We can ride to St. Ignace. Solid ice from here to there."

She scooted back the chair. "You mean we can actually take the sleds over."

"That's exactly what I mean."

He walked up behind her and put his cold hands on her warm neck.

She scrunched her neck into her shoulders. "That's not fair."

"Maybe not, but this is." He kissed her neck and then swept back her hair to kiss her cheek, enjoying the sweetness of her fragrance.

"What this?" he asked, when he looked at the computer.

"It's the Web site."

"Really?" He pulled up a chair beside her.

"This is the home page. It's a picture of the shop. Later I'll take one without the snow. And here's the picture I took inside."

"Nice," he said, amazed to see the detail of her photograph. "I can see the window I just hung."

She moved the cursor. "Here's the links. This one says Shop Online. The shopper will click here and I'll have categories of your products. And this will be good for people coming to the island or people who are browsing the Internet."

He hated to quell her excitement. "That's great, Christine, but—"

"I know," she said, hitting the close button and turning off the computer. "You want to go out on the ice bridge."

The fact that she'd sensed what he wanted gave him a good feeling. "Yes, but before we leave, I have a surprise for you." He stepped back and pulled a sheet of something from beneath his jacket.

She eyed it a moment until he handed it to her. Her heart lurched, seeing the amazing photograph of her red glove putting her last initial in the pristine snow. W. L. + C. P. Beneath the photo was Will's name and the title "Love on Cupid's Pathway." Love had come to her in this lovely place. "Your photo made it this time?"

"It did. And all because of those pretty red gloves."

Her eyes blurred with happiness as she wrapped her arms around Will's neck. "It was your sensitive photography."

He kissed the end of her nose. "It was that and love on Cupid's Pathway."

She grinned at his silliness and studied the photo

again, so proud that he'd finally had a winning entry in the calendar contest.

"Okay. Enough of this flattery. Let's take a ride. I want to get there before it gets dark." He gave her another hug. "Get ready, and I'll meet you outside."

"Give me a minute. I want to see if someone will come and stay with Grandma."

"We'll only be gone an hour or so. She can probably stay alone. Take the cell phone."

"I'll check with her," she said. She handed him the photograph, and he headed for the door to his apartment.

Inside his rooms, he slipped on his bib, then put on his jacket and zipped it. He slid the smock over his head and grabbed his helmet.

Christine had never experienced the ice bridge and had no idea what a relief this was to those who resided on the island. The ice had frozen enough to hold the sleds and the residents were free to zip over to St. Ignace for shopping or appointments, even go to a movie without paying the ferry or plane fare.

He opened the door to the house. "Ready?"

Footsteps banged down the stairs, and Christine appeared, bundled in her bib and jacket, her feet bound in boots. "I feel like a jumbo baby-blue pillow," she said, carrying her mittens and earmuffs.

"But a beautiful jumbo pillow," he said, giving her a gentle kiss.

"Grandma said she'd be fine, but I'll call her in a half hour or so just to make sure."

"She'll be great," he said, touched by Christine's concern.

Outside, Christine climbed onto her new, larger sled, but she looked confident. She'd caught on to sledding faster than the speed of Shepler's hydroplanes that brought visitors to the island.

He settled onto his sled, wishing Christine was tucked behind him, but he couldn't deny her the fun of driving her new sled. "Let's go," he said, motioning her forward.

The sleds pulled out to the driveway, but Christine halted. "Does the bridge begin downtown?"

"No, the British Landing. That's where the bridge has been marked out."

They sped onto the road, the wind in their faces, and headed up Hoban to Annex Road, then British Landing Road. He glanced behind him to see Christine smiling beneath her helmet. She waved, and he waved back.

When they arrived, he waited for her to catch up. "See the trees." He pointed to the line of discarded Christmas trees that residents used to mark the bridge.

"Somewhere along here are our trees," she said.

"It keeps us on the sure path for the sleds and pedestrians."

"Pedestrians?"

"Some people have the courage to walk the four miles across the ice." He leaned over and grasped her hand to kiss her glove.

"You're silly."

"Only when I'm with you."

"Look," she said, pointing across the frozen water. "The sun is setting."

He looked at the horizon, seeing the muted colors—corals, purples and golds reflected in the snow and ice. "It's like a rainbow almost."

"A promise." She squeezed his hand.

"We'd better go."

"Into the sunset," she called as he pulled ahead of her onto the ice.

Christine followed, gliding up alongside with a wide smile. The Christmas trees lying along the pathway flashed by, and once he was halfway across, he slowed.

"Let's stop and get out here," he said. He parked to the side in case another sled came along.

He climbed out, and Christine pulled behind him. He grasped her hand to help her off the sled onto the ice.

"Here we are standing on the Straits of Mackinac," he said, amazed at the thrill he had each time he experienced it.

Christine did a full turn and swung back with her face beaming. "It's awesome."

He took her hand and pulled off her glove to feel her warm flesh in his. "Not as awesome as you are."

"I love this place, Will—the island and the people."

Will broke into laughter. "If I remember correctly, you offered to cook me a seven-course dinner or whatever I choose if I ever heard you say that you loved it here."

"I did?"

He brushed her cheek. "I love food, as you know, but I have something else I love much better."

Her eyes narrowed, then she gave him a crooked grin. "You look guilty...like you have something up your sleeve."

"Nothing up my sleeve." He paused, his heart thundering beneath his down-filled jacket. "But I do have something in my pocket."

She frowned and followed his hand as he dug inside and pulled out the small velvet box.

Her eyes widened, and he handed it to her. She stood a moment, staring at the lid as if she were unable to move.

"Will." She looked at him, then the box.

"Open it," he said.

Christine inched the lid upward and peeked inside. The cathedral setting with its row of paved cut diamonds on each side of a princess-cut stone glistened in the setting sunlight. "It's beautiful. Gorgeous."

"You're far more beautiful."

He removed the ring from the box and knelt down on the frigid ice. "Christine, maybe you think I should wait, but I love you now, and I know our love will grow and grow with God's blessing. Will you be my wife?"

Her cheeks trembled as she looked down at him. Tears welled in her eyes, and she nodded. "Yes. Yes. I'll love you forever."

He rose, slipped the ring on her finger and drew her into his arms. Their lips met, and warmth spread through him into his heart.

Christine yielded to his kiss, her arms wrapping around his neck, her body straining upward on tiptoes to offer her love. She'd told him once he had Christmas in his heart, and today Christine filled it to the brim.

She had her own mind and plans, but God had given her path a turn and led her straight into his arms.

* * * * *

THE FOREST RANGER'S CHRISTMAS

Leigh Bale

This book is dedicated to Rose and Angie,
two bright lights in my life.

Many thanks to Mike Fritz, RPh, for taking the time
to answer my questions about pharmacies. And
thanks also to Julie Muhle for her medical expertise.

Rest in the Lord, and wait patiently for him.
—*Psalms* 37:7

Chapter One

❧

Jocelyn Rushton decreased her speed and switched on the windshield wipers as she entered the sleepy mining town of Camlin, Nevada. Home for the holidays. Or at least the only place on earth Josie had ever considered a real home.

As she turned down Garson Way, a siren sounded behind her. She peered into her rearview mirror at the squad car coming up behind her. Great! Just great. A speeding ticket to welcome her home.

The deep-throated noise escalated to a shrill whine. She slowed her compact car, the tires slicing through furrows of slush covering the black asphalt. Inching her way over into a drift of snow, she hoped she didn't get stuck in the frozen mud.

Red lights flashed and she shook her head. She hadn't been speeding. Not on these slick roads. Maybe she had a taillight out. Maybe...

The patrol car zipped past and Josie expelled a breath of relief. Then her mind went wild as she thought about where the police car might be headed. Her grandfather's house was on this street. He'd lived here most of his life. A cul-de-sac, with no outlet. What if...?

A blaze of panic burned through her chest. Glancing in her rearview mirror again, Josie pulled her car back onto the icy pavement and drove steadily toward Gramps's house. Forcing herself not to speed. Anxious to see Gramps and know that he was all right.

Rows of quaint little homes with spacious yards covered in pristine snow flashed past her window. Fresh wreaths of pine boughs and holly decorated almost every door front. The late afternoon sunlight illuminated strings of red, yellow and green Christmas bulbs hanging along each roof.

Her fingers tightened around the steering wheel as she forced herself to remain calm. To take deep, even breaths. In these slippery conditions, it'd do no good if she ended up sliding into the shallow irrigation ditch bordering the narrow road.

Finally she saw Gramps's white frame house. A bevy of ice-crusted vehicles sat parked out front. The squad car dominated the scene, perched at an odd angle in the driveway. It blocked a green Forest Service truck.

Josie pulled up in front of the house. Two elderly women wearing heavy coats scurried through the snow toward their cars. The siren still blared and they clapped their hands over their ears to shut out the deafening noise. No doubt they were eager to vacate the premises, now that the police officer was here.

Hearing the siren, neighbors came outside and perched on their front porches like gawking fowl. They crossed their arms against the chilly temperature and crinkled their noses at all the commotion.

Josie killed the engine and clicked off her seat belt.

She scanned the area for an ambulance, then remembered this tiny town didn't have one. Just a volunteer fire department, with the nearest hospital sixty-eight miles away in Bridgeton. One more reason for her to worry about Gramps. If he ever needed quick medical care, he could be in real trouble. And who would drive him to Bridgeton? With her living ten hours away in Las Vegas, Gramps was all alone. Something she hoped to change very soon.

She threw her car door open wide. Stepping out in her tennis shoes, she skirted a pile of slushy snow. She glanced at the roof of the two-story house, searching for smoke or some sign of a break-in. Except for a cluster of missing shingles on the west side, nothing looked out of place. No obvious reason that would warrant a cop.

Maybe Gramps had collapsed.

Lengthening her stride, she hurried toward the driveway. Her gaze scanned the yard...and screeched to a halt when she saw Gramps. In a flash, she took in his ruddy cheeks, lumpy coat, orange knit cap and black floppy galoshes. At the age of seventy-eight, he seemed perfectly strong and healthy. He stood beside another tall, muscular man Josie immediately recognized from her previous visits to her grandparents' home.

Clint Hamilton. The local forest ranger.

His drab olive-colored shirt, spruce-green pants and bronze shield lent him an air of authority. Even his broad shoulders couldn't withstand this intense cold. He jerked a heavy coat out of his truck and pulled it on, zipping it up to his chin. He towered over Gramps and the policeman, his muscular legs planted firmly beneath him. As he lifted his head and stepped closer to Gramps, he dominated the scene, strong and in control. But what was he doing here? And what did he want with her grandfather?

Josie's gaze shifted to Officer Tim Wilkins, one of her childhood friends. Another one of her failed relationships. If you could call a school dance at the age of sixteen a failure. They'd gone out twice, but she'd broken it off when he'd asked her to go steady. As a teenager, she'd tried not to hurt Tim's feelings, but she had. Her parents' nasty divorce, followed by her father's death a year later, had made her wary of falling in love. She'd promised herself she'd never get married if there was any chance it wouldn't last. If she didn't involve her heart, she wouldn't get hurt. It was that simple. Yet since that time, she'd been engaged twice. Her two ex-fiancés made her realize those relationships had been based on something other than love and respect. She'd wanted to be engaged, to feel normal and safe.

So she wouldn't be alone anymore.

Shaking off those somber thoughts, Josie refocused on the present. Tim was a grown man now with a family of his own, and she hoped he wasn't the sort to hold a grudge. In comparison to Clint, he looked rather silly, with his officer's hat perched at an odd slant and his hands resting on his thin hips.

Slogging through the foot-deep snow, Josie made a mental note to shovel it off the sidewalk before she unloaded her suitcase from her car. Her breath puffed on the air with each exhalation. As she bustled up the path, she surveyed Gramps's house one more time. A single strand of colored lights hung from a protrusion of rusted nails that edged the front porch. A skimpy showing compared to the rolls of bulbs Gramps normally stapled to the house every December.

This wouldn't do. Not at all. Josie had never hung lights on a house before, but she would learn how. And soon. No matter what, she wanted this to be the best Christmas ever. Because it might be their last here in Camlin.

A rivulet of meltwater ran from the gutters. Her gaze scanned the peeling paint and missing shingles. Without repairs, the moisture might soon invade the interior. Further proof that Gramps could no longer keep up the place on his own. He needed help. He needed her. She couldn't stand the thought of him collapsing on the floor of his house and lying there for days on end until someone found and helped him. But asking a man like Frank Rushton to leave his home and move with her to Vegas might ruin Christmas. Regardless, she had to do it. Because as much as she loved her job, she was tired of being on her own. If Gramps lived nearby, she could check in on him often. Neither of them would be alone anymore. It'd be good for Gramps. And good for her, too.

She hoped.

She shielded her eyes against the blare of red lights emanating from the squad car like the beacon of a lighthouse. The men were talking and gesturing, but she couldn't make out their words over the piercing squeal of the siren. It was so like Tim to leave it on. Even as a kid, he'd been loud and obnoxious. Always hanging around when Josie was in town to visit her grandparents.

She sighed inwardly, admitting she wasn't very good at relationships.

Tim's voice escalated as he shook a stern finger beneath Gramps's nose. When he reached to unsnap the leather tab over his holster, Josie's breath hitched in her throat.

She broke into a run.

"Officer Wilkins, I didn't expect you to come over here today." The forest ranger's voice boomed over the keening howl.

"Just helping to keep the peace," Tim said.

Ha! Not with all the racket his squad car was making.

Clint jutted his chin toward the neon orb flashing on top of the black-and-white vehicle, his brow furrowed in frustration. "Can you please turn off the lights and siren on your squad car? I can't hear what everyone's saying. And no guns will be necessary."

Tim's eyes crinkled in disappointment as he yelled his response. "Sorry about that."

He trotted back to his police car, puffing for breath as he passed Josie along the way.

"Hi there, Josie. Good to see you home," he shouted with a wave.

She nodded, too distracted to speak right now, her composure rattled. Her father had grown up in Camlin, where everyone knew almost everyone else, including a granddaughter who'd been visiting here all her life. That had good points and bad. The good was that most people here cared about her. The bad was that everyone knew her personal business, no matter how hard she tried to keep it private.

It didn't help that Gramps had a penchant for gossip.

He gestured to the side, where at least two dozen fir and spruce trees leaned against the chain-link fence that edged his driveway and bordered his front lawn. "I haven't done anything wrong, Ranger. I just cut fresh Christmas trees like I've done every year of my life since long before you was even a gleam in your daddy's eyes."

Trees? This was about Christmas trees?

The harsh sound of the siren died abruptly, and everyone in the yard exhaled with relief. Finally Josie could hear herself think.

"Gramps! What's going on?" She squinted at her grandfather until the red orb on the police car was shut off , then she blinked.

"Why, Josie. I didn't expect to see you here." Gramps engulfed her in a tight bear hug.

The scents of peppermint and arthritis cream assailed her nostrils. When Gramps released her, she drew back and gazed at his gruff face, looking for signs of distress. He wasn't a young man anymore, but he appeared strong, his cheeks flushed from the cold winter air. His steely gray eyes twinkled with joy and she couldn't help smiling back. How she loved him. How glad she was to see him again.

"Remember I called you last week to tell you I was driving in today?" she said.

He blinked and gave her an absentminded frown. "Oh, yeah. That's right. When did you get into town?"

"Just now. Are you okay?"

He waved a grizzled hand in the air. "Sure, I'm fine. How was your drive? Did you get caught in any snowstorms along the way?"

"No, but I—"

"How long can you stay?"

"About five weeks. But I want to talk—"

"So long? Why, that's wonderful news. We'll have so much fun. But we better go shopping. Ma always made a big ham for Christmas dinner, but maybe you'd like something else this year. What about prime rib? We can have whatever you like, as long as there's pumpkin pie and homemade rolls. You know your grandma made the best—"

"Ahem." The ranger cleared his throat. "Sorry to interrupt your reunion, Frank. But we've got to clear this matter up."

Josie gazed at Clint, recalling what Grandma had once told her about the man. A single father, with a cute little girl he was raising. Tall and well-built, with a blunt chin, short brown hair, and a dazzling smile that sucked the breath right out of her lungs. When he smiled, that is. But he wasn't smiling right now.

From her peripheral vision, Josie was conscious of Officer Wilkins joining them again. Without the wail of the siren, they automatically lowered their voices to a rational level.

"Can you tell me what this is about?" she asked, trying to calm her jangled nerves.

"Honey, you remember Clint Hamilton, the local forest ranger," Gramps said.

How could she forget? They hadn't said more than a handful of words to each other in the more than three years since he'd moved to town, but Josie would have to be a saint not to notice his slightly crooked smile and dark good looks. And she was definitely no saint. Not in this life, anyway. But since her broken engagement with Edward had been a mere eight months earlier, she wasn't interested in another romance. At least, that's what she told herself.

"Clint and his little daughter, Gracie, are members of my church congregation," Gramps continued. "You've met them a few times over the past years. They were at Ma's funeral back in September."

Ma. The affectionate name Gramps used to refer to

Viola, his wife of fifty-seven years. When she'd died three months earlier, something had changed inside Josie. She loved her job as a pharmacist, but suddenly work wasn't enough anymore. She wanted more, but wasn't sure what that might be. And so she'd decided to take a break and figure things out. Already, being here made her feel lighter inside. As though her presence really mattered. To Gramps, anyway.

She nodded at Clint. He'd been one of the pallbearers for Grandma's casket. And following the service, he'd shaken Josie's hand and offered sincere condolences for her loss. She'd looked into his caring eyes and felt her sorrow melt away. Then he'd stepped aside and she'd been blown back to her lonely reality.

"Clint, you remember my granddaughter, Jocelyn Rushton." Gramps bumped the ranger with his elbow and gave a sly grin. "She's sure pretty, isn't she? And a good cook and seamstress, too. Viola taught her."

Clint's gaze darted Josie's way. "Yeah, glad to see you again."

Momentarily distracted, Clint stuck out a hand for her to shake. While her cheeks heated up like road flares, he shot her a guarded look, his warm brown eyes sweeping across her face.

"Hi." Her voice sounded small and uncertain, not at all like the professional woman she tried so hard to portray. Then she realized she was staring. Oddly fascinated by the hint of stubble across his masculine chin. "Can you tell me what this is about?"

"Your grandfather is in a lot of trouble, Josie." Stepping near, Tim hitched up his waistband. The pepper spray, ammunition pouches, flashlight and radio on his police belt jangled.

Clint interceded. "I'm terribly sorry for all this trouble, Frank, but I've had a report of stolen Christmas trees."

Josie's gaze darted over to the row of spruce and fir. She didn't understand what was going on yet, but a twinge of alarm tugged at her stomach and she couldn't help feeling as protective as a mother grizzly. This was Gramps, after all. Not a stranger to these men. And certainly not a criminal.

"My grandfather would never steal anything," she said.

And she sure wasn't about to stand by while they accused him of theft.

Clint didn't like this situation. Not at all. And judging from the fierce glare on Jocelyn Rushton's face, neither did she. But even her frown couldn't diminish her pretty features. Curls the color of damp sand bounced against her slim shoulders. She looked casual, dressed in a waist-length coat, tennis shoes and blue jeans that fit her long legs in a firm caress. Her intelligent blue eyes sparked with annoyance. And he couldn't blame her. This was her grandfather, after all. If Clint didn't want trouble, he'd better do something to stop it. And fast.

"I'm sure Frank is innocent of any crime," he said. "But I've had a complaint that he's illegally selling trees. He's cut so many that I'll need to see his permits."

In unison, all eyes riveted back on Frank. The elderly man blinked vacantly. "Permits?"

"Yes, Frank," Clint insisted in a gentle tone. "You need a permit to cut each one of these trees. Do you have them?"

"Why, no, I don't," he blustered. "I've never bought a permit in the past. I just drive my truck up on the mountain and take what I want. It's not like I'm going into someone's backyard and stealing the trees."

Horror ignited in Tim's eyes. "Aha! That's a confession, Frank. We've got you now."

Josie's mouth dropped open in dismay and her beautiful blue eyes narrowed for a fight.

Oh, this wasn't good. Clint regretted telling Tim that he'd drive right over here and speak with Frank about the situation. As soon as Clint had arrived, he'd heard the blare of the siren and known Tim was on his way, too. Without him intending it, the situation had been blown out of proportion.

"Tim, let's hear what Frank has to say." Clint tried to calm everyone.

"Theft?" the older man said, looking confused. "I cut down Christmas trees to give to the widows down at the civic center. How is that a crime?"

Clint tilted his head to one side. Was this an act? Or did Frank really not understand about tree permits? Everything Clint knew about this elderly man told him he was painfully honest. But cutting trees without a permit didn't make sense, either. The whole situation gave Clint a bad feeling, as if he was about to get hit in the head with a brick.

"You took the trees without buying permits. That's called stealing," Tim crowed in victory.

Frank's gaze zigzagged back to Clint. "I can't argue with that, but it's what I've done all my life. Someone's got to cut trees for the widows in town. In my day, the dads used to go out with their sons. Now, parents are too busy to spend quality time with their kids and teach them to do a good deed for others."

Point taken. It reminded Clint that he needed to be a

better father to his own child. It wasn't easy being both a mom and dad to a seven-year-old girl, but he'd never stop trying. He'd failed to make Karen happy, but he wouldn't botch it with his daughter. Gracie was the light in his life. His reason for living. And right then, he decided to make time to cut down their own tree within the next few days, just as soon as she got out of school.

"I agree, Frank. But I still need to see your permits," Clint said.

"It's a clear case of theft." Tim pursed his lips almost smugly.

"It is not. My grandfather is not a thief," Josie cried.

She stepped protectively in front of Frank. Fire crackled in her eyes, absolutely stunning. But Clint reminded himself he wasn't interested. Not after his abysmal failure with Karen.

His heart couldn't take it.

He released a shallow breath and closed his eyes for the count of three. Technically, he could have Frank arrested. But he wouldn't do that. Not in a zillion years. Not only was Frank a good friend, but Clint could just imagine his supervisor's deep frown should this story hit the evening news. Clint could see the headlines now: Local Forest Ranger Has Elderly Man Arrested for Cutting Christmas Trees to Give Away to Poor Widows.

Clint shook his head. No sirree. He wasn't about to let this happen. Not on his watch.

"Look, Ranger," Josie said.

"Clint," he corrected.

"Look, Clint. I think this is all just a big misunderstanding. My grandfather didn't know he was taking the trees illegally. I'm happy to pay for them. If you'll just tell me how much." She dug inside her purse as though searching for her wallet.

Tim shook his head like a banty rooster. "It's too late, Josie. You can't steal trees, then buy us off. I'll have to take Frank in." He reached for his handcuffs.

"Officer Wilkins, please. Cuffs won't be necessary." Clint held out a hand, thinking the lawman had lost his mind. Maybe they all had.

Josie stared at Tim in shock. "This is ridiculous."

"I agree," Clint said.

"But, Ranger…" Tim objected.

Clint leveled his best warning glare on him and shifted his weight protectively toward Frank. Thankfully, the cop clamped his mouth shut. Without saying another word, Clint had effectively controlled the situation. He flashed a smile of amicable indulgence toward Frank. The last thing he wanted was for this good man to think he was being accused of dishonesty.

"Don't worry, Frank. I'm sure we can sort this out," he said.

Tim backed up, tossing a wary glance toward him. Clint had jurisdiction in this situation and the lawman could do nothing without his say-so.

"Frank, I was told that you were selling these trees for a profit. From what you've said, that isn't true." Clint spoke in a congenial tone, determined to keep the peace.

Frank shook his head. "Absolutely not. I've never sold a tree in my life. Who told you that?"

Clint's gaze wavered over the policeman for a fraction of a second. Tim had come to the Forest Service office less than an hour earlier to tattle on Frank. Unfortunately, the officer didn't have his facts straight. Or he'd possibly omitted a few things from his report. Right now, it didn't matter. Clint was not having Frank arrested.

"I realize now that was a mistake," Clint said. "A complete misunderstanding. But I hope you can see why I had to check it out."

Frank peered at the ranger with doubt. "It's not true. I give all the trees away, except for the one I set up in my own living room each year."

Clint reached inside his coat pocket and withdrew a slim pamphlet. Tree theft of any kind was a common occurrence that cost taxpayers millions of dollars every year. As the local forest ranger, Clint had to follow up and prevent theft whenever possible. "I'm afraid you need a permit. I'm surprised you didn't notice all the signs we have posted along the main road leading up into the mountains. You didn't see any of them?"

Frank shrugged his sagging shoulders. "Uh, sure, I saw the signs, but I didn't stop to read them."

"The lettering is quite large. We made the signs that way on purpose. You wouldn't need to get out of your car to read what they say. This tells you all about the permits." Clint handed him the pamphlet.

Frank barely glanced at the glossy paper. "How much is a permit? How do I buy one?"

Clint pointed at the brochure. "You can read all the information right there."

Frank stared at it blankly. "Uh, my glasses are in the house. I'll read it later."

Clint considered the elderly man carefully. A sense of doubt assailed him, a nagging suspicion he'd been fighting off for some time now. But he didn't want to embarrass Frank. Before he could act on his hunch, he'd have to get rid of the cop.

Reaching up, he clapped the policeman on the back. "Officer Wilkins, I appreciate you coming over here. But I believe it was a false call and I can take care of the situation from here on out."

"Are you sure, Ranger?" Tim drawled, his chest puffing out with importance. "I can haul the suspect down to the jail for more questioning, if you like."

"Suspect!" The word burst from Josie's mouth like a nuclear explosion. "Timmy Wilkins, this is my grandfather you're talking about. And you know perfectly well that you used to steal candy from Milton's Grocery Store when we were eleven years old. Who are you to accuse my grandfather of theft?"

"I, um, don't recall that." Tim ducked his head, his face flushing red as a new fire engine.

Clint shot Josie a quizzical look, wishing she wasn't here right now. He felt out of sorts around her. Around any woman, for that matter. Ever since Karen had died. But Josie had made a good point. Officer Wilkins wasn't without faults. None of them were.

"We're not arresting Frank." Clint's voice nailed the final verdict.

"There's no need to mollycoddle Frank just because we're all friends and neighbors. The law is the law and it can't be broken, even in a small town like Camlin," Tim said.

Josie shook her head, not accepting his sudden lapse in memory. "My grandfather has not knowingly broken any law. You're not taking him anywhere."

"Of course he's not." Clint tried to show a tolerant smile. "Officer, I'm sorry to have dragged you away from your busy day. Merry Christmas." He gave Tim's shoulder a gentle nudge toward the squad car, then turned his back on the policeman and indicated the house. "Frank, can I speak with you inside for a few minutes? Alone."

Clint sure didn't want Tim around for what he had to say next. Unfortunately, he had a feeling about Frank that would undoubtedly upset the elderly man and his fuming granddaughter even more. It'd be best to deal with the problem in private. Without anyone else present, including Josie.

But Clint couldn't back down. The issue was too important. He just hoped that, when he was finished with what he had to say, he and Frank Rushton were still good friends.

Chapter Two

"Sure we can talk, Ranger. Come on inside where it's warm," Frank said.

Clint glanced at Josie. "I'd like to speak with your grandfather alone for a few minutes, if you don't mind. It'll only take a minute."

She shook her head. "Sorry, but I'd like to be included."

He hesitated, frowning with displeasure, but Josie didn't give him the chance to argue. Frank lumbered toward the house and she followed, chugging through the snow like a bulldozer. Feeling as if the bottom of her world had just crashed through the floor. Dazzling smile or not, she wasn't about to leave Clint Hamilton alone with her grandfather. Not when he could change his mind and have Gramps arrested.

Gramps circled around to the side entrance into the kitchen. He opened the door, then stood back to admit Clint and Josie first. She wasn't surprised. Her grandfather was the kindest, most decent man she knew. Always putting others first. Generous to a fault. It wasn't odd that he cut and gave trees away to the local widows. And it didn't sit well with Josie to have him accused of theft. At least the ranger was being reasonable about the situation.

For now.

As she stepped inside, the warmth of the kitchen enveloped her. Then a sour odor like stale, damp socks struck her in the face.

Josie's gaze swept the normally tidy room in astonishment. Dishes crusted with food sat piled high on the stove and in the sink. A brick of cheddar cheese sat drying on the countertop, greening with mold. Several cupboard doors hung open. Moving past Clint, she reached up and closed them. Something crackled beneath her feet and she crinkled her nose.

Her mind churned, trying to make sense of the mess. Grandma had always kept a spotless house. Since her recent passing, Josie had come to visit Gramps twice. She'd cleaned his house each time, but it had never looked this bad. And she figured this was one more reason he needed her help.

Gramps indicated the chairs at the scarred, wooden table. "Take off your coat and have a seat, Ranger. You can talk freely in front of Josie. What did you want to say?"

Clint stood right where he was, his brow creased. He obviously didn't want Josie here, but she wasn't budging. As if realizing that, he indicated the rumpled pamphlet Gramps still clutched in his gnarled fist. "Frank, I don't mean to embarrass you in any way, but can you read that brochure to me?"

Frank's eyes widened. "Of course I can read it."

Yes, of course he could. At Gramps's age, his eyesight wasn't the best, but Josie knew he could read. And she couldn't prevent an annoyed frown from creasing her forehead as she looked at Clint Hamilton. Nor could she soften the demanding tone of her voice. "What exactly are you implying, Ranger?"

Clint shifted his booted feet, his persistent gaze centered on Gramps. "Truly, I don't mean to be rude, Frank, but would you get your glasses and read it to me now? Please?"

"Ranger, stop this," Josie demanded, openly hostile now.

Clint's gaze rotated to her, his dark eyes piercing her to the back of her spine. She expected him to make a biting remark, but he merely looked at her with a glaze of forced disinterest. As though he was trying not to like her.

"Please, call me Clint."

Not if she could help it. Not as long as he posed a threat to her grandfather.

"What is it you want, exactly?" she asked, bristling.

Clint's mouth tightened, but he had the decency to drop his gaze. "I don't want anything, but I'd rather have this discussion with Frank alone."

"I already said I'm not leaving," she insisted.

He dragged a hand through his short hair. "I'm sorry for that, but I need to know if your grandfather can read."

"Of course he can read. Why would you think he can't?" She leaned her hip against the counter and folded her arms, feeling irritable. She'd been worried about Gramps for several months now, and this volatile situation frosted the cake. With Grandma gone, Josie felt an urgency building inside her. To take care of Gramps. To keep others from hurting or taking advantage of him. To be with her family, little that she still had. And a nosy forest ranger would not get in her way of that task.

"Please, just humor me," Clint said.

She narrowed her eyes. "I thought you were his friend."

"Believe me, I am." Clint met her gaze again, the intensity of his eyes unwavering.

That was just the problem. She didn't believe him. Not when he dredged up things that didn't matter, let alone make any sense. Her past relationships had taught her not to trust easily. Especially men. In her life, Gramps had been the only man not to let her down.

And yet Josie couldn't deny a feeling of unease. She knew Gramps so well. The crinkle lines that framed his mouth whenever he smiled. The way his bushy eyebrows curved together when he was upset about something. The deep, rich timbre of his laugh. But now her mind sorted through the numerous times during her childhood when she'd asked him to read to her. Bedtime stories. Magazine articles. New books Grandma had bought for her. Gramps had always deferred, telling her a story from his memory or tickling her instead. Silly distractions she'd never suspected before. But that didn't mean Gramps couldn't read.

Or did it?

No, Josie had never heard anything so outrageous in her life. She refused to believe it. It couldn't be true. And yet an inkling of doubt nibbled at her mind. It'd be so difficult to hide a handicap like illiteracy. Gramps couldn't have made it through his long life without knowing how to read and write.

Or could he? What if the forest ranger was right and Gramps couldn't read?

Clint stepped back, giving Josie some space. She was visibly upset, with her blue eyes narrowed, her hands clenched. He would rather have this conversation without her present, but she'd made that impossible.

He considered leaving right now, without another word. He hated causing these people any more distress, especially after he'd accused Frank Rushton of tree theft. But he couldn't leave. Not now. Not in good conscience. Not until he knew the truth and did something to help Frank.

"Go ahead, Gramps. Read." Josie turned to face her grandfather.

Clint waited. When he'd seen Josie at her grandmother's funeral, he'd noticed the way her stunning eyes glimmered with tears, and the grief etching her delicate face. He understood grief and couldn't help feeling her loss.

But he'd heard that she was a career woman, one who couldn't seem to settle down with a man. From the tidbits of information Frank and Viola had told him, Josie's parents had divorced when she was thirteen. She'd been engaged twice, but it hadn't worked out. She'd quit on both guys just like Karen had quit on him. Apparently Josie had an aversion to marriage, which suited him fine. He had a child to protect, and he wasn't about to become Josie's third conquest.

She loved her grandparents, he had no doubt. And he couldn't blame her for feeling protective of Frank. No one lived in this small town and didn't hear what a kind, charitable man Frank Rushton was. But right now, Clint had a hunch. His own past experience with Karen told him he was right. Frank couldn't read. Not because he couldn't see well enough without his spectacles, but because he didn't know how to put the letters together to form the words.

"Please, Frank. Get your glasses and read for me," Clint insisted.

Frank's shoulders tensed, but Clint couldn't back down. As a ranger, he had an obligation to protect the national forest. It was his job. His first priority after Gracie. If Frank was going up on the mountain to cut trees, he needed to be able to read the posted signs. Clint also wanted to help Frank, if he could.

With a labored breath, the elderly man nodded, and his head drooped in resignation. "All right."

He disappeared into the living room. Josie stood beside the doorway, arms folded, her mouth set tight in outrage. Clint decided to be patient. He couldn't help feeling surprised to see her here. Christmas was still weeks away and he knew from talking to Josie's grandparents that she'd never spent this much time with them in the past. Not since she was a little kid. So why was she here?

"How's your work at the pharmacy going?" he asked, trying to make small talk. Trying to keep from becoming her enemy.

"Fine." Her clipped reply didn't encourage further banter.

"It must have required a lot of schooling to become a pharmacist."

"It did."

He thought about his own master's degree in geology. Even with his advanced education, he still felt like a fool in this woman's presence. All jittery and nervous. He could take or leave most women. But with Josie, something was different. Something he couldn't quite put his finger on. It was as though he knew her from some far-off memory. As if there was a magnetic attraction he didn't understand, yet couldn't deny.

"You're in early for a holiday visit this year," he said.

"That's right."

"Any special reason?"

"It's not your concern."

He rubbed his hand against his bristly chin. "Sorry. I didn't mean to pry."

She was a blunt little thing, he'd give her that. So blunt that she bordered on rude. But Clint got the impression it was all an act. A form of self-preservation. He could read it in her wary eyes. A mist of fear seemed to hover over her. And that brought out the protective instincts in him like never before. Safeguarding women was a weakness he'd never seemed able to overcome. His own mother had been widowed after Clint had graduated from college, so he came by the trait naturally. Mom had needed his help and he'd gladly stepped up to the task. But Josie was different. Caring for another woman would only bring him and his daughter more heartache. Something he must avoid like the plague.

Yes, he knew something was up. He could feel it in his bones. Even so, Josie was right. Her presence here wasn't his business. He tried to tell himself he didn't care, but he knew that wasn't true. She obviously didn't want to tell him about it, so he shut up.

A horrible silence followed.

Frank returned, wire-rimmed spectacles in hand. It took another two laborious minutes for him to clean them, then plant the glasses firmly on the bridge of his nose before he held up the pamphlet and stared at the words. His hand trembled, betraying his anxiety. But he didn't read. Not a single word.

Possibly because he was holding the pamphlet upside down.

Clint stepped forward and gently turned the leaflet right side up. With eagle-eyed focus, Josie watched every move.

She laid a hand on his arm. "Gramps? Read it out loud."

The tender gesture didn't go unnoticed by Clint. Maybe it was good she was here to offer moral support to her grandfather.

Frank whipped the glasses off his face and tossed them on the table. They clattered against the porcelain cookie jar shaped like a yellow pineapple. Josie gasped and stepped back.

Frank stared at the floor, obviously embarrassed. And Clint hated every minute of it, knowing he was the cause. Knowing he'd hurt this good man to the core.

"I'm sorry, Josie. The ranger's right. I can't read. Not a word," Frank said.

"Gramps!" A look of incredulity washed over Josie's face and she clapped a hand to her mouth in disbelief.

All the sadness of the world filled Frank's gaze, a lost expression Clint had frequently seen in Karen's eyes.

"Why do you think after your mom died your grandma and I pushed you so hard to do well in school?" Frank asked Josie. "We didn't want you to end up like me. Can't even read the daily newspaper. Uneducated and stupid."

"You're not stupid, Gramps. You're the smartest man I know," Josie objected in a passionate voice.

Clint agreed. "Definitely. You're very smart, Frank. Being able to read has nothing to do with a person's intelligence, believe me."

But a sick feeling settled in Clint's gut. He took no delight in revealing the truth. He'd suspected for a long time that Frank couldn't read. Too many clues had led to this conclusion. But now, Clint's heart tightened with compassion. He couldn't forget how Frank and his wife had lovingly provided child care for his daughter when they'd first moved to town three years earlier. Even when Clint had been called out overnight to fight wildfires, Frank and Viola Rushton had tended his little girl as if she were their very own. And look how Clint repaid them. By revealing a secret Frank had kept hidden all his life.

The elderly man lifted his gaze to Clint, his eyes filled with uncertainty. "What gave me away?"

Clint smiled warmly, trying to lighten the tense moment. Trying to show an increase of love toward this good man and his irascible granddaughter. After all, it was the Christian thing to do.

"To begin with, you held the hymnal upside down at church once. I've also noticed you can't seem to orient yourself in the scriptures. You flip through the pages and quote them from memory better than anyone I know, but you can't find a specific verse when the Sunday school teacher calls on you. And I've seen you at the power company, paying your bills in person, with cash, instead of paying online or mailing in a check, like most people do."

Josie narrowed her eyes. "How would paying with cash indicate he can't read?"

"My wife did the same thing. She always paid our bills in cash because she couldn't write a check." Clint had been proud of Karen's accomplishment when she'd learned to read, but he didn't like talking about her now. Even after seven years, the pain of how she'd died was still too raw, the guilt over her death still too fresh.

"I don't understand," Josie said.

Clint released a deep sigh. "Let's just say I recognized the signs. You fake it quite well, Frank. And today, when you claimed you hadn't read the tree permit signs up on the mountain, it all added up. Those signs are too large for anyone to miss, unless you can't read them."

And Clint knew firsthand what it was like to cope with illiteracy. Karen had been highly defensive about her disability and had found ways to hide it from other people. She'd constantly feared someone might find out and make fun of her. That, coupled with the physical abuse she'd endured as a child, had left Karen with no self-esteem whatsoever. Even after they'd married and she'd learned to read, she'd never gained much confidence. And no matter how hard Clint tried to convince her, she'd never really believed that he or God loved her.

Clint had failed to make Karen happy, but he was determined to make a difference for Frank.

"What now? Will you have me arrested anyway?" Frank asked, his bushy brows arched in misery.

Josie gave a sharp inhalation and Clint inwardly cringed. It was bad enough to reveal Frank's secret without worrying about Josie's disapproval. At least her concern for her grandfather appeared genuine. But Clint wished once more that she wasn't here to complicate the issue. Then again, maybe she could help remedy the problem.

"No, you're not going to jail." Clint stepped forward and rested a hand on the older man's shoulder. "I'm sorry, Frank. You can see now why I thought we should speak in private. I didn't want to advertise this. I just want to help."

Frank dragged back one of the chairs before dropping into it. He raked his fingers through his thin white hair, making it stand on end. Josie walked to her grandfather and rubbed his back, offering silent support. The man reached up and patted her hand, then leaned his elbows on the table, looking wilted with defeat.

Josie's caring gestures confused Clint. She was a beautiful woman, but a bit overbearing and brusque. He remembered the glow of pleasure that permeated Frank's face whenever he spoke about Josie and her career as a pharmacist. And then Frank's disappointment when she'd canceled numerous trips home because she was too busy working. Over the years, her absence had hurt Frank and Viola, though they'd never admitted it out loud. Of course, Josie lived in Vegas, a ten-hour drive one way. But since Viola had died, Josie had been coming around more often. At least this year Frank wouldn't be alone for Christmas.

"Frank, we have a learn-to-read program at the library downtown," Clint said. "I volunteer there almost every Thursday night. They're a great support group, but if you don't like that option, I can come here to your house in the evenings. I'd like to help you learn to read."

Frank stared at the dingy wall, his mouth taut. "I'm afraid I'm too old to learn, Ranger. It's too late for me."

Clint snorted. "No, it's not. It's never too late to learn anything. Not if you really try. And stop calling me ranger. We're good friends and you know my name."

Clint tried to sound positive, while avoiding Josie's glare. No doubt she was in shock, finding out the truth like this. Clint had felt the same way when he'd learned his new bride couldn't read. Having grown up in the poverty of a coal-mining community, Karen had been raised by an abusive stepfather. She'd been almost twenty-three years old before Clint had taught her to read. But even then, she'd never overcome the stigma. Depression had haunted her most of her life. Now, Clint worked at the local library in the learn-to-read program to honor Karen's memory. Because he'd loved her.

Because he'd failed to save her life.

"My brain doesn't work good like it used to," Frank said.

"Your brain works fine, and I'll prove it to you." Clint sat across from Frank and met the old man's gaze with a wide smile. "If you'll agree to participate in a reading program for just two months, I'll make the tree permit issue go away. In fact, you and I will deliver your trees to the civic center and hand them out to the widows tomorrow morning. I'll pick you up at 8:00 a.m. But you'd need to be in the reading program for at least eight weeks. Do we have a deal?" He thrust out his hand.

For several moments, Frank studied his face, as though thinking things over. "Do I have any other choice?"

Clint licked his bottom lip, not wanting to be too forceful. He had no idea what he'd do if Frank refused his offer. He'd probably let the issue drop and still give the trees away to the widows. He certainly wasn't going to call Officer Tim back to arrest the man. But learning to read would take time. It also could make such a difference in Frank's life. It could open an entire world. And Clint wanted so much to help.

To redeem himself for failing Karen.

"Everyone has a choice, Frank. Even you," he said.

"Are there other people that can't read in the program at the library?"

"Yes, two. Both are members of our congregation. So you already know them. And I'll bet they'd be happy to see you there, too."

Frank paused for several moments, as though thinking this over. Finally, he lifted his hand and they shook on it.

"All right, I may not be able to read, but I'm no coward. I'll go to the library."

A whoosh of air escaped Josie's lungs. "While I'm here for the holidays, I can help, too. And you're the bravest man I know, Gramps."

"I agree," Clint said.

"So what now?"

Clint stood and turned toward the door, pasting a generous smile on his face. "Now we go to work. I'll see you in the morning, and then again at the library at seven o'clock next Thursday night."

Josie nodded, going through the motions of listening. Her vacant look indicated she wished Clint would leave now. And he was ready and willing to oblige her.

Reaching for the doorknob, he paused long enough to bid them farewell. "Have a good evening. And merry Christmas!"

They didn't respond. A stunned silence filled the air with gloom. Josie stood looking at him like an ice queen, her blue eyes filled with doubt and some other emotion Clint couldn't quite fathom.

Fear, perhaps?

Clint didn't ask. As he stepped outside, the frigid air embraced him. It was still early, but darkness mantled the town. Christmas lights gleamed along the neighbor's houses across the street. Frost formed patterns of lace on the windshield of his truck. He climbed inside and fired up the engine before switching on the defroster. He decided it was quite a bit warmer out here than in Josie's frigid, glowering presence.

He hadn't meant to upset the pretty pharmacist, but he had. And for some reason, that bothered Clint intensely.

Chapter Three

Two days later, Josie stood with her shopping cart at the back of the only grocery store along Main Street. The place also served as a hardware store. Christmas songs blared over the loudspeaker, but she didn't hum along. The scent of freshly popped corn filled the air, along with the happy chatter of shoppers. In spite of all this, it still didn't feel like Christmas. Not to her. Not with Gramps in such a sour mood.

Looking down at her shopping cart, she studied the boxes of colored Christmas lights she'd selected. No matter what Gramps said, she was determined to hang them on his house. After what had happened with the ranger, he needed cheering up.

So did she.

Turning, she perused two fake Christmas trees. The pictures on the outside of the cardboard boxes were quite small and difficult to make out. A Douglas fir covered in heavy white flocking, and a spindly spruce. Both were poor imitations of natural Christmas trees. She could take one home and figure out how to assemble it, she had no doubt. But Gramps wouldn't like either tree in his living room. And she couldn't blame him. He'd had a real tree every year of his life and would settle for nothing less.

"You're Frank's granddaughter, aren't you?"

Josie turned. An elderly woman with cottony white hair, too much facial powder, and a merry dimple in each plump cheek smiled up at her.

"Yes, I am."

The lady's grin widened as she propped one hand against her thick waist. "I knew it. I'm Thelma Milton, one of Frank's friends down at the civic center. You and I have met a couple of times, but you probably don't remember me. I knew your grandma well."

"Yes, of course I remember. You were at Grandma's funeral."

"That's right. I was sorry to hear about your breakup with your last fiancé."

Josie tensed. No doubt Gramps had shared the news with all his cronies down at the civic center. The reminder hurt and made her wonder if she was doomed to spend her life as an old maid. How she wished she could meet just one man she could trust. A man who would love her unconditionally for herself.

"Frank told me," Thelma confessed. "And I say it's for the best. If a man really loves you, he wouldn't let a little thing like your work come between you, believe me. A beautiful girl like you deserves better."

Josie nodded, wishing it was that simple. But she'd rather never marry than end up in an ugly divorce like the one her parents had put her through. Of course, she wasn't about to discuss her broken relationships with a stranger.

"Yesterday, Frank and the ranger brought me the most

beautiful tree. Frank even set it up inside my house."
Thelma batted her eyelashes like a coy girl.

Josie swallowed a choking laugh. For some inane reason, she found the situation quite comical. True to his
word, Clint had picked up Gramps and the two of them
had driven over to the civic center, where they'd handed
out all the confiscated trees. Josie had remained at home,
sorting through piles of debris littering Gramps's house
to find the mop bucket and vacuum cleaner. His absence
had given her some time to clean house. It had also made
Gramps feel better, though the stress of learning to read
had settled over him like a fat rain cloud.

"I'm glad you got your tree up," Josie said, wishing
she had a tree for Gramps. Too bad the ranger had confiscated all of the trees he'd cut down.

Thelma stepped closer. "Frank tells me you're a pharmacist in Las Vegas."

"That's right."

"Do you like your work?"

"Yes, I love it," Josie answered truthfully. "And as I
remember, you own this store."

Josie showed her most friendly smile. After all, this
was one of Gramps's friends and the woman obviously
liked him.

"Yes, I do. Frank is so proud of you. You're all he talks
about. I'm so glad you came home for the holidays. He
needs some family around now that Vi's gone."

Vi. The name many people used for Viola, Josie's
grandmother.

"I'm happy to be here, too." The bite of guilt nipped
at Josie's conscience. She should have come to visit
more frequently. She missed Grandma so much. And it
dawned on her that losing his spouse must have devas-

tated Gramps. He didn't say a lot about it, but inside, he must still be shattered by grief. Josie didn't want the end of his life to be sad. She wanted them both to be happy. And Josie wasn't. Not anymore. Not while she was alone. But so far, she'd failed to find a man willing to commit to her permanently.

"I sure wish we had a pharmacy here in Camlin," Thelma continued. "I order my prescriptions through the mail. It's a real pain if they arrive late and I run out of my hormones."

"I'm sure that could be a big problem." Josie laughed.

"You could always open up a pharmacy here in my store. I wouldn't charge a lot of rent," Thelma offered.

Josie forced herself not to react. Rent wasn't the issue. Though she'd accumulated a modest savings account, she didn't have enough capital to stock the shelves with the basic medications people would need. Besides, spending the rest of her life in this one-dog town didn't appeal to her. "Thanks for the offer, but I'm happy with my job in Vegas."

"Oh, well. Have a merry Christmas. And give Frank my love." Thelma blew a sugary kiss before bustling down the aisle, leaving the cloying scent of gardenias in her wake.

"I will." Josie waved, then stood there and blinked for several moments. If she didn't know better, she'd think her seventy-eight-year-old grandfather had an admirer.

Josie shook her head. Men her grandfather's age didn't have girlfriends. Did they?

Above all else, she wanted Gramps happy. And a fake tree wouldn't make him happy.

Gazing at her options, Josie realized she took city shopping for granted. Living in Las Vegas, she could pull up to a spacious tree lot and pick out any one she wanted. The mild winters would be easier on Gramps's arthritis, too. Within minutes, they could visit a doctor and get his prescriptions filled. And she wanted that convenience for Gramps. A balanced diet wouldn't hurt him, either. She'd almost had a fit when she'd discovered he'd been subsisting on canned soup, potato chips and oatmeal. But how could she ask him to leave his world behind and move away with her?

"Hi, there!"

Josie whirled around. Clint Hamilton stood behind her, holding the hand of a little girl about seven years old with a cute button nose, flawless skin and a long, blond ponytail.

"Um, hi." Josie met his gaze and smiled uncertainly. Immediate attraction buzzed through her.

His unblinking eyes swept over her. He looked handsome and rustic dressed in a down-filled coat, cowboy boots and brown leather gloves. His gaze dropped away, and she couldn't help wondering what had produced the wariness in his warm, brown eyes.

She nodded at the melted droplets covering his broad shoulders. "Is it snowing again?"

"Just a dusting, but a storm is coming in later tonight." He showed a twinge of a smile, his cheeks slightly red from the cold.

"What's your name?" the little girl asked, her voice hesitant.

Josie's gaze lowered to the child, who was bundled up in a glistening red coat, matching rubber boots and a white scarf around her neck. She looked adorable. "Jocelyn Rushton. What's yours?"

"I'm Grace Karen Hamilton, but everyone just calls me Gracie."

"That's a lovely name," Josie said.

"This is my daughter," Clint supplied the introductions. "Gracie, this is Frank's granddaughter."

Understanding lit up the child's expressive eyes. "Oh, I recognize you. I've seen your pictures at Grandpa Frank's house many times."

Grandpa Frank? Over the years, Josie had heard other children in town call her grandfather by this name, but it seemed odd to hear it from the forest ranger's daughter. Obviously, the girl had been inside Gramps's home. Not surprising. Grandma and Gramps had many friends in this town.

"Is that right?" Josie felt the burden of Clint's gaze like a leaden weight. For some reason, the ranger made her feel as though he could see deep into her soul. And in all honesty, she feared what he might find there besides a bitter, unlovable woman who was emotionally inaccessible to others.

"Yeah, in his photo albums. He shows his pictures to me all the time. And Grandma Vi used to make me chocolate chip cookies," Gracie said.

"Ah, I see." Josie had also loved her grandmother's homemade cookies. In fact, she planned to make some while she was here. She wanted to bake and decorate and enjoy a slower pace while she could. In Vegas, she didn't have time for domestic chores, or anyone to cook for.

"I sure miss Grandma Vi," Gracie continued.

Josie did, too. More than she could say.

"She used to tend me every day while Daddy went to work," Gracie said.

Josie jerked up her chin in surprise. Why would a

woman of Grandma's advanced age be tending a young child on a regular basis? This revelation gave Josie the strange sensation that she was the outsider, not Gracie and her tall father. "Really? I didn't know that. She never mentioned it."

"Yeah, she was my favoritest babysitter ever in the world. I miss her a lot." No longer shy, Gracie smiled widely, showing a missing tooth in front.

A sinking despair settled in Josie's stomach. She couldn't help feeling as though she'd lost something precious when Grandma had died. But one question thrummed through her mind. Why had Grandma never mentioned that she was looking after a child every day?

Once again, Josie realized how little she really knew about her grandparents. Now that Grandma was gone, Josie regretted taking her for granted, and didn't want to do the same with Gramps. That was all about to change. Josie would have to tell Gramps about her plans to move him to Las Vegas. And soon. But she dreaded it. If he refused, she wouldn't make him go. And then what? Maybe she'd sit down and talk with him about it tomorrow or the next day. Together, they'd work something out.

"I got a new babysitter now. She's nice, too, but she doesn't make cookies like Grandma Vi did," Gracie said.

"Does your mom work, too?" Josie asked, wondering why the girl's mother couldn't watch Gracie during the day. In fact, hadn't Clint mentioned that he'd taught the woman how to read?

"No, my mom's in heaven," Gracie said.

"Oh, I'm sorry." Josie had forgotten Clint was a widower. She glanced his way, wishing she'd been more tactful. She understood firsthand the aching pain of losing people she loved, and didn't want to remind him.

Clint's eyes darkened and he shifted his weight uneasily. A guarded look flashed across his face and Josie regretted dredging up the topic.

Gracie shrugged one shoulder. "It's okay. I never knew my mom. She died when I was just a baby, but Dad says she loved me like crazy."

The girl slid her hand into her father's, seeming to take comfort from his presence.

Josie nodded in understanding. "I lost my mom and dad, too."

Now, why had she told them that? Normally, she kept her personal life to herself. Especially her childhood, which had been anything but happy. A disturbing memory of constant fights between her parents ripped through her mind. Angry words and hateful accusations, followed by her father leaving one rainy night just after Josie's thirteenth birthday. She'd never seen Dad again. He'd been killed in a car accident a year later. But not once had he called or written her. In fact, no man seemed to want her. First Dad had left, then two ex-fiancé's. Even Mom had treated her like a burden, and she'd grown up feeling unwanted.

She didn't want to dwell on those sad times, but they seemed imbedded in her soul. Something about Clint drew out her carefully kept secrets. Right now, she wished she could crawl into a deep hole and hide.

"Yes, I know," Gracie said. "Grandma Vi told me. She said you and me are kindred spirits because we both lost our moms."

Grandma had said that? Hmm, surprising, when Josie considered that her mother never cared much for Grandma. Mom hadn't gotten along well with her in-laws, especially after Dad had died. Now, Josie stared at Gracie, seeing a maturity in the girl's eyes that was much too advanced for her years.

Kindred spirits. That sounded like something Grandma would have said, but Josie couldn't equate herself with this little girl. After all, they were almost complete strangers. Yes, Josie understood loss. Her mom had been so busy working three jobs to put food on the table and pay the rent that she'd had little time for her lonely daughter. Growing up, it would have been so easy for Josie to become a rebellious teenager. Instead, she'd found approval through perfection. She'd spent most nights alone, reading books and doing homework. She'd had very few friends, but she'd earned top grades in math, science and chemistry. Seeking the love she so badly craved, she'd won the approval of her teachers. And during college, she'd avoided men and socializing. Nothing had seemed more important to her than school and work.

Until now.

"It's okay. I still have Daddy," the girl said.

Clint cleared his throat and glanced at the boxed trees before quirking his brows with amusement. "You need another tree? I would have thought with all the trees Frank cut down that you'd had enough for one Christmas."

Josie's face heated with embarrassment. He'd deftly changed the topic and she was relieved, but she hated that he'd caught her buying a fake tree. "Remember, you confiscated all the live trees, so we don't have one for our own Christmas now."

"Ah, I see. Well, that won't do." Understanding filled his eyes and he sent her a smile of empathy. "Where is Frank, anyway?"

She gave a scoffing laugh, finding the situation sadly

funny. "Outside in my car. He refused to come inside to pick out a fake tree. He's never had anything but a live tree and he's been grumbling for two days that Christmas is ruined without a real one."

She could buy a tree permit, but after what had happened the other day, she'd rather avoid the Forest Service office at all costs. She didn't want to take another chance on Gramps being arrested. Also, she had no desire to navigate the winter roads up into the mountains to cut another tree.

"We're going to cut our tree right now. Daddy needs to buy a new hand saw first." Gracie spoke in a tone that indicated a real tree was the only way to go.

Although Josie hadn't had a Christmas tree in her lonely apartment for the past three years, she agreed.

Clint chuckled, the sound low and deep. "There's definitely something to be said about having a real tree in your house on Christmas morning. But lots of people buy fake trees. Some are beautiful and look very real."

Josie stared doubtfully at her choices. "Just not these two."

"Yeah, these are pretty pathetic." He lifted a small saw with a yellow price tag emblazoned on the wooden handle. "I propose a solution. Like Gracie said, we're on our way up on the mountain to cut our own Christmas tree. I've got a chain saw and it'd be no trouble to cut one for you while we're there."

"Oh, I—"

"Hey!" Gracie cut in. "Why don't you and Grandpa Frank come with us? We have room in Dad's truck. Don't we, Dad?"

The girl looked up at her father, an innocent expression on her face.

Josie froze. She didn't know what to say. The deafening silence indicated that Clint was just as dumbstruck.

"Yeah." He spoke the word in slow motion. "Why don't you come with us? It'd do Frank some good, too."

Josie agreed. An outing might be just the thing to drag Gramps out of his surly mood. But that would mean spending more time with the attractive forest ranger and his cute little daughter. "I'm not sure we can. I've got to buy groceries first."

"Oh, please come with us, Josie. Please, please," Gracie begged, hopping up and down with anticipation.

Josie hesitated. If only the child wasn't so charming. And her father so handsome and brooding.

But Josie had to think. To discern if Clint's offer was authentic, or obligatory. She sensed a reticence in him. Not because of Gramps. Oh, no. Josie was almost positive that Clint had a problem with her. And she couldn't help wondering why.

This was a bad idea. Clint felt it deep in his bones. But Gracie had invited Josie and Frank, and Clint couldn't back out now. Not without possibly hurting Frank's feelings again. "Sure, why don't you come along with us? It'll put Frank back on an even keel with the Forest Service. And I'll even provide the thermos of hot chocolate."

Josie laughed, the melodic sound easing Clint's discomfort just a bit. "I don't know. I hate to impose."

He shifted his feet, surprised by her pleasant mood. He'd expected her to hold a grudge. And he liked that she was able to let it go. Nor could he deny the outing sounded fun. What could it hurt? It was just a tree-cutting party, after all. No big deal. Each year, he took Gracie out to cut down their Christmas tree. But this would be

he first time a woman accompanied them. And Frank,
 grandfather figure Gracie loved. Clint had to put his
ittle girl first. And as much as he hated to admit it, he
idn't seem to be enough for Gracie anymore. She was
etting older and growing up so fast. Maybe being with
ther people during the holidays would be good for her.

Maybe it'd be good for him, too.

"It's no imposition. Really. I even have several per-
nits, so it'll be perfectly legal." Clint reached inside his
oat pocket and pulled out three tree tags, dangling them
efore Josie's eyes as proof.

She chuckled at his attempt at humor. And it felt so
ood to hear a woman's laugh. Like coming in out of
ne cold after a freezing storm. Karen had been sullen,
aughing so rarely. Always deeply depressed. He remem-
ered making up jokes, and bringing her flowers every
aturday, just to see her smile. But laughter had evaded
er. Which was probably why he craved it so much now.

"I'd have to check with Gramps first," Josie said.

"Don't worry, he'll agree." Clint spoke with convic-
on.

"Okay, but I'll need an hour to take our groceries home
nd put our perishables away in the fridge. I've been
leaning the house for two days and we need to stock up
n a lot of supplies." She clamped her mouth closed, as
 she'd confided too much information.

Clint didn't mind. He'd seen the state of Frank's house
nd had his own concerns. Since Viola's passing, the man
vasn't taking care of himself. At his age, Clint could
nderstand why. He was glad Josie was here to aid her
randfather. But maybe she needed help, too. Clint had
oticed some shingles missing on Frank's roof. Not some-
ing Josie could repair easily. In this small town, you

couldn't just call a roofing company to come over and fix it. And it could become a huge problem if they got many more storms. Clint should do something about it. He had the time and knew what to do.

"I've been worried about Frank, too," he confessed.

Josie nodded. "He's competent enough, but I don' think he'll admit how frail he's become. He's not steady on his feet anymore."

"You're right. I've got some leave coming over the nex few weeks and would love to repair his roof."

He wanted to serve Frank, but he didn't want to be around Josie any more than necessary. Right now, tha couldn't be helped. She was here to visit and the work needed to be done. End of story. Besides, she'd be leav ing right after the holidays.

She hesitated. "I don't want you to feel obligated."

"I don't," he said. "Serving Frank is my pleasure. was assigned the task of looking in on him and Viola from time to time by our church leaders, but I'd do i even without that incentive. I've been checking on them for so long that they feel like family to Gracie and me."

"Oh."

And since the work was outside, Clint wouldn't need to mingle with Josie much. He'd show up, get it done and leave. Maybe a couple men from their congregation could help. Then Frank's house would be in good shape And the service would give Clint a warm feeling inside

Josie blinked her dazzling blue eyes. "That's very kind of you. Actually, I've been wondering who to call to do the job. I can pay for the supplies if you're sure you have the time."

He nodded. "I'm sure. Give me a day to watch the evening news. We're supposed to get another storm to night. As soon as we have several warm days to melt off the snow, I'll come over and do the work."

"I hate for you to take a vacation day for this."

"It's no problem, really. As long as you don't mind watching Gracie for me while I'm occupied up on the roof."

"No, of course not. Gracie is welcome at our place anytime." Josie smiled so sweetly at his little girl that it made his throat ache.

"Yay! I love doing jigsaw puzzles with Grandpa Frank." Gracie clapped her gloved hands together.

"And I think we'd love to go with you to cut a Christmas tree, too," Josie said.

Gracie hopped up and down with excitement again. "We're gonna have so much fun."

Clint rested a hand on his daughter's shoulder, forcing a friendly smile to his lips. "Okay, it's a date. Uh, not a date, but, well, you know what I mean. I need time to fill up my gas tank, so we'll pick you up at your place in one hour."

He blinked, feeling tongue-tied and foolish. What was the matter with him? After all, Josie was just Frank's granddaughter.

She nodded, seeming not to notice his awkwardness. "Thanks for your generosity. I have no doubt Gramps will like this. He's been in a real huff ever since he found out he'll have to go to the library on Thursday nights. Truth be told, I think he's kind of scared about learning to read."

"That's normal, but he's got nothing to worry about. Reading is easy." Clint waved a gloved hand in the air. "We'll walk him through the basics, teach him the skills he needs, and have him reading simple sentences by Christmas, mark my words."

"So soon?"

"Sure. Most people learn to read when they're a child. It just takes a little time to learn and practice."

"Good. I want him to at least be able to read the instructions on his medicine bottles."

From what Clint had seen, Frank also needed balanced meals and someone to clean his house regularly. Once Josie returned to Las Vegas, Clint worried what might happen to Frank. Maybe not yet, but sooner or later he would need more intensive care. Clint took a deep breath, hoping Josie would do right by her grandpa and figure something out for the elderly gentleman.

"If we can just get Frank to try reading, he won't regret it. It's indescribable how it feels when you can suddenly read traffic signs and labels without help," Clint continued in an animated voice. "The whole world opens up. Most of us take our ability to read for granted."

"Is that how your wife felt?" Josie asked.

"Um, yeah, she did." He pursed his lips and nodded, but he didn't enlarge on the topic. He could see the questions in Josie's expressive eyes. She didn't understand. Neither did he, but he wasn't about to try and explain it. Reading had made a difference for Karen. For a short time. But it had never been enough.

He hadn't been enough.

As if sensing his reticence, Josie stepped back and waved. "I better get going. We'll see you in an hour."

"Bye." Gracie waved back as she skipped after her dad.

"Goodbye, sweetie," Josie returned.

Taking Gracie's hand, Clint led her down the aisle. As

he reached the corner, he glanced over his shoulder. Josie stood watching them, her dainty brows knitted together in a frown. Once again he got the impression she was troubled by something. But he wasn't about to ask what.

A solid roof and a live tree for Christmas should definitely lift Frank's spirits. And that made Clint happy, too. But until the attractive pharmacist left town, he decided not to volunteer for anything else.

Chapter Four

An hour and fifteen minutes later, Clint gripped the steering wheel, still convinced this was a bad idea. He never should have invited Josie and Frank on this tree-cutting excursion. Oh, Frank was just fine. No problem. But Josie was a different matter entirely. Mainly because of what she made him feel whenever she was around. An uneasy premonition he didn't understand.

He parked his truck in the Rushtons' driveway and got out. Frank came from the garage packing a skimpy hacksaw, a buoyant grin deepening the creases on his face. Josie walked beside him, wearing a pair of earmuffs and a black coat with a white fur collar. They framed her delicate face perfectly.

His gaze lowered to her canvas tennis shoes. Not very practical for slogging through snow. "I'm afraid those little shoes won't provide much protection for you up in the mountains."

She gave a tepid smile. "They're all I brought with me. Don't worry. I'll be okay."

She turned away and he let the subject drop.

Gracie scrambled out of the truck and ran to hug Frank.

"Hi, sweetheart." He kissed her forehead.

"What's that for, Frank?" Clint pointed at the saw. Anything to jerk his focus away from Josie.

"Cutting trees, of course," he said.

Clint leaned against the right front fender of his truck and forced himself not to feast his eyes on Josie. Yes, he was physically attracted to her. He was a man, after all. But he knew his fascination with her was so much more. Whenever she was near, he felt a haunting familiarity. As though he knew her from some long-lost memory. A connecting of their souls. Irrefutable, and yet he couldn't quite put his finger on why or how. Something about her touched him deep inside and he felt drawn to her in a strangely powerful way. Her clean, bouncing hair, her expressive blue eyes filled with intelligence and...

Barriers.

No doubt about it. He didn't like this attraction he felt. Yet he couldn't seem to help it. After Karen's death, he'd made a promise to himself and his infant daughter that he'd never expose either of them to that kind of hurt again. Losing Karen was a heartbreak he just couldn't let go of. And so there'd be no other woman in his life. No more romance for him.

No more heartbreak.

He gave a nervous chuckle, thinking Frank's hacksaw wouldn't be of much use, except for removing slender branches from the trees. "You mean to tell me you used that wimpy saw to cut down all those trees you had here at your place?"

Frank tossed him a teasing frown as he spoke in a conspiratorial whisper. "No, I used my chain saw for that, but I ain't about to give you any more evidence to use against me, Ranger."

Clint laughed, noticing their exchange brought a wry smile to Josie's lips. It was good they could now find humor in the tree permit violation. But that didn't ease his discomfort around her. Not one bit.

They piled into his truck and set off. The ride up to Crawford Mountain took fewer than forty minutes. The girls sat in the back, with Josie behind Clint. He focused on the road, trying not to look at her in the rearview mirror. When the black asphalt gave way to gravel and then muddy ruts, he shifted his truck into four-wheel drive and slowed down to negotiate the windblown drifts of snow.

Frank had a satisfied smile on his weathered face. He seemed relaxed. Content to be here. And Clint wished he felt the same.

He tried to tell himself he was just self-conscious because of the tree violation and asking Frank to learn to read. But he knew this jittery feeling went deeper than that, and he wished he could shake it off.

He didn't have to insist they all wear their seat belts. They each strapped in, their heads bobbing gently as the vehicle bounced over deep potholes in the washboard road. Come spring, he'd send a Forest Service crew up here to even out the potholes.

The blast from the heater filled the cab with warmth and Clint switched it down a notch. The recent storms had blanketed the mountains in white. Though it was almost two in the afternoon, ice crystals clung to barren tree branches. Tall spruce and fir trees pierced the cerulean sky like elegant dancers. The river paralleling the road showed rocks and a shore that glistened like diamonds. He glanced at the crystal clear stream filled with frigid water. A beautiful winter scene. No prettier place on earth. Clint loved it here.

"Brrr, I'd hate to swim in that river." Looking out the window, Gracie gave a little shiver.

"I would, too," Josie agreed.

"But it's sure beautiful up here," Clint said.

Frank burst into a quick song, his bass voice vibrating through the air. It was a poignant verse about a young man stranded up on a mountain during a fierce winter storm. All the fellow wanted was to return to town and see his sweetheart one last time before he died. Instead, he froze to death and his shrieks of grief could still be heard on the mountain as the howling wind.

"You have a beautiful voice, Frank," Clint said when he'd finished the chorus. He'd always enjoyed Frank's singing in the church choir.

"But I don't like that song. It's so sad." Gracie's nose crinkled with repugnance.

"You're right. The young man forgot the most important thing while he was trapped up on the mountain alone," Frank said.

Clint felt both Gracie and Josie lean forward, eager to hear more.

"And what's that?" Josie asked.

"He forgot to pray."

She released a breath of cynicism and sat back. In his rearview mirror, Clint saw her tight expression. Hmm. She must not believe in the power of prayer. Her disbelief fitted his preconceived notions of her. A woman of the world, focused on her job and getting ahead. And certainly not what he would ever consider wife and mommy material for him and Gracie. But if what Frank had told him about her life was true, Clint figured she had a right to be cynical.

Gracie rested her miniature hands on the back of Frank's seat. "You think God would have helped the man down off the mountain if he'd prayed?"

"I do," Frank said.

Gracie touched Clint's shoulder. "But, Daddy, why wouldn't God help him off the mountain without him praying first?"

From Josie's skeptical expression, Clint could tell she wondered the same thing. Her doubt caused an overwhelming conviction to rise within his chest. In spite of how Karen had died, he felt God's presence in his life every day. The Lord had sustained him through a very dark time. Though he had his own failings, Clint couldn't help wanting to share his belief with others.

"He would have, if it had met His plan," he answered. "But I think our Heavenly Father is just like regular parents. Sometimes, He waits for us to ask for His help."

Gracie angled her head closer, resting her cheek against the shoulder of Frank's red flannel coat. "What do you mean, Daddy?"

Clint was aware of Josie waiting for his response with rapt attention. Her eyes deepened to a cobalt-blue and flashed with doubt.

"I sometimes stand back and let you figure things out on your own, right?" he said.

"Yes, sometimes. But you help me all the time, too."

"That's right. But I don't want to interfere if you don't want me to. I try to stand back and let you learn some things on your own, including how to ask for my help. And when you ask, I step right in, because I love you so much. Well, I think God sometimes does the same thing for us. He wants us to live by faith, so He stands back and waits for us to call on Him for help. We don't always know His plan for each of us, but I do know when we call on Him in prayer, He answers us. Maybe not the way we want, and maybe not on our timetable, but He does answer. Every time. It's our job to exhibit faith."

Speaking the words aloud brought Clint a modicum of peace. And it renewed his conviction that God loved him and Gracie. Clint knew the Lord wanted nothing but the best for them. And it also reminded him that he must not forget to call on God in prayer. To never give up hope.

Gracie sat back, thinking this over. "But your parents are dead. Who helps you, Daddy?"

"The Lord does. With God, I'm never alone." Clint peered in the rearview mirror at his daughter's puzzled expression.

He also noticed Josie, who stared out the window, seeming absorbed in thought. He wished she'd say something. Because he didn't know her well, he didn't want to push. At least not yet. Karen had been silent and deadly, keeping her feelings bottled up inside until they'd boiled over in tearful rage. Frank had never mentioned if Josie had a temper, and Clint sensed that wasn't her way.

Now, he was concerned. Gone was her cheerful smile; her forehead was creased with distrust. For some reason, Clint didn't like seeing this woman unhappy. And he hoped he hadn't said anything to drive her further away from God. He still had the impression that something was bothering her. Something big. But it wasn't his business to question her. He couldn't interfere. Not unless she asked him to.

Just like the Lord.

After finding a place to turn his truck around, Clint

parked in the middle of the deserted road. He doubted anyone else would come along and need to get by them while they were up on the mountain. If they did, he'd move his truck.

He killed the engine, then opened his door and got out. "Okay, ladies, you get the chore of choosing the trees. Make sure it's what you want before we start to cut, though. I only have three permits."

Frank gave an exaggerated cough, as though he was swallowing a heavy chortle. "No, we don't want any more extra trees to explain to the forest ranger."

Josie's chuckle sounded from behind him and Clint didn't even try to hide his smile. Yes, it was definitely good they could laugh about the situation now, and he liked that Josie had a sense of humor.

The foot-deep snow crunched beneath his boots as he stepped back to let the girls out. Josie climbed down first, tugging on her gloves, her breath puffing on the air each time she exhaled.

Clint looked at her tennis shoes and shook his head. He made a mental note not to let her stay out in the snow too long. Her feet would soon become wet and then she'd get cold.

If necessary, he had several pairs of dry socks in his fire pack in the back of his truck. Serving others came naturally to Clint and he couldn't help feeling responsible for Josie and Frank. It felt surprisingly good to have someone besides Gracie needing his attention. No matter what, Clint would ensure everyone here was taken care of while on this trip.

Sunlight sparkled off Josie's dark blond curls. The color of her eyes deepened to a sapphire-blue as she looked about. Twin circles of pink stained her pale cheeks. With the snow-covered trees as a stunning back-drop, she looked absolutely gorgeous.

Realizing he was staring, Clint looked away, so fast that he almost lost his balance in the snow. Clearing his throat, he clutched the handle of his chain saw tightly and wondered what was wrong with him. Josie was just Frank's granddaughter. Within a few weeks, she'd return to Las Vegas. Besides, he and Gracie had been on their own for years, and he liked it that way.

So why did he suddenly wish for more?

"I'm with Grandpa Frank." Gracie clasped the old man's hand.

"All right. Let's find the prettiest tree," Frank said.

Clint glanced at Josie. "I guess that means you're with me?"

A question, not a statement.

"Um, okay." She gave a noncommittal shrug.

He headed off, plowing through the snow with his boots to make a wide path for Josie to follow. Glancing over his shoulder, he saw her lift her knees high as she navigated the trail in her shoes. As they tromped through the drifts, she didn't utter a single complaint. Karen had grumbled about so many things. Now Josie's silence won a notch of respect from Clint.

"That one!" Gracie's shrill voice filled the air as she ran toward a bushy spruce standing along the roadside.

Frank followed, slogging through the snow in his black, knee-high boots. He brushed crusted ice off the tree's pointed top and held up the hand saw. "You sure?"

"No, this one. Oh, it's perfect." Gracie raced farther into the forest and stood beside another tree. "Or what about that one? It's so pretty."

"You can only have one," Frank called, as she darted from tree to tree.

Clint smiled, thinking perhaps it'd been a blessing that he was stuck with Josie. But poor Frank wasn't a young man anymore. It'd be easy for Gracie to run him ragged. "You're gonna have to choose one tree, so make up your mind before Grandpa Frank starts to cut."

"Okay," Gracie chimed.

"I like this one." Josie waved to Clint.

He whirled around as she pointed at a small fir with thick clusters of dark green needles.

"That's a good choice. Firs retain their needles longer and have a nice scent." He took a step, then heard Gracie call again.

"What about this one, Grandpa Frank?"

Frank lumbered after the girl, grumbling something about women never being able to make up their minds.

The child bopped hither and yon to inspect what seemed to be every tree on the hillside. Frank finally stood still, letting her have her fun, while waiting for her to decide.

"Gracie, settle on one tree and stay where I can see you," Clint called when she wandered too far off.

"She's a female, son. She'll never settle for just one tree. You should know that by now. But I've got a way to distract her." Shaking his head, Frank laughed and hurried after her. When he came near, he tossed the hacksaw aside and fell backward into the soft snow.

"Gramps!" Josie cried.

A burst of panic blasted Josie's chest. Gramps had fallen. He might be ill. He had a bad heart and she feared he'd left his medication at home. A nauseating lump settled in her stomach.

Paying no heed to the knee-deep snow, she lurched forward, and would have run to her grandfather if Clint hadn't held out a hand to stop her.

"He's okay. Trust me. Just watch a minute."

At that moment, Gracie pounced on Gramps. He caught the child and rolled, tickling her and laughing. Gracie shrieked, her voice rising through the treetops.

Josie relaxed her stiff shoulders, her heart still thumping madly. She glanced at Clint. "How did you know he was okay?"

Clint shrugged. "It's a game they've played before."

Understanding filled her mind. Memories washed over her as she listened to her grandfather's deep chuckles. When she'd been young, he'd played with her in much the same way. Making her feel loved and wanted. Helping her forget her sad childhood back at home.

"I guess I've missed a lot of fun times with my grandparents over the past few years. I've been too busy with work." Though she didn't want Gramps to get overly tired on this excursion, she was glad to see him having fun.

"You're making up for it now." Clint's words sounded a bit reluctant.

She turned, her gaze resting on him as he lifted his chain saw from its case. He used an Allen wrench to move the bar out and tighten up the chain. With a knit cap pulled low across his ears and his blunt chin sporting a hint of stubble, he looked completely masculine and content to be up on this mountain cutting trees.

"Better late than never, huh?" she asked.

"It's never too late with family." He spoke without looking up.

His words brought her a bit of comfort. And standing there in the forest, her feet cold in the snow, Josie realized her family meant everything to her now. Once Gramps was gone, she'd have no one left. No husband or children to call her own. And maybe that was for the best. Remembering her parent's ugly divorce, she decided being alone was preferable to being miserable in a bad marriage. Wasn't it?

She contemplated Gramps as he pushed himself up, brushed the snow off his blue coveralls, then followed Gracie over to inspect another tree.

"I worry about him." Josie spoke absentmindedly.

Clint looked up from his task. "That's as it should be, but I think he's doing okay."

"I don't agree. Not after spending two solid days cleaning his grubby house. I want him to move to Las Vegas with me. If he will, I've scheduled him to move into an assisted-living center in mid-January."

Clint dropped the Allen wrench, his brow creased in a startled frown. The wrench disappeared into the snow and he plunged his hand down to retrieve it. "I doubt he'll like that. It won't fit. Not for a man like Frank."

Hearing her own fears voiced out loud did little for Josie's self-confidence. Maybe she'd said too much. Maybe she shouldn't confide in this man. But she couldn't help feeling drawn to his open kindness.

"Have you told Frank about your plans?" Clint asked.

She shook her head, her eyes meeting his. "Not yet. I haven't found the right time. I'm hoping to convince him it's for the best. Then I plan to start boxing up his things while I'm here."

"And what about his house? I understand it's been in your family a long time."

She lifted one shoulder. The thought of never returning to Gramps's home made her feel suddenly sad, as if she'd be losing an old friend. "Keeping the house isn't as important as Gramps. I thought we could either close it up, rent it out, or sell it. It depends on what he wants to do."

Clint didn't respond. From his glum expression, she felt his disapproval like a leaden weight. And she didn't like that. For some reason, this man's opinion mattered to her.

"Have you asked the Lord what you should do?"

She snorted, brushing her long bangs out of her eyes. "You mean pray?"

Clint nodded, looking serious. And something shifted inside her. She longed to believe he was right. That maybe God did care about her and Gramps, and that He would help them if she just asked. But wretched experience had taught her otherwise.

"No," she said.

"You don't believe in God?"

She lowered her head, not knowing what to believe. Too much sadness clouded her life. But somewhere deep inside, she wondered if it wasn't too late to start trusting in God again. "Let's just say the Lord and I kind of leave each other alone."

"I'm sorry to hear that."

She didn't like this topic. As far as she was concerned, winning God's approval was just setting her up for another failed relationship. All her life, she'd worked hard to do her best. Trying to prove herself over and over again. In spite of her efforts, it had never brought her the love she craved. God didn't care about her. Otherwise, why had He taken her parents away when she needed them the most? Why had Daryl and Edward broken off their engagements with her?

Why was she so unlovable?

"I don't have a lot of options, Clint. I want to do what's right for Gramps, but I won't do something he doesn't like."

"Oh, he'll have plenty to say about moving to Las Vegas, I can promise you that."

That's what she feared. "I can't just leave him here all alone."

The ranger nodded. "I understand. And I don't envy you this problem. It's tough to know what to do when a family member grows old. From listening to the evening news, I know we've got an epidemic of senior citizens in this nation, many with adult children who don't want to take care of them. I'm glad you're not one of those. But first, you should ask Frank what he wants."

"I will. Of course I will. But please don't say anything until I have a chance to discuss it with him."

"I won't," Clint promised. "But I doubt he'll want to leave Camlin. This is his home."

"I know, but I live and work in Vegas. My job there is a good one and I love it. I have to earn a living and there aren't many options for me here in Camlin. As Gramps gets older, who will mow his lawn, clean his house or make sure he eats right? I've heard horrible stories of elderly people falling in their homes and lying on the floor for days until someone finds them. I don't want that to happen to my grandpa."

Clint glanced at her, his eyes filled with compassion. "Hmm, it sounds as though you've put a lot of thought into this."

"I have, believe me. I've visited a number of assisted-living centers in Vegas and made arrangements for Gramps to live at the best one. I just need him to agree, and then I'll call to confirm my reservation." Again, she had no idea why she was telling the forest ranger all this. He was much too easy to talk to. So open and honest. In spite of everything that had happened over the past few days, she felt as though she'd known him all her life. A crazy idea if ever she'd had one.

"I'm impressed," he said.

She tilted her head. "Why?"

He jerked off his right glove before twining his long fingers around the Allen wrench to get a better grip. "In all honesty, I didn't figure you really cared. I thought your grandfather was just a nuisance you'd rather avoid."

She sucked back a startled breath. "No! I love Gramps very much. I always have. But he's also a grown man with his own life. I don't want to take away his independence. I want to help him."

Clint met her gaze. "Good. I'm glad to know I was wrong."

"He's my grandfather. Why would you think I don't care about him?"

The ranger averted his gaze, seeming embarrassed to be caught judging someone else without all the facts. "Let's just say you haven't come around here much."

"That's because I have a job. Getting time off work to drive ten hours one way isn't easy. I can't help Gramps if he stays here. But if he moves to Vegas, I can visit him often and ensure he's well cared for." She couldn't help bristling with defense, and felt the hackles rise on the back of her neck.

"You make a valid point. There aren't many decent

job options in a town like Camlin. I didn't mean any offense. So, what are you going to do?"

She lifted her gaze to where Gramps was engaged in a snowball fight with Gracie, just as he'd done with Josie when she'd been young. "I'm going to try and convince him to move to Vegas with me."

Clint nodded. "That might be for the best. Just tell him the truth. All things are possible with the Lord. And don't worry. It'll all work out."

His optimism did little to inspire trust in Josie. For so long, she'd depended on no one but herself. It felt good to confide in someone, even if it was this stranger.

She shifted her weight uneasily. "I hope you're right."

"I am, but don't wait too long. It's best to say the words and get them over with. Then the two of you can plan together what to do."

"This one and that's it," Gracie hollered from the other side of the clearing.

"You're sure? No changing your mind again," Gramps warned.

"I'm sure." The girl nodded, standing straight and stiff like a little soldier.

Their voices echoed through the air. Good thing this wasn't an avalanche area, or they'd be buried under a river of snow by now.

Clint looked up, a smile curving his full lips. He stood and jogged over to his daughter. "I'm afraid that tree is too big for our living room, but it might work in Frank's house."

Everyone turned to look at Josie, silently waiting for her opinion. She studied Gracie's tree with a critical eye.

"Yes, it's very nice. That would be fine for us. And what about this one for your home? Will it work for you?"

Josie pointed at the smaller tree Clint had been preparing to cut, its thick branches weighted by snow.

Clint crunched his way back to Gracie's tree and knocked a waterfall of white off the branches. "This tree is lovely. Nice and compact, with soft bristles. What do you think, short stuff?"

He glanced at his daughter and waited. The child smiled widely, sending an arrow of emotion straight to Josie's heart. She sensed that bringing her and Gramps on this outing had made a big difference for the little girl, and Josie wasn't certain why. She understood feelings of loneliness and suspected perhaps Gracie missed her mom as much as Josie missed her parents.

Gracie shrugged happily. "Okay by me."

Clint arched one brow. "You're sure? No changing your mind once I start to cut."

"I'm sure." She nodded several times.

Now that it was settled, Frank held the first tree while Clint started up the chain saw and sliced through the slim trunk. The drone of the engine filled Josie's ears and she moved away. Sawdust spewed into the air. As the first tree swayed, Clint glanced around to find his daughter, and Josie realized he was always conscious of Gracie's whereabouts. His attentiveness toward his child made Josie like him even more.

"She's over here." Josie pointed to where the girl was rolling a hard-packed snowball around on the ground.

"I'm making a snowman," Gracie announced.

The girl continued her chore, building the base of the body. "Come on, Josie. Make a snowman with me," she called.

At first, Josie stared at the child in stunned disbelief.

Make a snowman? At her age? Absurd. She was too old for such nonsense.

Or was she?

No! She was on holiday and determined to have fun. That's why she'd come home. To be with Gramps and celebrate. To satisfy her craving for family. She just wished she'd bought a pair of winter boots first.

Trudging through the snow, Josie decided to ignore her frozen toes and preconceived notions about propriety. Instead, she rolled the middle section. Once it was ready, Gracie struggled to help her lift the heavy weight onto the base. As they slapped extra snow into the crevices to smooth out the roundness, Josie couldn't help feeling an element of satisfaction. This was just what she needed. A fun outing with her grandfather to remind her that life wasn't all work and no play. That maybe she wasn't alone in this world, after all.

Although it didn't make sense, Josie felt better having voiced her concerns to Clint. For so long she'd carried her burdens alone. No one to talk to. No one to brainstorm with.

No one who cared.

Clint had encouraged her to tell Gramps the truth and get it over with. But that was easier said than done. She'd never thought of herself as a coward, but now she dreaded a possible confrontation that might alienate her grandfather. No matter what, she didn't want Gramps to think she didn't love him.

She just hoped Clint was right, and everything would turn out right.

Chapter Five

"**D**addy, look at the snowman Josie and I made."

Clint turned at his daughter's call and watched Josie lift the snowman's head into place. "Yes, sweetheart. It's great."

But his eyes were on Josie. She'd removed her earmuffs and adjusted her hair back off her cheeks. The afternoon sun glinted on her blond curls. She exhaled and sniffed as she worked, her nose and cheeks red from the cold. Her lilting laughter filtered over him and he couldn't help smiling. Realizing he was staring, he jerked his attention back to Frank.

"Our girls are happy today," the older man said.

Our girls. Those words did something to Clint. A sudden rush of warmth flooded his chest. He tried to swallow, but a lump of emotion jammed his throat.

When he'd invited the Rushtons on this excursion, he'd thought it would be good for Frank and Josie to get away from their cares for a while. He hadn't realized how much he and Gracie needed it, too. He'd always taken his daughter with him for activities like this. They had lots of fun and spent quality time together, but something was always missing. And Clint knew what it was.

A mom.

Shaking his head, he picked up the hacksaw and trimmed off the scraggly branches at the base of the first tree. He'd been over this dilemma a trillion times before and didn't want to think about it anymore. He'd failed Karen. He didn't want to fail another woman. He wouldn't put Gracie through that kind of trauma. It was that simple.

"Something's bothering her," Frank said.

Clint looked up, his gaze zoning in on Josie like a heat-seeking missile. He didn't want to get involved, especially since she had confided in him earlier. But maybe it was already too late. He couldn't help caring about Frank and, by default, his pretty granddaughter.

"Why don't you ask her about it?" he suggested.

"Maybe I will," Frank said.

Clint just hoped Josie remained calm about the issue. From past experience, he found most women to be high-strung, emotional creatures. He'd grown accustomed to nervous suspicion in Karen's eyes. When she was happy, life was grand. But it never lasted long. After Gracie was born, postpartum depression had set in. He'd tried his hardest to provide emotional support. To give Karen the love and encouragement she'd needed and craved. But the demands of his job had constantly taken him away. He couldn't stay home and earn a living at the same time. In spite of getting her medication and a qualified doctor's care, Clint had never been able to help Karen expel the demons of depression that shackled her mind.

It'd been seven long years since Karen's death. Not nearly long enough for Clint to recover from the guilt.

Gracie had been so young at the time. Barely five months old. So innocent and lovable. A little girl who needed her mom. After Karen's death, Clint had wanted to give up. To quit. But he couldn't. He had Gracie to think about. He'd lived for her, determined to keep her safe and to raise her with all the love he could shower upon her.

Life hadn't been easy, moving on without Karen. Finding quality child care for his precious daughter. Meeting Gracie's needs while keeping his employer satisfied. But the Lord had buoyed Clint up. Through the power of prayer, he'd found the strength to carry on. To keep moving forward even when he floundered in the depths of despair. Gracie was always his first priority.

Now, Josie Rushton had entered his life like a blast of fresh summer air after a long, chilling winter. At first, he'd thought her career came first. But seeing how she acted with Frank and Gracie, he wasn't so sure. Discovering she was gravely concerned for Frank's welfare challenged Clint's preconceived notions about the woman. He certainly never would have suspected she wanted Frank to move with her to Vegas.

Clint briefly entertained the thought of asking Josie out on a date, but decided no. With a child to raise, he didn't have the luxury of going out with just anyone. He must be careful. Above all else, he had to protect Gracie, and the last thing they needed in their lives right now was another high-maintenance woman with deep emotional issues. That's what Clint feared Josie might be.

A sharp crack sounded as the second tree started to fall. Frank gripped the trunk with his gloved hands and Clint jumped out of the way. The tree dropped, its branches shivering as it hit the ground. Frank's breath rushed in and out of his lungs like a laboring ventilator.

Glancing at the elderly man, Clint wondered if this physical activity was too much for him. "You okay?" he asked.

Frank grinned, as though having the time of his life. "I sure am. I'm with my family. What could be better than that?"

Clint's heart gave a powerful squeeze. He loved this old man, no doubt about it. But for them to become a real family, he'd have to marry Josie. And that wasn't going to happen. Not now. Not ever.

Wondering how Frank had cut so many trees on his own, Clint took the brunt of the tree's weight. Without discussion, he dragged the fallen fir over to his truck and hefted it into the back. Within twenty minutes, he had the second tree loaded and ready to go.

"Who wants hot chocolate?" he crowed in victory.

Gracie squealed with excitement and Clint reached inside the truck for the thermos and cups. While his daughter stuck two rock eyes onto the snowman's face, Josie jabbed sticks into the rounded body for arms. Clint whipped out the camera he kept stowed in the glove box.

"Smile," he called.

The two girls posed together, with Gracie standing on a fallen tree trunk. At that height she was able to stretch her arm up and hold two fingers over the top of Josie's head.

When she discovered what the little girl was up to, Josie tickled her. "Oh, I'm going to get you now."

Gracie shrieked and wriggled away. Clint snapped several more pictures of the two chasing each other through the snow. They finally came running toward him, gasping from their exertions. Clint laughed, for no other reason than because he felt happy inside. He handed Josie a cup of chocolate and a pair of thick socks from his fire pack.

She lifted the gray wool between two fingers and stared as though she held a dead rat. "What is this?"

"Socks. Don't worry. They're clean."

She crinkled her nose with disgust. "But what are they for?"

"Your cold feet. For the trip home." His lips twitched, but he forced himself not to laugh.

"Thanks." She smiled, the expression lighting up her face and making her eyes sparkle.

Wow, she was lovely.

"I believe I'm going to need them. I can't feel my toes anymore," she finally conceded.

"Yeah, I'd hate to have to amputate. Why don't you climb inside the truck and I'll get the heater going. We need to warm you up."

As she headed for the truck, she laughed, not seeming overly upset by the discomfort. Again he couldn't help contrasting her positive attitude with how Karen might have reacted. The difference was amazing.

When Josie bumped into Clint and gave a nervous apology, he felt the overwhelming urge to pull her into his arms and kiss her. Right there in the middle of the mountain, with Frank and Gracie watching.

What an odd notion. Just thinking about it made Clint's face heat up like a flamethrower. And he realized in all these long, lonely years, he hadn't found one single woman who'd made him feel like laughing again.

Until today.

"Thanks for the Christmas tree. This outing meant a great deal to Gramps." It meant a lot to Josie, too.

Standing outside in front of Gramps's house, she smiled up at Clint and folded her arms against the chilly wind. The cold air stung her nose. After Clint had deposited their Christmas tree inside, she'd walked him and Gracie out to their truck, wanting an opportunity to thank the ranger for his kindness.

"All things considered, you're not quite the bully I first thought you were," she confessed with a smile.

He quirked one brow high and tried not to laugh. "Is that right? Well, I'm glad to hear it. I think."

She squelched a chuckle, thinking it was very good, since she'd be forced to work with him over the next few weeks while Gramps learned to read.

"I'll return your socks as soon as I can wash them."

He jutted his chin toward her feet, which were covered by the pair of blue fuzzy slippers she'd slipped on the moment she got inside. "Keep in mind that they're wool. They won't do well in your clothes dryer."

She nodded. "So noted. Thanks again."

"You're welcome." Clint flashed that devastating smile of his as he buckled Gracie into her seat and closed the truck door.

A bank of clouds brooded overhead. By morning, they'd have more snow. Thick shadows swallowed Clint's tall frame as he circled around to the driver's side. He brushed against Josie's arm and she caught his spicy scent of pine and aftershave. She backed up a step, trying to remember the last time a man had given her goose bumps just by being near her.

Like never. Not even her two ex-fiancés.

No, she shouldn't think such thoughts. Her dedication to her career had come with a price. But now, she couldn't help thinking that work wasn't what had destroyed her past relationships with her dad, mom and former fiancés. And God, too. Josie was difficult to love. She accepted that. But it didn't stop her from wanting it.

"You sure you can't stay for supper?" she asked. "It's the least I can offer after you helped us get our tree. I've got a beef stew simmering in the Crock-Pot and there's plenty for everyone."

Inside the truck, Gracie's eyes widened with enthusiasm and she bobbed her head up and down.

"Nah, we've got to get going," Clint said. "I took the afternoon off work to go get the trees, but now duty calls."

His generosity touched Josie's heart and she could no longer begrudge the illiteracy issue with Gramps. She realized Clint had nothing but Frank's best interests at heart. Rather than turning his back on the old man, Clint had shown an increase of love. He'd gone out of his way to help them get a Christmas tree. And he'd lent her a pair of warm socks. Such a simple act of kindness, but it meant the world to Josie. She couldn't think of the ranger as an enemy. Not anymore. But that didn't mean they were more than friends. And in a small way she regretted that.

Okay, in a big way. But she'd never admit it out loud.

Waving goodbye, she returned to the warmth of the house. Gramps helped her set the table, and laughed as they discussed their day.

"You should have seen your face when Gracie chose yet another tree," he said.

"Yeah, that little girl is something special."

So was Gracie's father, but Josie didn't say that.

"I'll have to dig out the ornaments so we can trim our tree," he said.

"I'll do it, Gramps. Where did Grandma store the decorations?"

"Up in the attic. But let's not tackle it tonight. I'm bushed." He yawned and stretched before sitting down at the table.

As she dished up the stew, Josie felt the same. Running around in the snow all afternoon had worn both of them out. In spite of the fuzzy slippers she now wore, she wondered if her feet would ever get warm again. Maybe after dinner she'd dash down to the general store before it closed. With another storm on its way, she would need boots tomorrow morning. "Our tree isn't going anywhere. I need to call and check in with my work, anyway. We can string lights and decorate the tree over the next few days."

If only she could forget the kind, enigmatic forest ranger who had just left Gramps's house, Josie might feel more at peace. She tried to tell herself she wasn't relationship material. After the cruel words Edward had said to her when he'd broken off their engagement, she had no desire to become romantically involved with another man ever again. Especially a widowed father with a little daughter to raise.

Okay, that wasn't true, either. But Josie figured if she kept telling herself that, she might actually start believing it. Eventually. After all, it'd do no good to hope for things that could never be. And yet she couldn't help feeling as if maybe, just maybe, she deserved one more chance at happiness.

Chapter Six

Clint tossed another load of laundry into the washing machine. He added a scoop of detergent, the fabric softener, then closed the lid. Stifling a yawn, he slid the milk jug back into the refrigerator and placed the dirty dishes in the sink. Turkey and cheese sandwiches with a bowl of chicken noodle soup. From a can. He'd included sliced apples and carrot sticks, to provide Gracie with additional nutrition. Nothing special like the tantalizing stew Josie had offered. Maybe he should have accepted and fed Gracie before they came home.

Then again, maybe not.

Poking his head into Gracie's room, he found it dark, except for a reading lamp on the nightstand by her bed. Dolls and stuffed animals crowded the top of her dresser. Books and games lined two shelves. He loved each and every drawing and finger painting she had plastered on her walls.

Gracie sat on the floor in her warm pajamas, holding a blue ceramic dish and a picture of her mother in her lap. He'd taken the picture of Karen the day they'd found out they were expecting Gracie. He'd been so filled with joy, but Karen had seemed reluctant. At the time, he'd written it off as nervousness over becoming a new mother. He hadn't fully realized yet that her problem went much deeper. That she actually feared she would ruin their baby's life simply because she was her mom.

"That's nice." He pointed at the blue dish with white speckles.

Gracie had made it last year in school. A Mother's Day gift for a mom she didn't have. Her teacher had told her to give it to her dad instead. Gracie had kept it, insisting she'd one day give it to her new mom, if she ever got one.

"You about ready for bed, pumpkin?" He stepped inside and picked up a few toys she'd missed when he'd sent her to clean up her room.

"Yep, I've even brushed my teeth." She gritted her teeth to show him her rows of pearly whites, and stuck her tongue into the gap where her front tooth was missing.

He laughed. "Good job."

She stood and placed the picture aside, skimming her fingertips over the glass pane, as though she were caressing her mother's face.

Clint had given her the picture two years ago, when she'd first started asking questions about Karen. He didn't want her to forget her mother or ever believe she wasn't loved.

From what Frank had told him, Josie had grown up believing she was an unwanted burden. Clint could understand how that might make her a bit antisocial. In spite of her emotional problems, Karen had loved Gracie very much. It was herself that Karen hated. She'd never believed Clint had loved her, either. And that tore him up inside. How he wished Karen could have seen herself the way he saw her.

The way God saw her.

"I miss Mommy," Gracie said.

"I know. Me, too."

"Someday I'm gonna give this to my new mom." She set the dish beside the picture.

Clint didn't say a word, his heart twisting into tight knots that made breathing difficult.

Gracie knelt beside the bed. He forced a smile and joined her there, pulling her close as they folded their arms and closed their eyes. Evening prayers were such an integral part of their nighttime routine that Gracie didn't even ask anymore. She just knelt down and began.

"Heavenly Father, thanks for the wonderful day we had and our beautiful Christmas tree. And thanks for letting Grandpa Frank and Josie come along with us. Bless Mommy and Daddy and me and help us to always be brave. And help Daddy to find us a new mommy, because we're lonely. In the name of Jesus Christ, amen."

"Amen." Clint opened his damp eyes.

He loved Gracie so much and she never ceased to amaze him with her honesty and compassion. But how could he tell her that there would never be another mom for her?

Gracie scrambled onto the bed and burrowed beneath the blankets. Clint sat beside her on the mattress. He snuggled the covers up around her shoulders, tucking her in.

"What was Mommy like?" she asked.

He knew the drill. Almost on a daily basis, his daughter asked the same question. But he didn't mind. He knew this was the only real connection Gracie had with her mother. Talking about Karen helped the girl feel closer to her mom. Helped keep her real and alive.

"Well, she was smart and pretty, like you. And she liked to ride horses."

Gracie's brows pinched together. "White horses?"

"Yes, and purple and green horses, too." He leaned forward until their noses touched.

"There's no green horses, Daddy."

He tickled her ribs and she squealed.

"How do you know?" he asked, laughing deeply.

She pursed her rosebud lips. "Everyone knows that, except you."

"Yeah, I guess you're right. But she loved the solitude of riding."

His daughter's eyes crinkled. "What's solitude?"

"Quiet. Privacy. Being by herself."

Karen had liked being alone too much, but Clint didn't tell Gracie that. Thankfully, his little girl had a special way of relating to other people, and wasn't at all like her mom in that regard. She was what her teacher at school called a "social butterfly." Clint didn't want to change that, apart from perhaps encouraging her not to chat quite so much during class time. Most people loved her and he wanted her to feel wanted and accepted.

"I like Josie," she said out of the blue.

He nodded, not surprised.

"Don't you like Josie?" she pressed.

"Yes, I like her just fine." But he couldn't help wondering where this was leading.

"When you go over to Grandpa Frank's house to fix his roof, Josie said she's gonna let me help her make Grandma Vi's chocolate chip cookies. And maybe some peanut brittle or pumpkin bread."

"Hmm. That should be lots of fun. And tasty, too." He appreciated Josie's generosity toward his daughter. Gracie loved everything domestic, baking included. Anything that might be interpreted as motherly. And once again he thought he might have misjudged Josie.

"I wish Josie could be my new mom. And I wish Grandpa Frank could be my real grandpa. Then we'd be a real family again. That would make Christmas so much more fun."

Oh, boy! This conversation was definitely taking Clint out of his comfort zone. Fast.

"I don't think that's gonna happen, pumpkin," he said.

"Why not?" Her unblinking eyes met his.

"For one thing, Josie lives in Las Vegas. She has her life there and we have ours here."

"Why can't we have our lives together?"

He raked his fingers through his hair, wishing his daughter wasn't quite so precocious. "It's not that simple. Josie's worked hard for her job there and I've worked hard for my job here. I know you and I both miss Mom, but we're doing okay on our own, aren't we?"

Gracie nodded and blinked her brown eyes, so much like her mother's. For a long time, he'd feared she might have also inherited Karen's depressive mood swings, but Gracie always seemed so happy and even-keeled. In retrospect, he realized why he'd fallen in love with Karen. She'd been so sad and vulnerable, and he'd wanted to protect her the way his dad had protected him and his mom. Always there. Always supportive and loving.

But Clint had failed miserably.

"We're doing okay, but we could be a lot better," Gracie said.

From the mouths of babes.

"I'm gonna ask Santa to make Josie my new mom," Gracie announced. "Then we can all be happier together."

Happier? He hadn't thought about it much. He worked and served each day, meeting his responsibilities. Trying to be the best father and forest ranger he possibly could. He loved his work, he loved his child and he loved God. That was all he needed in his life. But was he happy? Clint didn't know anymore. He sure didn't laugh much. Until today.

He arched one brow. "I'm not sure that's a good idea. You know Josie is just a friend, right?"

"But I want her to be more than just a friend. I want her to be my mom. You should ask her out, Daddy. On a real date. And buy her flowers and say mushy stuff to her."

Oh, yeah. This mommy discussion had gotten way out of control. But it sliced his heart to know his daughter had thought this deeply about the topic.

He sat back and took a long, settling breath. He wasn't about to lead his daughter on. With her usual candor, she might say something embarrassing to Josie. Better to nip this in the bud right now. "No, sweetheart. No dates. No flowers or mushy stuff. Frank and Josie are just friends we visit once in a while. Besides, Josie is just here for a short visit. She can't stay."

Gracie shrugged her slender shoulders and the carefully tucked in blankets drooped. "So ask her to stay."

Clint stared. Children saw things so simply. Their innocent minds couldn't always grasp the complications that adults packed into their lives. Either you were happy or sad. Hungry or full. Everything was black-and-white, with no gray areas. But Clint didn't have the luxury of seeing things that way. Not anymore.

"I'm not going to do that. Now, go to sleep," he said.

He stood and stepped over to the door, flipping off the light before she could comment any further.

As he walked out of the room, he heard her huff of impatience. Then her whispered voice filled the air like a shout. "I'm still gonna ask Santa to give us Josie and Grandpa Frank for Christmas. I've been good this year and we can make them happy, too."

Clint ignored that and headed down the hallway toward the living room. Brushing aside Gracie's coloring books, he plopped down on the sofa and switched on the evening news. He turned the volume down low, so it wouldn't disturb her. With any luck, she'd fall asleep soon.

He should go to bed, but Gracie's words troubled his mind. Why had she set her sights on Josie for a mom? They barely knew the woman. But that didn't seem to matter. He was attracted to Josie. Chemistry, Viola had called it. When a man and woman were drawn to one another for no obvious reason. A mating of their spirits.

But Josie didn't seem his type. No, not at all. She was too confident, educated, and set in her ways. Too determined in her goals. And he realized these were also just a few of the reasons he found her so attractive.

Laying his head back, Clint decided not to think about it anymore. He'd had his chance at happily ever after. Now, he had Gracie to raise. That was enough. It must be enough.

And yet it wasn't. No matter how hard he wished it was.

The next morning, Josie stood in the kitchen wearing her bathrobe and blue fuzzy slippers. Gazing out the window, she stared in awe at the stunning winter wonderland before her.

Ice crystals had gathered around the edges of the single-pane glass, forming intricate shapes. Six inches of new snow had fallen in the night, blanketing the world in white. As she stared at the hoarfrost clinging to the cherry tree in the yard, a reverent feeling settled over her. And for several moments, she found herself almost believing that God had created this beautiful world she lived in. That He wasn't a remote, uncaring God. That He loved all His children.

Including her.

The scraping sound of a snow shovel brought her back to reality. The neighbors must be out early this morning.

Reaching for a pan, she set it on the stove, then turned toward the fridge. She'd make Gramps his breakfast, then get dressed and venture out into the cold to clear their driveway and sidewalks. Later on, she planned to make peanut brittle. She'd found Grandma's recipe last night. Making candy would give her something to do until she could gather up the courage to speak with Gramps about moving to Las Vegas.

A figure moved past the kitchen window and she lurched around. Looking out, she saw Clint wielding his shovel like a tractor as he cleared tidy furrows along their driveway. At the sight of him, Josie's pulse tripped into double time. Before she could consider why seeing this man caused her breath to quicken, she glanced over at the garage.

Gracie followed behind her dad, pushing a child-size red plastic shovel. Amusement mingled with surprise inside Josie's mind. Clint didn't need to shovel their walks. Josie could do it. In fact, she relished the exercise. This man didn't need to keep coming over here to serve them. She could take care of Gramps. But she was glad Clint was here.

Abandoning breakfast for the time being, Josie hurried to her room, jerked on her clothes and pulled a brush through her snarled hair before racing downstairs again. She tugged on her coat and gloves, stomped into the new snow boots she'd purchased last night just before the store had closed, and hurried outside.

Standing on the front porch, she reached for Gramps's snow shovel, squinting against the haze of sunlight streaming through the trees.

"Hi, there." Clint stood at the bottom of the steps, wearing a black knit cap, gloves and his warm winter coat.

She returned his smile. "Hello. What are you doing here?"

He gestured toward a pile of snow. "Shoveling."

Obviously. She felt rather stupid for asking. Then she remembered he was here on assignment from his church. And she couldn't help wishing he'd come to see her again.

She struck a pose and gestured downward, to draw attention to her feet. "Do you like them?"

"Hey! You got some boots," he said.

"Yeah, I thought it was time. So now you don't need to shovel our driveway. I can take care of it."

He shrugged one shoulder and continued with his chore. "Just being neighborly."

Yes, and pushing her senses into overdrive. Did he even realize how attractive she found him?

"Are you neighborly to Gramps all the time?" she asked as she gripped her own shovel and stepped down beside him.

"I guess so, but this is a force of habit. I've been shoveling Frank and Vi's snow for three years now. Ever since we moved to Camlin."

"Really? I didn't know that. Part of your church assignment, I suppose." She'd assumed Gramps had done the chore, and vaguely remembered Grandma mentioning a kind man from her congregation who frequently shoveled their walkways for them. Now Josie realized it had been Clint.

"Hi, Josie!" Gracie came running, bouncing through the drifts of snow like a kangaroo.

"Hey, pumpkin. Walk around the edges so you don't pack down the snow we have to shovel," Clint directed in a gentle voice.

The smiling girl hopped off the driveway. "Sorry, Daddy."

Gracie threw her arms around Josie in a tight hug. At first, Josie stood there in stunned confusion, her heart flying up into her throat. She'd never met a more affectionate child. So open and honest. And Josie didn't know what to make of it. She'd never been hugged like this before. At least, not by someone other than Grandma and Gramps. And she silently admitted she quite liked it.

Lowering her arms, Josie pulled Gracie in close. "Hi, sweetie. Thanks for shoveling our driveway."

Gracie drew back and tilted her head in an impish smile. "You're welcome. We like doing it. Daddy says service is how we show people we love them. And we love you and Grandpa Frank a lot. Don't we, Daddy?"

The child looked at her father and waited expectantly. His gaze darted toward Josie, then dropped to the ground. "Yeah, of course we do."

Josie gave the girl another squeeze. "Well, I love you, too."

"See, Daddy? I told you so." Gracie tossed her father a victorious smile.

"Gracie..." he said in a warning tone.

The girl looked away, a bit contrite.

What was going on? Josie stared from one to the other in confusion. She sensed she was missing something here, but didn't know what. She hadn't meant to say she loved them, but the words had slipped out. She definitely loved Gracie. It was hard not to. But Josie wasn't sure how she felt about Clint. He was just her grandfather's friend. Right?

"We're gonna shovel all your sidewalks, too," Gracie announced.

"That's nice. Thank you," Josie replied.

The girl returned to her task, dropping the blade of her shovel into the snow and plowing forward. She made little growling engine sounds in the back of her throat, like a snowplow.

Josie laughed. "Like father, like daughter. But I fear she's enjoying her work a bit too much. I've never seen a kid so happy to help out like this."

A chuckle rumbled in Clint's chest. "Yeah, she throws herself into everything she does. But this is good for her. I'm raising a daughter."

Josie blinked. What did raising a daughter have to do with shoveling snow? "I don't understand."

He stood up straight and took a deep inhalation before adjusting his knit cap over his ears. "When you're raising kids, you've got to teach them service. And you do that by example. I'm not good at taking casseroles to sick people, but I'm great at shoveling driveways."

"Ah, I see." And his explanation warmed Josie's heart. From what she'd observed, Clint was an excellent father, loving and generous. And realizing how often he provided service to others brought a twinge of guilt. She couldn't remember the last time she'd done something for someone else just because she could. Just because they needed her. More and more, she was learning a lot from this kind man, and liking everything about him. But she couldn't say the same for herself. Edward had told her she was bitter and unlovable. That no man would ever want her. And though she didn't want to believe it, and her logical mind told her it was a lie, there was also a part of Josie that feared it might be true.

"Gramps is lucky to have you for a neighbor," she said.

Again, Clint flashed that winning smile that caused a blaze of lightning to crack inside her chest.

"No, I'm lucky to have Frank. He's a good man and I'm glad to know him," he said.

His rejoinder touched a chord inside Josie. How lucky she was to have Gramps as her grandfather. She wondered if it was luck or a blessing from heaven. Though she had little use for God, she was starting to think maybe she was wrong to have abandoned Him so long ago.

"Speaking of which, I'll go pick up the supplies to fix Frank's roof later this afternoon. The weatherman says the temperature is going to warm up now. I should be able to do the repairs within the next few days," Clint said.

"But I don't know what supplies we'll need."

He waved a hand in the air. "Don't worry. My dad was a good handyman who taught me a lot. I know what to do, and have it covered."

His confidence and generosity inspired trust in her.

Something she hadn't felt toward a man other than Gramps for a very long time.

"All right, but I'm paying for it," she insisted.

His lips twisted in a half smile. "Okay, lady. I won't argue with that."

Now that it was settled, he bowed his back and continued his work. Josie joined him, moving to the other side of the driveway so they didn't bump into one another.

Dipping her shovel into the fluffy white stuff, she lifted and tossed, ignoring the sting as wisps of wind blew the powdery duff into her face. "Wow, it's heavy."

He breathed deeply, speaking while he worked. "Yeah, a nice wet snow that should leave a good pack up in the mountains for our summer water supply. But it'll also create lots of greenery in the spring, to dry out by midsummer. That'll create a wildfire hazard, but we take the good with the bad."

She laughed at his analytical answer. "Do you ever stop being a forest ranger?"

He hesitated, looked up and flashed that devastating smile she'd come to enjoy. "Nope, I guess not. That's habit, too. I have to think about things like that in order to do my job."

And from what she'd observed, he was very good at everything he did. Dedicated, kind and hardworking. The kind of man she'd once dreamed of having for her very own.

Bending over, she pushed her shovel past an edge of broken cement and tossed the scoop of snow aside. "I don't know how you have time to raise Gracie, work your job and come over here to clear our snow and fix our roof."

"It's no trouble. I live just two doors down."

She jerked upright, looking to where he pointed at a white frame house with blue shutters at the end of the street. The sidewalks and driveway there had already been shoveled. Not surprising. She was fast learning this man was highly conscientious. A fastidious caregiver who never shirked his duty.

"I didn't know you lived so close by."

Of course, she'd never asked. After all, she wasn't interested in him or any man. Not when she had her own busy career and Gramps to focus on.

Yeah, and pigs could fly.

"It's handy for stopping by to check on Frank now and then," Clint said.

"And do you stop by often?" she asked.

"Probably a couple times each week."

She blinked in surprise, now understanding why he was so attached to her grandparents. But he wasn't coming around because she was here. This was his normal routine. An assignment from church. Yet she kind of wished he was interested in her, too.

They worked in silence for several minutes. Gramps soon came outside and waved to Gracie.

"While your dad and Josie work out here, why don't you come inside and help me fix breakfast, sweetheart?" he called.

The girl came running. The moment she disappeared inside, Clint glanced at Josie. "Have you told him yet?"

She whirled around, knowing he was referring to the move to Las Vegas. "Not yet, but I plan to sit down with him later today."

"Good. It's time." With a nod, he returned to his work.

Minutes later they finished their chore, leaned their shovels against the house and went inside. The air smelled of savory bacon. Gramps had eggs and pancakes warming on the stove. Gracie had just finished setting the table. Having Clint and his daughter here felt so normal.

Before she could blink, Josie found herself seated and listening to everyone's happy chatter as they ate breakfast together. They laughed at Gracie's nonstop banter and the pancakes Gramps had formed into animal shapes, complete with chocolate chips for eyes and broken candy cane pieces for the mouths.

Looking at the rounded circles of batter that made up the face and two ears, Clint chuckled. "Is this a mouse or a bear?"

"It's a mouse, of course." Gramps tucked his chin in, pretending to be offended.

"I love mine, Grandpa Frank." Gracie rewarded the elderly man with a hug and quick kiss on his cheek.

Josie smiled and bit into a crisp piece of bacon. She absorbed Clint's deep laughter like the desert sand absorbed rays of sunlight. A warm, giddy feeling settled over her. She couldn't remember the last time she'd sat down and eaten a meal with people she cared about. Like a real family. But then a tremor of warning made her shiver. Clint and Gracie weren't her family. Not at all. And this would end soon. She mustn't get too attached to the ranger and his sweet little daughter. No matter how much she wished she could.

Chapter Seven

Maybe Clint should have shoveled the sidewalks for Frank an hour earlier, before Josie was awake. Or not have come over at all. But he had seen the six inches of white new powder they'd received in the night, a wet, heavy snow that required lots of bending and lifting. And he couldn't help worrying about Frank and Josie. After all, Clint was stronger than either of them and he didn't want Frank out there shoveling at his age.

Having finished breakfast, Clint stepped outside on the back porch. His booted foot bumped a box of colored Christmas lights sitting by the screen door. The day they'd driven up on the mountain to cut their Christmas trees, he'd noticed Josie had some lights in her shopping cart. No doubt she was planning to hang them on Frank's house, but hadn't found the time yet. From what he'd seen, she'd had her hands full cleaning up the place. He had to give her credit. She'd done it. Everything looked as tidy as when Viola had been alive.

Again, Clint was impressed by Josie's thoughtfulness. But when he pictured her clinging to a ladder, trying to staple lights to Frank's eaves, he got a bad feeling inside.

What if she fell and hurt herself? What if she wasn't strong enough to make the staple gun work?

The thought of her injuring her delicate hands made him cringe. And right then, against his better judgment, he decided he'd better take care of the chore for her. It wouldn't take long. Gracie was occupied inside with Frank. Clint could get it done within an hour or so. The happy smile on Frank's face would make it all worthwhile. And secretly, Clint wouldn't mind seeing a bright smile on Josie's pretty face, either.

Without asking permission, he took the ladder and staple gun from Frank's garage and went to work. Minutes later, he was well into the job when the snap of the staples penetrating the wood siding brought Josie outside.

"What are you doing?" Standing on the sidewalk, she gazed up at him as she wiped her damp hands on a yellow dish towel.

"Putting up your lights." He forced himself not to look at her. Not to think she was attractive. Not to admire anything about her.

"I was going to do that tomorrow," she said.

"Now you won't have to. I'll have it finished within the hour."

"You've done enough already. Really. Stop and come inside."

"I'll be done soon." He kept working. Trying to tell himself he should quit and go home. But he felt compelled to be here. As though his future happiness depended on his service to this family.

"You're putting me further in debt. How will I ever repay you?" she asked.

Glancing over his shoulder, he grinned. "How about

giving me and Gracie some of that peanut brittle you're planning to make?"

She smiled back, looking completely feminine in her frilly apron and blue, fuzzy slippers. "I think that can be arranged. Especially since Gracie's inside helping me make it right now. But I have a feeling I'll owe you so much more than just a tin of homemade peanut brittle."

He shrugged as he threaded the lights along the living room window frame, and punctuated his words with blasts from the staple gun. "I also like divinity and pumpkin bread."

He shouldn't encourage her, but he loved homemade goodies. In fact, now that Vi was gone, he and Gracie rarely got such treats. He certainly didn't know how to make them. His cooking abilities were limited to mac and cheese, hot dogs, scrambled eggs and cold cereal.

Josie laughed, the sound high and sweet. "I think some pumpkin bread can be arranged, but I'm awful at making divinity. No matter how long I cook it, I can never get it to set up. It always tastes delicious, but you have to eat it with a spoon."

He chuckled. "Okay, definitely no divinity."

She folded her arms against the cold air. "You holler if you need help. I'll hear you through the window."

He nodded, but he wouldn't call. As she went inside, he felt a strange sense of elation, as if this was right where he belonged. But that didn't keep his old friend guilt from chewing at his mind. Clint told himself he was doing these service projects to help Frank and nothing more. Yet he couldn't help looking forward to seeing Josie again.

His jaw tightened. He was crazy to think such thoughts. He couldn't understand what had gotten into him. Then again, he knew exactly what the problem was.

He'd met a beautiful woman. The first he'd been attracted to in seven long, lonely years. And he wanted to pursue her. To ask her out. But he wouldn't. He couldn't take the chance of ruining her or Gracie's lives.

He shook his head. His wayward thoughts were an illusion that would only backfire on him down the road. Christmas brought the healing power of peace. It was a special time that promised joy throughout the year. But Clint knew better. It wasn't real or lasting for him. No matter how much he liked being near Josie, he could never be with her. Once the holiday ended, they'd each return to their normal lives. They'd pack up their Christmas ornaments and put them away, and Josie would go home. And Clint and Gracie would be alone once more.

Something was wrong. The moment Josie stepped inside the kitchen, she could feel an edge of tension buzzing through the air.

Gramps stood in front of a cupboard, the doors open. He held several cans of soup in his hands. More cans lay haphazardly on the green linoleum, as though they'd been knocked there.

"What are you doing, Gramps?"

He jerked around and another can thudded to the floor. It rolled and thumped against the base of the refrigerator. "I can't find my chicken noodle soup. You changed the labels on me."

A look of confusion crossed his face. Gracie's charming voice came from the living room, singing Christmas carols with some kid show on TV.

"What do you mean?"

"I don't recognize the labels. It's all different. I don't buy this brand of soup."

In a flash, Josie realized what had happened. She'd bought groceries and put them away in the cupboard. She'd obviously purchased a different brand of soup than Gramps was used to. Since he couldn't read the labels, he didn't know which can to choose for lunch. But his tension seemed more than just about soup.

"I'm sorry, Gramps. I didn't realize. Let me help you."

She reached to take the cans, but he jerked away. "Don't. I'll do it myself."

Stunned by his brusque tone, she pulled back and watched him.

The back door opened and Clint stepped inside and smiled. "Hey, Frank, I'm out of staples for the staple gun. If you don't have any, I can run over to my place to get some."

He froze, seeing Gramps's incredulous expression. No doubt sensing the anxiety in the room like a blast of chilly January wind.

Clint clamped his mouth shut and stood there, his snow-covered boots dripping onto the old, tattered towel Josie had laid in front of the door for this exact purpose.

"I'm useless. Good for nothing. I can't even find a can of chicken noodle soup," Gramps said.

He bent down to pick up the fallen items, his hands visibly shaking. What was wrong? Josie didn't understand.

She reached to help, wrapping her arms around him. Holding on tight as she offered reassurance. "You're good for everything. You're my grandpa and I love you."

He pushed her away and searing pain burned through his eyes. "If that's true, then why are you trying to get rid of me?"

Her mouth dropped open in shock. "What do you mean?"

He gestured angrily toward the phone. "The Sunnyside Assisted Living Center just called. They asked me to tell you they need a firm commitment by the end of today. Otherwise they'll have to release the room you've reserved to someone else."

Oh, no. A heavy weight settled on Josie's chest. This wasn't about soup at all. Not really. She didn't want this to happen today. Not like this. "Gramps, I didn't—"

He slashed a hand through the air, cutting her off. She flinched.

"I told them you only have one grandpa." Gramps's deep voice escalated. "And I said I sure wasn't gonna move into no cramped room in an assisted-living center. I thanked them for their time, but told them you wouldn't be needing the room, after all. Not unless you've got another grandpa I don't know about."

He arched his bushy brows, his expression stern, his steely eyes filled with hurt and betrayal. Without waiting for her reply, he slammed a can of soup down on the countertop, turned and stomped into the living room.

Josie couldn't move, as though her feet were nailed to the floor. She couldn't breathe. A hollow feeling settled in the pit of her stomach and she wanted to burst into tears.

She felt Clint's gaze like a leaden weight, and embarrassment heated her cheeks. She hated that he'd witnessed this scene. She looked up and blinked. Instead of censure and disapproval, she saw compassion written across his face.

"I know, I know. You don't have to say it," she said.

"Say what?"

"That I should have told him sooner. That I shouldn't

have waited so long. But I've only been home a couple of days. I haven't found the right time. I thought I was doing something good. Now it's too late."

She waited for Clint to scold her. To tell her she was inconsiderate and cruel. Instead, he nodded toward the living room, speaking in a soothing voice.

"Go in and speak with him now. It's not too late to explain everything. He knows you love him. Just tell him about your concerns and that you're worried about him. It'll all turn out fine."

Ha! She wished she could believe him. But his words of encouragement didn't inspire much confidence in her at this moment. Still, she appreciated his nonjudgmental attitude more than she could ever say.

"Gracie!" Clint called out. "It's time to go home, sweetheart."

"Ah, but I want to stay," she protested, clearly oblivious to what had occurred.

"Sorry, but we're leaving right now. Come on," he insisted.

Gracie groaned.

A long pause followed and the girl finally appeared in her stocking feet, dragging her red vinyl coat behind her. "But when can I come back and play with Josie and Grandpa Frank?"

"Maybe later," Clint said.

Josie watched in leaden silence while he helped his daughter tug on her boots and zip up her coat. He opened the door and ushered Gracie outside, but turned at the last moment to give Josie one last smile of support.

"Just tell him the truth. And remember that he loves you, too," Clint said.

He closed the door and she stood alone with her inner turmoil.

The truth. She didn't know what it was anymore. All her life, she'd worked so hard to get ahead. Memories of the loneliness and poverty she'd endured with Mom still haunted her. Now Josie had a good job that provided for all her needs, but she lived alone. Over the years, she'd grown more disenchanted with her life. Even her houseplants didn't seem to thrive. She'd never dare have a dog, cat or hamster. Or another boyfriend, for that matter. Ignoring her faults helped insulate her from the pain of failure. But she had to face it. She was antisocial and unlovable, just as Edward had said. What did her success matter if she had no one to share it with?

She inhaled deeply, trying to settle her nerves. Trying to formulate what she should say to Gramps. She had to speak to him now. No more delays. It wouldn't get easier by waiting.

Gathering her courage, she stepped into the living room. He sat in his worn recliner, staring vacantly out the window, his hands resting on his knees. She wondered how he'd gotten so old. All her life, he'd been the mainstay of her family. He and Grandma had been the only people in her life who had loved her unconditionally. So energetic and strong. So self-assured. He'd led an active, vital life. Always confident and in control. No matter what the problem, he had all the answers. But now he didn't. And neither did she.

Sitting on the sofa across from him, she clicked off the kid show on TV, leaving the room in a deafening silence. She realized even an elderly person needed reassurance sometimes. To know their life meant something to others. To feel loved and appreciated for the sacrifices they'd made and the good life they'd lived.

"Gramps, I'm so sorry. I didn't mean for you to find out this way. I wanted to sit down and talk with you about it first."

His gray eyes clashed, then locked with hers, and she inwardly cringed at the accusation and doubt she saw there.

"I never thought my own granddaughter would want to lock me away in an old folks' home." His voice was harsh with anger.

She flinched, thinking how heartless it sounded when he put it that way. "I would never lock you anywhere, Gramps. I love you."

He snorted. "Is that why you came here? To pack me off to that place?"

"No! I came to spend the holidays with you. To be near you. I'd love for you to live in Las Vegas with me, but I won't make you do something you don't want to do."

"Why would you ever think of putting me in an old folks' home?"

"It's not an old folks' home. It's an assisted-living center."

He shrugged. "It's the same thing to me."

She couldn't argue with that. She told herself she must be patient with him. He'd received a series of harsh blows lately. Grandma's death months earlier, having to learn to read, and now this. Josie wanted to encourage him. To make him understand how much she cared. That no matter what, she'd never desert him. Not ever.

"You'd maintain your independence there and have an apartment all to yourself," she said. "You could come and go as you like. But you wouldn't need to worry about yard work anymore, or shoveling the snow, raking leaves or mowing the lawn."

His mouth dropped open in shock. "But I love working in my yard, Josie. It's what keeps me young and strong. And who'd tend Ma's rosebushes if I left here?"

Rosebushes? Josie hadn't thought about that. And that's when she realized a house wasn't just a place where you lived to keep out the cold. It was a home you built with your loved ones day after day. Planting flowers. Repairing leaky faucets. Painting walls and hanging curtains. The place where you ate your meals and gathered together in the evening with your family, to share your life. Where you built all your hopes and dreams and then brought them to fruition.

She couldn't blame Gramps for wanting to stay. But that didn't change the fact that he was getting older and needed more care.

"There're lots of people your age living in this center, Gramps, so you'd have lots of companionship. You could cook or take your meals in the dining hall with the other patrons. They have fun activities for you, too. You'd be busy all the time, but if you got tired, you could rest. The weather is so much warmer there, and I'd be able to visit you every week. We'd be able to spend more time together."

And she wouldn't be worried he might collapse and not be found for hours or days, until it was too late to rush him to the hospital for help.

He lifted a gnarled hand. "I have lots of companionship right here in Camlin. All my friends at church, and down at the civic center. They care about me, Josie. They're good to me and I love them. I don't want to leave."

She nodded in understanding. "Then you don't have to go. I just thought it would be good for both of us. My intentions were never to lock you up and abandon you there. Not ever. And if you don't want to go, you won't. So that's the end of it. Now that I know how you feel about it, you'll stay right here."

The harsh lines around his mouth and eyes softened. "Good. I'm glad we got that settled."

She was, too, although it wasn't the outcome she'd hoped for.

She reached out and folded her hands over his. "I love you, Gramps. I just want what's best for you. I want to take care of you...."

He jerked his hands away. "I don't need you to take care of me. The good Lord does that for me. And I'm strong yet."

"I...I didn't mean it that way, Gramps."

His expression softened. "I know, muffin. I'm sorry to be so touchy about this. But I'm not afraid. God has never let me down. Not once. I'll stay right here until the day I die."

And she dreaded that day. But she envied Gramps and Clint their faith. How Josie wished she could trust God the way they did. But that would mean giving the Lord another chance, and she didn't know if she was ready for that step. Not yet, anyway.

"I've been living in this house for seventy-five years. I was only three when my folks moved here. What were you planning to do with my home?" Gramps asked.

Josie took a deep breath before letting it go. "I thought of several options. We could close up the house, rent it out, or we could sell it."

"Sell it? Why, this house has been in my family for

years." Horror ignited in his eyes and he glared at her as if she'd just asked him to shoot off his own foot.

She held up her hands. "So we won't sell it. We could keep it and visit anytime you like. I'd drive you home."

He snorted. "You rarely have time to visit me now. What makes you think you'd have time to drive me home to visit an empty old house?"

Oh, that hurt. Because he was right. And they both knew it. Josie couldn't deny it. Living so far away made visiting here difficult. Things always kept getting in the way. But she realized work couldn't fill up all the empty places inside her heart. Not anymore. Only love could do that.

"I'm sorry, Gramps. I just want to do what's best for you. I'm worried about you."

"You don't need to worry about me, Josie. I can accept God's will. And you should accept Him, too. In the meantime, I'll live right here to the best of my abilities."

That was just it. She couldn't accept it. Because when Gramps died, she'd have no one left. She'd be by herself.

Truly and wretchedly alone.

Chapter Eight

❧

That night, Josie couldn't sleep. Oh, she wanted to. In fact, she needed rest. Badly. Too many long hours at work had taken their toll. On top of it, she was worried about Gramps. She also felt discontented with her life, yet wasn't sure what to do about it. Not a good recipe for an insomniac like her.

Reaching over, she flipped on the lamp sitting on the table next to the bed. She blinked as her eyes accustomed to the dim light, then sat up and glanced at the clock. Two thirty-three in the morning and she was wide-awake.

The chilly air forced her to drag the heavy quilt up to her shoulders. Dressed in a warm nightgown, she wiggled her toes, glad she'd decided to wear socks to bed. She knew Gramps's penchant for turning down the heat at night. Having worked his entire life as a custodian for the local elementary school, he'd earned a modest living for his family. Although they'd always pinched pennies, he and Grandma Vi had been happy, sharing a love few people ever understood. Even so, Josie couldn't help wondering how he kept his indoor pipes from freezing.

What should she do? In Vegas when she couldn't sleep,

she'd normally get up and read, clean her small apartment, exercise, or drive in to work. Something constructive to distract her from being alone. But she'd wake Gramps if she started jogging around the house.

In retrospect, she marveled that Gramps had gotten along all his life without being able to read. How had he paid his bills or read the labels on his medications? How did he follow traffic signs or know which legal papers to sign?

Grandma Vi. She must have known the truth and helped him. But now she was gone, and Josie realized with churning clarity just how much Gramps had relied on his wife. It made Josie feel empty to think she might never have that intimate relationship with a man in her life.

Reaching over to the bedside table, she picked up a black Bible sitting there. She brushed her fingertips across the dusty, cracked cover and fanned the yellowed pages. Opening it, she read her grandmother's name etched in the top right corner: Viola Clements Rushton, 1951.

Grandma had always loved God and lived her life in service to Him and her family. Though Josie didn't have much use for the Lord, she respected her grandmother more than anyone else on earth, except Gramps.

As she flipped through the pages, the book naturally opened at a particularly tattered page. The twenty-second chapter of Psalms. She read the first verse, which was underlined in red ink.

"'My God, my God, why hast Thou forsaken me? Why art Thou so far from helping me, and from the words of my roaring?'"

Josie closed her eyes, squeezing tears from between

her lashes. A strangled groan of anguish came from her throat. How often had she felt this way? As though the Lord had completely forgotten her. As if she didn't matter, or God didn't love or care about her one iota.

Opening her eyes, she almost shut the book. Her heart felt so heavy with sorrow that she didn't want to read on. But she couldn't put the Bible down, compelled to read on.

Her gaze skimmed the words one by one and paused on the eleventh verse.

"'Be not far from me; for trouble is near; for there is none to help.'"

Yes. That was exactly how she felt right now. Fretting over Gramps. Worrying about his well-being. Feeling adrift personally and professionally. Aching with loneliness. And yet she had no one to blame but herself. She wanted to change. To make her life different somehow. To have friends and a family of her own. A man who truly loved her without reservations. But how should she start?

"'Show me the way, Lord. Show me what I must do,'" she murmured in a heartfelt prayer.

She turned the page and read more. "'The Lord is my shepherd; I shall not want. He maketh me to lie down in green pastures: He leadeth me beside the still waters. He restoreth my soul....'"

Her voice broke, shredded by emotion. And then she wondered, had Gramps felt this way, too? When he was a young man eking out a living for his family and hiding his frustration over his illiteracy? Perhaps even more recently, since Grandma Vi had died? Surely he'd felt forsaken at times in his life.

Josie didn't know. She'd never asked him about it. He always seemed so happy and content. So strong and supportive. But surely he had his down times, too. Everyone did. Even Clint Hamilton had undoubtedly needed God's comfort when he'd lost his wife and struggled to raise his daughter alone. And Josie couldn't help pondering if maybe, just maybe, Gramps and Clint were skilled at putting on a good front.

Hmm. Maybe other people felt lost and alone like she did. Though she'd always gone to church with her grandparents, she'd never considered herself a particularly religious person. She'd prayed during several critical times in her life, but God never seemed to answer her. So she'd quit trying. Why bother? Her words never reached heaven. If they did, the Lord had chosen to ignore her.

Tonight, as she thought about Gramps and Clint, the Bible verse brought her some comfort. As though her life was in God's control, even if she couldn't see it.

Josie set the book aside, thinking she was becoming overly sentimental now that she was home again. Flipping the heavy quilt back, she slid her feet into her fuzzy slippers and trudged downstairs. Maybe some warm milk would help her sleep.

The dark stairs creaked as she made her way down to the living room. The sound of scratchy static on the TV set drew her attention and she switched it off. Turning, she was surprised to see Gramps still reclining in his easy chair, fully dressed in his blue overalls, and fast asleep. A loud snort filled the room as he shifted position.

His spectacles rested on the bridge of his nose, and his face looked serene. Drawing near, she saw that he held a wide photo album in his lap. The faint light from a reading lamp sprayed across the book. He'd obviously been looking at the pictures when he'd fallen asleep.

The album lay open on a page that showed a beautiful photo of Grandma Vi at age sixteen, when she and Gramps had first met. Gramps's fingertips rested against the picture, just at the hollow of Grandma's throat, as though he'd been caressing her face.

Adoring her.

Glancing at her grandfather, Josie saw the toll the years of living had etched on his face. The sparse, graying hair, the grizzled cheeks and deep laugh lines around his eyes and mouth. He'd once been so muscular and young. So handsome. Grandma had always called him her "confident captain." But without Grandma here to read for him, he wasn't as confident anymore. And no matter what he thought, Josie had noticed he moved slower and seemed more fragile.

Vulnerable.

She couldn't bear to hurt him. She'd give anything if she could protect him.

Moving carefully, she slid the photo album away before covering him with a warm afghan. Slipping his spectacles off his face, she set them beside him on the table. Then she retrieved her glass of milk and took it and the photo album upstairs with her.

The mattress squeaked as she sat down on her bed and sipped her milk while she perused photos of her family members. Pictures she was familiar with, having viewed them with her grandparents on numerous occasions.

Strangers, every one.

Except for her parents and grandparents, she didn't know any of these people. And yet she did. Grandma Vi had told her all their stories. This was her family. Her heritage. As Josie gazed at their faces, the ache of overwhelming loss shadowed her heart.

She closed the album, too heartsick to view any more.

She wondered what had happened to cause her parents' divorce. How had they allowed their love to die?

Josie's mom had raised her alone, working all the time, indifferent and remote. Angry at the world. And for so long, Josie had thought her mom hated her, too.

No wonder Josie had cherished the summer months when she could be in Camlin with her grandparents. It had been an escape. A place to feel happy and secure.

As she set the album down and turned off the light, Josie realized how unhappy her mother had been. But her anger had never restored her marriage or brought Dad back. And it had never made her mom whole. So if anger wasn't the answer, what was?

On Thursday night, Josie drove Gramps to the local library, arriving promptly at seven o'clock. Because he was so nervous, and it was too cold to wait outside in the car, Josie walked inside with him. Helen Mulford, the organist from church, greeted them at the front counter.

"Hi there, Frank. And who's this stranger with you?" Helen, a woman of perhaps sixty years of age, winked at Josie, her cheeks plumping with her smile. As a good friend of her grandmother's, Helen knew exactly who Josie was.

"Hi, Helen. It's so good to see you again." Josie gave the matronly lady a tight hug. Like always, the woman smelled of chocolate brownies.

"She's visiting for the holidays. Staying with me for several weeks," Gramps said, his chest puffed out with pleasure.

He didn't mention that Josie wanted him to move to Vegas, and she was grateful her grandfather wasn't one to hold a grudge.

Helen leaned her elbows on the counter and leveled a cheerful gaze on Josie. "That's great. Maybe you can join the chorus for the program we're giving on Christmas Eve."

Josie hadn't thought about that. Only once had she attended the Christmas Eve program with her grandparents. Gramps had a beautiful singing voice and always sang at least one solo. Josie had never been able to attend the practices before, but now she couldn't help anticipating the event. "I'm not a very good singer, but I'd love to try."

Helen's eyes widened. "Good. Frank has the schedule. Just come to the practices with him and we'll bring you up to speed on the songs. We're having a cookie exchange after our next practice, so bring a plate of cookies wrapped up for someone to take home, and another plate for everyone to sample."

"She's a great cook, like Vi." Gramps jerked a thumb toward Josie.

A flush of pleasure flooded Josie's cheeks. The activity sounded fun. Some of her best memories had been at home, cooking with Grandma. Now that Vi was gone, Josie cherished those times when they'd been alone together in a warm kitchen that smelled of yummy things to eat. But she wasn't used to mingling with lots of people in a social gathering. What if her singing was off? What if her cookies weren't up to par?

She told herself that was silly. She'd made Grandma's cookies zillions of times. She could do this. No problem. She refused to let her fear of failure darken her life anymore. "I'll be there."

"Good. I'm so glad you're home for the holidays. I don't know how you drive in all that city traffic. Las

Vegas is such a big place. Too many people for me. I'd be lost if I had to live there."

Josie had to admit driving in Camlin was a lot less stressful. But she loved her job. And a city was an easier place for her to get lost in. Now, she wasn't sure she wanted to hide out anymore.

"Clint said you'd be coming in for reading time, so let me take you back, Frank." Helen stood and walked around the counter, carrying a slim booklet with her.

"I'll wait out here," Josie told him.

"You're not coming with me?" A look of sheer panic filled Gramps's eyes, and his voice was unusually high and nervous.

"I'd just be in the way, but I'll wait for you. I won't leave."

He took two shallow breaths, then nodded, his brow furrowed with determination. He hesitated, his leathery hands fluttering apprehensively, as though he was being forced to go into surgery without anesthesia. And that's when Josie realized how difficult this was for him.

Not in a million years would she have guessed her grandfather was afraid. But Josie could see it in the way his eyes darted toward the door, as though he'd like to make a run for it. It didn't matter that reading was easy for most people. Or that Clint was trying to help him live a richer, fuller life. Gramps had never done this before and was terrified of failure.

Just like Josie.

A feeling of compassion churned inside her chest. "It's going to be okay, Gramps. But I can come with you, if you really want me to."

He coughed to clear his voice, obviously trying hard to be brave. "No, muffin. You're right. I'll be fine."

Muffin. His nickname for only her. Standing a bit straighter, he marched down the hall behind Helen, looking rather like a soldier being led to the gallows.

Josie hid a bittersweet smile. Though she felt empathy for her grandfather, she couldn't help finding the situation a tad amusing. Clint had said Gramps should be reading small words by Christmas. What a great gift for her grandfather. She just hoped he applied himself. And every evening, she planned to sit down and read with him, to ensure his success.

Perusing a rack of mystery novels, Josie selected one and turned to find a comfy chair where she could relax for an hour. It'd been ages since she'd read for pleasure, and she anticipated it with relish.

"Hey, you're not coming back?"

She whirled around and found Clint standing behind her, dressed in a pair of faded blue jeans, cowboy boots and a blue flannel shirt. She had the maddening impulse to rest her hand against his chest, to rub the soft fabric—a crazy thought that caused a flush of embarrassment to heat her cheeks. He quirked one eyebrow and she couldn't help smiling at his endearing expression.

"I didn't know I was invited," she said. "I thought there'd be teachers for Gramps and that I'd be in the way."

"We have some literacy tutors here to help, but family members make the best teachers. Why don't you come on back? Then you'll know how to spend the time when you're reading with him at home."

Without notice, Clint reached out and took her hand. The warmth of his fingers made her arm tingle, and her heart gave a powerful thump.

"But I...I don't know how to teach someone to read."

He gave her a warm smile. "It's okay. I'll show you what to do. Come on."

Lulled by his soothing voice, Josie nodded, then reached inside her purse and pulled out the woolen socks he'd lent her the day they'd cut their Christmas trees. She held them up. "Before I forget. I washed them, but let them air dry so they wouldn't shrink. Thanks for the loan."

"You're welcome." He released her hand and took the socks. Then he led the way past the stacks of books and down a short hallway to a conference room set up with desks and chairs. Several people, including Gracie, sat waiting quietly, their gazes trained on Josie as Clint escorted her to where Gramps sat off by himself, frowning.

Gracie waved and grinned. Josie smiled, then settled in her seat, resting her hands in her lap. Clint seemed so encouraging and confident. Not at all like Edward. Somehow she knew Clint wouldn't let Gramps fail. And that knowledge brought her a modicum of peace.

She stared straight ahead while Clint stepped to the front of the room and picked up a book. The front cover showed a young woman hugging an elderly lady, both with giant smiles on their faces. The title was *Teach Someone to Read.*

As Clint had them each introduce themselves, Josie told herself she could do this. With two advanced degrees in the sciences, she was educated and knew how to read. Surely she could help Gramps learn. How hard could it be?

And that's when she realized she was just as petrified of this process as he must be. With one big difference. Josie knew what Gramps was missing. And no matter what, she was determined to help him with kindness and compassion. Nothing else mattered right now.

"To begin, let's run through the alphabet." Clint stood at the front of the classroom with a welcoming smile. Three students and their tutors gazed back at him. Frank was new, but Clint knew what to do to start him off right. Josie could help. Yet her presence made Clint nervous as he directed everyone to open their reading manuals.

Picking up a pointer stick, he indicated an *A* on the dry-erase board. He spoke the letter out loud, then had the class repeat it, eventually moving sequentially through the entire alphabet. Frank blinked nervously, his gray eyes narrowed on the letters as though they were some strange puzzle he must figure out.

"Now, let's break up into our learning groups and go to work."

Clint joined Josie and Frank. Gracie followed him, huddling close against Josie's side. The woman accepted the child's presence without question, and Clint couldn't help thinking the two had become inseparable.

The other students and tutors already knew what to do. He figured Josie needed some guidance if she was to help her grandpa effectively.

Pulling a chair up to their desk, Clint leaned close, speaking in a subdued voice that wouldn't disturb the other students. "Frank, can you tell us a little about your life as a child?"

The older man studied the eraser on the end of his pencil, thinking it over. "Well, I was six when my daddy died. Mother took in washing to make ends meet. I was the eldest and times were tough. At first I looked after my younger brother, Bert. Then I started working at the mine to help Mother put food on the table."

Josie blinked, and a sad, strangling sound came from her throat. "I never knew any of this, Gramps. What did you do at the mine?"

"I started out as a water boy. Mother always planned to send me back to school one day, but it never happened. I guess I got less than a first grade education. Not much, I know. But times were awful hard back then."

"I'm sorry, Gramps."

He patted Josie's hand. "Don't be, muffin. No sense in regretting our lives. We just need to learn from things and move on. There's been a lot of good in my life, too."

Clint liked Frank's attitude. He remembered his own shock after he'd married Karen and discovered she couldn't read. But that wasn't the worst of it. When he'd learned that she also suffered from chronic depression and bipolar disorder, he'd been discouraged. But he'd loved his wife and had tried to help.

It hadn't been enough. And his failure still caused an ache in his heart.

"Why didn't you ever tell me all this?" Josie asked.

"Dropping out of school wasn't something I wanted to talk about," Frank said. "But it wasn't all bad. My family was poor, but we were close and looked after one another."

"I vaguely remember Uncle Bert," she said.

A solemn smile creased Frank's face. "Bert was a good brother. We loved each other dearly. People do what they gotta do to help each other survive."

Clint figured that was true. He thought about Karen and how she'd coped with the abuse she'd suffered during her youth. As an adult, she'd hidden her sorrow locked deep within her heart. On the surface, she'd appeared happy and normal. But inside she'd simmered with rage and insecurity. As time passed, her anger had burst forth and she'd never been the same again. Unable to forgive. Unable to heal.

Clint shook his head, focusing on Frank. "What are you interested in reading?"

A hopeful smile curved his lips. "I've always wanted to read the Bible. And the newspaper. You think that's possible?"

"Absolutely. Once you learn to read, there's nothing you can't do."

"I can teach you the alphabet song. It's easy, Grandpa Frank," Gracie offered.

Frank smiled at the child. "I'd like that, sweetheart."

Hmm. That might be a good idea. Due to lack of child care, Clint had to bring Gracie with him to the reading program at night. She was an obedient child and it posed very little problem. And Frank responded so well to Gracie that he might actually see part of this learning process as a game if Gracie taught him a few things.

For the next few minutes, they sang the alphabet song together. Frank joined in, and after going through it numerous times, he had it down pat.

Conscious of Josie watching them, Clint had Frank write his name. Pressing his tongue against his upper lip, Frank held the pencil between his fingers and etched the letters in a tidy cursive with very little flourish.

"That's nice, Gramps. You have lovely penmanship," Josie praised. "And I think you're holding the pencil correctly. How did you learn to sign your name?"

Frank beamed. "Ma taught me. She also taught me words like *danger* and *stop,* so I wouldn't get hurt at work. She tried to teach me more, but we were always so busy that we finally just let it drop."

Clint appreciated the way Josie praised her grandfather. Frank needed reinforcement. Inwardly, Clint thought about how hard life must have been for the elderly man. Working at the mine at such a tender age, he'd never had a real childhood. Too much responsibility for such a young kid.

Just like Karen. With the exception that Frank had kept his faith and lived a full, happy life.

Clint glanced at Josie, wondering if it had been the same for her. Oh, she'd had educational opportunities, that was true. But she'd lost both her parents too young. Frank had told him how hard Josie had worked to put herself through college. Studying all the time. Earning scholarships to pay her tuition. Working side jobs to pay the rent. That could put a lot of pressure on a young woman, but it also built character and a good work ethic. Josie had succeeded, and Clint was proud of her accomplishments.

But she'd lost her faith somewhere along the way.

"Life can be so unfair, but you never complain," Clint said.

Frank shrugged. "What's there to whine about? God is so good to me. And I don't want to ever forget that."

Looking up, Clint saw Josie listening intently, her forehead creased with thought. He did some thinking of his own. With Frank's example to inspire him, he made a silent vow to complain less. To be more grateful for the people and opportunities life brought his way.

By the end of the evening, Clint had provided Frank with eight slim books written for beginning readers. "This is just a loan. Take them home and read them with Josie several times. When you bring them back next week, I'll give you some different ones."

Frank's brows darted upward. "Read them?"

"Yep. She'll help you get through each one. Sound out the letters of the words. I have a feeling it'll come fast for you."

Josie nodded, flipping through the pages of a rudimentary book about a man hitting a ball with a baseball bat. "None of the words in these books is over three letters, Gramps. That should make it easier for you to sound them out. I'll make sure we read and write together every night. Or no dessert after dinner." She flashed an impish grin at her grandfather.

Frank gave a mocking frown. "Well, I don't know if I like that."

As Clint walked Frank and Josie out to their car, Gracie waited inside. The cold night wind struck him like a polar vortex. They each zipped up their coats, their breath puffing on the air, their noses red.

"Thanks for your help, Ranger," Frank said.

"Yes, thank you very much," Josie chimed in.

Clint met her eyes. "You're welcome."

He wanted to say something more, but didn't know what.

"Bye, Grandpa Frank," Gracie called from the doorway, waving one of her fluffy red gloves.

"Good night, sweetheart. See you later," Frank returned.

Gracie had hugged Josie earlier, a content smile on her face. As if they were close, and family. But they weren't. Clint had to remember that.

And then the Rushtons were gone. As Clint watched them climb into Josie's car and drive away, a warm, buoyant feeling settled in his chest. He'd enjoyed tonight and felt good about what they'd accomplished. Frank had a long way to go yet, but they would help him. Above all, Clint didn't want him to get discouraged.

"I still think you should ask Josie out." Standing on the curb, Gracie looked up at her dad.

Clint heard her, but didn't respond. He shuffled one foot against the black ice and stared down the vacant street.

Gracie slipped her hand into his and he squeezed it tightly. The two of them had each other, and she was his entire world. But he still felt empty inside. As if he was just going through the motions and missing something important in life.

During their reading time, Clint had forgotten his sad past and the way Karen had died. He could almost pretend he hadn't failed her. And he found himself wishing Frank was Gracie's real grandpa and Josie was...

What?

A friend. That's all she could ever be. Yet in his heart of hearts, Clint wished they could be so much more.

Chapter Nine

Josie shivered in the cold car and flipped the defroster on high. The crackling of ice sounded beneath the tires as she pulled out of the parking lot. Looking in her rear-view mirror, she saw Clint and Gracie standing together on the sidewalk, holding hands.

A strangled cough rose up in Josie's throat. She liked the forest ranger and his little girl. A lot. Maybe too much. She liked the way Clint had patiently tutored Gramps. The way he spoke so kindly to each of them as he'd explained what they must do. The way his warm eyes crinkled at the corners when he smiled.

Shaking her head, Josie focused on the slick road. Gramps sat bundled in his heavy coat as he gazed out the windshield, subdued and quiet.

"You did well tonight, Gramps," she said.

He made a growling comment in the back of his throat.

"What was that?" she asked politely.

"I'm never gonna learn to read."

"Of course you are. Don't be so pessimistic." She spoke in a buoyant tone, trying to be positive. Trying to mimic Clint's optimism.

"I'm too old," Gramps said.

"You're never too old to learn. That's a fallacy. Instead, why don't you try to have fun? You're not alone in this. Clint and I are gonna help. And Gracie, too."

No, they weren't alone anymore. Funny how she'd come to rely on the enigmatic forest ranger so quickly. Without coming on too strong, Clint seemed to know just what to say to steer them toward success.

The sound of the engine and gushing air from the heater filled the void of silence. Gramps stared out the dark window, his profile etched with vulnerability.

"You really think so?" he finally asked in a contemplative voice.

"I know so." Her heart gave a powerful tug. He needed her strength to face this great hurdle.

Reaching across the seat, she folded her fingers around his hand, giving him comfort the only way she knew how. "It's going to be okay, Gramps. I promise."

He squeezed her hand and nodded, speaking in a voice roughened by emotion. "Of course it is, muffin."

She chuckled, noticing how he squinted as they passed a bright streetlight.

"Are your eyes hurting you?" she asked.

"No."

But she wondered if he would tell her if they were.

"I think I'll make you an appointment to see about getting you a new pair of glasses. We can drive into Bridgeton to see an eye doctor. You've used the same reading glasses for years and years," she said.

Another grumble emitted from Gramps's chest.

Before he could argue, she hurried on. "And I think I'll make Grandma's lasagna for dinner tomorrow night. How would you like that?"

His face brightened just a bit. "Sounds good. I haven't had Ma's lasagna since she passed. How long did you say you can stay with me, honey?"

She glanced in her rearview mirror as she flipped on her blinker and made a right turn. "As long as it takes."

"As long as what takes? You didn't get fired, did you?"

She whipped her head toward him. "No, of course not. I simply had a lot of vacation time saved up, and I intend to use every bit of it."

She needed this break. Had hungered for it, in fact. When the time came, it would be so difficult to go back to her lonely existence in Vegas, but she'd have to. Like everyone else, she had bills to pay. And knowing Gramps wouldn't be going with her made her feel lonelier than ever.

The moment Josie and Frank stepped into the cultural hall for choir practice on Saturday night, Clint's senses hiked into overdrive. Standing at the front of the stage with Tom Baker, he cleared his throat, feeling suddenly out of sorts.

"There you are, Frank. We've been running through that new song I told you about." Carl Wilkins, the director, waved him over.

Dressed in her winter coat and black fluffy earmuffs, Josie carried a large basket to the front row of the auditorium. Several choir members sitting there greeted her. She smiled and answered their questions, hugging a couple of the women. They were all friends of Frank and Viola Rushton. No doubt Josie knew them from her visits home.

Her pale skin gleamed in the dim light, radiant and angelic. She lifted the muffs off her head and shrugged out of her coat, revealing a beautiful red sweater beneath. It framed her pale, flawless skin perfectly. Her black jeans fit her legs and hips to perfection. Her clean hair bounced against her shoulders. As she folded her coat and set it aside, her long lashes swept downward. How could a woman have such beautiful, expressive eyes?

Clint's throat tightened, dry as sandpaper, and he swallowed. Seeing Josie so feminine and lovely caused his insides to churn, like a long lost memory he couldn't let go of. He'd almost forgotten the intimacy of being with a woman. The hushed voices and soft kisses in the middle of the night.

A giddy rush of adrenaline coursed through his veins. He felt like a schoolboy about to ask the prom queen for a dance. Oh, yes. He'd love to ask Josie out on a real date. And then what? What if they fell in love?

Wearing blue coveralls and a blue flannel shirt, Frank lumbered down the aisle before stepping up onto the stage.

Carl handed him some sheet music. "Frank, you'll be singing bass, Tom will sing tenor and Clint will sing baritone. Let's take it from the top."

Clint glanced at Frank, who calmly stared at the pages in his hands. He showed not a single glimmer to indicate he couldn't read the words before he lowered the sheets. "I'm afraid I forgot my glasses. I can't read this."

Oh, yes. Frank was good at this. He'd spent a lifetime hiding his disability.

"I'll help him," Clint offered.

Carl nodded at Helen, who sat behind the piano on the side of the stage. When Carl lifted his hands in the air to direct the song, Josie sat up straight, her face creased with concern. She glanced at Clint, her eyes filled with pleading. And without asking, he knew exactly what she was thinking. She didn't want to reveal Frank's secret and embarrass him. Neither did Clint.

They shared a significant look no one else noticed. Clint inclined his head and gave a little calming motion with his hand, offering reassurance the only way he knew how. She sat back, seeming to relax.

Trusting him.

"I think it would help if we play through the piece and say the words together just once," Clint suggested.

A look of impatience crossed Carl's face, but he nodded. "Oh, all right."

Nodding at Helen, Carl indicated that she should play the music. As the dramatic notes filled the stage, the men spoke the words out loud together, keeping time with the rhythm.

"Don't go too fast during the second measure," Carl interrupted. "This is a reverent song. Almost a lullaby. I want you to sing nice and slow."

They began again, the men holding the chords in perfect harmony. And when they finished, a moment of profound silence filled the auditorium.

"I think I've got it" Frank broke the quiet.

"Good. Let's take it from the top, then." Another nod at Helen, and Carl led them through the song twice more.

By the third time, the song went more smoothly— a beautiful, worshipful piece about the three wise men coming to visit the baby Jesus the night He was born.

Frank didn't need to be told the words twice, and Clint silently noted that the man had an amazing memory. Probably a skill he'd gleaned over the years in order to accommodate his illiteracy.

As he sang, Clint glanced up and saw Josie studying them. Sitting at the front of the audience, she looked up at him. He stuttered and felt suddenly awkward. His voice wobbled and he missed his notes. He'd never felt nervous singing before, but with Josie's eyes boring into him like a high-speed drill, his hands shook and felt cold and clammy.

"No, no." Carl tapped the music stand with his pointed baton. The piano stopped abruptly. "Clint, you need to concentrate on your notes more. You're off tonight."

He certainly was.

"Sorry. I'll do better." He flashed a nervous smile, but inwardly, he was trembling. What was it about Josie that disconcerted him so much?

They went through the song one more time. Clint refused to look at Josie, which helped him concentrate. It wasn't perfect, but he made it to the end.

"Practice at home," Carl ordered. Then he turned toward the auditorium, where the chorus members sat waiting. "Okay, let's have everyone come on up and take your places."

Josie stood with the rest, looking uncertain as she picked her way among the crowd.

"Josie!" Gracie ran over and took her hand.

Smiling widely, Josie leaned down and spoke to the little girl, but Clint couldn't hear their words. When they came up on stage, Gracie joined the other children, while Josie stood nearby. Clint tried to focus on the director as he told them each where he wanted them situated for the opening number.

"Thanks for covering for Gramps." Josie spoke next to him, whispering for his ears alone.

"You're welcome. You doing okay?" Clint murmured.

"Yes, I'm fine." She glanced at him, clutching her hands together.

"How did your conversation about moving to Las Vegas go with Frank?"

"He's still a bit upset, but I think he's forgiven me." She spoke low, her gaze focused on Carl.

"Did you two work everything out?"

"He's not leaving Camlin, if that's what you mean. But we certainly haven't worked everything out. I need to find someone to bring in meals for him once I'm gone. He's been living on oatmeal, cookies and chicken noodle soup."

He felt her pain. From the deep creases in her forehead, fretting over her grandfather was starting to take its toll on her.

"I'll ask around for you. We'll find someone. How's his reading coming along?" Clint asked, trying to hold his sheet music steady.

"Good. He's trying hard. In fact, I'm surprised at how fast he's learning. He's memorized the alphabet and the sounds each letter makes, and we've started putting them together into small words. The flash cards you gave us help a lot."

Clint nodded, liking this news. "Have you seen the light bulb flash in his eyes yet?"

She tilted her head and he caught the tantalizing lemony scent of her hair. "What do you mean?"

"Usually when people start learning something new, a light clicks on inside of them and it shows in their eyes. It's like they're all aglow with happiness."

"Hmm, I've mostly just seen a lot of frustration and grimaces from Gramps." She laughed, the sound charming.

"Don't worry. It'll happen soon enough."

Clint remembered seeing that light click on in Karen's eyes when she'd read her first beginner's book and actually understood the simple story. It had been the highlight of her education, all because she could now read rudimentary words and comprehend them. That was before Gracie was born. Karen had even talked about taking a college course, and he'd encouraged her. But she never did. Her insecurities had gotten the better of her.

"You don't know someone in town that I can pay to go in and clean Gramps's house once a week, do you?" she asked.

"As a matter of fact, I do. Rachel Burdett cleans my house. Since she lives right across the street from Frank, I'm sure she'd—"

"Ahem!"

He looked up. Carl stood at the front of the stage, tapping his foot impatiently as he glowered at them with disapproval. All eyes were trained on them. A couple of men chuckled and nudged each other, while the women tossed Josie knowing glances. Since Clint was a highly eligible bachelor, no doubt they were conjecturing over whether he was interested in Josie. And he was. But not in the way they thought. This was just a friendship, nothing more.

Clint swallowed and gave an apologetic smile. "I'm sorry, Carl. What did you say?"

"Can you stand over here with Frank and Tom, please? Then you'll be ready for the wise men number when it's time." Carl pointed a stiff finger at the floor.

Clint tossed a meaningful look at Josie. "We'll talk about this later."

"Okay. Thanks." She nodded and he stepped away.

As Carl led the choir through a series of simple Christmas carols, Clint stood beside Frank and sang his parts.

From all outward appearances, he was focused on what he was doing. But inside, he felt the thrum of electric shock currents zipping through his arms and legs. He found himself glancing repeatedly at Josie. From his peripheral vision, he was conscious of her every move. Of her innocent expression as she sang the chorus to "Silent Night." He caught the high, clear melody of her voice during "O Little Town of Bethlehem." Being near her wasn't getting any easier.

Clint was watching her again. Josie could feel his eyes on her as she carried her basket of snickerdoodles to the refreshment table following practice. She knew it without looking his way, probably because she'd been watching him, too. Every chance she got. Surreptitious glances when she didn't think he was looking. Feasting her eyes on his clean-shaven face and slicked-back hair. And she didn't understand her obsession with the guy. He wasn't special. Not so unique.

Who was she kidding? He was gorgeous, kind and wonderful. And hands off for her. He had a child to think about. He wouldn't be interested in the likes of her.

Or would he?

When they'd finished their practice, the choir members headed toward the outer foyer for the cookie exchange. Josie reached inside her basket, lifted out a paper plate filled with soft cookies, and set it on the table. She then carried her basket to the sampling tables, where red and green cloths had been laid out, and chunky pinecones, Christmas ornaments and candles served as centerpieces.

A dull roar of happy chatter filled the air along with the crisp aroma of cinnamon and cloves. Kids raced among the crowd to attack the refreshments, their mothers calling for them to slow down.

Josie lifted a silver tray of cookies out of the basket and set it on the table. As she tugged off the plastic wrap, she bumped into someone.

"Excuse me." She jerked around and found herself gazing up into Clint's expressive eyes.

He stood close. Too close. And she stepped back.

"Sorry. It's rather crowded in here." He gave a nervous laugh.

She smiled. She couldn't help it. "Yes it is."

"Hi, Josie." Gracie squeezed between them and snatched up one of her cookies.

"Hi, sweetie."

"Mmm, snickerdoodles. And they're homemade." The girl took a big bite.

Josie brushed her fingers through Gracie's long blond hair. "Hey, you did a good job tonight singing with the kids' choir."

Her face flushed with pleasure. "Thanks. So did you."

As Clint set his offering on the table, Josie glanced at his bag of packaged cookies and arched her brows. "That's cheating, you know. Store-bought cookies aren't gonna cut it with this crowd."

He gave a sheepish grin. "Yeah, sorry about that. But trust me. You don't want to eat my homemade cookies."

"He burned them." Gracie crinkled her nose. "And they weren't really homemade, anyway. They were one of those tubes of cookie dough you buy at the store and bake at home."

Josie narrowed her eyes, as though this were a grave insult. "Hmm, so you were gonna try and pass off store-bought cookie dough for your own, huh?"

Clint's face flooded with color. He reached over and pulled Gracie close, placing a kiss on her forehead before whispering loudly enough for Josie to hear. "Remember, that was just our secret, sweetheart. You're not supposed to go around telling everyone."

A laugh burst from Josie's throat. "Well, I must admit, store-bought cookies are good, too."

"Not as good as these are." Gracie held up the half-eaten snickerdoodle before moving on down the table.

"No more than three cookies," Clint called after her, and she groaned. He turned back to Josie, not quite meeting her eyes.

She chuckled. "I'm glad to discover you have at least one flaw. I was beginning to think you were perfect."

In every single way.

"Oh, no," he assured her. "Just ask Gracie. She'd be happy to tell you every one of my faults in great detail." A wry smile curved his mouth and he shook his head, his face still bright with embarrassment.

Josie didn't believe him. From what she'd observed, Clint *was* the perfect man. It was easy to see why Gracie adored her father. And for three crazy seconds, Josie felt an intense longing to feel his strong arms around her, feel the steady beat of his heart as she rested her cheek against his solid chest. To hear him speak her name with a sigh.

Stunned by her wayward thoughts, she looked away, her cheeks flaming with a blush.

"Gracie's playing the part of an angel in the program," he said.

Josie glanced back at him with interest. "Have you made her costume yet?"

He shook his head, looking mildly concerned. "Last

year she was an elf, and Viola made her costume. I'll have to get someone else to do it this year."

Not surprising. Most men were not seamstresses.

"Why don't I make it for her?" Josie offered.

He blinked in surprise. "You know how to sew?"

"A little bit. Does that surprise you?"

"Yes," he confessed.

"Grandma Vi taught me. Her old sewing machine is still sitting right where she left it, in the back bedroom, and I have the time. I'm sure Helen will help me if I run into difficulty. Besides, it's a great way to repay you for all the work you've done around Gramps's house."

Clint smiled with relief. "That would take a huge load off my mind. I have no idea what marabou trim is, much less how to sew it onto white satin."

She chuckled. "Don't worry. I'll take care of it."

Drawing a deep breath, he leaned nearer. "While we have a moment alone, I was wondering if you might also be interested in—"

Josie felt a hand tugging on her arm.

"Hi, Josie!"

She turned and found Thelma Milton, the owner of the grocery store, standing beside her. Thelma smiled widely, showing smudges of bright red lipstick on her front teeth.

"Hello, Thelma." She greeted the lady cheerfully.

"Mrs. Milton." Clint nodded at her, then stepped away to speak with someone else.

Josie watched him go, wondering what he'd been about to ask her.

"These are for Frank. I made them special just for him." Thelma handed her a plate wrapped in shiny tinfoil.

Focusing on the woman, Josie sniffed the contents and

lifted her eyes in question. "Thank you, but wouldn't you like to give them to him yourself?"

"No, I don't want him to think I'm being too forward. They're chocolate chip. Vi's recipe."

Josie wasn't about to tell Thelma that she'd already frozen dozens of the same cookies for Gramps. He was planning to hand out some to their neighbors as a holiday gift.

"Oh, I'm sure he'll love them. That's so thoughtful of you," she said instead.

Yep, Gramps definitely had an admirer.

Thelma waved a hand in the air. "Oh, it's nothing, really. Vi always brought me a plate every year. It's just not the same now she's gone. I miss her so much. She was a good friend to me when my Harry passed away two years ago. I'm just trying to return the favor now that Frank's all alone."

Josie caught the sincerity in Thelma's voice and couldn't help liking the woman. She was fast coming to realize that elderly people needed companionship just as much as younger folks. Just because they got old didn't mean they didn't still need others. "Yes, I miss her, too."

"You sing soprano, right?"

Josie nodded. "But not very well. I tend to crack on the high notes."

"Oh no, dear. You sounded great to me." Thelma reached for a pecan brownie and took a bite.

Josie didn't respond. She knew she couldn't sing well enough for a solo, but she could carry a tune and did well enough in the chorus. And that suited her just fine. It felt good to be included in the festivities.

"Where'd that grandpa of yours run off to?" Thelma's

gaze scanned the roomful of people while she munched on her brownie.

Josie swiveled around to help her look. "I'm not sure. He was here just a few minutes ago."

"He promised to go caroling with a group of us from the civic center next week. He said he'd pick me up. I was wondering what time."

Since she was at least five inches taller than Thelma, Josie pointed to where Gramps stood beside the punch bowl, with Clint and Tom. "There he is."

"Of course. Talking with the other men." Thelma's voice gushed with admiration.

Josie watched as Clint dipped out a cup of red punch for Gracie. The girl laughed at something he said, and Clint gave a wry grin before he handed her the cup. Watching the two interact, Josie felt as though she was eavesdropping on something private between them. And yet she liked how Clint treated his daughter. He seemed to be more than just Gracie's daddy. He was also her best friend.

At that moment, he turned and glanced Josie's way, almost as if he'd felt her gaze. Across the expanse of the cultural hall, their eyes met. Embarrassed to be caught gawking, Josie gave him a half smile, then jerked her head around and pretended to be absorbed in her conversation with Thelma.

"Gramps looks like he's having fun," Josie said.

"Yes. He's such a nice man. I think I'll go and confirm the time he'll be picking me up for our caroling trip. We're old fuddy-duddies, but you should plan to join us. Excuse me, dear." Thelma scooted away, making a beeline for Gramps.

"Hi, Josie."

Helen Mulford took Thelma's place, crowding close as she reached for a napkin.

"Hi, Helen." Josie folded her arms and leaned against the wall, feeling nervous with all these people around, yet still enjoying herself.

"How's Frank's reading coming along?" Helen spoke in a low tone.

Josie appreciated the woman's tact. Until Gramps learned to read, she didn't want to advertise his disability to the world. She thought about the quiet hour she'd spent with him last night, helping him sound out each letter of the alphabet. And when they got home tonight, they planned to read again before going to bed. His eagerness to learn inspired Josie, and she couldn't help feeling proud of his efforts.

"Very well," she whispered back. "In fact, he's learning so fast that later tonight I'm planning to help him tackle one of the remedial readers we borrowed from Clint."

"Oh, that's wonderful," Helen said. "Once he starts reading small words, the bigger words will come quick enough."

Josie took that opportunity to mention the angel dress she was planning to make for Gracie.

"How nice of you to sew it for Clint. If you need any help, you just give me a call. It's no trouble at all. And this is for both you and Frank to enjoy. Merry Christmas."

The woman handed Josie a bag filled with candied popcorn balls wrapped in plastic. Although Josie didn't want any more goodies around the house for Gramps to gobble down, she smiled graciously and accepted the gift. "Thank you so much."

"I'm Marylou Calhoun." An unfamiliar woman suddenly inserted her hand between Helen and Josie. Dressed in blue jeans and a tie-died blouse, she chewed a piece of gum with her mouth open. "You must be Frank Rushton's granddaughter. I've heard a lot about you."

Startled by her forward manner, Josie took a step back.

"Hi there, Marylou." Helen smiled and provided a short explanation to Josie. "Marylou bought the Sunglow Café downtown. It just reopened again after being completely renovated."

Josie shook the woman's hand. "How nice."

Especially since it was the only diner in town. Josie hated to see any of the local businesses closing up shop. The fact that the restaurant had reopened was a good sign the poor economy was recovering, if only a little bit.

"You looking for a job, honey? I'm hiring waitresses," Marylou said.

"No! Josie isn't gonna be one of your waitresses," Helen interrupted. "She's a pharmacist in Las Vegas."

Marylou's eyes widened. "A pharmacist, huh? I'll bet you make loads of dough."

Josie blinked. She sensed the woman was harmless enough, but couldn't get used to her blunt candor.

"Of course she does. She's had lots of schooling and works hard," Helen said.

"I sure wish we had a pharmacy here in Camlin," Marylou grumbled.

"Me, too," Helen agreed.

Josie didn't see how she could open a pharmacy here. Maybe in a few years she'd have enough capital saved to try such a venture.

"Heaven knows we can use some young women in this town. We need more little kids bopping around the place," Marylou said.

Helen swatted the air. "Oh, phooey. You just miss those grandkids of yours. But Josie isn't even married, Marylou. She's not gonna have any kids, yet."

Marylou shot a look over at Clint, then winked at Josie. "We can sure fix that problem. That is one mighty fine looking man, honey. He's single and built in all the right places. And I believe you've already caught his eye. Do you need pointers?"

Josie would have laughed, but Marylou had hit a little too close to home. "No, thank you."

"She's not interested," Helen interjected. "She just broke up with her fiancé."

Marylou glanced at Josie. "Your fiancé, huh?"

"Yes, this is her second broken engagement," Helen said. "She needs time to heal. Frank told me so."

Josie's face flooded with heat. Was there anyone in town Gramps hadn't told her business to? She edged away from the table, longing to escape.

"Oh, I'm sorry to hear that." The café owner placed a conciliatory hand on her arm. "But don't you worry. The best cure for a broken heart is to go out with lots of other men. That'll show whoever broke your heart that you don't care one bit. And you'd have a lot of fun in the process."

But that was just the problem. Josie did care. Perhaps too much.

"She doesn't need a man. She's a pharmacist and can support herself," Helen said.

"Everyone needs a man," Marylou said.

Something deep inside Josie rebelled at this. No, she didn't need a man. But she wanted a family of her own. Someone to share her life with. That was all.

The women continued speaking as though she was

actually participating in their conversation. Before long, two other neighbors swung by to give Josie a package of fudge and homemade caramels. Grateful for the change in topic, she accepted their offerings with a smile. Their consideration touched her deeply and she found herself chatting and laughing as though she'd lived here all her life.

She compared this outpouring of attention with her lonely existence in Vegas. No one ever brought her homemade gifts at Christmas. It occurred to her that in order to receive, she needed to give. If she wanted to have friends, she needed to be a friend.

Starting tomorrow, she'd finish baking her loaves of pumpkin bread. Grandma always did a ton of baking during the holidays. Josie planned to continue the tradition. She had an angel dress to sew and deliveries to make, starting with Clint and Gracie. It was the least she could do to say thank you for all Clint had done for them. Gramps could help. He loved visiting with his neighbors and could make the deliveries. And it'd give Josie another opportunity to visit with Clint and Gracie.

Deep inside, Josie knew nothing could ever come of her relationship with the handsome forest ranger. Nothing but a distant friendship. And that left her feeling sad and empty inside.

Chapter Ten

The next morning, Josie started work on Gracie's angel dress. Thankfully, the choir director's wife had done the shopping and provided the pattern, fabric and thread, so that each child would be dressed the same.

By midafternoon, Josie stopped to help Gramps decorate their Christmas tree. While he strung the lights, she climbed into the attic to retrieve the ornaments. Flipping on the light, she gazed about the dreary space in surprise. Dust motes filtered through the threads of sunlight that peeked through the grimy window. Cobwebs and filth covered every surface. The cold caused her to shiver. As she crouched down and perused the stacks of boxes, she realized this was a big fire hazard. Forget a lighted match. All they needed was spontaneous combustion to burn down Gramps's house. She made a mental note to clean out this storage room before she returned to Las Vegas.

She lifted the lid to an old wooden trunk. A cloud of dust flew upward toward her face. She coughed and sneezed, waving a hand to clear the air. Peering inside, she saw a stack of old letters tied with a faded blue satin ribbon. Curiosity got the better of her and she lifted them out, noticing the dates, and that they'd been written by her parents before they'd married.

Love letters from the past.

Opening several envelopes sequentially, she scanned the yellowed pages. Loving words flowed from one sheet to the next. Her mother's words, expressing hope and joy for her life with Josie's father. Josie devoured every sentence like dry sand soaking up rain.

Before she knew it, she'd read seven letters. Her mom had written two letters for every one written by Dad. Separated when he'd gone off to college, she'd missed him and longed for the day when they could be together always. Likewise, Dad could barely concentrate on his school studies, he'd missed his sweetheart so much.

Sitting there in the dust and cobwebs, Josie found tears flowing down her cheeks. For the first time in her life, she realized how young her mom had been when she'd been divorced with a young child to raise. Too young. And Josie didn't understand why. All she remembered were the noisy fights filled with hateful words. And then the divorce and Mom's constant anger afterward.

Josie never saw her father again. When Gramps telephoned a year later to say that Dad had died in a car crash, Mom had responded stoically. Then she'd hung up the phone, walked to her bedroom, closed the door and sobbed uncontrollably. Josie had remained outside in the hallway, curled against the wall, her face buried in her hands. Longing to go to her mother. To be comforted. To know everything was going to be okay. But it wasn't. And four short years later, Mom had died of a heart attack.

They'd all been cheated out of a happy family life

together. If Mom and Dad had stayed together, things would have been different.

Never had Josie missed her father more than right now. If he'd lived and stayed with her mother, Josie's childhood would have been more carefree. Once Dad graduated from medical school, they would have had more money to pay the bills. Mom could have stayed at home more. Josie might even have some siblings to love. They would have been happy.

But all the would have's and could have's wouldn't help them now.

"Parents shouldn't outlive their kids, and kids shouldn't have to grow up without their parents," she murmured beneath her breath.

She wondered if her folks had had any inkling that they would both die young. What might they have done differently if they had known? What words might they have said to each other?

"Hey, sweetheart! You coming down?" Gramps called from the bottom of the stairs.

Josie swiped at her damp eyes. "Yes, I'll be right there."

In a flurry, she found the box of ornaments and placed the letters on top as she climbed down the ladder to the second floor. Depositing the letters in her room to finish reading later, she scurried downstairs with the box of colored bulbs.

The tree stood in one corner of the living room, the lights aglow. Gramps had turned on an old cassette of Christmas carols. "Rudolph the Red-nosed Reindeer" played in the background and Gramps sang along in his rich, bass voice. The house smelled of pine needles and the cinnamon rolls she'd popped into the oven just before she'd climbed into the attic.

"I got the rolls out," Gramps said.

"Oh, I forgot. Thanks, Gramps." She'd been rather distracted.

He inspected the tree, then turned to get her opinion. "It's pretty, huh?"

"Beautiful." A poignant feeling of love overwhelmed her and she hugged him, determined not to live her life with regrets. To cherish the people in her life now, while she had the time.

"I love you, muffin."

"I love you, Gramps."

As they stood there gazing at the lights, Josie realized she'd hardly thought about her job at the pharmacy over the past few days. Tomorrow, she'd call and check in with them.

And then a thought struck Josie. If she died, what would happen to Gramps? Who would take care of him as he got older?

The Lord. That's what Grandma would say. He was there for all His children. All Josie had to do was trust in Him. But Josie hadn't thought about God in years and didn't know how to start trusting in Him now.

"It's the prettiest tree I've ever seen. I'm so glad I'm here," she said.

And she meant it. Every word.

"Hey, sweetheart. You okay?" Gramps drew away, his gaze focused on her face. No doubt her eyes were red from crying.

She hugged him tightly, breathing in his spicy cologne, cherishing his presence like never before. "I'm just great. Thanks for letting me be here with you."

"Of course. This is your home. You're welcome any-time, muffin."

She laughed, a pang of nostalgia swamping her with memories. Gramps teaching her to fish. Grandma teaching her about the atonement of Jesus Christ and how to pray. Her grandparents had been her dearest friends. Yet she'd turned her back on God. He'd let her down, so she'd decided to ignore Him. But now, Josie wondered if she was wrong. Maybe, just maybe, Clint was right and God was waiting for her to call on Him again. Maybe God hadn't abandoned her, after all. Hmm. It was something to think about.

That night, Josie and Gramps sat on the couch and laughed as they sang songs and ate chunks of homemade peanut brittle. When she finally went to bed, Josie spent another hour pouring over her parents' letters. Laughing when they teased each other about some silly joke they'd shared. Crying when they talked of their future plans and how much they loved each other.

Poor, lonely Mom. How she must have regretted the divorce after Dad had died.

Waves of compassion crashed over Josie. She no longer saw her mother as an angry, bitter woman. but rather as a human being with failings and regrets of her own. And for the first time since Dad had died, Josie thought perhaps she may have unfairly judged her mom.

Chapter Eleven

The next morning, Gracie knocked promptly at ten o'clock. Josie opened the front door, her gaze locking with Clint's as he stood behind the little girl. And wham! Josie's senses careened into high gear.

"Hi, Josie. I'm ready to try on my angel dress." The child pushed open the screen door and skipped inside, a huge smile on her face. She tugged at her knit cap, but the long ties held firmly beneath her chin.

Conscious of Clint shifting his booted feet on the welcome mat, Josie hunkered down on one knee to help Gracie undo the knot. "Hi, sweetheart. We'll try on the dress first. Then I'm making cookies and divinity. You want to help me?"

The knot came free.

"I thought you weren't going to make divinity," Clint said.

Josie pulled off the cap and strands of Gracie's soft, clean hair lifted into the air with static electricity. "I thought I'd try it one more time. If the house catches fire, you'll know I've cooked it too long."

He laughed, the sound vibrating through her.

"Sure, I want to help," Gracie responded with enthusiasm.

After a warm hug, the little girl zipped into the living room, as though searching for her dress.

"Wait until I'm there. I don't want you to get stuck with pins," Josie called after her.

Clint gestured toward his daughter. "You sure you're up to watching her?"

"Oh, yes. It's no problem, really. We're going to have lots of fun. I fear you're getting the short end of the straw with repairing the roof in this cold weather." Josie stepped out onto the porch with him.

"No problem here. We've had several days of sunshine, so the roof is clear of snow." He picked up a small white bucket.

"What's that for?" she asked.

"Garbage, to put the decayed shingles in after I remove them from the roof."

Josie wrapped her arms around herself and peered at him as he hopped down off the porch in one graceful lunge. She couldn't help admiring his long, muscular legs and wide shoulders as he picked up a ladder and leaned it against the siding. A heavy tool belt hugged his lean hips. Armed with a bundle of new shingles, nails and a thin piece of metal flashing held beneath his left arm, he gripped the ladder with his right hand and stepped up on the bottom rung.

"You sure it's safe to climb up on the roof loaded down with all those tools?" She touched his shoulder.

He jerked his head around, lost his balance and dropped the box of nails. It hit the snow-covered ground and burst open, the metal spikes peppering the area.

"Sorry! I didn't mean to startle you." She scurried to help him gather up the nails.

"It's okay. Guess I'm a bit clumsy today." He gave a nervous laugh.

"As long as you're not clumsy up on the roof. It's a long drop down."

"Don't worry. I'll be fine."

Fearing he might think her a bit too forward if she fretted over his safety, she looked away. But inside, she knew she'd be heartbroken if something bad happened to this kind man. Gracie needed him. Having lost her own dad, Josie understood that very well.

Together, they plucked the wayward nails from the snow and deposited them back in the box. Gazing up into Clint's warm brown eyes when they'd finished, Josie felt as though the summer sun was shining down on her after she'd survived a long frigid winter. A happy feeling pressed in on her. A unique emotion she hadn't felt in...

Never. Not once in all her life had any man made her feel this way. Not even her two ex-fiancés.

She stepped back, wondering what being near Clint did to her senses. He seemed so grounded. Even when he lost his balance and dropped a box of nails, she felt complete confidence that he knew what he was doing, and would take care of everything.

An odd thought, surely. She had no idea what made her think such things.

"Thanks." He smiled down at her, stepping closer.

"You're welcome." Her lips parted. As she gazed up into his eyes, a sudden breathless tension overtook her. She felt lost and found all at the same time.

"Hey there, Clint!"

Josie jerked back as Doug Parson and Mike Burdett

walked up the driveway, neighbors who had lived on this street as long as she could remember. Doug worked for the state road crews as a supervisor and Mike owned a trucking company. Each man carried a variety of hammers and other tools. Josie had already spoken to Mike's wife, Rachel, about cleaning Gramps's house every week, once Josie returned to Vegas.

"Hi, Josie." Mike grinned at her.

"Hi, Mike. You two gentlemen here to help out Clint?"

Doug nodded, flashing a half smile. "Actually, Clint's doing all the work. We're just going to inspect it to make sure it's up to par."

Josie laughed at Doug's teasing, impressed that these men would take time out of their busy day to help her grandfather. "Thank you so much. I can't tell you how much Gramps and I appreciate your help."

"Ah, it's no problem. Your grandparents have sure been there when my family needed help over the years." Mike brushed aside her praise.

"Yeah, mine, too," Doug declared.

No doubt Clint had called them together. Their generosity touched her deeply. Once again, Clint's service reminded her that there were kind people in the world. That she wasn't alone. And she made a resolve to lessen her hours at the pharmacy and start looking for ways to help others. It was time she had a life outside work.

"Good morning, neighbors. You ready to tackle this job?" Gramps appeared, dressed in his winter clothes and packing a beat-up red toolbox.

"Oh, no. Not you." As he passed by Josie, she grabbed his arm and tugged him back.

His mouth dropped open in surprise. "I'm gonna help."

"No, you're not." She could just imagine her elderly

grandfather plummeting off the roof into a snowbank, followed by a frantic race to the hospital in Bridgeton.

"I'm sure not gonna sit inside while all the men are out here working," Gramps said.

Josie rested her hands on her hips. "Well, you're certainly not going up on the roof, either."

They stood there facing one another, a silent battle of wills waging between them. Finally, Gramps relented. "Okay, I won't go up on the roof. I can just be their fetch and carry man."

She tilted her head and peered at him with suspicion. "You promise?"

He pursed his lips, his gaze dropping to the ground. He grumbled something about sitting around like an invalid while everyone else did the work, but finally nodded. "I promise."

He stomped off to join the other men. Looking up, Josie's eyes met Clint's and he winked at her. "Don't worry. I'll make sure he stays safely on the ground."

A gentle comfort settled over her and she smiled as the four men huddled together to discuss their repair strategy. Josie took that as a cue to go inside.

Gracie sat before the coffee table, leaning her elbows on top, with her chin in her hands. A bored expression clouded her eyes until Josie appeared. Then the girl stood up straight, a bright smile flashing across her face. "Where's my dress?"

Josie laughed. "It's in the back bedroom. Come on. Let's go see if it fits."

Taking Gracie's hand, she led her into the back room. The dress fit beautifully, except the hem was too long.

"I'll have to shorten it," Josie said, and reached for the pin cushion.

The girl swirled and swayed, making the taffeta swish around her spindly legs. "Oh, it's so pretty. Daddy will think I'm beautiful."

"That's because you are," Josie said.

"Thank you."

Another hug followed. Josie set the length of the hem, relishing this special time with Gracie. Pretending for just a few minutes that she was her mother.

Soon, they retired to the kitchen. An occasional thump and tapping on the roof told her the men were hard at work. As she reached for the flour and mixer, Josie couldn't help feeling a sudden warmth deep inside her soul. The sense that God loved her, and had sent good men over to repair Gramps's roof and this endearing child for Josie to love.

Grandma had told her the Lord used other people to perform His work. Maybe even Josie was God's tool to help Clint, by making the dress for Gracie. She'd never thought of it that way before. And right now, she knew Gracie needed time with a mom. It felt so good to fill that role for the little girl.

Thirty minutes later, Gracie stood on a stool happily stirring sugar into the batter. "Dad and I are gonna go visit Santa down at Milton's grocery store when he's finished with the roof."

"Oh?" Josie looked up as she reached inside the fridge for the eggs and milk.

"Yep, and I know just what I'm gonna ask Santa for, too."

Josie hid a smile, wondering if she dared ask. She waited, thinking the girl might volunteer the information. She thought about the little porcelain doll, books, games and hair ties she'd purchased the day before to give the girl, and figured Gracie was at the age when she loved doll houses, nail polish and pretend makeup, too.

"And what would you like this year?" Josie finally asked.

"I can't tell you. It's a secret." The girl hummed a tune as she popped several chocolate chips into her mouth and chomped down.

Josie shrugged this off. Maybe Gracie feared she might not get what she wanted if she told anyone but Santa.

When they pulled the first batch of cookies out of the oven, Gracie sampled one with relish.

"Careful, it's hot," Josie warned.

"Mmm, these are the best cookies I've ever had."

"They are?" A feeling of harmony settled over Josie. For some reason, the little girl's approval meant everything to her.

"Yes. Can I take some to Dad and the other men?"

"Sure." Josie helped Gracie pull on her coat, then got a plate out of the cupboard and layered cookies on it before handing it to the girl.

"Careful, now. Hold the plate with both hands so they don't spill." She opened the door and the girl carried her offering outside. The screen door clapped closed behind her.

"Those are for me?" Josie heard Gramps's gravelly voice coming from the front yard.

"Yep, and the other guys, too. Josie and I made them," Gracie said.

Josie could just imagine the men devouring the soft cookies, and a smile of satisfaction curved her lips.

The buzzer sounded and she pulled the next batch out of the oven. As she sat at the table and placed dollops of

dough onto the pan, she accidentally knocked Gracie's
red gloves to the floor. When she reached down to pick
them up, a white piece of paper fell out of one glove. Josie
couldn't help noticing Santa's name scrawled across the
front flap in a child's handwriting. She didn't mean to
pry, but the letter lay open for her view and the request
was quite short. Expecting a request for various dolls and
games, she quickly scanned it.

Dear Santa,
I've been extra good, so I know you'll grant my
wish. I want Josie for my mom. Dad doesn't think
I know he's lonely, but he always looks so sad when
we're at home. And Josie and Grandpa Frank are
lonely, too. We need to love each other. We should
be a real family. That's all I want.
Gracie Karen Hamilton.

Her hands trembling, Josie folded the letter and tucked
it back inside the glove. Glancing over her shoulder, she
felt a wave of guilt and helplessness. She shouldn't have
read the letter. No wonder Gracie didn't want to tell her
what she wanted for Christmas.

It touched Josie deeply to know that she was Gracie's
Christmas wish. That the little girl thought enough of
her to want her for a mommy. And realizing these things
made Josie wish her life could be different. That perhaps
she and Clint could...

No! She mustn't think that way. It wasn't possible.
She lived in Vegas. Clint lived here. It would never work.

But in her heart of hearts, Josie couldn't help wishing
she could be Gracie's mother. She envisioned marrying
Clint and celebrating next Christmas like a real family,

right here in Camlin. They'd be so happy and in love. And he wouldn't mind that she was unlovable and emotionally inaccessible. But that would mean she'd have to abandon her job in Vegas.

She shook her head, returning to reality. She'd messed up with her other fiancés. Her career had kept getting in the way. Clint and Gracie deserved someone that could be there for them at the drop of a hat. Not a workaholic who didn't know when or if she'd be home to fix supper in the evenings. Besides, Clint wasn't interested in her. His service here at Gramps's house was a church assignment, nothing more.

And now what? How could Josie pretend she didn't know the letter's contents? How could she pretend she didn't know Gracie's true feelings? Or ignore her own loneliness?

And worse yet, how could she ever look at Clint in the same way?

Sitting at the table in Frank's kitchen, Clint bit into a piece of divinity and smiled with satisfaction. Doug and Mike had already left, each carrying a plate laden with mounds of chocolate chip cookies and candy Josie had presented to them for their families to enjoy. In spite of telling himself this service project was just about taking care of Frank, Clint enjoyed Josie's appreciation. Karen had always hidden out when people came to their home. Instead of scurrying to the back of the house somewhere, Josie had stayed out front and showered them with kindness.

Standing at the kitchen sink wearing a gingham-checked apron edged by red rickrack, Josie looked domestic and attractive. A strand of long hair hung across her flushed cheek, and Clint's hand itched to reach out and feel the silky texture between his fingertips. It'd been so long since he'd held a woman in his arms, and he couldn't help wishing...

"*Hop*. That's the word you want, Grandpa Frank." Gracie's voice came from the living room, where she was practicing reading with Frank. Her voice brought Clint back to reality.

"I'm so relieved that's finished and no one got hurt. In these slick conditions, you could have fallen off the roof," Josie said, oblivious to his wayward musings.

"Actually, the roof is completely dry. The sun has done its work over the past few days, but the weatherman is forecasting another storm on its way. We got the work done just in time," Clint said.

"Thank goodness. Were the shingles in bad shape?" Josie asked as she dried a clean mixing bowl with a dish towel.

"Not as bad as I thought. We had to replace quite a few and repair the flashing around one of the vents. The rest of the roof appears to be sound. If we had ignored the problem, it could have easily worsened. I didn't want Frank to have a leaking ceiling come February or March. Once the snow melts off in the spring, I'll check it again, just to be sure. We can do more thorough repairs then."

For some reason, he felt like talking. It was almost as though a surge of adrenaline pumped through his veins. He looked up and noticed a sheen of moisture in Josie's eyes. She turned away, as though embarrassed by her emotions. He could tell she was touched by this outpouring of love from her neighbors. And wham! A lightning bolt struck him from across the room. This was where he belonged. Here with this woman.

He choked on his cookie and coughed. She stepped near and pounded him on his back. "You okay?"

He nodded, thinking he'd lost his mind. "Yeah, I'm fine. Your divinity is delicious. Very sweet."

"Thanks." She smiled and went back to washing dishes. He watched her for several minutes. When he wasn't trying, he felt as though he'd known Josie all his life. Felt he could say anything to her and she'd understand. But then he remembered his failings with Karen and he felt suddenly out of place. If that wasn't bad enough, Josie would be leaving soon. It'd do him and Gracie no good to become overly attached to her.

"Why haven't you remarried, Clint?" she asked.

He blinked, stunned by her question. He coughed again, trying to find his voice.

"I'm sorry. I shouldn't have asked that." Her face flushed a pretty shade of pink.

"No, it's okay. Although it is a very personal question." He wasn't sure he was ready to discuss his personal life. And yet he longed to confide in Josie.

"And?" she persisted.

"Truthfully, I haven't remarried because I figure I don't deserve a second chance."

"You mean because your first wife died?"

"Yes, but also because of the way she died."

"And how was that?"

He hesitated a long time. "She took her own life."

Okay, he'd said it. But the words seemed to pour out of his mouth without his permission.

Josie flinched, her eyes filled with sadness. "I'm sorry, Clint. Suicide can't be easy on the loved ones left behind."

"Yeah, tell me about it. And what about you?"

"Hmm?"

"Why haven't you married? And don't tell me it's because you haven't met the right man yet."

Her gaze slid to the ground, but not before he saw the regret and disillusionment in her expressive eyes. "Actually, I've dated a lot. I've even been engaged twice."

"Really? And what happened?" he pressed.

"Me. I happened."

He quirked one brow. "I don't understand."

"In case you haven't noticed, I'm a bit of a perfectionist. Working all the time. Everything in its place. Neat and tidy. No room for error. You could say I worked a lot of late hours."

Clint understood that dilemma. Especially during the summer months, when he worked some very long days.

"I failed. I couldn't make them happy." Her voice sounded small and wounded.

Clint couldn't help comparing her doubts with his own. He couldn't make Karen happy, either. "What do you mean, you failed?"

She hesitated, her shoulders tense. "My last fiancé told me I worked too much and was bitter and unlovable, and that I'm emotionally inaccessible."

Unlovable? Inaccessible? Clint laughed, not believing that at all. Not when Josie had little trouble confiding in him. In fact, he'd never met a more loving, caring woman in all his life. Completely adorable and lovable.

"I doubt that. Not from my experience," he said. "Maybe it wasn't you. Maybe your fiancé wasn't the right man for you, after all."

She gave a scoffing laugh. "I don't know anymore. It doesn't matter now. But lately, I wonder if he was right. I have stopped working such long hours. I love my job, but it doesn't keep me warm at night."

Clint rested his hand on her arm and gave a gentle squeeze. "I sure would never describe you as bitter or unlovable. In fact, you're just the opposite."

Oh, boy. Maybe he shouldn't have said that. He jerked his hand away, realizing he was letting down barriers he couldn't afford to loosen.

"Thanks, but I doubt Edward would agree with you."

Clint lifted one shoulder. "Edward doesn't matter now. He's in the past. Give it time. You'll find someone else. Someone even better."

But he didn't want her to find someone else. Not unless it was him.

She looked skeptical. "I'm not so sure."

He snorted. "An attractive woman like you? Believe me, he's out there just waiting...."

Clint stopped and clamped his mouth shut, realizing what he was saying. He didn't want to have this conversation. No, sirree. He claimed to have faith in God, but maybe he didn't. Not fully. Not enough. Not if he couldn't forgive himself. A wave of fear washed over him. Speaking his thoughts out loud would bring him nothing but heartache. He just couldn't let go of the guilt.

"Sorry," he blurted like a fool. "I didn't mean to imply anything. It's just that if I loved a woman like you, nothing as simple as you working late would get in the way of me being with you. I think if Edward had really loved you, he would have been more supportive. Instead of complaining, he should have brought you dinner at your work."

Josie flashed a timid smile. "Thanks for saying that. And no apology is needed. Every woman likes to be told she's attractive."

But now that he'd said the words out loud, they were

firmly implanted in his mind. He couldn't take them back, and he knew they'd haunt him for a long time to come.

He didn't know why he wanted to reassure her, but he hated the sadness in her big blue eyes. Maybe it was because of his past relationship with Karen. Because he understood what Josie was feeling. The regret and sorrow. He tried to tell himself he hated to see her unhappy, and was just trying to make her feel good about herself. But he knew better.

He cared for this woman. A lot. Probably too much. More than he was prepared to cope with right now.

"You're still young and there's plenty of time to find that one person to call your own," he said.

She studied him for several moments, her eyes peering deep into his soul. "It sounds like you should take some of your own advice, Mr. Ranger."

He didn't like where this conversation was going and decided to change the topic.

"Yeah, maybe I should. You want to see the roof?" He ducked his head and picked up his tool belt to take outside with him.

"Sure!" She removed her apron, then reached for a sweater hanging from a peg by the outside door.

After stepping out onto the porch, he led her over to the sidewalk, then pointed up at the roof, where the new shingles were visible from their vantage point.

As he explained the work they'd done, she again expressed her gratitude. And once more he felt that full, enveloping warmth of pleasure suffuse his entire chest. As though this was right where he should be. With Josie.

The muffled sound of the buzzer on the clothes dryer

sounded from inside and she whirled around. "That's permanent press."

They walked back inside and he closed the door while she headed to the utility room to get the clothes out. Clint was about to join her when Frank appeared.

Jerking his thumb toward the doorway, the older man frowned. "Why don't you ask my granddaughter out?"

"Huh?" Clint's mind spun dizzily. He couldn't think of anything more intelligent to say.

"You heard me. Ask Josie out on a date."

Clint stood against the wall, feeling dazed. "I'm afraid marriage isn't for me, Frank."

"Bah! Who said anything about marriage? Just ask her out."

"Frank, at my age, asking a woman out can get serious very fast. And I can't let that happen again."

"That's baloney. You're young and handsome and you've got a little girl who needs a momma. My Josie needs a family, too. You're perfect for each other. You just don't know it yet. But every minute you waste figuring it out is a minute you could be living happily ever after. Believe me, life is short. You never know when it'll come to an end. You should be happy every minute that you can." Frank waved a hand in the air before jerking open the refrigerator door and pulling out a carton of milk.

As the man retrieved two glasses, then stomped back into the living room, a stutter of confusion filled Clint's mind. For years, he'd tried to tell himself he must remain single and focus only on raising Gracie. It was the best way. Right? Of course right! But now, that idea no longer held any appeal.

Chapter Twelve

Late Saturday morning, Josie sat curled up on the sofa in the living room, reading from the book of Psalms. Sometimes Gramps practiced his reading from the Bible, speaking the words out loud as she helped him sound them out. The fact that it was Grandma's birthday today made the Bible even more precious to Josie. Reading from it seemed to bring her closer to her grandmother. The poignant words seeped deep into Josie's soul. She hungered for the knowledge they imparted. Reading the passages, she started applying the principles to her own life, and saw ways to make herself a better, happier person.

Gramps stepped in from the kitchen and stood in the doorway, considering her. She looked up and smiled.

"Is something on your mind?" she asked.

"Yeah." He held her gaze for several moments, a look of compassion on his face.

"It's Grandma Vi's birthday today," she said. An overwhelming feeling of love encompassed her heart.

"So it is. You up to taking a little ride with me?" He

smiled and popped a piece of toast with raspberry jam into his mouth.

Placing the book aside, she uncurled her legs and sat forward on the couch. "Sure. When did you want to leave?"

"In ten minutes."

Not a lot of notice, but at least she was dressed. She had tossed a load of laundry into the washer and swept the skiff of snow off the front porch.

Curious about their destination, she indicated her clothing. "Am I dressed okay?"

"Yep." Chewing the toast, he headed toward his bedroom.

"I'll be ready." She stood and went to the closet to stomp on her snow boots and put on her coat.

Gramps soon returned, dressed in his winter gear. He went outside to fire up his truck and turn on the defroster. By the time Josie joined him, a warm jet of air filtered through the cab.

"Where we going?" she asked as she buckled up.

"You'll see."

She sat back, enjoying the quiet companionship of being with her grandfather. They didn't speak as he drove down Main Street. It had snowed again, but melted off the road, leaving the black asphalt gleaming. Shoppers bustled along the sidewalks as Gramps pulled up in front of the general store.

"Why are we stopping here?" she asked, confused.

He opened the door, but left the truck running. "You'll see. Wait here. I'll be right back."

Puzzled by his mysterious manner, Josie decided to enjoy the surprise. As he went inside the store, he waved at a couple of friends who were leaving. True to his word, he returned minutes later carrying four small, potted red poinsettias.

Tugging on the handle, Josie opened the door for him and he passed her the flowers.

"These are nice." She set the pots on the floor between her feet so they wouldn't tip over.

"Red was always Ma's favorite." He climbed inside, put the truck in gear and drove on.

"What are they for?" she asked as she admired the vibrant color of the soft petals.

"Not what. Who."

She crinkled her forehead. "Who are they for?"

"You'll see," he repeated.

He headed out of town, making a turn near the feed and grain store. As they rounded the bend near the outskirts, she realized where they were going.

The cemetery sat off to one side of the road. Fields lay before her, swathed in snow and segmented by one-lane dirt roads pitted by mud puddles. Headstones laden with melting ice dotted the expansive area. A black wrought-iron fence surrounded the perimeter, the spiky tips reaching upward toward the gray, clouded sky.

Gramps pulled inside the main gate, then drove two rows down and three over before he shut off the engine.

Josie didn't need to ask what they were doing here. Gramps obviously wanted to visit Grandma Vi for her birthday. The sentimentality of it warmed Josie's heart. How she wished she had someone to love and dote upon the way Gramps had always doted on Grandma.

Without a word, he climbed out and came around to open Josie's door for her. She handed him one of the poinsettias.

"Bring two of them and leave one behind for you," he said.

She smiled, touched by his gift. "Thank you, Gramps." She kissed his weathered cheek and a rumbly sound of pleasure came from the back of his throat.

After she'd scooped up two of the plants, he took her elbow and assisted her across the uneven road. As she neared her parents' graves, an uneasy feeling crawled up her spine. A dark fog filled her mind, the memory of funerals, tears and loneliness. She'd first lost Daddy, then Mom and then Grandma Vi. And by Josie's way of thinking, that was way too many funerals for someone her age to have to attend. Knowing she'd one day have to bury Gramps almost broke her heart.

Scrunching her shoulder up, she tried to wipe her suddenly damp eyes. Though her grandparents had brought her here throughout the years and told her stories about her family members, Josie didn't like this place. Even though her loved ones rested here, it was just another reminder of all that she'd lost, and that there was still more to lose.

They tromped through the fresh snow as Gramps led her to Grandma's grave. Ignoring the dampness, he knelt down and jerked the knit cap off his graying head in a show of respect. The right knee of his blue coveralls soaked up the moisture, but he paid it no mind. With his gloved hands, he brushed snow off Grandma's headstone. His fingers lovingly caressed Vi's name before he set one poinsettia on the ground. Bowing his head, he held the cap in his lap.

"Happy birthday, Vi. I hope it's the best day ever for you up in heaven. And merry Christmas, too." His low voice sounded thick.

Watching him, Josie felt a deep reverence for the love and esteem he'd shared with her grandmother. Josie wished she could comfort him somehow, but had no words to speak. Deep in her soul, she carried an abiding faith that death was not the end. Her reasoning mind could not accept anything less. And if that was true, then families must be eternal.

Once again, Josie couldn't help wishing she could share her love with one special man. Someone she could love more than life itself. Someone who would mourn at her grave if she died.

"This is another reason I can't leave Camlin." Gramps didn't look up as his voice surrounded her. "I need to be here for Vi. To visit her every week."

Josie rested a hand on his shoulder, her feet crunching in the snow as she shifted her weight. "I know, Gramps. You don't have to leave. I understand."

And she truly did. For so long, Josie had lived her life isolated, and thinking other people were holding her back. That she didn't need anyone. That she was better off alone. Now, she realized how wrong she'd been. The quiet support and encouragement she'd received all her life were invaluable. Her family had given her wings to fly. To grow and become a better person. To reach her goals. The realization of how much she appreciated them made her shiver.

"Gramps, why did they divorce?"

He took a deep inhalation before letting it go. "Who knows? Money problems. The stress of life. Selfishness is always at the core. I've never heard of a divorce where one or both partners weren't being selfish in some way or another."

She supposed that was true, and resolved to be more giving, more selfless.

"I realize Dad was your son, but why didn't my mom like coming here to visit you and Grandma after he died?"

Gramps took another deep breath. "She did back when they were first married, and you were born. But after the divorce and then your dad's death, I think it hurt her too much."

"Why? What happened?"

Her grandfather shrugged his drooping shoulders, his breath puffing on the air. "I think coming here was a reminder of everything she'd lost. It was too painful for her. Suddenly, she couldn't seem to get along with your grandmother anymore, but I think that was just an excuse not to stay. We always welcomed her with open arms."

Josie figured her mom must have been riddled by guilt. For years after she'd died, Josie made so many excuses not to come home. To stay away. Because she'd feared the pain of losing the very people she sought to avoid. Maybe she was just like her mother—cold and remote. Angry and unforgiving. And that frightened Josie. Because she didn't want to end up being alone all her life.

Until she'd met Clint Hamilton and his sweet little daughter, she had given up hope of ever marrying. But now she couldn't seem to think of anything else. What was it about the two of them that made her want to love again? To put her family first, above everything else, including her career?

She didn't know; it just seemed to be happening that way. But that didn't mean she knew what to do about it.

Pray.

The thought came to her so suddenly, a still, small voice deep within her heart.

"One time, I drove by the cemetery after your mom had dropped you off at the house for a short visit," Gramps said.

"And?"

"And I saw your mom here, lying across your father's grave. I stopped to comfort her, but it did no good. She was inconsolable. I think she regretted the divorce. Your dad died believing he'd be able to get her back one day. And maybe deep in her heart, your mom believed it, too. But death stole that chance from them. It was too late to make things right. And I think that's one reason your mom was so unhappy in life. She was racked by guilt. She'd lost your dad and couldn't make it right. Not in this life, anyway."

Josie blinked back sudden tears. The thought of Mom lying here, mourning the husband she'd lost, was almost too much to bear. In the past, it would have galvanized Josie's commitment not to love again. To remain aloof and protect her heart. But not this time. In the past few weeks, something had changed for her. She'd always believed in God and the atonement of Christ, though she hadn't always shown it. But now, she no longer wanted to wallow in guilt and past regrets. She wanted to live. To take the chances that might lead to her happiness.

Bracing one hand against the headstone, Gramps climbed to his feet and wrapped an arm around Josie's shoulders. "Your mom and dad loved you very much. I hope you know that."

No, that wasn't completely true. "Dad never came to see me after the divorce."

Gramps jerked his head around. "He did, but your mom wouldn't let him see you. Every time he called or sent you a gift, she refused them."

Oh, no. It couldn't be true. But it must be. Josie realized that now. Her mom had been so filled with anger that she'd made everyone else miserable, too. "I never knew."

Standing there in the cold field, she gazed at the trio of graves. One day, Gramps would rest along Grandma's right side. And Josie dreaded that day like the plague.

"I used to think Mom hated me," she said.

Gramps snorted. "Of course not. After your dad died, I think you were the only thing that kept her sane. Different people react to loss in different ways. Your mom lived for you, but it was hard. She didn't have much and we didn't have much to offer her, either. She worked hard to provide for you, and never gave up trying until the very end. I hope you'll always remember that."

His words sank deep into Josie's soul. Suddenly she understood all the sacrifices Mom had made for her. Working extra hours at her various jobs so she could take time off to attend one of Josie's field trips or science fairs. Although dark circles of fatigue marred her eyes, Mom had never voiced a single word of complaint. She just did it.

Maybe Gramps was right. Maybe Mom hadn't known how to show her inner feelings very well. Maybe Josie had read the situation all wrong.

And for the first time in a long time, she felt a peaceful feeling settle over her, as if arriving safely at her destination after a long and harrowing journey past a dangerous cliff. It must be the fledgling knowledge that God loved her. That she wasn't alone as long as she accepted the Lord into her life. A new concept that brought her a lot of comfort.

Reaching out his arms, Clint swung Gracie free of his truck and whirled her around. She squealed and clung to him. The pompom on top of her red knit cap bobbed wildly.

"Daddy, put me down," she cried.

He set her on her feet, his laughter mingling with hers in the crisp morning air. He took a breath, the frozen breeze biting his nose and lungs.

"When we're finished visiting Grandma Vi, maybe we'll have lunch at the Pizza Shop in town. Would you like that?" Picking up the single white rose he'd laid on the dashboard earlier, he slammed the truck door and took Gracie's hand in his.

"Sure. Can we invite Grandpa Frank and Josie?"

He released a deep sigh of frustration, his boots sinking into the snow of the cemetery as they rounded a tall, barren cottonwood. For some reason, he just couldn't get it through Gracie's head that they didn't need to spend every free moment with the Rushtons.

"I don't think that's a good idea...."

He froze in midstride, staring straight ahead. Frank and Josie stood together beside Viola's grave, their arms linked, their heads bowed as they spoke quietly together.

Great! He should have thought about this. Of course Frank and Josie would be here visiting today. It was Viola's birthday, after all. But Clint thought Frank usually came in the afternoons.

Reticent to interrupt, Clint opened his mouth to suggest they come back later.

"Josie!" Gracie yelled.

Too late.

The woman lifted her head, her eyes wide with surprise.

Jerking her hand free, Gracie took off at a run, galloping across the snow-covered cemetery. Not even considering that this was a place of respect.

"Gracie! Stop," Clint called after her.

She tripped over a low headstone and went down. As he ran to help, she pushed herself up and brushed at the snow covering her pants and coat.

"Hey, sweetheart. You okay?" Josie reached the child first.

"Uh-huh." Gracie nodded.

Clint didn't like this behavior at all. He bent over and inspected her. "*Are* you all right?"

She nodded and smiled.

He hugged her, then gave her a warning look. "Okay, but remember where we are. People's family members are buried here. Be polite and don't go running across the cemetery like that again."

She gave a little nod. "Sorry, Daddy. Can I take the rose to Grandma Vi now?"

Chuckling at her exuberance, he handed it over. Gracie held it up for Josie's inspection. "We brought Grandma a rose for her birthday."

"You did? That's so nice of you."

Whirling about, the girl picked her way carefully over to the road and then raced toward Frank.

"Hi, Grandpa Frank. Look what I got." Gracie's voice carried across the field, her enthusiasm contagious.

She launched herself at him. The elderly man opened his arms to receive her. "Hi, sweetheart. I'm so glad you came."

Turning, Clint smiled at Josie and gestured toward his recalcitrant daughter. He felt suddenly shy again, like an awkward schoolboy. He longed to take her in his arms and feel her melt against him. "We didn't know you'd be here, too. We didn't mean to intrude."

"It's no problem. Gramps and I were almost finished. You're lucky you caught us," Josie said.

Lucky. Yes, maybe so. He couldn't ignore a sudden feeling of excitement pulsing through his veins, as well as the danger signals ringing inside his head. Big-time.

"Are you here just for Grandma Vi, or is Karen buried here, too?" Josie turned and looked around the cemetery, as if she might spy Karen's grave.

"No, Karen is buried in Caldwell, Idaho. We don't get to visit her often, so we visit Viola instead. But I don't want Gracie to forget her mom." He spoke in a soft voice that wouldn't carry to his daughter.

"I can understand why. Caldwell's a long ways away from here." Josie also lowered her tone.

He hitched one shoulder. "It's where we were living when Gracie was born."

"Is that where Karen was from?"

"No, she grew up in a small coal mining town in Oklahoma." He didn't like talking about his wife, but he couldn't seem to shut off the flow of information.

"Ah, and what brought her out west?"

"Me. We met while I was working for the Forest Service. She had a part-time job bagging groceries at the general store. We hit it off immediately."

And he'd married her two months later. She'd been desperate to escape her life, and he'd provided the way out. He'd been so drawn in by her wide, soulful eyes and soft voice. He'd loved her instantly. Or at least he'd thought it was love. After their marriage, he'd locked his heart to all other women. Her gentle innocence had cried out to him. He couldn't seem to help himself. It had been his privilege and joy to sweep Karen out of the poverty she was living in and make a life with her. He didn't find out about the abuse she'd suffered until months later, when she was pregnant with Gracie. By that time, he was committed. This was his family and he'd do anything for them. He'd refused to give up on Karen. Even if she gave up on herself.

"She suffered from a deep depression. I couldn't make her happy." The moment he said the words, Clint regretted them.

Josie stared at him, as though not knowing what to say. "I don't believe that. Sometimes it's not so simple. You know that, right?"

He didn't nod or flex a single muscle. He wanted to accept what Josie said, but he couldn't. His guilt wouldn't allow it.

"Depression can make people mentally ill, Clint. I know you must have done everything you could for her," Josie said.

"You're very kind," he said. "And in my mind, I know you're right. But in my heart, I feel like I failed her. Like I should have been able to do something more to help her."

"Like what?"

Faced by Josie's blunt question, Clint wasn't sure. And that did something to him inside. He felt a softening, as though the chunks of ice encasing his heart had shifted somehow and were breaking loose.

"I'm not sure. But something," he said.

She looked to where Frank was pointing out various graves in his family plot, telling Gracie about each person's life.

Watching them, Josie made an offhand gesture. "You know, I've been so alone at times that I've often felt like I was in the middle of an ocean and had crossed halfway, but I still had half an ocean to go before I could make it to shore. And there I was, drowning. As though my face was covered with water and all I had was a straw to breathe through."

She turned and faced him, her eyes filled with conviction. "And then I came home to visit Gramps. And you and Gracie were here. You've helped Gramps and me when we needed you most. You've been our friend. I'm so sorry for your loss, Clint. But I have to tell you that you have friends here, too. You're not alone. And maybe it's time you cut yourself some slack and let go of the guilt. I have so many faults of my own, so I'm not in a position to judge. But I have learned that life is short, and wallowing in guilt isn't the way God wants us to live our lives."

He stared, stunned right down to his toes, and unable to say a word. His first instinct was to tell Josie to mind her own business. That she had no right to say such things to him. But then he realized she was right. She'd spoken the truth. And that softened him as nothing else could.

"You got your faith back," he said.

She lifted one shoulder. "Yes, thanks to you."

"Me?"

"You encouraged me to pray. It's a work in progress, but I've also been searching the scriptures and trying to give God a second chance. And then I discovered that He never really left me. It was me that left Him. But now I want to come back."

"I'm glad to hear that."

She turned and waved to get Frank's attention. "Gramps! I'm cold. I'm going to wait in the truck."

He nodded, and Josie glanced at Clint. "See you later."

"Yeah, later." He stood there, still amazed by what she'd said.

Frank slogged through the snow toward Clint. The two men greeted one another, but Clint felt like a wooden soldier just going through the motions.

"See you tomorrow," Frank said as he passed by on his way to join Josie.

"Yeah." Clint stared after the man, his mind broiling in confusion. At this point, he didn't know what to think. Or feel. Or say.

Tomorrow was Sunday. Church. No doubt Frank and Josie would be there. And as Clint walked over to join his daughter, he couldn't decide if that made him happy or sad.

Chapter Thirteen

The next morning, Josie sat in the front seat of Gramps's truck and shivered. Somber clouds scudded across the sky like dive bombers, just waiting to open up and let them have it again. Another storm was on its way, but that didn't diminish Josie's spirits. As someone who'd lived her entire life in the western United States, she figured it wasn't Christmas without snow. She just wasn't sure she liked this much of the white stuff.

Gramps stood outside, scraping frost off the windshield. He wore a yellow knitted scarf around his neck, handmade by Grandma Vi. He refused to let Josie clean the windows, for fear she might muss her pretty dress and high heels. Knowing she might see Clint at church, Josie couldn't bring herself to wear her practical, but dowdy snow boots. Though she tried to tell herself she didn't care if she caught the handsome forest ranger's interest, her vanity said otherwise. Of course, after the blunt words she'd spoken to him yesterday, she wondered if he'd ever talk to her again. She'd just make sure she held on to Gramps's arm as she teetered up the walk into the church.

Looking out the windshield, Josie noticed the frayed edge along one sleeve of Gramps's gray suit coat. It was definitely time to get him a new one. Grandma Vi would be mortified to have her husband going to church looking anything but his best, and Josie agreed.

Hmm. That gave her an idea for Christmas.

The warmth of the old defroster hadn't kicked in yet, but the cold wasn't the problem. Huddled in her coat, Josie felt nervous energy tingle down her arms. She couldn't remember the last time she'd been to church. Years earlier with her grandparents, during one of her short visits home. But she couldn't say when. Just that it had been way too long. The thought of going caused a strange, happy contentment to bubble up inside her. Then she feared God might disapprove of a sinner like her darkening the doorstep of the church.

Maybe she should stay home.

Gramps climbed inside the truck and slammed the door. "Brrr. It's cold as brass underwear out there." Fisting his hands together, he blew warmth onto them.

Josie gave a nervous laugh. "Gramps, maybe I shouldn't go."

He barely spared her a glance as he put the truck into gear. "Nonsense."

And off they went. Too late for Josie to change her mind now. Besides, she knew having her along brought Gramps a lot of joy. It wasn't often he got to go to church with a family member. She realized this wasn't just about her. Gramps was lonely, too. He liked her company. She could see it in the way he held his head high and whistled Christmas carols as he drove down the street.

"Gramps, you know I've been reading Grandma's Bible recently."

"Yes." He lifted one bushy eyebrow.

"Mostly the verses about God forsaking me."

"Ah, you've been reading Psalms twenty-two and twenty-three."

"How did you know?" Josie asked.

He hunched his shoulders. "I memorized those scriptures at my mother's knee, and I often think about them. They've sustained me during my life. Especially lately, since I lost Vi."

"Really?"

He nodded and began reciting the Lord's prayer out loud in his deep, bass narrator's voice that sounded as though he should be on TV.

Josie didn't move. Didn't breathe or twitch a muscle. His words held her spellbound. The emotion in his tone immobilized her. And when he'd finished, she sat frozen in her seat.

"A month after Ma died, I thought God must have forsaken me," he said. "How could I live without my dear wife? We'd been together for over fifty-seven years. How could I go on without her?"

Josie blinked and sent tears tumbling down her cheeks. "Oh, Gramps. I never knew."

He reached over and squeezed her hand. "But then you would call at just the right moment to lift my spirits. And then you came home for Christmas. Maybe you didn't know how much I needed to see you, but the Lord did. He sent you to me, Josie. You're an answer to my prayers, muffin."

She gave a croaking laugh. "I've never been an answer to anyone's prayers before."

"Sure you have, sweetheart. You've done so much for me. You were too young to remember, but your mother needed you once your daddy died. Nita wasn't taking good care of herself. Without you, I doubt she would have survived as long as she did."

"Mom needed me?" Josie tilted her head, hardly able to believe this.

"Oh, yes. More than ever.

She had no doubt Clint must have felt lost when Karen died. As though his world had ended and he couldn't go on. Yet he had. Because Gracie needed him. Because the Lord expected him to carry on to the end. And that made Josie respect Clint even more.

"Thanks for telling me, Gramps. I love you."

He smiled and squeezed her hand again. "I love you, too."

They'd reached the church. The redbrick building stood alone in a wide field. Sunlight gleamed against the damp pavement. During the summer months, green grass surrounded the area, a fun place for large barbecues and rousing games of baseball. As Gramps parked the truck, then opened the door for her to get out, Josie felt jittery. He led her inside the warm foyer and she stomped her heels on the black floor mat to get all the snow off her feet. Soft organ music filtered through the air, creating a reverent atmosphere.

"Josie! Grandpa Frank!" Gracie raced over to them, throwing her little arms around Josie's waist.

"Hi, sweetheart. You sure look nice today." Josie hugged the girl, her gaze sweeping over Gracie's fire-engine-red jumper and black tights. Her long pony tail bounced with each stride, and a floppy red flower was attached to the scrunchie at the back of her head.

"You look pretty, too. Doesn't she, Daddy?" Gracie whirled on her father, her face etched with expectation.

Josie looked up, to see Clint standing near the doorway talking to Mike Burdett.

"Yes, very pretty." Clint's gaze traveled over Josie, down her legs to her high heels.

"Is my angel dress almost finished?" the girl whispered, as if it was a secret she was keeping from her dad.

"It is," Josie replied.

"Oh, goodie. I'm gonna look so beautiful."

"Yes, you are." Josie squeezed her hand.

"Hi, Josie. How's the roof holding up?" Mike stretched out his arm.

"Just great. Thanks again for all your help." Unable to think of anything more intelligent to say, she smiled as she shook his hand.

Feeling Clint's gaze on her, Josie smoothed her fingers over the front of her floral print dress, a flush of heat searing her face. Why his compliment would cause such a reaction, she couldn't say. She only knew she liked it. A lot.

"Well, I better round up my family. The service is about to start," Mike said as he went inside the chapel.

Standing beside Clint, Josie swallowed, feeling giddy and uncertain of herself. As he shifted his weight, she gave him a double glance and caught the clean scent of wintergreen mouthwash. He looked so different today. She'd gotten used to seeing him in his Forest Service uniform or casual blue jeans. Today he wore a black pinstripe suit, shiny wing tip shoes, a white oxford shirt and red paisley tie. He appeared handsome and festive, his short hair slicked back with a bit of gel. He looked good. Too good.

Gracie hugged Grandpa Frank with enthusiasm. "Hi, Grandpa."

"Hi there, sweetie pie. You getting excited for Santa to come to your house?"

"Yes, I am." The girl pointed at Josie and gave Gramps a knowing look. The elderly man winked in response.

Frank looked up at Clint. "I hope you're planning to come over for Christmas dinner after the program on Christmas Eve."

"Oh, yes," Gracie said.

Clint looked doubtful and opened his mouth to speak, but Frank cut him off. "I won't take no for an answer. Josie's cooking us a feast," the older man said.

Clint blinked. "Okay, I guess we'll be there, then."

"Good." Frank grinned widely.

Josie didn't know if this was a good idea. Clint looked reticent, his brows bunched in a deep scowl. She didn't want to force him to share Christmas Eve with them, but she wouldn't deny she wanted him and Gracie there. Having a child in the house for Christmas would make the holiday even more special.

"Gramps, maybe Clint and Gracie have their own Christmas traditions," she said.

Clint met her eyes and heaved a deep sigh. "Actually, eating one of your nice meals might be refreshing for a change. You already know I'm not much of a cook."

His words pleased her enormously and she couldn't help anticipating the holiday with him.

Gracie tugged on Frank's coattail. He leaned down, and she cupped her mouth with one hand and whispered loudly, "I delivered my letter to Santa, just like I told you."

"You did, huh? That's good."

"Yeah, and he said he'd see what he could do."

Josie stared at her grandfather. Had he known about

Gracie's special Christmas wish? Why hadn't he told Josie? She didn't dare say anything, for fear she might upset Gracie. She glanced at Clint, wondering if he knew about it, too.

"Come and sit with us. I'll tell you all about it," Gracie insisted as she latched on to Gramps's big hand and tugged.

"Okay." A deep chuckle rumbled in his chest as he let her lead him into the chapel.

Josie watched them go with misgivings. Then she glanced at Clint and shrugged it off. "Looks like we're sitting together."

"Yeah, it looks that way." He cupped her elbow and indicated she should precede him to the pews.

As they entered the chapel, several people Josie didn't know turned and stared at them, then ducked their heads together to whisper among themselves. Thelma Milton waved from across the room and nodded in approval. Helen Mulford sat up front playing the organ, her face creased in a knowing smile.

Josie looked away, a flood of warmth heating her cheeks. No doubt the gossips would have a good time discussing her and Clint sitting together.

Clint leaned down and spoke close to her ear, his warm breath brushing against her face. "You sure you want to sit with Gracie and me? Looks like we'll be the topic of discussion all over town for the next week."

Oh, let them talk. Josie didn't care. Not today. Clint's touch brought her a deep sense of fulfillment, as though she belonged here with him. A crazy notion, but irrefutable proof that they'd become close friends. Yet he seemed reticent. As though he didn't want to be with her.

"It's okay. It won't last long," she said.

As they approached, Gracie slid close to Gramps. Josie had no choice but to sit sandwiched between Clint and the little girl. As the prelude music ended, Josie was surprised to discover she felt perfectly at home. She listened to the service, and a peaceful feeling settled over her. Like a homecoming. As though she'd never been away. An odd notion, surely, but undeniable all the same.

Midway through the program, the church choir sang "Hark the Herald Angels Sing." With several elderly people among them, they weren't the best in the world, but their vibrant voices meshed together in perfect harmony. Like angels singing praises to God, their words pierced deep into Josie's heart. She'd never heard anything so beautiful in all her life. And the sermon on Christ's mission here on earth left her feeling calm and quiet inside, as though all was right in her world. In spite of her fears and worries, God lived, and loved her. He was here for her and had everything in His control. All she had to do was rely on Him.

Easier said than done. But Josie was trying. She wished Clint lived in Vegas and wasn't hung up by guilt. But he was, and he lived in Camlin. And they couldn't be more than friends.

He leaned close and whispered, "You okay?"

She blinked and nodded, realizing tears filled her eyes. He must have seen them. As she responded, she again caught his clean, spicy scent.

"Yes, I'm just enjoying the meeting."

A smile creased the corners of his mouth. "Good. I'm glad you're here."

"So am I."

And she meant it. But realizing what she'd just admitted, her breath froze in her throat. Except for Gramps, she couldn't remember a time in her adult life when someone had told her that they were glad she was there. It meant a lot to Josie. It meant everything. If only it could last.

By the time Sunday school was over, Clint couldn't fight it anymore. His attraction for Josie had become a powerful energy he couldn't deny. And yet he must, for Gracie's sake as well as his own. And telling Josie she looked pretty, and that he was glad she was here, and agreeing to share Christmas dinner, wasn't helping him fight that magnetism.

Standing in the outer foyer while he waited for Gracie, he leaned back against the wall and slid his hands into his pants pockets. Josie stood close by, waiting for Frank. Clint told himself it was just because she didn't know many people here, so she seemed to gravitate to him like a lifeline. But deep inside, he wished it was because she...

What? Wanted to be around him? The way he wanted to be with her?

"She's always such a happy kid." Josie indicated Gracie as the girl skipped down the hall with her friend Jenny Fletcher.

The girls' teacher called them back, indicating they'd forgotten the pictures they'd drawn during their Sunday school class. Even this far down the hallway, Josie caught the melodious sound of Gracie's laugh. The kids disappeared inside their classroom again, no doubt gathering up their artwork.

Clint nodded, his gaze pinned on the doorway where his daughter had disappeared. "That's mostly due to you."

"Me?"

"Yes, she's grown quite fond of you."

Unfortunately, so had Clint.

Josie's eyes glowed with pleasure. "I'm fond of her, too. Very much."

"And I appreciate that," he said. "The time you've spent with her baking cookies and making her angel dress has been therapeutic for her."

"It's been my pleasure. I can understand her wanting to bake, especially at Christmastime. I've been feeling the same way for a long time now. It's been refreshing to cook and sew, and spend time at home for once."

He tilted his head in confusion. "You don't do those things when you're in Las Vegas?"

"I'm afraid all I do when I'm at home is work. I rarely take time to bake cookies or go shopping. I guess it's because I live alone. Although I may start making baked goods to take to my coworkers at the pharmacy. That sounds nice. I think I need more balance in my life. Not so much work," Josie said.

He nodded in agreement. "I know what you mean. It's hard when you're trying to get ahead in your career. Work can easily take over, but that's not healthy. We have to fight to keep some balance."

"Yes, especially someone in your situation. It can't be easy raising a little girl all by yourself."

"It's definitely worth it, though. But there *are* times when I wonder if God has forgotten about us. Then I look into Gracie's eyes and I realize that isn't so."

Josie's own eyes crinkled. "You surprise me, Clint. I never thought anything could rattle your strong faith."

He glanced her way before his gaze slid to the floor. At one time, he'd thought the same. Since Karen's death, he'd learned that wasn't true. "I do have a strong faith, but I have bad times just like everyone else. Sometimes

I'm tested and my trust in the Lord slips a bit. It takes constant vigilance for me to stay strong."

And confessing all this to Josie was like admitting to his mother that he'd just robbed a convenience store at gunpoint. Not a pleasant admission at all. If only Josie wasn't so easy to talk to.

She hesitated, biting her bottom lip. From the flash in her expressive eyes, he knew she wanted to say something more, but was trying to choose her words carefully.

"Thank you for telling me that, Clint. I'll admit I've come to look up to you, and it helps give me hope to know someone as strong as you has trials just like me."

Her words made him like her even more. She seemed so approachable and human. Someone he could relate to. Someone he could confide in. Not at all the stuck-up, high maintenance woman he'd once thought she was.

"Coming home for the holidays has taught me a lot about my faith lately," she continued.

He arched one brow. "Oh? How so?"

"Well, I've discovered that you don't build faith when the sun is shining bright and all is right with the world. Faith comes in the darkness, when we're most vulnerable and must depend upon God to pull us through."

Her words sank deep into the farthest reaches of his heart and anchored there. Inspiring him. Offering him hope. When he'd first met this woman, he'd never expected her to teach him about God. But that's exactly what she'd just done.

"That's so true. I'm glad you've regained your faith," he said.

She gave a dazzling smile. "It's not perfect, but it's coming along. The main thing I've noticed is that my life doesn't seem so hopeless anymore. I don't know how everything's going to work out for Gramps and me, but I feel more excited by the possibilities."

How Clint envied her discovery. His own life wasn't great, but it was going along okay. He had a challenging career and a beautiful little daughter, but it just wasn't enough anymore. Not for him. He felt as though something was missing, something he needed if he was ever to feel whole again. And he suspected that something was Jocelyn Rushton. But it would do no good to dwell on something he couldn't have. She'd be leaving soon. He couldn't pursue her. He just wished he could get her out of his mind once and for all.

Chapter Fourteen

Josie shifted the strand of red-and-gold garland across the windowsill in the living room. With barely a week before Christmas, she was having the time of her life sprucing up the house for Gramps. Tomorrow they would drive to Bridgeton for some last-minute shopping. And she couldn't wait to pick up the special gift for him she'd ordered online at the department store.

Holding several pins in her mouth, she tacked the shimmering filaments into even swags across the window. She stood on the step stool and tugged to take up the slack on one drape and make it even with the others.

"How does that look, Gramps?"

He cleared his throat. "A little more to the left."

He sat in his recliner behind her, giving her instructions as she fought to get the decorations just right.

She pulled a little more. "Is that better?"

"It's too—" The sound of papers hitting the floor interrupted the flow of words.

"What, Gramps?" She stuck another pin into the wall to hold the garland secure.

He didn't respond and she cast a sideways glance over her shoulder. "Gramps!"

He lay curled on one side in his chair, clutching his left arm, his face contorted with agony.

Hopping off the stool, she rushed over to him. "Gramps, what is it?"

"My…arm. Hurts," he gasped.

Heart attack!

Josie didn't wait another moment. Racing to the bathroom, she jerked open the medicine cabinet. A tube of toothpaste hit the floor with a thud. Prescription bottles clattered into the porcelain sink. Josie paid them no mind. What she wanted was nitroglycerin, but she already knew from past conversations that Gramps didn't have any. He'd told her he didn't need it anymore. That the doctor had given him a clean bill of health.

Yeah, right.

Instead, she clasped the bottle of baby aspirin in her hand. Running back to the living room, she popped the lid and pushed two tablets into Gramps's mouth.

"Try to chew them up and swallow," she encouraged, caressing his face with her hands.

He did his best, wheezing for breath. When he got the aspirin down, she grabbed the phone.

"Hold on, Gramps. I'm getting help. Just hold on."

She dialed Clint's number, her mind churning. If only there was an ambulance in this town. Dialing 911 would just bring Officer Tim to her door. That didn't inspire a lot of confidence in her. The nearest hospital was in Bridgeton, a sixty-eight-mile drive away. And Josie was determined to load Gramps into her car and drive him there as quickly as possible.

"Come on. Come on," she urged, as the phone rang and rang.

Clint's voice mail picked up. He wasn't home. Probably at work. She clicked off, not leaving him a message.

Her mind raced. Who else could she call?

She dialed Mike Burdett across the street, hoping against hope that he was home. If nothing else, he could help her get Gramps into the car.

"Hello?" Rachel, Mike's wife, answered the phone.

In several clipped sentences, Josie explained the problem.

"Oh, honey. I'll send Mike right over."

"Thanks, Rachel." Josie dropped the receiver back into its cradle and hurried to the hall closet, where she retrieved a warm quilt to wrap around Gramps.

"Mike's on his way," she called urgently over her shoulder. "He'll be right here. How you doing?" she asked, wanting Gramps to know she was there for him. Wanting him to hear her voice and take hope.

"It...hurts," he wheezed.

Her heart plummeted. She ran back to him, kissing his face, smiling at him, urging him to hold on.

The next fifteen minutes whizzed by in slow motion. Mike finally arrived and helped her load Gramps into her sedan. A fissure of fear caused Josie's stomach to contract. Gramps breathed easier and seemed to be in less pain, but his pallid face told her he wasn't out of danger yet.

What if this was the end? What if she lost him? She just couldn't take it. Not at Christmastime. Not now.

Not ever.

"I can ride with you," Mike offered, once they had Gramps buckled into his seat.

She quickly tucked the quilt around him, to keep him warm. With her purse slung over her shoulder, she slammed the door and rounded the car to the driver's seat. "Thanks, but I don't think that's necessary. We should be fine now. Can you call the hospital for me and tell them what's happened and that we're on our way?"

"You bet. Just drive safely. Thank the Lord the roads are clear today." He nodded and stepped back.

Yes, thank the Lord.

Josie fired up the car. Hyperconscious of Gramps's comfort, she cranked the heater on high. She pulled out of the driveway, fighting off the temptation to speed all the way. As they left town, the slick roads cleared to damp black pavement and gratitude suffused her. If they could just get to the hospital in time...

She glanced over at her grandfather. His eyes were closed and a shiver of dread swept her. "Gramps? You okay?"

"Sure. Just dandy." He opened his eyes with a wan smile.

She gave a nervous laugh and reached over with one hand to squeeze his arm. "You hang in there for me. We'll be to the hospital in just a few minutes. Everything's going to be fine."

She kept talking, wanting him to cling to life until he could receive proper medical attention.

"Thanks for being here." He spoke without opening his eyes. His breathing sounded a bit better.

She flashed a sarcastic smile, trying to lighten the moment and inspire confidence in both of them. "Oh, I wouldn't miss this for the world."

And then she wondered what would have happened if she hadn't been here.

She tried not to contemplate what might happen once she returned to Las Vegas and Gramps was all alone. She couldn't think about that now. She needed to concentrate on her driving. On getting Gramps to the hospital safely.

The short trip seemed to take hours. When she pulled up at the emergency entrance to the hospital, a man and woman wearing blue smocks bustled out and took over. Josie helped them load Gramps into a wheelchair. He was conscious, but he fell back into the seat and closed his eyes, his face creased by utter exhaustion.

As they whisked him away, Josie's heart pumped hard in her chest. She would have followed, but a receptionist at the front counter intercepted her, asking for medical and insurance information. Josie watched helplessly as Gramps disappeared through two wide swinging doors. A feeling of complete panic clawed up her throat.

Was this the last time she'd ever see him alive? There was so much more she wanted to say to him. So many things she wanted to share.

Hot tears burned the backs of Josie's eyes. Her hands trembled as she opened her purse and reached inside for her wallet. And that's when she prayed, silently in her heart. A plea that God would preserve her grandfather's life and help him get well. She needed Gramps. Needed him like flowers needed rain and sunshine. If she lost Gramps now, she'd lose everything.

She staggered against the front counter.

"Hey! You all right?" the receptionist asked.

No! Josie wanted to cry. A dull throbbing pounded against her temples. The thought of losing Gramps was almost more than she could take. She didn't know how she did it, but she took hold of herself. If Clint was here, she'd feel stronger. She knew it instinctively. His presence always brought her peace. Within a few short weeks, she'd come to rely on him so much. Just his advice and companionship had given her the strength to regain her faith.

But her relationship with the forest ranger couldn't continue. She knew that, though she tried to ignore it. Soon she'd return to Las Vegas. All good things must come to an end. And standing there in the middle of the busy emergency room, with the phones ringing and the voices of complete strangers surrounding her, Josie had never felt more alone in all her life.

Clint's boot heels pounded the tiles of the hospital floor as he hurried down the hall. It'd been over an hour since he'd gotten news of Frank's collapse. Clint had torn out of his house, gotten into his truck and driven to Bridgeton without considering the ramifications. All he knew was he needed to reach Josie. To make sure she and Frank were safe.

Pausing next to a decorated Christmas tree in the main foyer of the emergency department, Clint got his bearings. He stepped over to the reception counter and asked directions to Frank Rushton's room.

"Are you a family member?" the receptionist asked.

"No, but we're close friends. Very close." The last thing he wanted was to be told that he couldn't see Frank.

The receptionist smiled. "Down the hall, to your right. You'll see a waiting room where you should find Mr. Rushton's granddaughter."

After striding down the corridor, Clint rounded the corner. His gaze swept the myriad people lounging in chairs and sofas in the waiting room.

Josie wasn't there.

Whirling back the way he'd come, he scanned the hallway for some sign of her. His gaze screeched to a halt beside a door. She stood leaning against the wall, her hands clasped in front of her, her head bowed as if in prayer.

Seeing her brought Clint instant relief. But what about Frank? He was the last family Josie had. If they lost him, she'd be all alone in the world.

Not if you stay by her side.

The words came unbidden to Clint's mind, but he refused to let them take root. Warning bells jangled inside his mind.

He walked toward her, not wishing to intrude, yet needing to know if Frank was all right. Clint's mind told him he shouldn't be here. He shouldn't get more involved than he already was, but he couldn't bring himself to leave. And his misgivings wreaked havoc within him.

Josie looked up, visibly shaking. Fatigue shadowed her beautiful blue eyes along with translucent tears. Fear and utter desolation etched her features. Her porcelain skin was almost void of color. The strain of today's events caused her mouth to tighten.

A surge of protectiveness rushed through Clint. He yearned to take her in his arms. To share her burdens and keep her safe. But that was a fallacy. He'd shared Karen's burdens, but that hadn't stopped her from taking her own life. Nor could he prevent bad things from happening to Josie, either.

"Clint." She breathed his name, but he heard it just the same.

"How is Frank?" he asked as he joined her, praying silently the elderly man would recover.

She shook her head. "They haven't told me anything

yet. I'm sick with worry. I don't know what could be taking so long. What are you doing here?"

"You called me."

Her eyes widened in surprise as she wiped her nose and sniffed. "But I didn't leave a message. How did you know?"

"Caller ID. When I couldn't reach you at Frank's house, I phoned Mike Burdett. He told me everything."

"And you came." Her voice sounded tremulous. In a sudden burst of emotion, she flung herself into his arms.

He held her as she sobbed against his shoulder, obviously overwhelmed by her ordeal. It felt good to be needed. To have a woman depend upon him. To trust him. Somehow it lessened the sting of how badly he'd let Karen down.

He wrapped his arms around Josie's trembling back. The intimacy of cradling her close and comforting her like this did something to him inside. This was what he'd yearned for over the past few weeks. To have her pressed against him. He could almost feel his frozen heart thawing. His gaze lowered to her lips and a sense of longing slammed through him—so powerful that he almost kissed her right there in the hospital for all the world to see. The scent of cinnamon and allspice clung to her clothes and hair. The fragrance of home and hearth. He never wanted to let her go. And yet he must.

"There, there. It's gonna be okay. I promise." He didn't know what else to say. Each of them must die, and he knew it might very well be Frank's turn. But Clint's faith gave him the hope that death was not the end, but rather the beginning.

He loved Frank like a father. The fact that Josie had tried to call him when Frank collapsed touched Clint on a deeply protective level. It indicated she trusted him. That she'd reached out for help. Something Karen had never done.

"You okay now?" he asked.

"Yes." Josie took a shallow breath and gave a jerky nod.

"I got here as fast as I could."

"Thank you for coming. I can't tell you how much I appreciate it." Regaining her composure, she drew back and wiped the tears away with her fingertips. Mascara smudged her eyes.

"You're welcome. I couldn't stay away." He took hold of her chilled hands, trying to warm them with his larger ones.

His confession caused a sting of warning to race up Clint's spine. He loved her; he knew it now with perfect clarity. He loved her more than he could comprehend. But what if he couldn't make her happy? What if they got engaged and she broke it off? Or if they married and she died, or decided to leave him later on? Divorce or death. He couldn't take that chance again. If he were alone, that would be one thing. But he had to think about Gracie and the havoc such trauma might wreak on her young life.

"Where's Gracie?" Josie asked.

His wayward thoughts caused the sizzling heat of embarrassment to flood his face. He hauled in a deep breath, trying to settle his nerves. "Rachel Burdett's watching her until I get home. I'm sure she's having fun playing with the three Burdett kids."

"I guess you were worried about Gramps." Josie's voice cracked and so did his heart.

He tilted her chin up so that she met his gaze. "I was

worried about you, too. What you've been through today hasn't been easy. I didn't want you to be alone."

A wobbly smile curved her lips, and in her eyes, he saw her disbelief. "No one's ever come to be with me like this before. I don't know what to say. I've intruded on your life so many times already, yet you always make time to be there when I need you most."

Yes, and he'd loved every minute of it. Cutting Christmas trees together, shoveling snow, roof repairs and eating Frank's pancakes. But Clint couldn't say that out loud. He'd already said too much.

"It's no problem. Come on." Taking her hand, he led her down the hall to a secluded spot where they could sit and talk privately until the doctor came out to see them.

"I can't believe you actually drove here to Bridgeton," she said as she slipped off her shoes and settled on a chair. She curled her legs beneath her, looking small and vulnerable.

The sharp pain of loss stabbed his heart. He couldn't make everything up to Karen, but he could sure make a difference for Frank and Josie Rushton. "Serving you and Frank has become kind of cathartic for me. It's a way to lessen my own grief."

A silvery tear plummeted down her cheek and she shivered. "I'm sorry you have to see me like this. And I'm sorry you're still grieving for Karen."

He licked his bottom lip. "I sometimes wonder if I'll ever stop feeling guilty for her death."

Josie tilted her head. "Why, Clint? From what you've told me, you did everything you could to help her."

"I tried. I really did. But it wasn't enough."

"Can you tell me what happened?"

No, he didn't want to. But something about this moment had drawn them close together. The possibility of losing Frank had become too real for both of them.

He took a deep breath and let it go. "The first few months of our marriage, we were happy. Then we had the new baby and a promising future. Everything was going great, but Karen couldn't see it. It's as if she was two different people. Depression lived inside her. She was diagnosed with a serious case of bipolar disorder. Medication helped some, but she wouldn't take it regularly. She slept all the time. I was working long hours, gone all the time. Don't get me wrong. I know Karen adored Gracie. But postpartum depression complicated the problem. When I was called out on a wildfire, I thought Karen was getting better. She was getting up in the mornings, doing the laundry and cooking dinner. She became quieter, less complaining. I later learned that was a sign she'd pulled further inside of herself. I wasn't there when she needed me the most. I guess that's why I'm determined to be here for you. Because you need me."

There, he'd said it. And he couldn't help contrasting Josie with Karen. Both women had suffered from severe loneliness. Neither one had enjoyed a happy childhood. But where Karen had shut herself off from the world and wallowed in her own grief, Josie had pushed forward, serving others. She'd never given up hope or stopped trying. She'd refused to quit. In Clint's view, that was a distinct difference.

"What happened when Karen died?" Josie asked.

He gave a scoffing laugh, unable to forget the last time he'd seen his wife alive. She'd been holding their infant daughter close to her chest and had given him a halfhearted smile and a kiss goodbye.

"I was called out on a wildfire in Montana. As I

crossed the tarmac to get on the chopper, Karen held Gracie up and waved her little arms at me. Karen looked happy, if a bit pale and tired. I told her to get some rest. We were planning a trip to Yosemite once I returned." He paused, the memories washing over him like a cold rain. "I was only gone one day when I received news that she'd taken our daughter over to the neighbor's house, then went home and drowned her sorrows in a bottle of sleeping pills."

Josie cringed. "Oh, Clint. I'm so very sorry."

He clenched his eyes closed. Josie needed him to be strong right now. His old faded problems didn't matter anymore. But oh, how he wished he could let them go.

"You're a remarkable man to have survived that and be doing such a great job with Gracie," she said.

"I haven't made it, yet. I keep battling between compassion and anger toward Karen. I don't know if I'll ever understand why she couldn't cope. Why weren't Gracie and I enough to make her happy? Why did she have to take her own life?"

Josie reached out and rested her hand on top of his. Her touch sent tingles of warmth shooting up his arm. "I don't know all the answers, Clint. I do know depression is very real. As real as any other illness, like diabetes or cancer. Our modern medicine doesn't know everything. Our minds and bodies are complicated machines. But you've taught me that God is the great equalizer. I think because of the atonement of Jesus Christ, all of us can receive forgiveness for our failings. And if you really believe that, then you should forgive Karen. You should forgive yourself, too. Let God be the judge. You don't need to carry this burden anymore."

He flashed her a smile. "For someone with fledgling faith, how'd you get to be so smart?"

She gave him a shy, sidelong glance. "You taught me."

He reared back, surprised by that. He thought about what she'd said and realized that forgiving Karen was easy. After all, she'd been mentally ill when she'd died. Not in her rational mind. But forgiving himself was much harder. He wanted it so much, craving redemption like a starving man craved bread. "Sometimes I think I was trying to fix Karen. And when I couldn't, it devastated me. It left me believing I'd failed her miserably."

"No, you didn't fail. I know you well enough to know you tried your hardest."

Not hard enough. In retrospect, he thought perhaps that had been his attraction for Karen. He was the great protector, after all. His entire purpose was to make her whole again. But now, he knew only the Lord could do that for her. And for him.

Clint had a lot to think about.

"Does Gracie know about Gramps?" Josie asked.

"Yes. As soon as I know he's all right, I've got to call her. I suspect the whole town knows about it by now and they'll be waiting for news."

She chuckled, seeming more at ease now that he was here. "She's a sweet little girl. You're lucky to have her."

Thinking about his daughter made him laugh. "Yeah, I know it."

"Maybe it was for the best that Edward and I broke up. He never wanted children."

Clint looked at her closely. "And you do?"

She nodded. "I do. Yes. Maybe someday. But it's not looking too promising at this point in my life. I'm getting older."

"You still have time."

She shrugged. "I hope so."

"You'd make a great mother."

"You think so?" A gentle smile curved her lips.

"Yes, if the way you treat Gracie is any indication."

Josie hesitated for several moments, as if thinking this over. "Thanks for saying that, Clint. I can't tell you how much I needed to hear that right now. But Gracie is so easy to love."

"She certainly is."

And so are you, he thought to himself.

He couldn't help thinking how much Josie had overcome. Frank had recently told him a lot about her unhappy life. Clint thought of his own happy memories from his youth and wished he could share them with Josie. But he feared getting close. She'd already gone through two fiancés and Clint didn't want to be the third. Besides, the end of the holidays would come soon enough. And then Josie would return home. And that would be that.

Chapter Fifteen

"**M**s. Rushton?"

Josie turned and saw a doctor standing in the doorway. He was wearing a white jacket and holding a clipboard, and had a stethoscope dangling around his neck. Both Josie and Clint popped out of their seats and hurried over to him.

Finally some news.

"I'm Jocelyn Rushton." She clenched her hands, prepared for the worst. She took comfort from Clint's silent support, highly aware of him resting one strong hand on her shoulder. She couldn't believe he'd driven all the way to Bridgeton just to be with her during this difficult time. She fed off of his presence, feeling better.

"I'm Dr. Crockett, your grandfather's doctor. Frank is all right. His EKG and blood enzymes tell us he suffered a mild heart attack. He's resting comfortably now." Dr. Crockett's thin brows arched with his smile.

"Oh, thank the Lord." Relief swept her body and she released her breath in one giant whoosh. She hadn't been aware she'd been holding it in while she awaited the final verdict. Now, she had so much to be grateful for.

"He doesn't appear to have any arterial blockages," the doctor continued. "I want to keep him in telemetry to monitor him overnight. If all goes well, he can return home tomorrow afternoon. I know it's difficult during the holiday season, but I would suggest that he lower the intake of fat and carbohydrates from his diet. I'm also concerned that he hasn't been taking his heart medication."

She tilted her head, conscious of Clint doing the same. Both of them were startled by this news. "What heart medication? I didn't know he was supposed to be taking anything."

"I prescribed a blood thinner for him almost two years ago. This might not have happened if he'd been taking it regularly."

A sick feeling settled in Josie's stomach. Maybe Gramps had stopped taking his medicine after Grandma died, because he couldn't read the label. Josie wasn't sure what his reasons were, but she intended to find out.

"That won't be a problem anymore. I'll ensure he takes it from now on," she promised.

Dr. Crockett shifted the clipboard in his arms. "Good. I'm glad to hear it. I'll write you out a new prescription. You might want to fill it here in Bridgeton before you return home to Camlin."

"I'll do that," Josie said.

"You can both go in and see Frank now."

"Thank you, Doctor." She smiled, grateful for the Lord's intervention today.

The doctor left them and Clint squeezed her arm. "You see? I told you everything would be fine."

"Yes, you did." She couldn't help returning his smile.

"Do you mind if I come with you to visit the ol' codger?"

She laughed, feeling giddy with relief. "Of course not. You and Gracie are like family, Clint. Come on."

Together, they walked down the hall. After finding out which room Gramps was in, they went to see him in the ICU. A strand of holly and red berries had been strung along the top of the white curtain that partitioned his bed off from the rest of the room.

He was wearing a hospital robe, and most of his body was covered by several thin blankets. The upper portion of his chest lay open to view and was taped with a twelve-lead EKG heart monitor. His left arm rested by his side and had been hooked up to an IV. His eyes were closed, his face serene.

The moment Josie touched his hand, he turned his head and looked at her. "Hi, muffin." His voice sounded raw and tired.

"Hi, Gramps." She leaned down and kissed his whiskery cheek.

"How are you feeling, Frank?" Clint spoke beside her.

"Great, though I wouldn't want to run any marathons today." He showed a weak smile.

Clint and Josie laughed and she decided Gramps's attempt at humor was a good sign.

"I think I'll call home and tell everyone the good news. Gracie's awfully worried about you," Clint said.

Gramps blinked. "You tell her not to worry. I'm looking forward to reading with her again as soon as I get home. We've made it a contest, but she can still read faster than me."

"Don't worry. You'll catch up soon enough." Clint stepped out of the room, and Josie took that opportunity to speak privately with Gramps.

"Dr. Crockett said you haven't been taking your heart medicine."

Gramps looked away, his chest expanding as he drew a deep breath. "I can't afford it, honey."

Oh, no. Josie couldn't believe she'd missed this detail. Suddenly she understood all the extra payments in his bill drawer when she'd brought his accounts current. She'd written the late notices off as a casualty of his illiteracy, but now realized it wasn't that simple. Her grandfather had been in financial need and she hadn't even been aware of it. For whatever reasons, he hadn't felt that he could consult with her over his troubles.

And something else nibbled at the back of her mind.

"Is that why Grandma was watching Gracie while Clint was at work? To make some extra money on the side?"

He nodded, his gray eyes filled with affection. "But it was no bother. We loved having Gracie in our home. She reminded us of you when you were little, and she filled up our hearts with love."

Josie could understand. It's how she felt about the little girl, too. And she'd be reticent to let that go when she left town again.

"We can definitely afford your prescriptions, Gramps," Josie insisted. "I wish you'd told me you needed money to pay for them."

"I didn't want to bother you, muffin. You've got your own life and concerns. You don't need an old man hanging on you like a giant leech."

"Gramps! Don't say that. You're no bother. You *are* my concern. I'm going to make sure you have everything you need. I've already contacted Carol Yerington. She's going to come in and check on you every day and bring in your lunch and dinner, too. And Rachel Burdett is going to clean your house once a week. Don't you worry about the expense. I've got it covered."

Gramps gave an impatient gesture. "Oh, phooey. I don't need all that nonsense."

"Yes, you do, so don't argue. You need to eat something besides soup, oatmeal, pastries and bacon. Please don't fight me on this. It's the concession I need from you if you're going to stay in Camlin when I return to Las Vegas." Careful of his IV and other lines, she hugged him to soften her rebuff. "I can't lose you, Gramps. We need to keep you healthy. We're a team. We can do this together. Okay?"

His eyes shimmered with gratitude. "You sound just like your grandma. And just now, you look like your momma, although you have your daddy's eyes."

Josie laughed, fighting back the tears. "That's one of the greatest compliments anyone's ever paid me. I so want to be like all of you."

They hugged again and she wiped her eyes.

Clint returned and they talked a little while longer. Josie held Gramps's hand and laughed when Clint described Gracie's enthusiasm at finding out Frank was going to be okay. Thirty minutes later, Josie could see that he was tired and needed rest.

After saying good-night, Josie walked Clint out to the main lobby. Like a wind tunnel, drafts of icy air whipped past them each time someone walked through the dark outer doors. Josie shivered and Clint removed his coat and whisked it over her shoulders. The gentlemanly gesture pleased her enormously. His coat smelled of his clean, spicy scent and she took a deep inhalation.

"Thank you," she said, and curled her arms within the warm folds.

"You sure you want to stay here all night? You won't get much rest in the hospital waiting room." He slid his hands into his pants pockets and hunched his shoulders, an indication that he was cold, but would sacrifice his own comfort for hers.

With a bit of reluctance, Josie relinquished his coat and handed it back to him. "I'm not budging. Not until I can take Gramps home."

He took the coat, but didn't put it on. He hesitated, as though he longed to stay here with her. And that meant everything to Josie. It was odd, but when she was with him, she felt strangely calm and settled. As if everything in her life made sense. Her fears and doubts faded away into perfect clarity of thought. It was as if they were old and dear friends, familiar and safe. But now he needed to leave. She didn't want him driving home on slick roads in the dark.

"You better get going. Night is coming on and you'll need to watch out for black ice."

Lifting his hand, he brushed her cheek with his fingertips. "You take care of yourself."

Currents of electricity shot through her. She squelched the desire to hug him.

"I will." She gave him a warm smile and nudged his arm. "Go on, now. I'm fine. Really. And tell Gracie we'll be home tomorrow night."

"All right." He turned and walked toward the doors. They slid open and he passed through to the damp sidewalk outside.

Josie crossed her arms and braced herself against the rush of freezing wind. She paused there for several moments, waiting. Before he got into his truck and pulled away, he looked back at her over his shoulder. She knew, because she watched to see if he would.

He lifted a hand in farewell, and she waved back. Once he drove out of the parking lot, she finally realized she hadn't eaten all day. Though she had little appetite, she realized her body still needed nourishment.

Alone in the hospital cafeteria, she ate a light dinner of tomato bisque, chicken salad and a slice of pumpkin pie with whipped cream on top. It sure wasn't as good as Grandma's recipe.

As she picked at her food, Josie mulled over what Gramps and Clint had each told her about their lives. They were remarkable men and she respected them both. When she went home to Las Vegas, she was going to miss them so very much. And Gracie, too. In fact, Josie didn't know how she was going to stand it.

Three days passed before Clint saw Josie again. Three tortuous days during which he purposefully stayed away, even though he knew Frank was out of the hospital and back home again.

Instead of going over to visit, Clint called and spoke with Frank by phone. Gracie went over to visit, but Clint immersed himself in work. An excuse to stay away from Josie.

It didn't help. On Christmas Eve, Clint thought about bowing out of the Christmas pageant, but knew they were depending on him. He had to go.

He drove Gracie to the church, arriving twenty minutes early. The pageant wouldn't last long. Less than an hour, so that people could go home and enjoy the evening with their families.

As Clint pulled into the parking lot, he noticed Frank's vehicle parked nearby. The doctor had agreed it would be okay for Frank to attend, but he was not to participate in the program, other than to sing the three wise men song with Clint and Tom.

As they walked to the inside foyer, Gracie held Clint's hand. Once inside, she broke away, rushing off to find Josie, who had brought her angel dress. Clint anticipated seeing his daughter in the outfit for the first time. Yet he couldn't get excited about the event. Not when he knew Josie was leaving in a few days.

Pasting a smile on his face, he retreated to the cultural hall. The choir members waved and chatted with him, but he couldn't remember a word of their conversations. His mind felt fogged by confusion. All he could think about was Josie and how he must get through this evening without blurting out how much he loved her.

The long curtains had been pulled across the stage. People stood around visiting and choosing the best seats in the wide auditorium. In a small town like this, it didn't matter what denomination you belonged to. Everyone flocked to the little redbrick church to enjoy the celebration of Christ's birth.

Wearing his Sunday suit and a red tie, Clint scanned the audience until he picked out Frank and Tom, dressed much the same. For their performance later on, they would don long robes and headbands, and hold gifts meant to resemble gold, frankincense and myrrh.

He mingled with the members of his congregation on stage, waiting for the performance to begin. He saw Josie, but ducked away, avoiding her. Nervous energy thrummed through his veins, but not because of his performance. Josie stood nearby, her presence setting him on edge.

She looked up and caught his eye, giving him a wistful smile. Clint gave one sharp nod before jerking his head away. He had no idea how he'd get through Christmas dinner later on that evening, but he must. He'd have to smile and pretend he was having a wonderful evening celebrating the Savior's birth, when all he wanted to do was cry. If it wouldn't break Gracie's heart, he would have canceled. Being with Josie simply prolonged the inevitable. Even if he could believe she'd never leave him, they couldn't be together. Not in a long-distance relationship. It'd be painful to walk away, but he didn't believe he had a choice.

The reverent hum of the choir sifted across the stage in the church auditorium. Clint stood at stage left with Tom. Frank sat on a cushioned chair between them.

When Gracie filed out with the rest of the children's chorus, Clint stared in awe. Against the backdrop of the deep green curtain, her white satin dress glimmered in the pale lights. Josie had French braided the girl's blond hair and coiled it on top of her head. Adoration gleamed in his daughter's eyes. As she stood beside the makeshift manger Clint had helped the other men construct for this presentation, she sang hosannas to Christ the king.

She glanced his way, her eyes glimmering with happiness. She brushed a hand down her beautiful dress, as though seeking his approval. An emotion of pure love bubbled up inside of him and he nodded and mouthed the words, *You're beautiful.*

A flush colored her cheeks and her smile widened.

Lifting his head, Clint looked at Josie and found her watching him. She stood at the back of the raised platform with the rest of the choir members, almost hidden from view. He knew she didn't feel confident about her singing voice, but she'd still joined the chorus. And knowing she'd taken the time to create such a perfect dress for his daughter touched his heart on a deeply personal level.

She smiled and nodded in encouragement as Gracie sang her lines. Between Josie and his daughter, Clint didn't think he'd ever seen anything more wonderful in all his life.

How he loved them. More than anything else in the world. He couldn't fight it anymore. The feeling encompassed his heart, so powerful that it almost hurt. He loved Josie, even knowing he would soon lose her. It was Christmas Eve, and within a few short days, she'd be going home to Vegas. Leaving him and Gracie alone.

A hushed reverence settled over the congregation as the chorus deepened, then reached a crescendo. When Frank began to sing, Clint had to jar himself back to reality.

He was up next.

Frank's deep bass voice carried throughout the hall, thrumming across the expanse of the room in a beautiful serenade of devotion. Clint sang his lines next, followed by Tom. Then the three men sang the melody together, their voices vibrating on the air in perfect harmony.

The words of the song anchored within Clint's heart. His love for God almost overwhelmed him, yet he couldn't seem to trust the Lord enough to let go of the past. When he thought of Karen, needles of grief pierced his heart. He longed to throw off the shackles of guilt, but didn't know how. His doubts ran too deep to push aside.

Instead, he fought back his emotions as he lifted his

voice in praise and adoration. Yet it was bittersweet. Clint's joy for Christ's birth and mission on earth mingled with his frustration at losing Josie. He thought about asking her to stay, but knew he couldn't do that. It wouldn't be fair to her. She loved her job in Vegas and had few prospects here in Camlin.

Somehow from the ashes of his past, Clint must build a future for himself and Gracie. He needed to forgive himself for the past. It was time. Long overdue. And yet he couldn't seem to let it go.

If he could make it through until Josie left town in three days, he'd be okay. But then he'd be without her. And that thought left him feeling numb and hollow inside. Empty and alone. Within his mind, Clint could reconcile no other outcome. He must let her go.

It was already too late. Because losing Josie was going to break his heart no matter what. And after tonight, he was determined never to see her again.

Chapter Sixteen

Something was wrong. Josie could feel it like a tangible thing.

Following the Christmas program at church, she and Gramps had headed home. Clint and Gracie followed in his truck, driving in tandem to Gramps's place. Yellow, red and green lights twinkled on the house. When she opened the door to the kitchen, warmth spilled out, and the tantalizing aroma of prime rib made her stomach rumble. She'd already made the cranberry salad and set the table, adding an extra leaf to fill out Grandma's lacy tablecloth.

Discarding her coat and gloves, Josie immediately set about laying out their meal. Clint and Gracie came inside, carrying a couple gifts.

"Make yourselves at home," she called over her shoulder as she slid the yeasty rolls into the oven to warm.

Clint and Gracie disappeared into the living room with Gramps. Within minutes, Josie had pulled the meat and potatoes from the oven.

"Come and eat while it's hot," she called.

They sat down together and Gramps offered a blessing on the food. He gave thanks for the bounty they enjoyed, for the Savior's birth, and for family.

They enjoyed a sumptuous feast, including homemade pumpkin and pecan pies with whipped cream. But Josie couldn't taste a thing.

Frank and Gracie chattered away, recounting every moment of the Christmas pageant. The oohs and ahhs of the audience. The quiet reverence as Frank and Clint sang their parts in the wise men song.

"It was beautiful," Josie said.

She'd never forget Clint's rich, vibrant voice as he sang with Gramps. In those moments, a peaceful feeling had settled over her and she'd felt close to her Savior. She couldn't explain it, but she knew God loved her. And she loved Him. But when she thought of leaving town, her throat jammed with emotion. She loved Clint and thought him the most amazing man she'd ever met. How could she leave and forget the integral part he and Gracie had come to play in her life?

"You definitely did a good job, Daddy." Gracie leaned against her father as he sat at the table and wrapped his arm around her.

His smile was subdued. "So did you, honey."

"I think we all did well tonight. Especially Josie, with this delicious feast. To Josie. My beautiful girl." Frank held up his glass of Grandma's fine crystal.

Clint and Gracie reached for their glasses to join the toast. A flush of satisfaction warmed Josie's face. Clint took a sip of sparkling cider, but he didn't meet her eyes. Ever since they'd confided so much to each other at the hospital, he hadn't been the same. So reserved and withdrawn, so far away... It was as though she couldn't reach him anymore.

Oh, why pretend she didn't understand? No doubt he regretted confiding so much to her. They both needed to take a step back. As much as she'd like to stay here in Camlin, she couldn't. She had to earn a living and help provide for Gramps. But lately, she'd started looking at her job differently. She thought of all the people she got to help every day. The consultations she had with numerous customers, some of them gravely ill. But each of them had lives of their own. They needed her help. And in distributing their medications, Josie was able to ease their plight, if only a little bit. To help them feel better. To make a difference.

No longer did she view herself as working behind the scenes. She *wasn't* alone. She mingled with dozens of people every day of her life. She'd just never seen it before—the good work she could do for them. The caring and service.

But leaving Camlin wouldn't be easy. Not now when she knew what she was giving up. In fact, it'd be the most difficult thing she'd ever done. And lately, she'd been praying for a miracle. A way for her to earn her livelihood as a pharmacist here in Camlin. And the greatest miracle of all…for Clint to love her, too.

Their meal ended all too soon. Gramps and Gracie retired to the living room. Gramps put on his old cassette of Christmas carols and the music sifted through the air.

Josie cleared a few perishables away from the table. Clint didn't speak as he helped her, covering a couple dishes with plastic wrap before stowing them in the refrigerator. They were both somber and overly quiet.

As she turned toward the doorway, Josie almost tripped over the step stool. What was it doing here? Gramps must have been using it, and forgot to put it away.

Folding it up, she stowed it in the closet, then stood next to Clint in the doorway. Gramps sat in his recliner beside the Christmas tree, with Gracie in his lap. Wearing expectant grins, they gazed at Josie and Clint.

Josie angled her head in confusion.

"What are you two up to?" Clint asked.

Gramps pointed over their heads. In unison, they looked up. A sprig of mistletoe hung directly above, tied with red, curling ribbon.

"Now you have to kiss her, Daddy," Gracie ordered with a laugh.

Clint stiffened and backed up, his eyes opening wide in surprise. Josie would have moved away, but the door frame jammed against her shoulder blade and she couldn't get past without brushing against Clint's broad chest.

Their gazes clashed, then locked. He dropped his arms to his sides, his lips slightly parted in shock. Currents of energy hummed between them. She could feel it rushing at her like a living being. Her heart gave a maddening thump, and her emotions churned inside her like curdled milk.

He took a step closer, lifting a hand to gently squeeze her upper arm. In this light, his eyes looked black as olives, and mesmerizing. He lowered his head, his warm breath whispering across her face. Her pulse kicked into triple time and a hungry longing slammed through her.

He kissed her, a quick, soft caress that ignited a yearning deep within Josie to hold on tight and never let him go. All rational thought evaporated from her mind.

Clint drew back, looking down into her eyes. Josie felt lost. Felt as though they were the only two people in the world. Then Gracie clapped her hands and Gramps gave a deep laugh of approval.

Clint jerked back as though he'd been scalded. Hot embarrassment singed Josie's cheeks and she whirled away.

"Okay, you've had your fun," she scolded Gramps and Gracie in a gentle tone.

Clint turned and sat in a chair on the opposite side of the room. Sensing he didn't want to be near her, Josie took a seat on the edge of the sofa. Gramps reached down and plugged in the tree. White, green, red and gold Christmas lights twinkled. He picked up the Bible and flipped through the pages. With Gracie's help, he read the nativity scene from the book of Luke. The story of Christ's birth.

Listening to his tentative, halting voice as he recounted the story of the three wise men, Josie's eyes misted with tears. She loved this story, but hearing it in her grandfather's gruff voice had an extra special meaning this year. Gramps could read. His accomplishment almost overwhelmed her with joy and frustration. If a man his age could learn to read, then why couldn't she figure out some way to work and live here in Camlin?

Gramps led them in singing several carols. Josie barely heard the words. She forced herself not to look at Clint. Her stomach churned with nervousness.

When they were finished, Gracie turned to Gramps. "Now?" she asked.

He nodded. "Yes, now."

Gracie slid off Gramps's lap. Josie expected the girl to lunge at her own gifts. Instead, she reached for a small wrapped parcel, which she handed to Josie.

"This is for you. I made it myself. Open it first."

The child's consideration touched Josie's heart. She loved this girl and couldn't help thinking how much she'd miss her and Clint once she left town in a few days.

Gazing down, Josie saw the sides of the wrapping paper were folded over haphazardly and sealed with gobs of tape. A crinkled bow perched on top, affixed with more clumps of tape. Josie laughed, having no doubt Gracie had wrapped it herself. Clint sat on the sofa and leaned forward, resting his elbows on his knees. He tilted his head to one side, twin creases furrowing his high forehead.

At Josie's expectant look, he shrugged. "I have no idea what it is."

He glanced at his daughter, his eyes filled with questions.

"It's a surprise," was all Gracie would say.

Filled with mystery, Josie pried an edge of paper free of the tape and ripped it open. Dropping the casing of gift wrap to the floor, she held a small blue dish with white speckles. The sides were slightly uneven, and indented with small finger marks. As if Gracie had molded the clay and created the dish herself.

A shallow gasp came from Clint, but when Josie looked his way, he sat motionless, his face completely blank and pale, his shoulders rigid. Something about his demeanor told her this wasn't an ordinary dish. It was special, but she didn't understand the significance. Or why Clint seemed upset.

Something was wrong here. Something Josie didn't understand.

Gracie waited for her verdict. And she wasn't about to disappoint the girl.

"It's absolutely beautiful. I love it," Josie said, meaning every word. No one had ever given her something like this. Something that was a part of them.

Gracie smiled with pleasure. "You can set it on your

dresser and put your earrings in it. I made it myself. And every time you see it, you can think of me."

Josie hugged the girl tightly. "I will. And I'll treasure it all the more. Thank you. It's wonderful."

"Really? You like it?" Gracie looked up and smiled, her eyes shining with joy.

"Really. It's the loveliest present I've ever received. And knowing you made it means even more to me." And she realized it was true. If she had to choose between her savings account and this child's gift, she thought she would choose the dish.

She'd choose Clint, too. What did her job matter if she couldn't be with the man she loved? She'd been hurt before, but she had to tell Clint how she felt. That she loved him. That she wanted to take one more chance. If only he was willing to do the same.

"Come see what we got for you." Gramps drew the child over to open the oodles of presents they'd wrapped for her.

Josie studied the dish more intently. The shiny ceramic finish felt smooth against her fingertips. She turned it over and read the childish writing on the bottom: "To Mom. Happy Mother's Day. From Gracie."

Josie's mind spun. Her throat felt suddenly dry as sandpaper. Her eyes widened and she glanced at Gracie, then over to Clint. He met her gaze for just a moment, his eyes dark and filled with misgivings. Then he looked away. He sat there, watching his daughter, as she plopped down on the tan carpet and happily opened a box filled with toy dishes and a miniature oven made especially for kids.

"Oh, I love it," Gracie exclaimed. "Now I can bake cookies just like Josie does."

Hugs and more exclamations followed as Gramps helped the child remove the packaging, and showed her how to work the oven. Josie didn't hear their words. Not even when Gramps opened the new dress suit she had purchased for him. Her ears felt clogged, as if she were underwater.

Gracie handed her a gift from Clint. Floating on autopilot, Josie tore back the cheerful wrapping and gazed at the silver-framed picture of her and Gracie, taken the day they'd cut Christmas trees and built a snowman. It was such a personal reminder of a wonderful time. Josie loved it, thinking the gold watch she'd purchased for Clint paled in comparison.

She looked up, but found him occupied with his daughter. When the girl moved away, Josie stepped near and placed the blue dish safely aside on Grandma's hutch, where it wouldn't get broken.

"Thank you for the picture. I'll cherish it always," she said.

"You're welcome. And thank you for the watch." Clint held up his left wrist, with a half smile that didn't quite reach his eyes.

"Did you know about this?" She indicated the blue dish.

He lowered his head and nodded. "But I didn't know she was going to give it to you."

Josie gazed out the window, at the darkness of the town, and the Christmas lights flickering on the house across the street. "She made it for her mom, didn't she?"

He didn't answer, but he didn't have to. Josie knew it was true. Coupled with Gracie's Santa letter, Josie understood the significance of the gift. Its meaning seeped deep into her soul. Out of all the women in the world, Gracie had chosen her.

"I wish I could be her mom." Josie spoke low, so Gracie and Gramps wouldn't overhear.

Clint stood abruptly, as though he didn't want to hear her words. He paused, looking across the room for several heart-pounding moments. Josie waited, a hard lump forming in her throat.

"It wouldn't work. I…I just can't." His eyes looked flat and guarded.

"Why not?" She hoped and prayed he wouldn't reject her, as everyone else had done. If only he could let go of his painful past. If only he'd let her in.

He met her eyes. "You've been engaged twice already. What would be different this time?"

She gave a rasping laugh. "I think you've misunderstood something, Clint. Yes, I've been engaged twice, but I never broke it off. They did."

"They did?" His expression clouded with disbelief.

"Yes. I was willing to get married. I know my faith hasn't always been strong, but I do have values. My first fiancé never really wanted to marry me. We were engaged three weeks. He just thought I'd move in with him once he proposed. But he was wrong. I want commitment from the man I love. I've already told you my second fiancé didn't want children. When he found out I did, he ended it, not me."

"And why do you think being with me would be any different?" Clint asked.

"For one thing, you're not a jerk."

He gave a harsh laugh. "I'm not so sure about that. I don't think I can give you what you're looking for. What you really deserve."

"What do you mean?"

"I may not be able to offer you the commitment you seek. I have to put Gracie first. I can't do anything that might jeopardize her happiness."

"And you don't think I'd make the both of you happy?"

"It's not that. I...I just can't afford the risk. She's already lost one mother. I can't take the chance that she might lose another one."

Josie turned with another question on her lips, but he moved away. He wouldn't meet her eyes. He seemed stiff and unapproachable. Closed.

"I think it'd be best if you took the dish back," Josie said.

He shook his head. "No, that would hurt Gracie too much. She wants you to have it."

Josie accepted his final word without argument, but inside she was screaming. She felt as though she was usurping Karen's place, and she wasn't welcome. If Karen was alive and Clint had divorced her, Josie might know what to do. But she didn't know how to fight against the woman's memory or Clint's guilt over her death.

As they finished opening their gifts, Josie was grateful for Gracie's consuming presence to conceal the underlying tension between her and Clint. But it didn't escape Gramps's notice. He shrugged into his new suit coat to try it on. When Josie stepped into the kitchen momentarily to fetch a black plastic garbage bag to stash the used gift wrap in, he intercepted her on the pretense of asking if she thought the coat fit.

"It's beautiful. You look so handsome," she told him as she smoothed the fabric over his chest.

He patted her hand, a look of concern creasing his brow. "You okay, muffin?"

"Yeah, sure." She nodded and pasted a smile on her face, but she couldn't fool Gramps.

"She's just a lonely little girl who wants a mommy," he said.

"I know, Gramps. And I can't tell you how badly I wish I could be that for her. But there's no sense in wanting something that can never be. Not if Clint won't let it happen."

Her grandfather opened his mouth to say something, but she stepped away and returned to the living room, feeling as though she was merely going through the motions. And later, as Clint bundled Gracie up and prepared for the short drive home, Josie watched him with misgivings.

She longed to tell him that she wanted to be with him. And to ask if maybe he could love her, too. She'd already opened the door, but he hadn't wanted to step through it. He'd have to reconcile Karen's death in his own mind, first. If he ever could.

As it stood, a life together wasn't going to happen. Not for them. And Josie couldn't help thinking this was the best and the worst Christmas she'd ever had.

Chapter Seventeen

Over the next two days, Josie put away the Christmas ornaments, paid the bills, washed all Gramps's laundry and stocked his kitchen with groceries. As he helped her put the food away in the cupboard, he stared at the cans he held in each hand. Amazement crinkled his brow.

"I can't believe it."

"What?" She slid a loaf of bread onto the counter and turned.

He held up the cans, his eyes shining with awe and wonder. "I can read these labels. This one is vegetable beef and this one is chicken noodle. Ma would be amazed if she knew."

Josie hugged him. "She knows. And I'm sure she's proud of you, Gramps. I know I sure am."

He placed the cans inside the cupboard and closed the door. "You don't have to leave, you know," he said.

"I know. But I do, Gramps. I have to go back to work."

His eyes misted and he brushed at them with one hand. "I'm missing you already."

He pulled her into his arms and held her close. For a

few moments, Josie felt like that little girl he'd been comforting all her life.

"You could come visit me in Vegas for a couple of weeks," she suggested. "It's much warmer in the winter months. We don't get much snow."

"I think I'd miss the snow. It wouldn't feel like home."

Yes, he was probably right. But she couldn't think about it that way. Leaving was hard enough already.

She turned to fold up the plastic bags and put them away in the broom closet. A good excuse to hide her tears. "I'll be back in two weeks. As the weather gets warmer, I think I'll thin out the tulip bulbs in Grandma's garden. It's getting a bit overgrown."

"That would be nice. You gonna say goodbye to Clint and Gracie before you go?"

She shook her head. "I don't think so. Gracie called me this morning and was in tears over the phone. I doubt a personal visit to say goodbye would make things any easier on her."

Or me, for that matter.

"You know, sometimes folks don't seem to know what's best for them. Sometimes they need a little help to figure things out."

She tilted her head. "What do you mean by that, Gramps?"

He shrugged. "Oh, nothing. Just the ramblings of an old man."

He turned and walked into the living room, and she let him go. If he was referring to her and Clint, she'd rather let the subject drop. Pursuing Clint when he obviously didn't want to be with her would do nothing but bring them both more unhappiness and embarrassment. She didn't want to go, but she had little choice.

Or did she?

She thought of staying and trying to live on Gramps's meager retirement funds. Her modest savings account could help supplement them, but she had no idea what they'd do when the money ran out. Gramps needed his medicine. They needed clothes, electricity and food. She'd feel like a freeloader if she cut into his skimpy income without earning her keep. And without a job here in Camlin, she couldn't earn a dime. Which meant she needed to return to Vegas, where she had a good job waiting for her.

That night, they spent a quiet evening at home, watching TV and chatting together about her return trip in two weeks. It wouldn't be easy, but she figured she'd have to drive home at least once a month to visit. Long, tiring trips that would sap her gasoline budget as well as her energy. But it'd give her something to look forward to. And it'd be worth it to ensure Gramps had what he needed. In the meantime, she'd call him every other day, just to make sure he was doing okay.

If only she dared call Clint. Just to hear the smile in his voice. To know he was still there. But that would only prolong the pain.

The next morning, she loaded up her car and kissed Gramps goodbye.

"I love you," she said.

"And I love you, muffin."

Opening the door, she glanced in the back. A heavy quilt had been spread across the seat. Gramps had mentioned it earlier. He'd put it there, in case she broke down and had to sit in the freezing cold while she waited for a tow truck.

Thinking little of it, she climbed inside, waved and

drove down the street. Looking back in her rearview mirror, she studied Gramps's lone image, trying to commit it to memory. At his age, this could be the last time she ever saw him, and she didn't want to let it go.

Sudden tears burned her eyes and she brushed them away. She couldn't help gazing at Clint's house with longing. Were he and Gracie inside? Or had he gone in to work that morning? How she wished he could let go of his guilt over Karen's death. How she wished she could convince him to take a second chance on love. To trust the Lord to heal his broken heart.

In an effort to distract her morose thoughts, she turned on the radio. Over an hour later, she was driving through a mountain pass and could get nothing but static. She flipped the radio off and heard a rustling in the backseat. Probably her Christmas gifts settling with the movement of the car.

Focusing on the slick road ahead, Josie paid it no mind, until the noise came again. She glanced back. The heavy quilt bunched and moved, as though something beneath it was alive.

Josie gave a startled yelp. What on earth?

The movement ceased abruptly. What was going on?

Josie pulled over and stopped the car. She got out, sucking back a quick breath as the winter wind cut through her with full force. Her teeth chattered as she stepped over a mud puddle and opened the back door. Reaching inside, she grabbed a handful of the quilt and gave a hard jerk.

"Gracie!"

The girl popped up off the floor. She was wearing blue jeans and her shiny red coat, and her hair stood on end, filled with static electricity from being beneath the quilt.

"Hi, Josie!"

"What are you doing here?"

But Josie didn't need to ask. In a flash, her mind filled with understanding. And the resulting ramifications.

The little stowaway sat up on the seat and folded her arms, her jaw locked with determination. "I decided if you're leaving Camlin, then I'm leaving, too."

Josie shivered in the cold. Waving the girl over, she climbed in beside her and sat down, pulling the door closed so they could talk for a few minutes without freezing to death.

"Your dad will be so worried about you. Does he know where you are?"

Gracie shook her head. "No, he wouldn't let me come, if he knew."

Oh, no. Clint must be worried sick by now. And Josie didn't want him to think she'd kidnapped Gracie. In a few minutes, she'd whip out her cell phone and try to call him…if she could get a connection here in these mountains.

"But if you leave Camlin, what will he do without you? Don't you love your dad?" Josie asked, trying to get the girl to think about what she'd done.

"Of course I love Dad. But don't you love him, too?"

What a blunt question for such a little girl. "Yes, I do."

Why deny it? Gracie knew the truth. Kids had an uncanny way of seeing things adults tried to hide. Everyone thought children were so resilient, but they weren't. Not really. They just didn't have a choice. They had to survive what the adults in their life forced upon them. But children knew things. Especially a child as smart as this one.

"I knew you loved Daddy. And he loves you, too," Gracie said.

If only that were true. "You know I'll have to turn around and take you back," Josie said.

Gracie nodded, a satisfied smile curving her lips. "Yes, I thought so."

Josie stared at her in surprise. Then she couldn't help laughing. She hugged Gracie, unable to stay angry at her no matter how hard she tried. Especially since they loved each other so much.

"I love you, Josie. I don't want you to leave." The girl's voice was muffled against Josie's blue sweater.

"I know, honey. I love you, too. I don't want to leave, either, but sometimes we have to do things we don't want to do."

Gracie drew back, her high forehead creased with confusion. "Why?"

"Because adults have to earn a living. And my job is in Vegas." Josie didn't know how to explain to to her about guilt, fear, responsibility, bills and all the other difficult things she would undoubtedly learn about as she grew older. Or explain that the girl's father couldn't seem to heal from the guilt he felt over her mother's suicide.

Josie took a deep, settling breath. "Okay, climb up front. We've got to take you back home."

She opened the door. A blast of chilling air caused her to hurry. Gracie scrambled overtop the seat backs and slid into place.

With the doors closed, Josie gripped the steering wheel, shaking her head. She couldn't believe this had happened. No doubt Clint would be worried by now. She reached for her cell phone and tried to call. As suspected, she couldn't get any reception on this lonely mountain pass.

"Put on your seat belt," she told the girl.

Gracie complied and Josie started the engine before edging back onto the road. She did a U-turn and headed back toward Camlin.

Minutes passed. The closer they got to home, the more anxious Gracie became—staring out the windshield, shifting in her seat, fidgeting nervously.

"You okay?" Josie asked.

She glanced over with a worried frown. "You think Daddy's gonna be mad at me for what I did?"

Josie reached out and clasped the girl's hand. "Don't worry. He loves you. I think right now he just wants to know you're safe. So stop worrying."

A short time later, they entered the Camlin city limits. Josie drove down Main Street and onto Garson Way. She could see Clint's house a quarter mile away.

The wail of a siren sounded a moment later. She stared into her rearview mirror at the police car coming up fast behind her.

"Oh, no. Not again," she grumbled.

She pulled over on the side of the road and waited for Officer Tim to get out of his squad car and saunter over. Rolling down her window, she pursed her lips. She didn't have time for this nonsense. She needed to get Gracie home.

"Hi, Tim. What's up?" she asked, trying not to be rude.

He bent his head down and met her eyes, then glanced over at Gracie. His face tightened and he moved back. "Can you step out of the car, ma'am?"

Her shoulders slumped. "If you're going to give me a ticket, just do it. I've got to get Gracie home, Tim."

"So, now you're into kidnapping, huh?"

"What?" Her mind raced in confusion.

Tim raised his hand to cup his gun holster, his brows

lifted in a demanding expression. "Clint called to report Gracie was missing. I need you to get out of the car. Now."

"Wait! I can explain. She's a stowaway, Tim. She climbed into my car before I left town. I was an hour down the road when I found her in my backseat. I'm bringing her home."

She'd never seen Tim like this before. Her mind ran wild with what could happen next. And honestly, she was a little afraid.

Lifting his hands to rest against his hips, Tim jingled the handcuffs. A car whizzed past, the driver craning his neck to see who Tim had pulled over this time. Mortification heated Josie's cheeks.

"Gracie!"

Josie turned. Clint came running toward them. He must have stepped outside his house, seen the cop car and noticed his daughter inside Josie's vehicle.

The little girl threw open the door and raced toward her father. In the middle of the street, he scooped her up and hugged her tight.

"Oh, I was so worried about you. I've been searching and calling everyone we know. Where have you been?" he asked, kissing her face.

"Daddy, you're squashing my eye."

He finally set her on the ground. Josie got out of the car. By this time, Gramps had seen them and was walking toward them at a fast clip.

"Clint, she climbed into my backseat and hid under a blanket. I didn't know she was there," Josie explained.

Taking Gracie's hand, he walked over to her, listening.

"So, this isn't a kidnapping, after all?" Tim said, looking disappointed.

"No!" Josie, Clint, Gramps and Gracie answered in unison.

Tim raised his hands, as if to ward them off. "Okay, I get it. I'm just glad everything worked out and she's all right."

"Me, too. Thanks for helping us find her," Clint said.

Tim shifted his weight, a cocky smile on his face. "Anytime. That's what I'm here for. Keeping our city safe."

Chuckling, the cop walked back to his squad car, got inside and drove away.

"Come on. Let's get inside where it's warm," Clint urged.

While Clint and Gracie walked with Gramps the short distance to his house, Josie hopped into her car and pulled it into the driveway. Inside the comfy kitchen, Gramps got out a pan and glanced at the little girl. "You want to help me make some hot chocolate while your dad talks to Josie for a few minutes?"

Gracie nodded, then leaned close and cupped her mouth to hide her loud whisper. "It worked, Grandpa Frank. Josie brought me back home. But I'll bet Daddy's gonna ground me for a year."

Josie froze, as though her feet were stapled to the floor. "Gramps! Did you know about this?"

He cleared his throat, his face flushing a deep, burgundy red. "We didn't mean any harm by it. It was the only thing we could think of to get you two to listen to reason."

At first Clint stared in stunned surprise. Then he threw back his head and laughed deeply. "So, you two planned this together? Unbelievable."

Josie agreed. But having almost been accused of kidnapping, she wasn't amused.

"Look, you two love each other and should be together." Gramps lowered his bushy brows in a stern frown and waggled a finger at them. "Gracie and I know it, and so do you. So stop fighting it. Now go into the living room and figure out a way to work this out between you."

"That's right, Dad. You taught me that you can't run away from your troubles. You've got to work things out." Gracie gave a firm nod.

Oh, boy. Josie couldn't believe this. She felt like a naughty kid being told to go to her room…by her elderly grandfather and a seven-year-old child. But Josie was a grown woman. And her heart couldn't take much more of this.

Turning, she went into the living room and sat on the sofa. Her body trembled from nervous energy as well as from standing outside in the freezing cold. She didn't know what to think anymore.

A movement in the doorway caught her eye and she looked up. Clint stood there, watching her. The sounds of the fridge door opening and Gracie's voice coming from the kitchen told Josie that Gramps was making his hot chocolate.

"I'm sorry about this," Clint said.

Josie stared at him, wondering what more she could say. Maybe it was time for her to listen instead.

He peered at her. "Are you okay?"

"Yes."

He slid his hands into his pockets and came to stand directly in front of her. "I don't think they meant any harm, Josie."

"I know."

"And...and I need to ask your forgiveness."

She lifted her gaze. "For what?"

"For being a fool."

What did he mean? She tilted her head, more confused than ever.

"I don't know how I ever let you leave. In fact, when I looked outside this morning and saw your car was gone, I panicked. I realized I might have lost one of the best things that ever happened to me."

She leaned forward, her senses on high alert. "You did?"

"Yes. I called to Gracie, to tell her to get ready to leave. I was going to drive to Vegas and convince you to come back with us. But Gracie was gone. I knew she was upset, but didn't realize how much. None of the neighbors had seen her. And the thought of losing either of you scared me more than anything I've ever faced before."

Josie became very still. Listening. Barely breathing. Barely daring to hope.

"I don't want to lose you," he said. "Not ever again. I can't control whether you're happy, whether you love me or whether you stay or go. You'll have to decide those things for yourself. But I do know I can't bear to let you leave without telling you how I feel. I love you, Josie. That's all I know. I'm not sure what to do about your job in Vegas. Or how it'll all work out. I just know I can't lose you again."

She held up a hand to interrupt him. "Wait. Did you just say you love me?"

He paused. "Yes, very much."

"But what about Karen and...?"

"Karen's gone. I can't bring her back, and I love you.

Whatever the future brings, I'm going to trust in the Lord. I'm going to trust in you, too."

"You are?" His faith touched Josie deeply. Like a precious gift she must protect and never take for granted.

He gave a shuddering laugh. "Yes, and I feel so free. For the first time in years, I feel free and forgiven."

Sudden tears burned her eyes. "Oh, Clint. I'm so glad."

He knelt before her and reached up to take her hand. "Would you consider staying here in Camlin? With Gracie and me?"

She released her breath in a quick exhalation. Her heart stopped beating, as though it waited for the earth to start rotating on its axes again. "What...what exactly are you asking me?"

He leaned near, a nervous smile teasing his lips. "I love you, Josie. So very much. I don't want to lose you ever again. Will you please marry me? And make me the happiest man on earth?"

Her mouth dropped open in shock. This was what she wanted, but it was entirely unexpected. He'd let go of his guilt over Karen's death. Josie didn't know how, but she understood the unconditional healing power of God's love.

"Say yes, Josie. Say yes!" Gracie stood in the doorway with Gramps. Both of them were smiling like crazy.

Josie laughed, overwhelmed with sudden bliss. She paused for a moment, wondering if this was real. Or if it was a dream. "Oh, yes. Yes, I'll marry you. I love you, too. More than I can ever say."

"Hooray!" Gracie jumped up and down. Gramps's laughter filled the room.

And suddenly, Josie was in Clint's arms. He kissed

her and she felt his strength surrounding her. Her heart felt overpowered by happiness.

"I'm worried," he whispered against her ear.

"About what, my love?"

"I don't know what to do about your career. I don't want to take that from you. I know you love your job as a pharmacist."

A scoffing laugh escaped her throat. "Not as much as I love you. And I'm not worried. I know the Lord will take care of that for us. Let's just trust in Him."

He smiled into her eyes. "Okay, sweetheart."

And as he kissed her again, she truly believed what she'd said. She didn't know how, but God knew. For now, no more words were needed. Josie's heart was overflowing with joy. And she realized she'd just been given her heart's desire.

Chapter Eighteen

One Year Later

Josie sat on the couch in Gramps's house and cuddled against Clint's side. He wrapped one arm around her shoulders and pulled her close. Resting his hand across her slightly rounded abdomen, he gently caressed her baby bump as they watched the New Year's Eve program on TV.

Looking across the room at Gracie, Josie couldn't contain a smile of contentment. In spite of it still being early, the girl had fallen asleep in the recliner. Sitting on the coffee table in front of them was a variety of chips, dips, salsa and finger foods. A barrage of party poppers waited for the midnight hour. They were having a quiet evening at home to celebrate the beginning of a New Year. With her husband's baby moving within her, Josie could barely contain the peace and happiness she felt.

"Where'd Frank go?" Clint asked as he placed a warm kiss on her lips.

She threaded her fingers through his hair, enjoying the hushed relaxation after such a busy holiday season. This past year had been hectic and wonderful, but the next year promised to be even better. "I don't know. He was here a few minutes ago. He must have gone into his room."

Returning her husband's kiss, she marveled at all that had transpired in her life. With Thelma's capital, she'd gone into partnership with the woman. Last April, she'd opened her own pharmacy downtown in the grocery store. She'd married Clint in June, with Frank acting as best man and Gracie as the cutest flower girl ever. Josie had spent the chaotic summer setting up her store and caring for Gracie, while Clint was called out to fight wildfires. Gramps helped as much as he could, mostly by watching Gracie. In retrospect, Josie couldn't believe all they'd accomplished together. The Lord had truly parted the waves and provided a way for them to reach all their dreams.

Now, she was about to become a mother for the second time. Because she would always consider Gracie her first child. And being a wife and mother exceeded all her expectations. Nothing in the world could compete with the joy she felt over those accomplishments.

She glanced at Gracie, so innocent and wise. If not for her persistent wish for a mommy, Josie might still be living in Vegas. Alone. Without a family of her own.

"Everyone's asleep. Maybe we should go back over to our place," Clint suggested as his lips covered hers in a warm kiss that almost sizzled her toes.

"Ahem! I'm not asleep. Not by a long shot."

They broke apart as Gramps burst into the room. Josie jerked upright and smoothed the large T-shirt over the swell of her unborn child.

"Gramps! Are you going out?"

Frank stood beside the coat closet, dressed in his best

Sunday-go-to-meeting suit and the new red tie Gracie had given him for Christmas a week earlier.

"As a matter of fact, I am." He reached inside the closet and pulled out the black dress coat Josie and Clint had given him. Clean shaven and smelling of spicy aftershave, he looked ready for a night on the town.

Clint's brow crinkled. "Where you going, Frank?"

"Down to the civic center. It so happens that I have a date."

Josie sat up straight, stunned down to her kneecaps. "A date? With whom?"

Gramps flashed a cheesy grin and waggled his eyebrows. "Thelma, if you must know."

Josie and Clint looked at each other and she had to cover her mouth to contain a chuckle. Gramps had a date. She could hardly believe it. He hadn't said a word about it to her, but she figured he was a bit old to ask her permission.

"Well, um, have fun," she said.

Clint laughed. "Yeah, have a good time. And don't stay out late."

Gramps harrumphed as he shut the closet door and picked up the keys to his old rusty truck. They jingled in his hand as he stepped away. "I intend to have fun. Don't wait up for me. And I will definitely be home late."

He slipped into the kitchen, and Josie heard the outside door open and close. A rush of frigid air marked his passing. Outside, the sound of the truck engine fired up, accompanied by headlights that soon faded away.

"Well, what do you make of that?" Josie looked at her husband, startled by this new turn of events. Just when she thought God couldn't surprise her any more, something else happened to prove her wrong.

A wide grin spread across Clint's face. "I think it's great. Frank's got a girlfriend."

"You don't think they'd... No, of course not."

"What?"

"You think they might decide to get married? At their age?"

Clint laughed and nuzzled her neck. "Why not? Life's too short not to enjoy. You like Thelma, don't you?"

She relaxed, breathing in his warm, clean skin. "Of course I do. She's a wonderful woman. But I guess I figured Gramps was finished with all of that."

"Why? Just because he's a senior citizen doesn't mean he should stop living. And I have no doubt it won't change his feelings for Vi one iota."

Josie hadn't thought about that. "You're right. What Gramps and Grandma shared was remarkable. Nothing will ever change that."

"It just goes to show that you're never too old to find true happiness with the one you love."

She gave his shoulder a playful swat. "Oh, you."

"Besides, we're finally alone." He cast a quick glance in Gracie's direction. Then he pulled Josie close and kissed her thoroughly.

She didn't fight him. No, not at all. Not when her heart was singing to the starry sky above. This was what she'd prayed for. What she'd always wanted. A family of her own. And the sweet, enveloping love of a good man who cherished her above all others. What more could she ask for?

* * * * *

"Get back!"

Definitely a female voice, from the other side of the barn. He walked around the barn. If someone had asked him to guess what he might find there, he wouldn't in a hundred years have guessed correctly.

A young Amish woman—Plain dress, apron, *kapp*—was holding a feed bucket in one hand and a rake in the other, attempting to fend off a rooster. At the moment, the bird was trying to peck the woman's feet.

"What did you do to him?" Daniel asked.

Her eyes widened. The rooster made a swipe at her left foot. The woman once again thrust the feed bucket toward the rooster. "Don't just stand there. This beast won't let me pass."

Daniel knew better than to laugh. He'd been raised with four sisters and a strong-willed mother. So he snatched the rooster up from behind, pinning its wings down with his right arm.

"Where do you want him?"

"His name is Carl, and I want him in the oven if you must know the truth." She dropped the feed bucket and swiped at the golden-blond hair that was spilling out of her *kapp*. "Over there. In the pen."

Daniel dropped the rooster inside and turned to face the woman. She was probably five and a half feet tall, and looked to be around twenty years old. Blue eyes the color of forget-me-nots assessed him.

She was also beautiful in the way of Plain women, without adornment. The sight of her reminded him of yet another reason why he'd left Pennsylvania. Why couldn't his neighbors have been an old couple in their nineties?

"You must be the new neighbor. I'm Becca Schwartz—not Rebecca, just Becca, because my *mamm* decided to do things alphabetically. We thought you might introduce yourself, but I guess you've been busy. Mamm would want me to invite you to dinner, but I warn you, I have seven younger siblings, so it's usually a somewhat chaotic affair."

Becca not Rebecca stepped closer.

"Didn't catch your name."

"Daniel...Daniel Glick."

"We didn't even know the place had sold until last week. Most people are leery of farms where the fields are covered with rocks and the house is falling down. I see you haven't done anything to remedy either of those situations."

"I only moved in yesterday."

"Had time to get a horse, though. Get it from Old Tim?"

Before he could answer, a dinner bell rang. "Sounds like dinner's ready. Care to meet the folks?"

"Another time. I have some...um...unpacking to do."

Becca shrugged her shoulders. "Guess I'll be seeing you, then."

"Yeah, I guess."

He'd hoped for peace and solitude.

Instead, he had half a barn, a cantankerous rooster and a pretty neighbor who was a little nosy.

He'd come to Indiana to forget women and to lose himself in making something good from something that was broken.

He'd moved to Indiana because he wanted to be left alone.

Don't miss
The Amish Christmas Secret *by Vannetta Chapman,*
available October 2020 wherever
Love Inspired books and ebooks are sold.

LoveInspired.com

Mikey's fingers contracted. "Suppose I told you that the
hotel I own is actually a casino," he said slowly, "and it's
in Las Vegas?"

Bernie's eyes widened. "You own a casino in Las
Vegas?" she exclaimed. "Wow!"

He laughed, surprised at her easy acceptance. "I run it
legit, too," he added. "No fixes, no hidden switches, no
cheating. Drives the feds nuts, because they can't find
anything to pin on me there."

"The feds?" she asked.

He drew in a breath. "I told you, I'm a bad man." He
felt guilty about it, dirty. His fingers caressed hers as they

neared Graylings, the huge mansion where his cousin lived with the heir to the Grayling racehorse stables.

Her fingers curled trustingly around his. "And I told you that the past doesn't matter," she said stubbornly. Her heart was running wild. "Not at all. I don't care how bad you've been."

His own heart stopped and then ran away. His teeth clenched. "I don't even think you're real, Bernie," he whispered. "I think I dreamed you."

She flushed and smiled. "Thanks."

He glanced in the rearview mirror. "What I'd give for just five minutes alone with you right now," he said tautly. "Fat chance," he added as he noticed the sedan tailing casually behind them.

She felt all aglow inside. She wanted that, too. Maybe they could find a quiet place to be alone, even for just a few minutes. She wanted to kiss him until her mouth hurt.

Don't miss
Texas Proud *by Diana Palmer,*
available October 2020 wherever
Harlequin Special Edition books and ebooks are sold.

Harlequin.com